STARRED REVIEW

The Host Rises
K.H. Brent
iUniverse, 433 pages, (paperback) $22.95, 9781532014710
(Reviewed: December 2017)

K.H. Brent's stellar debut novel, the first installment in his Promised Land saga, is a page-turning fusion of apocalyptic fiction, science fiction and mainstream thriller. It's set in a near-future where the world's population, on the brink of self-annihilation, is effectively reshaped by a group of seemingly godlike invaders who forcibly bring "a promise of peace."

The Host Rises takes place in a dystopia where ignorance and apathy have flourished, turning America into a fearful, narrow-minded theocracy. Much of the population has become "Virtuals," spending the majority of their time in artificial realms while their bodies wither away in virtual living compounds.

The world is irrevocably changed when the Seraphim, members of an entity known as the Host, give humanity an ultimatum: End all conflict and turn all military assets over to the United Nations in 48 hours or be destroyed. When the population of an entire town is instantly killed after not complying, the rest of the world's governments quickly fall into line.

A year after the "Peace" has been established, the world is markedly different. There are no nations, only regions. English is the global language. Food production is being radically improved and global warming is being addressed. But there are those who don't trust the seemingly benevolent Host and are covertly attempting to understand its real motivations. Special agent John Harriman and journalist Grace Williams have been investigating the Host from the beginning. When they uncover its true origins, they must attempt to stop its masterful plan before it's too late.

The writing is fast-paced and full of driving energy, propelling the book through a wealth of plot twists. Reminiscent of Arthur C. Clarke's seminal 1953 novel *Childhood's End*, Brent's book is everything good science fiction should be: powered by deeply considered speculation, relentlessly thought-provoking and, above all else, visionary.

Bottom line: *The Host Rises* is better than the majority of science fiction releases currently on the shelves. Yes, it's that good.

BlueInk Heads Up: The Star designation is offered with the recognition that copyediting issues remain in need of attention, including improper use of the possessive apostrophe, comma mistakes and word usage errors.

Also available in hardcover and ebook.

EDITOR'S NOTE- Copyediting issues corrected with this revised edition.

Kirkus Indie Review
THE HOST RISES
Book One of the Promised Land Series
K. H. Brent

August 25, 2017
BOOK REVIEW
In this debut novel and series opener, humanity struggles to
adapt to a strange, otherworldly entity's presence and its self-
imposed — but not entirely welcome — plan to save the world.
In the near future, numerous people experiencing a quick,
stabbing pain in the abdominal area become part of a global
event. Someone takes credit for the apparent attack, calling it a
demonstration and promising to reveal all at the forthcoming
United Nations General Assembly. It's there that a "saucer
shaped craft" arrives and a humanlike being emerges — the
Voice of the Host. The Host has an ultimatum: earthlings will
cease all hostilities or be destroyed, much like members of a
violent faction whom the entity later kills simultaneously. Parts
of the Host's planet-saving strategy are beneficial, enlisting Wil,
a Virtual (his time is largely spent in virtual reality), to combat
starvation by developing optimum crop production in VR for
real-world application. Many, however, are resistant to the
Host, seeing it as either a dominating alien or some sort of
demon. Col. John Harriman and others, meanwhile, hope to
reclaim freedoms taken by the Host, which intends to
implement a world government. Taking down the entity will
necessitate studying its superior technology — as covertly as
possible, of course. Brent delivers a worthy novel, with tension
derived from the Host's ambiguity and a dialogue-heavy
narrative of characters' varying theories. For example, there are
alternating signs of extraterrestrial and religious origins; human
Directors working for the Host have "halos" over their heads,
which are reputedly devices linking each person to the entity.
Two romances in the story are rather conventional (meeting the
parents is a significant step in both) but nicely contrast with the
titular character. Wil and Sonya, for one, meet in VR but
gradually join reality, while sometime assassin Harriman and

—

war correspondent Grace, with violent conflicts now absent, lose their livelihoods. Elucidation on the Host is striking, but the ending is truly remarkable and a stunning preamble to Book 2.

A smart, delightfully offbeat tale with shades of sci-fi and military action.

Kirkus Indie, Kirkus Media LLC, 6411 Burleson Rd., Austin, TX 78744

indie@kirkusreviews.com

—

FOREWORD
REVIEWS   THE INDIE WE LOVE.

Clarion Review ★ ★ ★ ★ ★   SCIENCE FICTION

The Host Rises

K. H. Brent
iUniverse (Aug 26, 2017)
Softcover $22.95 (462pp)
978-1-5320-1471-0

Introspective and action packed, The Host Rises is a deft start to a new science fiction series.

An implacable alien force arrives to usher humanity into an era of peace in the thrilling *The Host Rises* by K. H. Brent.

In the not-too-distant future, Earth is reeling from catastrophe after catastrophe. Corporations coalesce into megacorporations with influence enough to unseat governments.

Grace thrives as a war correspondent traveling from conflict to conflict, while John slips in and out of global conflicts on secret missions. Wilson lives in a virtual world, only leaving for food and hygienic considerations. The three find themselves connected when an extraterrestrial force arrives on Earth to enforce peace at any cost.

Seemingly omnipotent and able to strike down countless threats, the Host demands that human beings put aside violence or face instant execution. Earth enters a period of peace, but dissidents threaten to unravel everything.

The Host Rises is the first book in the Promised Land series. It does a great job of introducing characters and setting scenes. It's also chock full of both thrilling action and contemplative moments. From exploding battlefields to efforts to solve the food crisis, there is never a dull moment. The book's cliffhanger ending is appropriate, satisfying, and engaging.

John and Wilson shine in their roles. John starts out as a human weapon; the president points him at whatever threat needs to be taken care of. Over the course of the novel, he struggles with war and violence and his place in both. A twist near the end adds intensity to his backstory and sets up the conflict for the next book.

Meanwhile, Wilson barely escapes the lure of the virtual world, but he ends up studying with AIs that are modeled after history's greatest minds to solve the world's food crisis.

The point of view moves between characters to flesh out events thoroughly, particularly when John or other military characters step into the spotlight. Military jargon and tactics are used freely and only explained when needed, allowing events to unfold appropriately.

This is also science fiction with an important perspective. In between its unusual aliens and new technology, characters grapple with moral and ethical issues. John's cold, unfeeling executions are coupled with his increasing difficulty at staying distant from his actions.

Wilson, too, forces himself to learn and understand as much as possible in the hopes of helping an unstable world. Issues of economics, philosophy, and human nature are confronted. Intense world building adds to the book's appeal.

The Host Rises is a deft start to a new science fiction series, both introspective and action packed.

Promised Land
By
K. H. Brent

Book One: The Host Rises

THE HOST RISES
Book One of the Promised Land Series

Follow KB Brent for more on the Promised Land series, other works, and for commentary on the issues of the day at khbrent.com.

For
Matthew & Michael-
who made time to help me...

Prologue: Three Years Before The Peace

Grace exploded into the room.

"Fabio, I've found them! It's about an hour's drive. Venha vamos! Agora!"

The young man, who had been sleeping peacefully on one of the beds, sat up with a startled shout.

Grace moved swiftly through the room to the closet, unbuttoning her dress and kicking off her heels. Grabbing a heavy, black shirt from the closet alcove, she looked at Fabio again.

"We don't have much time. Something big is about to happen, and I need to be there. Get up and get your shit together!"

Slowly, Fabio climbed out of bed, reaching for the clothes pile on the floor.
"Eu quero café, por favor."

Grace, having already slipped on a pair of black pants, scowled as she laced her boots.

"Ugh! Brazilians! No concept of urgency. It seems that the only people in this country who move fast are eco-terrorists."

"Well, senorita, they have a sense of purpose that the rest of us do not possess," replied a groggy Fabio. "After all, they believe that they are trying to save the planet."

"I think that when these people kidnap one of the wealthiest families in the country and hold them for ransom, there might be a little more to it," shot back Grace. "Get the equipment."

Fabio shrugged and picked up a backpack stowed in the corner of the room.

"Can we get something to eat as well? Eu quero comer."

Grace rolled her eyes. "God, I miss Red! We'd be halfway there by now."

"But then you wouldn't have your reliable guide and translator," countered the young man with mock bravado.

"Fabio, we've been dicking around here for two weeks while you run up the expense account and we've got nothing to show for it. It's pretty obvious what your game is. We'd be here another two weeks if I hadn't come on to Silva," she said.

"How was dinner? See! You have eaten, and here I am starving. It's not fair," complained Fabio, putting on his jacket.

He grinned at her. "You probably ate well as the new mistress of Commander Silva.

—

"Say that again, and I'll put you through the wall. Silva's a pig," responded Grace with disgust. "And I am *not* his mistress. That thought makes me want to vomit. I simply went to dinner with him... at his estate. Thank God the man can't hold his liquor. Toward the end, he started bragging, trying to impress me. He wouldn't be able to do it with anything else. Dumbass passed out before anything happened. Fell over into my lap."

She paused in her preparations.

"I might have to burn the dress."

Recovering, Grace opened the door and, with Fabio following her, spilled out into the hotel's corridor. They made their way to the parking lot.

"So, where are we going?"

"About an hour south of the city. They're holed up in a villa that Silva says looks like a fortress. Way too big of an operation for the locals. They don't want to risk making a mess of it and getting the family killed. Then again, paying the ransom is out. That would simply encourage the kidnappers to do it again."

"Are we just going to knock on their door?" asked Fabio. "I don't think that is a good idea, senorita."

Grace gave him a deadpan look as she opened the passenger door to their Range Rover.

"You'd be surprised how well that might work. These people thrive on publicity. The world sees them as terrorists and bandits. If they really are about saving the planet, then they need some serious rebranding. Who better to do that than Grace Williams and NNI?"

The young man listened as he hopped into the driver's seat and started the vehicle. "Grace Williams and Fabio Dutra," he corrected, grinning at Grace. "What's the address?"

She touched her Magi-Watch, synching it to the Rover's GPS.

"These people aren't aware of anyone knowing their location, especially the state police. If we actually *were* to walk up to the door for a statement, we would have blown their cover. They'd probably kill the hostages and us, too."

Fabio's grin faded. "Ok, so we are going to die."

"Just so you're clear, that's *not* the plan. Start the car. Let's get going."

Grace continued as they left the lot, "The Cabral's are not just one of the world's richest families. They are also important leaders within Brazilian evangelical Christianity."

"Yes, everyone knows that."

—

2

"Well, what you don't know is that it also makes them very important players within American, evangelical Christianity, which is much more politicized than it is here. In particular, Tiago Cabral is good friends with James Roberts, one of the most influential men in American religion. That also makes him one of the most influential men in American politics."

Grace paused and looked at the young Brazilian. "Are you still with me?"

"Yes, querida but why am I still driving to my certain death at the hands of eco-terrorists?"

"You're not. James Roberts and his group were huge contributors to the campaign of one Samuel Hiram Craig."

"The new American president," said Fabio, eyes intent on the road.

"Yeppers! Guess who's coming to dinner?"

"My English just quit on me, Miss Grace. What is a *yeppers*; and you already went to dinner. As for me, I still need coffee very badly."

Grace laughed. "I'm sorry, Fabio. Guess who's coming to rescue our hostages?"

Fabio looked away from the road and at Grace wide-eyed. "The Americans!"

"That's right! The Americans," she repeated. "Now, eyes on the road."

"It's Brazil. No one keeps their eyes on the road."

"Please, these cars down here still aren't automated, and I don't want to get into an accident before I break this story," pleaded Grace sarcastically.

"We voted as a nation not to let cars drive themselves. We don't trust them," defended Fabio.

"As awful as everyone here is at driving, I think I would have voted for the robot cars. That would most assuredly boost the national life expectancy rate. Anyway, our pig of a commander let it out that there is an American spec ops unit getting ready to assault the villa at around three this morning. That gives us about an hour to get there and an hour to hoof it into position so that we can capture the firefight," speculated Grace.

Fabio slowed the car. "Miss Grace, I am sorry, but I do not want to get in between people who are shooting at each other. I do not get paid well enough to die."

—

3

Grace flashed him the smile that had helped to make her famous. "Don't worry, I do this all the time, and I'm still here."

Her companion was unmoved. "No querida! These are not *gangues das favelas*. I can buy my safety with those people. You cannot reason with these eco-terrorists, and the Americans will see everyone in the area as a terrorist and shoot them. There is nothing in this world worth dying for."

They rode on silently for a few moments.

Sensing the depth of his fear, Grace offered up a compromise.

"Look, we have to get off the main road to find the villa. Get me close, and I'll walk the last kilometer alone. When it's over, we'll do the production and upload together. You'll get both a story credit and paid as well."

Fabio contemplated the offer for a moment.

"I will do this for you, Miss Grace. I will take you there and wait," he said finally.

"I still need to stop for an espresso."

"Pull over here," commanded Grace an hour later.

Fabio was confused. "We are still at least five kilometers from the road. You won't make it on time."

"I need to get ready here," replied Grace.

Fabio brought the Range Rover to a stop. Grace jumped out, grabbing the backpack from the rear seat. As Fabio shadowed her, she sat it on the hood and opened the top flap. Reaching inside, Grace pulled out a black baseball cap and put it on, stuffing her ponytailed, blonde hair inside. Taking out a Bowie knife, she strapped it to her right hip and thigh. Rummaging around in the bag, Grace then found a small jar and opened it to reveal a clear jelly. She scooped the jelly with her fingers and rubbed it on her face. Fabio looked on quizzically.

"Kills the heat signature. Clothes dampen the rest of it; special made," she explained, vigorously rubbing in the gel.

"How did you know you would need these things?" he asked.

"I've been at this for a while. In most war zones, a combatant can kill you without ever having to see you. They just zero in on your heat sig and send in an RPG. This stuff is standard issue if you want to live through a firefight."

"But I don't have any of these things."

Grace gently put her hand on his arm. "You were never coming with me. I couldn't ask that of you. You're going to stay with the Rover, and if I'm not here by dawn, you're going back to the hotel and contact the network. I'll be back, though. In the meantime…"

She handed him a pair of glasses.

"Put these on and touch them here," she said pointing just in front of her right temple.

Fabio did, and a green glow illuminated the world before him.

"Night-vision glasses," said Grace.

"Aren't you going to need them for yourself?" he asked.

"Later yes. For now, you'll need them more because you're driving. One last thing, find me a big rock."

Fabio looked around, picked up a round stone the size of his fist and handed it to Grace. She walked around to the back of the Range Rover and proceeded to smash out the taillights. Satisfied, Grace tossed the stone aside.

"You can't turn off brake lights," she said as she passed the perplexed Fabio. "Let's go. You *can* turn off the headlights. Do that before we start."

Reentering the car, they continued into the moonless night. Ten minutes later, a T-road came up on their right.

"Pull over a couple hundred meters past the road," requested Grace. Fabio complied.

"I'll be needing these now," Grace said taking the glasses off Fabio's face. She opened the door and stepped out, shouldering the backpack.

Grace spoke quietly, "GPS says the villa is about a kilometer up that hill in a clearing. I'm going to see if I can grab a vantage point to get some good video-while being careful not to run into our *friends*. I'll see you in a few hours."

"Via com Deus, Miss Grace."

Acclimating to the green glow of the glasses, Grace began up the gentle slope. She made good time up the hill as the terrain was clear of dense brush. *Probably landscaped at some point*, she ascertained. That presented a problem- no groundcover meant hiding in the bush was out if a patrol came by. She might be able to find a tree to press against but would be a sitting duck for anyone with their own night-vision specs. She guessed that likely to be a certainty.

Grace approached the hill's crest, slowing her pace and going into a crouch that soon became a belly crawl as she reached the top. What she saw made her understand why the locals had washed their hands of the situation.

The eco-terrorists had chosen their defensive position well. The villa sat on a terrace at the top of the hill encircled by what Grace guessed to be a twelve-foot perimeter wall. Surrounding it on the three sides, she could see an open lawn at least three hundred feet deep. It was a perfect killing zone; a small force would be cut to ribbons crossing it. A large-scale assault might breach the wall but also ensure the hostages' execution.

No wonder the Brazilians had punted. Maybe the Americans had too- she had yet to see movement in the surroundings, or maybe they were just that good. Grace couldn't wait to see what they had planned, but for that she needed elevation.

Grace scooted back into the woods until she could stand upright without being seen. Looking around, she found her hiding place- a large canopied tree with low branches. It had to be tall; at this angle, Grace knew she was going to need to get up at least thirty feet to have any view of the compound's inner courtyard.

Without the night-vision glasses, she would never have attempted the climb. Grace knew that trees are far from sterile environments. In fact, they're rich biomes teeming with life. In Brazil, much of that life could be very dangerous. She took great care to survey each handhold before proceeding. The last thing she wanted to do was run across a brown recluse spider.

Halfway up, Grace saw the tree viper and knew it was going to be a problem. The vibrations from her movement had alerted it. It was wrapped tightly around the branch just above and to the left, waiting for her to come within striking distance. Attempting to move to the left or right of it proved fruitless- the viper mirrored her motion, blocking the way.

Grace knew that she couldn't share the tree with such an aggressive predator. Even if she could get around it, there would always be a chance it would wander into her perch later. That would get her killed.

At this point, finding another tree was also out of the question. According to Silva, the assault should be starting within minutes. She was running out of time. There was only one option.

Bracing her legs and lower torso against the branches, Grace slipped off the backpack, ever watchful of her opponent. Securing it to her left forearm as a shield, Grace unsheathed the Bowie knife.

God, I hope they don't find my bloated carcass in the morning, she thought, taking a deep breath.

Grace began thrusting the shielded arm back and forth, attempting to tease the viper into striking the backpack. Seconds later, the agitated snake took the bait, lashing out and driving its fangs deep into the satchel.

Grace pulled the backpack towards her and with the knife slashed down at the still attached viper. It sliced completely through, inches from the back of its head.

The viper's body went limp immediately, its head remaining firmly joined to her improvised shield. Grace waited until she was sure all life had drained away before prying the knife blade between its mouth and the fabric. She hesitated and debated wrapping the head in something to keep as a trophy. Deciding against it, Grace flicked the head away. She heard it fall softly through the branches. Sheathing the knife, she slid the backpack on and resumed climbing, turning her attention to the villa.

She didn't know how high up she was when the courtyard of the compound came into view. In the green glow of the glasses, she could just make out figures walking. From this viewpoint, she spied at least one guard on each wall.

Grace did her best to secure herself into a bough, again removing the backpack and pulling out the tablet. It was a bit low tech- unable to uplink live and without the production apps of newer models, but it did have top notch resolution with both infrared and night vision capabilities. It was just what the doctor ordered for this type of shindig. Grace set it up, zooming in on the courtyard. Not wanting to miss a thing, she started rolling.

Then she waited.

***

John Harriman and Walt Stevens studied the 3D projection on the pad before them. Securing the intelligence from the drone had been slow; it needed to penetrate the villa's thick walls without its prop noise arousing suspicion.

Typically, the drone could hover over a target to gather intel but, in this case, that had proven impossible. The compromise had been to get the drone into position at a higher altitude and airspeed, cut the engine a few clicks away, and glide silently over the villa at two hundred meters. It was tricky business, the pilot back at Langley had her hands full keeping the plane on its flight path and at times in the air. Patience and innovation eventually secured their three-dimensional snapshot.

"Nineteen, judging by the heat sigs. Against six of our Meat Eaters," said Stevens. "Do you want to pull in the picket?"

"No, let's stick to SOP," replied Harriman, shaking his head. "All we need are more bad guys joining the party unannounced."

They looked on in silence.

"These are the assets," said Harriman pointing to the orange figures in the center of the display. "They never move. We know there are five hostages in total and eight bodies in this room. That makes a total fourteen baddies."

"That's tough, John. A soup sandwich."

Harriman sighed.

"Yep. Well, this is the mission, straight from the CIC," he said, continuing to study the image silently.

"Walt, how many flies do we have?"

"Six, sir."

"Ok, we've got six targets inside, three in the room with the assets and three close enough to terminate the assets if we screw the pooch," postulated Harriman. "The flies will take out the targets inside. Philips and Hawke can get elevated here and here, and pink these four on the walls. That leaves the four in the courtyard. We blow the front door, pink the baddies on the deck and get two of us in on the assets while the others neutralize the last two bad guys."

Stevens nodded as Harriman explained the plan, eyes fixed on the display. "Four on four, advantage Meat Eaters. Gotta get the timing of the flies right. You can't leave anyone inside alive, or we're fucked."

He looked up at Harriman, "What if the place is spiked?"

Harriman's focus remained intently on the pad. "The flies will recon the interior before we hit them. If there's an IED, then I'll get there and disarm it."

"Let's hope there's no dead man's switch," countered Stevens. "I'd hate to have to pick up all your pieces, sir, much less have to report back to the CIC that he's lost his Hammer."

—

8

"Stop! I hate that nickname. If you were still a grunt, I'd bust you down," snapped Harriman, finally looking at his companion.

"Ah, but we're all secret squirrels now, and you can't," replied the smiling Stevens.

Harriman remained sober.

"If one of those baddies does have a deadman's switch, then we never stood a chance. Still, we've gotta go in. Round up our little dicksticks and brief them. I'll call Mother."

The Miniaturized Aerial Surveillance and Ordinance Units were affectionately known as *flies* by their operators for the obvious reason that they were designed to look like a large housefly. The tiny drone's purpose was

two-fold- the first being the proverbial *fly on the wall*. It could freely gather intelligence without notice in any accessible space. That could usually be accomplished by accessing an open door or window. Once inside, the fly would utilize the ventilation system to find its target. This mobility allowed a fly to follow the object of its surveillance undetected.

The second use was as a weapon- each unit contained enough high explosive to blow a hole in a man's head.

Harriman needed these particular flies for both purposes.

The miniature drones had entered the villa through various open windows, one at a time so as not to arouse suspicion. Harriman and Stevens watched the six split screens on the monitor before them; a monitor viewed through specialized glasses that provided the display's lighting. Anyone stumbling across them would have witnessed two grown men staring at a black pad. From the villa, they remained unseen.

As they watched the six screens, two of the flies were still moving into position. The remaining four had now found resting places on the ceilings of their targets' rooms. Three were in the room occupied by the hostages, each settling into a spot on the ceiling that provided the maximum view of the room. Harriman could see the five hostages- Tiago Cabral, a woman whom he knew from the briefing file was Cabral's wife, Maria, a boy of around seventeen would be the son, Jose, and the twin girls, Flavia and Flora, fourteen.

The family was sitting on a couch, gang chained at the waist and feet to a bar on the floor and watching a large monitor mounted to the wall. The setup allowed them some mobility- from Harriman's viewpoint they could get up and walk around in a small area containing a dining table. It wasn't enough to reach either the door or their captors, seated at a second table. Two of the guards were absorbed in their virtual watches; a third was looking at the wall monitor as well. All were armed with pistols. A shotgun was propped up in the corner.

The fourth fly parked itself in a room with a solitary occupant, a woman looking to be in her thirties, reading.

"I'll be damned! Is that an actual hardcover book?" asked Walt Stevens incredulously.

"Seems to be," said Harriman.

"It would be a shame to blow that brain out of her head. Such a Renaissance woman!"

Harriman shook his head. "Nope. Everything must go. Besides look over there."

Stevens's eyes narrowed behind his glasses.

"There's our spike."

"Mother, can you zoom in on D-five, grid point twenty-one by thirteen? IED detected and detonator type needs to be determined," said Harriman to the drone's pilot in Langley, Virginia.

"Roger that, Red Hen," crackled a woman's voice in their earpieces. The grid point suddenly enlarged to fill the screen.

"Wireless trigger, standard cellphone detonator," stated the Langley pilot.

"Concur," replied Harriman wearily.

"They just have to phone it in. Our soup sandwich just became a shit sandwich," Stevens said dryly.

"Maybe not. Let's figure out who's in charge. They might be the only one with the number. So long as they aren't on the deck..."

The two continued watching as the sixth fly settled into position over a heavily armed man in the anteroom. Number five continued to follow a heavyset man from the anteroom into the woman's room. The fly made it inside and took its position on the ceiling. From both monitors, the two men watched as the woman put down the book and stood. She walked to the man and kissed him, then fell to her knees in front of him.

Harriman and Stevens looked at each other.

"Bingo!" said Stevens.

———

"Angels, status?" asked Harriman.

"An angel rises in the east," sounded a voice over the earpiece.

"Another rises in the west," chimed in a second voice.

"Confirmed. We go at three ten hours. Primaries are the corners. Mother, keep an eye on number five," said Harriman.

"Will do. Go at three ten hours local. Good luck, Red Hen."

"And you, Mother."

He looked at Stevens. "We've got four minutes."

The two moved to join the rest of their squad. Jim Anderson held the rocket launcher. Teresa Zane waited beside him, arms resting on the FN-SCARP attached to her body armor.

"Fire it, drop it, get to the breech double time," instructed Harriman. "I've got the assets, you secure the courtyard and then my six."

"Hoo-ah!" affirmed the others quietly.

"Here we go," said Harriman, watching the pad. On the monitor, he saw all six flies, five finding resting places on the back of each target's skull.

The sixth fly's camera told a different story. Harriman saw the boss turn his face to the fly, arm moving forward. The screen went black except for a pinpoint of light.

"Shit!" said Harriman.

In synchronicity, all six cameras went black as the ordinance of each fly was delivered to its target.

"A one. Target neutralized. Acquiring second target."

"A two. Target neu…."

Harriman didn't wait to hear the rest. "Open the door Jim!" he said, throwing away the glasses and taking off at top speed toward the villa.

He heard and felt the shell fly past him, crossing the yard and impacting on the large, wooden door. The gateway was immersed in a rising wall of flame, the door disintegrating before him.

He looked over to see Walt Stevens keeping pace five meters to his right. Harriman realized that Anderson had fired the grenade between them.

"That was too close," Stevens said breathlessly. "I'm gonna have a talk with that boy."

"Didn't give him much choice," said Harriman between breaths.

The two made it to the smoldering entrance, pressing against the wall on either side of where the door had once stood.

11

They both reached for a concussion grenade from their belts. Stevens motioned a three count with his hands. They pulled the pins, threw their grenades opposite of each other into the courtyard, and waited.

The blast shook the walls with a deafening force. Both men jumped into the courtyard. Harriman's side was empty. He heard the pop of Steven's SCARP, turning in time to see a lone figure slump to the ground, a small rose forming on his forehead. Zane and Anderson burst through the entrance behind him.

"Go!" yelled Stevens. "We'll finish it!"

Harriman ran to the villa's entrance and kicked in the door. The anteroom was empty of anyone alive- the body of the lone guard was face down on the floor with the back of his head missing from the fly's nasty bite. He raced down the hall to the room with the IED.

Entering the room, Harriman knew that he and everyone else would soon be dead. On the floor was the boss, his crotch bloody from the detonation of the woman's fly, his right hand and most of his forearm missing. His look was that of a desperate animal- eyes wide and breathing hard, fighting for every precious second of what remained of his life. He was staring intently ahead at his left hand.

In it was a cellphone.

Harriman could see that he had dialed a number. With his thumb, the boss pushed the green button that would connect the call and end their world.

Harriman leapt across the room toward the bomb. He grabbed the attached cellphone and tore it away from the device, throwing it with all his strength across the room. It began to ring in midair and shattered against the wall.

Realizing that the bomb would not go off, the boss began crawling across the room. Harriman could see his goal- a holstered nine-millimeter pistol on the floor. Harriman walked towards the gun, knowing he would easily make it there before the bleeding, broken man on the floor.

A shot rang out, and the front of the boss's head exploded in a mélange of red and pink. Harriman turned to see Stevens in the doorway.

"All sales are final," he said, smiling. "Area is locked down. Anderson and Zane are securing the assets."

Harriman leaned against the table, catching his breath.

"Jeez! That was way too close! Thank God for shitty cell service."

12

Stevens looked at his watch. "Under five minutes. Not bad for a bunch of old guys."

"Preparation wins the game. Call in the birds and pop smoke."

Zane stuck her head through the doorway.

"Sir, we have a problem... oh! Outstanding work!" she said looking over the room.

"You know, Terry, these people have mothers," replied Harriman, slightly annoyed. He resisted nonchalance over killing. "What's the problem?"

"Sorry, sir. Picket brought in an intruder from just off the main road. He was parked a couple hundred meters from the access road. Speaks English pretty well. He claims to be waiting for someone."

"Another terrorist?" speculated Walt Stevens. "That's easy enough. Let's shoot the fucker and blow this pop stand."

Harriman put his hand up. "Wait a minute. There's the matter of whom he's waiting for, and I'm not so keen on offing him that quickly. If he's a terrorist, he could provide valuable intel on this group... something this one is no longer going to able to provide, Walt."

"That's just it, sir. He's not with this group. Says he's waiting for Grace Williams," said Teresa Zane.

"Oh, shit!" cried Stevens throwing his arms heavenward. "Oh shit!"

"Who's Grace Williams?" asked Harriman innocently.

"Don't you watch the news, John?" Stevens was incredulous.

"She's a VIP with Net News International, sir," replied Zane. "Focuses mainly on foreign stuff, war zones, civil wars, revolutions... kind of what we do sir," said Zane. "Made her name covering the Basque war. One tough bitch."

"Well, we can't kill *her*," moaned Stevens.

"She doesn't know that," countered Harriman. "Besides, we have to find her first. Let's see if we can leverage her partner. Where is he?"

"On the front lawn, sir."

"So he hasn't seen anything inside. Let's keep it that way and maybe no one else has to die." He turned to Stevens, "Still gotta pop smoke and call in the birds. Get on the horn to the locals, too."

"On it."

"Terry, let's go see our interloper."

The two walked out of the villa and onto the now, well-lit lawn beyond the perimeter wall. On his knees, hands zip-tied behind his back, was a young man who looked to be in his early-twenties. Harriman could tell he was terrified. That was good.

He stopped in front of the man, sizing him up. Thin and small with a boyish face... this fellow was no fighter.

"Who are you?" Harriman inquired in his most demanding voice.

"My name is Fabio Mariano Dutra from Sao Paulo and I am not a terrorist. Please do not kill me."

Harriman was glad their captive was looking down. He was having difficulty keeping a straight face interrogating what he had quickly surmised to be a harmless interloper.

"How do we know that? Do you know what happens to terrorists?"

The young man shrank. "No, please! I am a V-Stream producer for NNI, and I am here waiting for Grace Williams. Please! Do not kill me! I am not a terrorist! I swear!"

"Where is Grace Williams? Why would she be here?"

"The state security commandant told her that they had found the Cabral's and that the Americans were coming to free them tonight. I..."

"What?" Harriman broke in. "Are you telling me that Commander Silva leaked this operation to a reporter?"

"Sim, senior," answered Fabio looking up for the first time. "She can be very... persuasive. She convinced me to wait for her, and I am a true coward."

That asshole! thought Harriman, seething that his unit had been compromised.

"Where is Grace Williams? Tell me, or I'll shoot you in the head and leave you here to rot," threatened Harriman.

Fabio whimpered, "Please! I do not know. She left me and walked up the hill. I have not seen her since. She wanted video of the hostage rescue."

Playing a hunch, Harriman took out his sidearm and pointed it at the young man.

Fabio began sobbing loudly.

"Grace Williams," Harriman shouted into the woods, "you've got until I count to ten to show yourself or I'm going to blow this boy's brains out just for fun."

—

14

"Hold on," came a woman's voice from the gloom. "Don't shoot. I'm coming out, hands up."

A figure emerged from the dark, walking slowly, hands raised in surrender. Moments later, the woman came into full view in the light.

"*That's* Grace Williams," said Terry Zane. "Toughest news bitch out there. Goes into all the hotspots and she looks like that."

"Whoa!" said Harriman under his breath. "Ok, I get it."

***

Grace had recorded the entire firefight from her perch. What perplexed her was the ease in which the inner villa had been taken. She speculated that someone on the inside must have been a traitor to the cause- turning on his compatriots and killing them. That would explain the bursts of light from inside the house just before the RPG hit the door.

It was an amazing piece of video. She'd probably never know who the two spec ops heading for the door were but they had huge balls. Capturing the RPG splitting the air between them might win her a Pulitzer. The entire operation had lasted only a few minutes, which was perfect. There would be almost no editing required and her voiceover would be over the top of it... or a bumper at the front and back. She hadn't quite made up her mind yet.

She was still rolling for the hostages to exit or their bodies to be brought out when she saw the two figures walking across the yard. The one in back was a spec op, she could see an assault rifle hanging from his abdomen. The other in front was a prisoner, hands tied behind his back. Grace zoomed in for a better look. It was Fabio.

Grace had already climbed down from her perch and was standing in the shadow of the woods when she saw the one in charge point his pistol at Fabio's head. She smiled, knowing that both she and the young Brazilian were safe. She waited to be called out- appearing out of nowhere might get her shot. When it came, Grace raised her hands and slowly stepped into the light, moving toward the assembled party.

Grace did a quick sizing up of the leader, just under six feet and roughly one hundred eighty pounds. Like most spec ops, he was solid as a rock. Not a pretty boy but sharp, good looks, dark hair, likely in a military cut under his cap. He looked to be in his mid-thirties. Having seen him in action, she was impressed.

"My associates tell me that you are somewhat famous, Ms. Williams," he began.

15

"Somewhat," Grace replied. "May I lower my hands?"

"Of course. We have a bit of a dilemma. You see, we aren't really here, yet you have evidence to the contrary. We need to confiscate your camera."

Grace had expected that.

"I'm afraid it's out there… somewhere," she said motioning toward the woods.

"Ms. Williams, this isn't a game. I need that camera and anything else you possess that has documented this incident," he said calmly.

"Why? Anyone can see you're either specs or spooks and you just performed some freaking incredible acts of bravery. Why not let the people back home know? Hopefully, you saved the Cabral's. Good for you, Captain… do you have a name?" asked Grace.

"No, and I'm afraid you are mistaken in your assumption. This operation isn't sanctioned by the government of the United States, and no one here is currently a member of any branch of the U. S. military. We're all private citizens.

"People can't know about this for two reasons. First, we have to maintain a low profile in order to continue our work. If our faces were to be seen, it would put us in danger.

"Second, we are operating within a sovereign nation, and the last thing *anyone* wants to do is embarrass the government of that sovereign nation with video of foreigners conducting a paramilitary operation within its borders," he said firmly.

"Well Captain… *Anonymous*, we really do have a problem because I busted my ass and risked my life for that video and it's the best thing I've done in two years. I'm not chucking it away because some spook is worried about whether or not I got his good side," Grace retorted just as firmly. "If this isn't a spec op, then you don't have the authority to detain me."

"No, I'll just shoot you and your friend here," he said, pointing at the now silent Fabio. "The Brazilian state police are on their way and what they'll find are two *very* stupid journalists who made the mistake of getting caught in the crossfire. Who is to know any better?"

"Ah but then you still wouldn't have the camera and video would you?" She countered. "Big woods out there, lots of hiding places. Other people know why I'm in Sao Paulo… who knows who might stumble across it? Same problem for you."

"True but I could take some satisfaction in killing you."

Grace looked the man squarely in the eyes.

"You're not going to kill me," she said in a steady voice.

"Lady, you have no idea what I'm capable of," he shot back. "Don't push your luck."

Another man walked briskly into the group. She assumed from his manner he was the second.

"Locals will be here in thirty, birds in ten."

The one in charge nodded without taking his eyes off of Grace. She had an idea.

"Look, if you don't want to take credit, fine. I'll stream the story and give it to the Brazilians. I'll say that it was their spec ops that took out the compound. I get my story, the Brazilians save face, and you get to slip back into the fog," said Grace.

She could sense he was working it over. She decided to push a little harder.

"This is going to help embellish your cover story; actual video of the Brazilians storming the compound. I can get an interview with their commander describing the assault. It's a win-win."

"Why should I trust you to keep your word?"

She knew she had him. "Because I'm trusting you to keep yours. Besides, you won't kill if you don't have to. I know your type."

"My type? What makes you think I wouldn't kill the both of you and fly off into the dawn without a second thought?"

Grace beamed him *the smile.*

"I saw from the woods. Fabio was never in any danger. You didn't chamber a round before pointing your pistol at him."

The man broke into a genuine grin. Still holding his sidearm, he fired a shot into the ground away from the group. Grace lost her smile, looking at where the bullet had struck. His didn't waver.

"Ms. Williams, in my line of business, there's always a round in the chamber," he said to her, holstering the weapon. "We have a deal, but if you go back on it, I will hunt you down and kill you. It'll be as easy as eating pancakes. Understand?"

Grace never lost her composure. "I do. You can review every second. I will delete anything you consider to be compromising."

"Be assured that I will." He looked at the guard standing over Fabio. "Cut him loose but don't let him wander." To the woman beside him, he said, "Go help Ms. Williams find her lost camera."

Grace relaxed as the situation de-escalated. She laughed.

"You called in the state police? That means I have to deal with that pig Silva again."

The man shot her a deadly look. "I'm afraid you'll be interviewing his EXO, Ms. Williams. Commander Silva will be leaving with us. We don't tolerate security breaches. They can get my people killed."

He continued to look at her darkly and Grace understood. Silva was about to *accidently* fall out of a helicopter. She turned to the woman, motioning toward the woods. "Shall we?"

The two began walking together into the red glow of the coming dawn. They were halfway to the woods when the woman sheepishly spoke up.

"Can I get your autograph?"

PART ONE

Chapter One

She felt the vibration of the shell as it went past, dividing the air with a whoosh. Instantly, it brought forward a childhood memory of a baseball hit to her in left field. That familiar buzz, resonating from the ball's stitching as it cut through the dense air.

Though the explosion was well behind them, the concussion knocked her around. It seemed to take forever to regain her balance. Looking back at what had once been the outer wall of a house, she thanked their luck. It was gone.

The escort squad scattered for cover wherever they could find it. Small arms fire rang out; they were seemingly surrounded. Regaining focus, she realized that it was coming from the houses ahead and to the right.

It was a weak ambush. So far, only a single RPG had been sent their way and maybe a half dozen AK-74's now popped off. She figured it was probably a scout and scavenge unit. Assuming that her escort was a platoon with slightly better firepower, she felt pretty good about their odds. Still, she had been around long enough to know it only takes one stray bullet to become a piece of meat.

This was a hit and run; a tactic regularly used to degrade government units. Pick one or two off here, take out a unit commander there. She had seen it before in other war zones… in other countries… around the world. It was too familiar.

The platoon began returning fire. It was a typical firefight between what for all practical purposes were two groups of scared and angry men with guns. No rhyme or reason, just terrified souls barely out of their teens firing blindly around corners and over stone walls at nothing in particular. It would be over in a few minutes- the rebel patrol would cut out amidst the confusion, hopefully with no one killed.

She continued to take cover behind a wall. The soldier acting as their interpreter crouched a few feet away. From time to time, he would stick his AK-74 around the corner and get off a few rounds. Not one to die for his cause. She liked that.

"Gracie, why do we keep signing up for this?" She looked over at Kearney. He had his camera out panning the platoon as it fired back. He had been quick on it, by her count less than thirty seconds had passed since the grenade hit. John had been through it before too. He looked her way with *the face*- a wild-eyed symbiosis acknowledging that your life could end in a microsecond blended with the rush of never feeling more alive.

"Over here, Red!" She saw no reason to waste an opportunity. The firefight meant nothing in the grand scheme of the war, but it would play big back in the real world.

Kearney turned the camera towards her. These days, Grace thought they looked a lot more like an old style tablet with a handle. It was a mini production suite. John could take video of the scene and use the touch screen to add whatever effects he needed. He could edit and upload to satellite a report from the battlefield within minutes of it happening, or instantly as raw footage if he wanted to capture the moment for the viewers back home. It was a far cry from shoulder borne digitals she had started out with years ago.

He held the camera with his left hand, raising his right to cue her. "In five, four, three…"

"Grace Williams for NNI, your eye on the world, reporting from Akhalskaya Province, Turkmenistan, with producer John Kearney. We are embedded with Turkmen government soldiers, who are at this moment engaged against rebel forces we believe to be from the Shia Army of God.

"Both sides have been battling fiercely for control of the villages in this region and we find ourselves caught up in an ambush as we travel through the town of Baharly. The town is close to the front but was believed to be firmly under government control. This firefight comes as a surprise to us as we make our way northeast to Serdar.

"So far, the fighting has gone on for several minutes with neither side making gains on the ground. Casualties could be high. For now, we will bring you the dramatic scenes of this battle." Grace paused to give Red a chance to work the camera off her and back onto the firefight.

He gave her a sarcastic smirk. "Casualties could be high?

"Dramatic license. Sounds like it's just about over."

"That's the *second* most dangerous time in a firefight."

Grace hunkered behind the wall while Red grabbed video of the chaos. Within minutes, the shooting subsided and the platoon slowly reformed. A quick head count determined no casualties. Grace assumed they wouldn't find any dead rebels either.

Their interpreter for this hayride was a short, impressively built young man named Nazar. He made his way over to them, grinning as he approached.

"I am so glad to see that you are not dead! It makes me happy that we do not have to carry your bodies back down the mountain to Ashgabat." The grin got a little wider, showing off a rough set of tobacco-stained teeth.

"Thank you, Nazar. We are happy as well not to leave your bullet-riddled corpse here unburied and be forced to take up with the rebels."

The brawny interpreter broke into a full laugh. Grace grinned back.

Some Turkmen might have taken offense at her brazenness, but Nazar had spent four years in London studying finance before everything had fallen apart. He understood the sarcasm of Westerners.

"I believe that should such a thing happen, Azat Mohamed would not hesitate to turn a beautiful Chinese woman over for his men to use as a sex slave." He drifted for a second; she could tell that he was contemplating the idea. Cocking his head toward Kearney, "And I believe that your red head would decorate a post in his camp."

"American. Korean-American," she corrected. "So were those Army of God troops we just danced with?"

"I don't believe so. Azat's men are fanatics. They would have died before retreating and would have enjoyed taking American hostages for propaganda. These were probably Russian or Ukrainian Orthodox Army scouts. They're more likely to hit and run." The grin returned. "They appreciate living to fight another day, as do I."

Nazar grew serious again.

"The AG, they do what we are taking you to see."

The three of them moved toward one of the ancient troop carriers that acted as the unit's transportation. Others loaded into the jeeps that accompanied it. They had stopped at the outskirts of Baharly to stretch their legs after passing through the town. The rebel patrol must have seen the opportunity for an ambush with the small convoy rowed up like ducks. The RPG was probably intended for their troop carrier. Grace thanked Providence for poor marksmanship.

As they settled into the APC, Grace thought about the motivations of young men who had once played together as brothers on the soccer pitch to now kill each other for their god.

God. Shia Army of God, Orthodox Army of God... what a joke. Except for Azat Mohamed's group of fanatics, this war had nothing to do with God. It was a proxy war between regional powers over the vast energy reserves located throughout the country- and who profited from them.

It's always about money.

Turkmenistan was the last place Grace or anyone else expected to blow apart. From the fall of the Soviet Union until a few years ago, everyone had gotten along. Overall, it was a homogeneous population, roughly eighty percent Muslim. Of that, eight out of ten were Sunni, those along the border with Iran naturally tended to be Shia.

It was in the midst of a modernization program, funded primarily by revenue from vast natural gas reserves when the trouble had begun.

Turkmenistan was a rising star in Central Asia. The population was poor, but not impoverished. The government subsidized electricity and heating oil. It had free, universal education. There was economic development, a building boom, and a tourism industry.

Ironically, the unraveling began with the implementation of democracy. The parties had coalesced not around mutual political ideology but instead ethnic, sectarian, and religious identities. Groups forced to get along under the former, authoritarian regime now openly expressed their disdain for each other. The moderates were shouted down. In her experience, Grace had found that they always were.

Two years ago, Party of God leader Azat Nurali and Christian Democrat Party leader Dmitri Kalashnikov stood up in the Meiji and walked out with one-quarter of the country's representatives. Within days, Balkanskaya province declared independence. Then the northeastern section of Balkanskaya sheared away, declaring itself the Central Asian Republic. Turkmenistan shattered into a Christian north, Shia west and Sunni east. What was left of the Meiji immediately authorized the army to put down the uprising.

As Grace knew, it's never really that clean and straightforward. For one, a significant portion of the army leadership was comprised of Russians and Ukrainians, many in command positions. Weeks before parliament had disintegrated, a large number of the officers secretly began moving themselves, loyal troops, equipment, and munitions westward. The call to defend the nation was met initially with a vacuum of confusion.

Then there was the politics… and economics… of it all. The Christians and Shias were indeed strange bedfellows. It was no secret that the Shias were supported by Iran while the Christians took their marching orders from Russia. These two states being regional rivals made their proxies' co-operation even stranger.

Russia's leaders, increasingly belligerent in their efforts to recreate the old empire, had their eyes on Turkmenistan. A foothold, gained through the country's ethnic Russian population, was a good start toward eventual annexation.

As the nation with the largest concentration of Shia Muslims, Iran had a strong desire to support Shias worldwide. With the Muslim world embroiled in its own version of the Hundred Years War, Iran openly sought allies. Partitioning southern Iraq had created a puppet state and buffer zone to the west. Now, it had the opportunity to weaken and shear away one-third of what had been a mostly Sunni state and create another buffer to the north.

Those massive gas fields in the Karakum Desert... Russia wanted a proxy state directly west of it. A martial move to the east could easily secure both the energy and the profits for the big bear.

All that gas and oil moving north on a pipeline through Uzbekistan was something neither the Turkmen nor the Iranians could accept. The Turkmen had their own pipeline passing through Balkanskaya to ports on the Caspian Sea. Another pipeline under construction would soon link with those in Iran. Both were now lost with the insurgency of the Shia. Even if the Turkmen retained control of the gas fields, distribution deals with the Iranians and their Shia puppets would be inevitable.

It's always about the money.

War comes and the people pay. People who were friends and neighbors, did business with each other, married each other. Now, they scatter from hatred and death- dealt to them by former friends, solely because an ancestor long ago had chosen a particular way to pray. The people always pay the price; in blood and with their homes. Seeking refuge in enclaves set aside for them, only to wither away.

Ethnic cleansing as a form of natural selection. Grace had covered enough of these to know the endgame.

A once peaceful little country descending into Hell.

They continued to trek through the dusk, down foothills and onto the western steppes towards their destination- the town of Serdar. Though it was a part of Balkanskaya province, the townspeople there had resisted joining in the secession.

Turkmen forces had just retaken the region, previously controlled by the AG. When the rebels withdrew, the Turkmen had found evidence of atrocities. War crimes being committed against civilian populations in a war zone was to be expected. What made this a story was the scale. The Turkmen claimed the entire town had been massacred- more than ten thousand people.

The rumors were less than twelve hours old and, time being of the essence, NNI immediately pulled Grace and John off a political story in Alexandria and flew them into Ashgabat.

This was what they did, why they were the best at it. Grace had cut her teeth in Syria in the twenties. Later, she had met and teamed up with Kearney covering the Basque conflict. A familiarity with war zones kept them wary but not fearful. Like any good soldier, they had trained themselves to mentally step back from constantly lurking death to focus on the job at hand. This time was no different. They would drop in, get the story, and move to the next big thing. It had been this way for more than a decade.

Grace looked over at the big Irishman. His back was propped up against the APC's wall. A duffel bag shoved behind him acted as a makeshift cushion. Kearney's head drooped into his chest, eyes closed. She heard him snoring and smiled; Red could always catch sleep no matter where he was. Panning the APC, she saw the half-dozen soldiers in various states of recline grabbing whatever slumber they could in the red glow.

Though exhausted, Grace couldn't do that, in part because she had to be more conscious of her surroundings. She wouldn't have been the first female war correspondent to be raped by her escort. In most of the places they worked, she was the exotic-looking Westerner. A mix of Korean-American mother and English father had provided her the best physical features of both races. The mélange had given her a striking Eurasian beauty, canopied by straight, blond hair that fell just below her shoulders. While she did respectfully adopt traditional garb in the more conservative regions, some men still saw her as nothing more than a decadent Western whore- theirs for the taking.

Grace had taken to carrying an eight-inch military knife on her person. When in robes, she concealed it in a sheath strapped to her right calf. She knew how to use it as well. It was subtle yet effective- a sidearm could make her look like a combatant instead of a correspondent. The knife didn't carry the same connotation, but it did even things up. Now, she had a prick too, and it wouldn't be a good time for anyone who tried to use theirs on her.

This trip, the knife was strapped to her hip and thigh in plain sight. The Turkmen had been Soviets for decades and were relatively secular. These weren't Wahabists- for most Turkmen Sunnis, their religious practices were the Muslim equivalent of being Lutheran. That gave Grace an opportunity for practicality; she was able to wear camo pants and military boots. She kept warm in a standard issue field jacket with her only concession to femininity being the blue blouse underneath. When the camera came on, the jacket came off, and viewers got a little eye candy with their carnage.

She turned back to the matter at hand. Massacre on a scale so massive that the Turkmen claimed it would be a game changer. The Iranians and Russians would no longer be able to argue that they were merely offering assistance to peoples desiring self-determination. They would become de-facto supporters of genocide.

For the Turkmen, this would be huge for their propaganda effort. The West was reluctant to take sides; no one wanted an east-west proxy war in Russia's backyard. Besides, the Americans had their hands full in Africa, matching the Chinese move for move in a half-dozen brush wars.

The systematic murder of thousands of innocents would conjure up the specter of Rwanda, Bosnia, and Cambodia. There were still many alive who could remember those days and the millions who died from western paralysis. Then, the alibi was feigned ignorance. A lack of timely news coverage coming out of those killing fields had allowed the world to claim no interval to act.

That excuse wouldn't cut it these days. Net News International and other web-based services put coverage in real time. Within hours, this story would be uploaded into the NNI video stream for viewing... potentially by billions. The Americans and EU would be hard pressed not to step in. Even the UN might come to an agreement on this one. Holding the moral high ground, Turkmenistan could get the global consensus and military assistance that it had been pleading for to turn the war in its favor.

Grace could see through the viewport that it was now completely dark. Judging from the sounds and headlights flickering through the slit, she guessed that they had joined up with a convoy.

She closed her eyes momentarily, right hand resting on the hilt of the knife.

They opened when she could no longer ignore the odor. She knew what it was but had never been hit with something this pervasive. It was the smell of putrefying meat.

Every once in a while, a quizzical person would ask her what was the most memorable aspect of being in a war zone. For Grace, it was the smell of the bodies. She would try to describe it for them. A dead cat left in the sun for a few days. A malfunctioning freezer full of rotting meat- the acrid, sickly odor smacking you when the lid is opened, bringing bile to the top of your throat. Instinctively telling you to run as far away from it as possible. A fragrance denoting finality.

The visuals of bodies rotting, blackened, and bloated, flies and maggots crawling through exploded stomachs or pulled apart by scavenging rodents; those were horrific, but eventually the casual viewer could become desensitized to such imagery. After all, they were not much more shocking than a lot of zombie videos that had been such a rage years ago.

Grace wondered how popular those shows would have been if viewers could smell the zombies as well.

The soldiers were now pulling bandanas out of their pockets. A small plastic bottle was making the rounds- each soldier shaking a few drops onto their cloth and passing it on. The aroma of peppermint fought a losing battle with the stench.

Grace took out her bandana and another small bottle from the side pocket of her camo's. Popping the top, she put a few drops in the tri-fold and wrapped the bandana around the lower half of her face, tying it bandit style. Hers was cinnamon, a surgeon's trick she had picked up from a forensic pathologist. Live bodies smell bad enough when sliced open; dead ones smell worse. Peppermint isn't strong enough. Cinnamon burns the nose a bit, but the strong odor overpowers the rot as opposed to blending with it.

Inevitably, there would be those moments when she would have to pull down the mask to show her face for the camera. That would come later, and she had time to psych herself up for it. She was happy that Red didn't have to suffer through that torture.

The APC lurched to a stop. She could tell through the slit that it was daybreak- there was a lot of movement outside. One of the men began winching the rear ramp down; the electricals had ceased to function long ago.

It was as though a camera was wiping down the opening scene of a movie. First, the cloudless, azure sky breaking through the red light of the APC. Into focus came the tops of heads flying back and forth, seemingly disembodied. Slowly, the rooftops and walls of the town in the background came into view, the heads now gaining torsos and arms. As the ramp touched the ground, full-bodied men came into view- as did the corpses.

In the foreground, soldiers were carrying the dead past the opening of the APC, moving left to right. No body bags or stretchers- one man on the arms and another on the legs. Heads bobbed lifelessly in rhythm with the strides of the living. A lone soldier passed, carrying what had once been a child in his outstretched arms.

Looking past the foreground, Grace saw the scattered bodies on the hill before her. Working her vision back toward the town, she could see dots of color blending into blotches and swaths, contrasting with the green of the hillocks. Initially, her mind tricked her that these were reds and yellows from autumn leaves. Upon mentally registering the blends of blues and whites, she knew it was something far different. The swaths spiraled and trailed back towards the town, a kilometer in the distance. Within the lovely, bright colors were hundreds... thousands of dead. It resembled a Monet when viewed too close up; everything blurred together into an exquisite mishmash of color with all form lost.

It was the most horrific scene Grace had ever witnessed. She suppressed the urge to vomit. Others stumbled out of the APC and did just that.

When confronted with unimaginable carnage, there's an initial revulsion and flight reflex. Momentarily, the veneer of culture rejects reality and physically manifests itself in vomiting, uncontrollable tears, or screaming.

Then something kicks in, and people do their jobs. Grace used to think it was training but, time and again, she had witnessed civilians transform themselves within moments, from a quivering, incoherent mess to moving bodies and digging graves.

Grace thought that it was a unique ability people had to disconnect from their humanity, making a mental adjustment to get through any situation. It was how we were able to kill each other, or how we could start looking at a dead child as just another carcass to be disposed of. Some part of their psyche went into a box, to be recovered later when they were beyond the horror's reach.

The damage would manifest later- in nightmares and tears, drinking and drugs, anger... and hatred.

This scene was almost too much. That was another thing about people: lose a single celebrity to cancer and thousands of strangers will come together to pay tribute to his life and donate to his charity. Tell them that the lives of twenty thousand strangers were just extinguished by an earthquake and they'll shrug their shoulders, unable to comprehend.

Red was already out and shooting, starting with a pan of the low hills before them. He then moved to shots of recovery teams carrying bodies toward the large cremation pits that had been set up downwind of the road. He was doing his job. Hers would be to make people care.

Nazar came up on her right and touched her arm. Such an action would normally be considered taboo, but Grace saw the pain in his eyes. It was not an act of intrusion, but instead one of inclusion.

"I will find someone for us to speak with," he said through the bandana. His eyes became a stone. He turned and began walking toward a group of large tents silhouetted in the sunrise.

Grace reached into her side pocket, taking out a notepad and pencil. In the real world, it would have been a mic transcribing her words into text. In a war zone, things as fragile as a virtual notepad or Magi-Watch broke. She had learned over the years to trust paper. Of course, she used waterproof pads because it could always be wet somewhere. The pencil was a standard number two that she could sharpen with her knife when needed.

Grace walked around the immediate area making notes. Kearney needed time to get the visuals- his time to shine. Hers would come soon enough.

Making her way down the hill closest to the APC, she saw what must have been a family- a woman and three children lying close together. The mother and two of the kids were lying with their heads facing the bottom of the hill; giving her the mental image of sledding down it. Grace could not see the mother's face. It was buried in the grass. The children's faces were turned as if sleeping on their stomachs. One had a frozen grimace that looked as though he were grinning. The other had no eyes- scavenging crows had plucked them out.

They were traditionally dressed; dried blood stained their garb. The exit wounds were surprisingly large.

A few meters behind them was a third child, a boy she guessed, lying spread-eagled and face up. He seemed to have been killed while contemplating a cloudless sky. Half his head was missing. It looked like the work of a fifty-caliber machine gun.

She wondered- why would the Army of God waste large-caliber bullets on defenseless civilians? It was terribly inefficient. It seemed to be more an act of irrational anger as opposed to cold-blooded murder.

Something else struck her- there were no girls, at least not teens or young adults. Grace could guess what had happened to them.

She heard Nazar calling from the roadside. Beside him stood three men, one was Red setting up the shot. Another carried a rifle, probably a guard. In the middle, shorter than the others was an officer. Grace briskly walked up the hill toward them.

Nazar spoke first, "Grace Williams; it is my privilege to introduce General Ali Puntjar, supreme commander of the western region."

Grace had learned early in her career that an interpreter was merely a tool. She kept her eyes fixed upon the general. The commander extended his hand. He looked directly into her eyes, speaking in Russian.

Grace found it ironic that these men, whose ancestors had been Mongolian invaders and who had later adopted Islam, would converse in European Russian. She couldn't think of a better example of people adapting to their environment despite their genetic point of origin. She smiled behind the bandana as she took his hand in greeting.

"The General offers his welcome. He says it is a great honor to meet the famous Grace Williams."

"The honor is mine, General. I only wish we could have met under a more social circumstance. What we see here is unimaginable." Grace waited for the back and forth of Nazar and Puntjar. The General spoke uninterrupted as he released her hand and turned towards the town in the distance. He gestured as he spoke, hands opening wide as if to take it all upon himself. His tone was steady and reserved, doing his best to wear the mantle of leadership.

"This town had been reluctant from the beginning to join in the rebellion. Sunni and Shia had lived here in peace for hundreds of years. The town council made it clear that they would not resist occupation, but they would also contribute none of their young men to the rebellion. For many, Serdar was a symbol of hope that we could live together again as one nation." General Puntjar's eyes grew sullen as he continued with Nazar interpreting.

"Azat Mohamed sent his men to occupy the town when the battlefront had formed to the east, using it as a staging area. From what we have been able to discover, the townspeople did not interfere. A few days ago, our forces broke through the lines. Seeing that retreat was inevitable, Azat Mohamed decided to repay the town for their lack of enthusiasm. He ordered everyone slaughtered.

He had his troops pull back and surround the town. Then his men began going house to house, killing everyone within. Soon the whole town was gripped in panic. Many of the men tried to fight back, but they were all killed. Those you see before you on the hills were escaping from the murderers who were going through the town. They were driven toward machine gun nests as they fled. Those who pretended to be dead had their heads clubbed as the monsters went from body to body."

The General's face grew darker as he tried to control his emotions.

"We entered the town yesterday and found this. There were more than ten thousand souls in Serdar." He stopped for a moment.

Grace noticed that John had been recording the General as he spoke. Several men had formed around them in a semi-circle. Some held rage in their eyes; others held back tears.

"General, have..." Grace broke off in mid-sentence and clutched at a fire in her abdomen. The pain was so bright and hot that it bent her forward.

Oh God! I'm shot!

Chapter Two

Wil stood across the street from the Blue Heron's entrance, the evening breeze blowing his hair gently. He finished his cigarette and took a deep breath of fresh air before starting toward the door. He was late.

The teal door was weatherworn, its paint peeling slightly. Wil couldn't help but crack a smile. *Beautiful detail,* he noted in admiration. The bar inside was even better, being slightly seedy but not quite a dive. Lots of black, chrome and mirrors. A parquet dance floor anchored the center of the room, the strobe light reflecting off the overhanging mirror ball. A variety of beautiful people danced to retro disco music. In the booths, couples and larger groups were laughing and pawing at each other over drinks.

Very vintage, he thought, *but why the hell is it called the Blue Heron?*

He found Sonya sitting at the bar, engaged in conversation with a couple. She was exceptional tonight dressed in a purple, sequin dress and matching pumps. The front was cut practically down to her belly button, and every time she turned, the fabric would separate from her breast to reveal a nipple. The dress's slit complemented tan and taut thighs. Her blonde hair was feathered to perfection.

This is so not me, thought Wil. *Why do I let her keep talking me into this?*

Still, he couldn't help but get stirred up looking at her. He hoped she got as hot for his avatar.

Sonya must have sensed him coming, turning to flash a smile. No matter the shell, the face was always the same. "Hi, babe! Kinda late, aren't we?" She gave him a kiss on the lips- hot and quick with just a hint of tongue. A tease for what was to come.

"Wilson Ramirez, meet Penny and Nick Starr. Penny, Nick, Wilson." She pulled him towards her, more to showcase him for her newfound friends than anything else.

"Wilson. My... don't you look like the main course!" exclaimed Penny with a wry smile. She leaned into him, brushing her hand past his cheek. Her wrist smelled of musk. He loved musk.

"Keep your big meals, dear," crooned Nick, sliding an arm around Sonya's waist. "I prefer a little dessert myself."

That tipped him off; they were 'bots. The pickup line was a bit too clichéd. These worlds always made him uncomfortable. He was a lot shyer and more self-conscious about sex than Sonya but she liked coming here to pass the time, and he did his best for her sake.

AI or not, Penny was one fine-looking woman. A natural redhead with even more natural-looking breasts busting out of a halter top dress. Secretly, he couldn't wait to get his hands on them.

He played along. "Just call me Wil. So what's everyone drinking tonight? I'm going to have a scotch." He motioned towards the bartender. "Johnny Walker Red, double, on the rocks." He looked around, eyes inquiring.

"Sex on the Beach," Sonya said over the roar. The music was obnoxiously loud.

"Sloe gin fizz and a rum and coke," said Nick. The bartender nodded and began preparing glasses. *She's a fine looking thing as well*, thought Wil. Short and stacked. He wondered if she was an avatar or AI.

He looked back to Sonya, whose right hand was helping Penny's rub Nick's crotch. "So this is the swinging seventies. I can see why you like it."

"The sixties were swinging, but by the seventies, they had it down to an art form. It's before AIDS ruined sex. Come closer, dear." She reached down with her left hand to massage his crotch as well. It felt incredible.

The bartender came back with the round. Nick reached into his sports jacket for his wallet.

"This one is on me. How quickly can we get *you* on me?" he cracked, eyes betraying a lust for Sonya.

Sonya took her hand away from him and picked up her drink. Rising, she said, "Let's move the party indoors."

They worked their way through the crowded room, Sonya in the lead. Halfway to the other side, Wil realized that Penny had gotten in front of him and had deliberately slowed down in order to press her incredible-looking rear against him. It was working- he hadn't been this excited in a long time.

Sonya was the best. She knew how to get him going with an experience like this, something he would never do on his own. That was why he loved her.

They finally made it to a wall of doors on the other side of the room. Sonya and Nick kept opening and closing them as they moved down the wall. Once, Wil was able to see inside one of the rooms before the door closed. He couldn't count how many naked bodies he had seen and in more positions than he knew. Sonya finally found a room she liked and the foursome poured through it, laughing in anticipation.

Inside the chamber was a huge, pink, satin sofa with big, soft pillows. It was three-quarters of a semi-circle, enveloping a wood and glass table. Behind them was a circular bed; its surface seemed to bob up and down gently. He glanced quizzically at Sonya.

"It's a waterbed. Big deal in this era." She smiled as she first sank into the sofa and then popped forward towards the table. Nick had found a spot next to her. "Don't worry. You'll get to try it out soon enough." She turned her attention to Nick. "How about a little blow, hon?"

Nick pulled a sandwich bag filled with white powder from his coat pocket. He reached for a mirror on the table and poured out a sizable amount. Taking a razor blade from the table, Nick started chopping and forming lines on the mirror.

"You're going to love this baby." Sonya mewed, taking a sip from her drink.

"I know what cocaine is," Wil replied.

"Sure baby, but have you ever fucked on it?" He saw that Sonya could hardly contain herself. "You can fuck for hours and hours!"

They all sat close together on the sofa. Penny had slipped next to him but slid slightly behind him, swaying back and forth slowly. He could feel her hard nipples through his shirt. Nick presented the lines and a rolled up twenty, handing it and the mirror to Sonya. She took a line up each nose and let out a rebel yell.

"Jesus Christ! What a rush!" She began slipping out of her dress as the mirror went around the table.

Penny took her turn, handing the mirror off to Wil. He took a hit up each nostril and felt an immediate flood of power. He looked over to see that Penny was now naked. She began to loosen his belt. Across from them on the couch, he could see that Sonya and Nick had wasted no time. Her head was bobbing up and down in his naked lap.

Penny quickly slid his pants and shorts down, teasing him with her breasts. He put his hand on her naked back.

35

"God, you're huge!" she said. "I can't wait to feel that inside me. Let's start with a little taste…" It was true. He looked up at the mirrored ceiling, and his shell was the epitome of a perfect human body in every way.

Penny got on the floor and moved between his legs. She reached back to the mirror and rubbed her fingers in the cocaine. Then she began rubbing the coke onto him.

"This is going to keep you going all night," she said. "Just give it a minute to go to work."

He began to go numb, but it wasn't really numb at all. He could still feel all that tension, needing release. Penny moved her head between his legs and went to work on him.

Sonya had crawled on all fours next to him. Nick had gotten behind her. She kissed Wil deeply on the mouth. Her tongue was like velvet.

"Happy birthday, baby," she whispered in his ear. "We're going to fu..."

"I'm sorry Wilson, but we have to go back now. Your time is up," came the familiar voice. He looked up to see the angel floating above him. She reached out and pulled him into the black.

Wil awoke from the Virtuality with a jolt. For a moment, he couldn't focus on where he was. A side effect of the trip.

He felt the coffin's movement and realized he was being pulled from the rack with the rest of the row. The top slid back, and there was his attendant. She began disconnecting him from the box.

"Hello, Wil, time to get up and move around a bit. Got to clean up some as well. There's a hot shower waiting for you in the other room and then some solid food." She smiled at him vacantly in the way that all nurses did- polite, but without warmth. Never get too close to the subject, just do the job. Wil got it. He was just a patient to be processed. He had been here for two years, and she had never told him her name. Wil didn't care.

Nameless helped him up and out of the coffin. It took him a moment to get his legs under him- one of the effects of spending sixteen hours a day on his back. Within moments, the strength returned to them... as much strength as he had.

The others in his row were being assisted and brought out as well. This row had thirty canisters in it: fifteen men and fifteen women. Sonya was in this group; it was how they had met. It didn't have to be that way- he had met lots of people from all over the world. His wife in the farm world was boxed in a San Francisco facility.

He saw that everyone had made it back. As time went on, that wasn't always the case.

They shuffled in mass toward the locker room, no one speaking. Separating by sex, they went into the showers on either side of the room. Inside was a clothes hamper where Wil could deposit his robe. He did so, walking naked the rest of the way.

The water was soothing hot, and he soaped down. Still soapy, he washed his hair and then rinsed it all away. Towels were waiting in the locker room on the benches. Wil walked past a mirror, stopping to look. He was just under six feet tall, but couldn't straighten his back. That cost him three or four inches. His hair was thinning. He was what they used to term *heroin thin*. The penis that had been Penny's envy in the erotica world was, in reality, shriveled and impotent.

Today was his twenty-second birthday.

Wil toweled off and found his locker. It opened with his thumbprint, fresh clothes waiting for him. He dressed and headed for the cafeteria. There, he found Sonya.

She was small and heroin thin as well. She had no breasts, no hips, her clothes hung from her. Her face was gaunt and hollow, but he could tell that she had once been very pretty. When she saw him, she smiled, being careful not to show her teeth.

"What shitty timing," she moaned. "I was getting ready to pound you into next week, birthday boy!"

Wil grinned back at her. "Didn't look like it was me you were pounding, my dear."

"I was getting to you. There's nothing better than being the meat in a sandwich,' she shot back.

He laughed. "Sonya I love you, but you can be such a slut."

Her demeanor darkened. "No, I'm not. I've never even had sex... just inside the box. In there it isn't real... and it doesn't matter. I don't even know if that's what it really feels like. Hell, even our friends were just algorithms."

"Well, I have, and I can tell you that they've done a great job with it."

"Oh... no wonder it's such a popular pastime." Her coyness returned as she smiled.

They had found their way to the cafeteria. Other rows that had come out were mingling with their own; the area was soon filling up with several hundred people. They moved together to the serving line. Today, they were having meatloaf.

"There was an old joke my grandfather told me about meatloaf again," Wil said. "It was from some old movie about a guy getting eaten by a transexual." He looked at Sonya with his most serious face. "Maybe they keep recycling him."

"Stop! I have to try and eat this shit. You aren't helping."

They found a table and sat down together. They were lucky to have found each other and become friends. Many people ate alone and then crawled back into the box. Wil felt sorry for them.

They looked at each other and picked at their food. It was hard to eat. It wasn't anybody's fault. RLC had tried to provide the best that it could, and he was grateful. Outside, food was expensive, and a lot of people were hungry. It was just that, inside the box, they could eat steak and lobster, or lamb chops, or barbecued ribs and chicken, or fillet of sole. That was the appeal of Virtuality.

In reality, it was meatloaf and probably not made with actual meat. Much as people hated the box, it wasn't hard to figure out where they'd rather live.

Sonya looked up. "How would you like to have some ice cream, birthday boy?"

"Sure, just tell me where to meet you, and we'll go for some."

"No, not in the box. Real ice cream."

Wil was perplexed. "I... I guess so. Where are we going to find real ice cream? They can't even get meatloaf right."

"Let's go down the street. I saw a place when I first came here. We can go there."

Wil leaned forward across the table until he was almost close enough to kiss this girl. "You want to leave?" he whispered.

"Why not? We can come and go as we please. We aren't in prison," countered Sonya. "I even hid some cash away outside just in case I ever wanted to get out of here for good."

—

Wil's eyes widened. He never knew what to expect from this creature. "You're serious... leave the compound?" The handlers wanted them to spend some time every day outside on the grounds, but no one ever walked through the gate into the real world. Not that you couldn't if you really wanted to. Sonya was right- this wasn't a prison, it's just that no one ever left. There was no point- nothing was waiting outside the gate except hardship and misery. The box took the hardship out of people's misery. Once inside, they could choose their poison. So what if most only lasted a few years in the box? At least they weren't bored to death while on the way to their deaths.

Now, here was Sonya proposing a real adventure. Wil couldn't recall the last time he had been outside; he had come here at nineteen after he learned that he had missed out on a chance at college and that there were no available apprenticeships for his class year. He wasn't brave and couldn't see himself as a soldier. It was either struggle on the street or go into the box. Virtuality seemed the better choice. Being on the street meant a good chance of getting mixed up in crime. Those who were caught ended up in the box anyway, the one with the nine circles of Hell. From what he understood, there was a special place they sent you to that fit your crime. For eighteen hours a day, you were virtually punished for your sins. The way Wil figured it, better to be in Virtuality enjoying your sins than suffering for them. Besides, there were other worlds he could go to where he felt important. The sex worlds were fun but for Sonya.

Sonya was growing impatient. "Come on, Wil. We have to start prep soon. It's now or never."

"I don't know. Virtuals get treated like shit outside. Maybe we can find a nice world with the best ice cream and cake."

"No! That isn't real, it's just a brain trick and no matter how good it is, it's still just a trick. I'm sick of it, and I want to taste real ice cream. You can stay here if you want... I'm going out."

"Ok Sonya, I'll come too." As much as he was afraid of reality, Wil was even more afraid of something happening to her. She was all he had. "Get your coat. I'll meet you at the front in ten minutes."

Sonya gave him a tight-lipped smile. "There ya go!" She stood up from the table, half full plate in hand. "We are going to have so much fun!" She practically ran to the garbage can.

Wil stayed an extra few minutes to finish dinner before heading back to his locker. Inside were the clothes he had arrived with and a bag of extras that the handlers had told him to bring as well. He didn't bother with putting on his street clothes- they wouldn't have fit him anymore anyway. His shoes did still fit, and he slipped those and his heavy coat on. Last was a baseball hat in an attempt to conceal the ports on his head.

They were the unique, identifying mark of the Virtuals. Normals didn't require the ports to use the box- but there was more prep involved. The Virtuals spent their lives in the box, RLC had surgically implanted the access ports as a convenience for the caregivers.

There were three: one at the base of his skull, one on top of his head, and one in his forehead. The first two could be hidden in his hair, but the one in front was just below the hairline and reminded him of a third eye. For that, he needed the hat, and he pulled it down tight over the port.

Looking in the mirror with his coat and hat on, Wil convinced himself that he could pass for a Normal.

He found Sonya waiting for him in the lobby by the front entrance, dwarfed in her coat. A large, blue, knitted hat was pulled over her head, brown hair cascading onto her shoulders. Even though Sonya was average height for a woman, she looked like a girl, maybe thirteen or fourteen. Wil knew that wasn't possible; you couldn't go into the virtuality program unless you were eighteen but he suddenly realized he didn't know how old she was.

Wil thought she was beautiful. He just didn't know how to tell her.

Sonya stretched her arms out to meet him. "Come on birthday boy! Let's go for a little walk." She took his hand- for all of their trysts in virtuality, he had never actually touched her in reality. It made his heart jump to be touched by another human being for something other than *maintenance*. Her hand was clammy at first, but quickly warmed to his.

They pushed out the front entrance, down a set of stone steps and onto the grounds. It reminded Wil of a park; there were trees full of gloriously fiery leaves contrasting with the still green grasses and hedges. Benches were scattered along brick walkways, people sat alone or walked the paths. The air was surprisingly fresh for Chicago, and its chill slapped at his bare face. "It's cold," he said to no one. He knew that it wasn't really that cold, but with no body fat, the wind chill cut right through him.

"Oh no!" his companion cried, pulling him along. "We're not going back. In fact, you and I are going to run right through that gate and get my money. C'mon!" Sonya picked up speed, dragging Wil along.

What the Hell, he thought, matching her pace. They quickly came upon black, iron gates set into a redbrick wall. With one final rush, they burst through.

The next second, Wil was flying downward into the ground. Something had stopped his legs and tripped him up in mid-stride. Instinctively, he put out his hands and felt the burn on his bare palms as he hit the concrete of the sidewalk. The fall knocked the wind out of him.

Jesus! he thought in a panic. *Maybe they really won't let us leave!*

***

Around 5:30, Philip Janikowski took his best girl for a walk.

October was bringing cooler, shorter days and he had taken a light jacket to combat the crisp breeze. He padded down the sidewalk with Virginia by his side; she always thrilled at a chance to get outside. Every so often, she would turn to look at him with her large brown eyes. He imagined that she loved him as much as he did her.

Philip always took these moments to admire his girl's form. In his mind, she couldn't have been a better example of perfection. Virginia possessed the triangular, bat ears and long snout of a Sheppard, her black nose spackling into gray and brown. Her coloring then morphed into the black bandit's mask, split with a streak of white that the best specimens of the breed possessed. Her eyes were dotted over the top with two small patches of brown, giving the illusion of eyebrows.

41

Virginia's head flowed into a thick neck and broad, powerful chest tapering into a thin, muscular torso, and finished with equally impressive haunches. Her strength, even at forty pounds, was that of a dog twice her size; betraying the dingo in her lineage. If it weren't for the coloring, she would have easily passed for that wild dog.

Her body was covered in a somewhat short-haired, gray coat; but it wasn't a solid color. It was more like black hair mixed unequally with white and mottling into blackish spots. Not solid black, though, it reminded Philip of the photographic negative image of a cheetah's coat.

The mottled black and white coat ended at her feet in a trace of brown and white, more in the front. As Australian cattle dogs go, his Virginia was magnificent!

Philip's only gripe was the way her instinct took over at the beginning of every walk. Virginia would always dart in and out of his legs, nipping at his heels with her teeth. It didn't hurt, but it was annoying. Once they got going she would fall in by his side, occasionally dropping back to once again weave in between his feet until assured that her master was still moving in the right direction. They were nicknamed Blue Heelers for this habit, but she had never been trained to it.

Philip found this behavior fascinating. Here she was in a Chicago suburb having been born, raised, and lived in the city for almost five years. Not once had this dog ever seen or experienced anything remotely resembling a farm or livestock. Even so, she instinctively herded him along as though he were a cow.

Some behaviors are deep in the genes, he surmised. It was something she was driven to do by God's programming.

They moved along at a solid gait, fast enough to keep the dog satisfied that it was performing its duty but leisurely enough to admire the brilliant palette that autumn had provided. This season, the leaves were full of color and hardy enough to remain bound to their branches. Fiery reds dominated the landscape, blending to perfection with oranges and yellows. The reddish-orange dusk sky enhanced the show even further.

Philip always loved this time of the year. When he was a kid in high school, there had been Friday night football games with dances afterward. He and his friends would spend some of those nights stalking the Iowa cornfields, shucking ears for their hardened kernels. Then, they would lie in wait in tall grasses next to the bridge. It was wonderful- just the right temperature with none of the bugs that would have inhabited the riverbank in summer. Each time a car came by, they would toss handfuls of corn over the wall and wait for the clatter of their ordinance on the windshield and body of their target.

Most of the time, the cars would slow then continue on their way. A couple of times a night the car would stop- the driver jumping out to curse and scream at his invisible antagonists. They might spend a minute or two standing on the bridge making threats, but nothing would come of it. Who wanted to chase ghosts through the grass in the blackest night? He did remember the night they hit a County Mountie by accident. The cop's searchlight had raked the banks below the bridge for what seemed like hours before moving on. He and his friends stayed motionless deep in the blowing grasses, terrified to breathe. He kept that memory as one of his best.

Philip's reminiscence was interrupted by the vibrating of his Magi-Watch; on its face was the image of his only son. "Answer phone," he said to no one. Campbell's disembodied head and shoulders appeared translucently before him in his glasses.

"Dad, don't forget that we have to meet with my teachers at 7:30. "

"I haven't. Just out walking the dog. I'll be back." Philip knew that this was a make or break meeting for his son. He was a few points off the marks needed for financial assistance for college, and they were hoping for a letter of recommendation from his school faculty to put them over the top. School was so expensive these days that only those with top grades or a lot of money were guaranteed a spot. Campbell was close enough on the marks to make a second tier school, but without financial assistance, even that would be out of reach. He could read the tension in his boy's face.

"Campbell, relax a little. Your teachers like you. It's all going to be fine." Philip did his best to reassure- though he knew that it might not be fine at all. They needed some luck as well.

"I know. I hope so," Campbell tried to smile. "Just don't want to be late, ok?"

43

"See ya soon. End call." Campbell's projection ended. Again Philip focused on the view.

Fifty feet in front of him, a middle-aged Asian couple had stopped walking toward him and decided to jaywalk the street. That somewhat irritated him, but he understood. Virginia had never made an angry move at anyone, but she had a vicious look about her that frightened people. He felt that those people tended to be from parts of the world where dogs weren't held with the familiarity as they were here.

Philip knew that deep down people were the same, and he preached it to his kids, but he missed how things used to be in the neighborhood. Back then, when he passed people on the street, they would look him in the eye with a smile and say hello.

These days, they turned their heads away and refused to acknowledge his existence. The women were the worst- always behaving as if they were about to be raped. He snorted in disgust.

There were so many things about the *new* look of the neighborhood that irritated the hell out of him. He understood immigrants. He realized that the country was built on immigrants. Everyone's family had been immigrants at some point. His own grandparents had left Poland to escape the communists- electing to settle in Chicago because there were so many other Poles in the city. His parents had been the ones choosing to move out to Davenport and join the Church when he was a kid.

The Poles, Italians, and Portuguese… they had all tried to fit in. They wanted to assimilate and become Americans as fast as possible. Sure, they had kept some of their cultural artifacts, but they had learned to play baseball and football.

These new people didn't even try. They kept wearing clothes from the old country. They wouldn't learn English. They would go into the schools and demand their kids to be taught in their own language… and the schools would do it! The thought of it drove him crazy.

Now, instead of baseball and soccer, the fields were being used for cricket. The old Italian and Polish restaurants were being replaced by curry and shawarma.

Still, he took comfort in that they would always be second-tier citizens.

They had reached the end of the block, and it was time to make a left turn. Philip realized that he been so lost in his thoughts that the walk had now gone autopilot. He had let Virginia take the lead... right past the Virtuals' compound.

The sign outside read *Center for Virtual Living: Oak Park Facility... An RLC Community*; *RLC* being the Resource Living Corporation.

RLC was one of the world's largest multinationals, but as far as Philip was concerned, it was the work of Satan. He hated that this place was so close to his home and family.

RLC had started out as *HeadGames,* and Philip had been a huge fan of the *Critical Mass* series when he was a kid. He would spend hours trying to beat the games on extreme to make it to the special cut scenes embedded at the end of them.

When HeadGames developed *immersion* technology, it allowed gamers to put themselves directly into the action. At first, headgear was utilized to get the immersion effect, and the games were pretty simple.

Then it introduced the cranial interface; a huge leap forward in technology. A person could no longer distinguish reality from *Virtuality*.

He remembered when Virtuality had taken over Hollywood. Why just watch a movie when one could be in it? There were still folks around like Philip who didn't trust the experience and kept to their 3D helmets, but most people had gone over to the cranial interface. Philip considered it to be the Mark of the Beast.

He thought the box was even worse. He thanked God every morning that he had chosen to be a tradesman. Plumbers couldn't be replaced by robots yet, and it had placed his family firmly in the middle class. He thought of all they had known who had made the wrong choices and been swept into the box by economics.

As a loyal party member, Philip understood the importance of the Resource Living Centers to maintaining the status quo. There were simply too many people for the number of available jobs. The military was full up- even Campbell would have a rough time enlisting with the backlog of applicants.

When he was a younger man, there had been a great deal of unrest and bloodshed, as the idled had angrily taken to the streets over the government's seeming lack of interest in offering solutions.

—

He had understood that position- it wasn't the fault of the mega-corps that they were obligated to provide the highest possible profits for their shareholders. It was the cornerstone of a system he believed in as much as he believed in God and America. If people couldn't learn how to adapt to an ever-changing economy, then it also shouldn't be the government's responsibility to take care of them. He didn't expect a handout- although the Faith Subsidy did help smooth things out during slow times.

Still, Philip recalled images of the corpses of the rich hanging from lampposts like blackened, overripe fruit. There had been no choice but to accommodate those with limited futures. RLC's Virtual Living Centers had come along a just the right time to solve the problem for both the mega-corps and the governments of the world.

The sales pitch was simple: why suffer through the miseries of reality when you can live any life you want... and live it much better... in Virtuality?

For most, there wasn't much need for convincing. People could have the body they wanted and live in the time and place of their choice. They could be with friends, eat steak and party or screw the gorgeous person or persons of their desire. All the while their body is being maintained and nourished by attendants in an immaculate, climate-controlled building.

The alternative was to live in a rent-controlled ghetto; fighting and struggling with the neighbors in a perennial competition to keep from starving or being shot to death. It was an easy decision.

The best part for all parties involved was that RLC had arranged with the government to subsidize every aspect of a tenant's stay. RLC took care of it all, daily nourishment and housing, medical care, clothing, attendants.

Philip got why the politicians were ecstatic. For every person who entered into virtual living centers, the government saved thousands annually in food stamps, Medicare, Medicaid, Social Security (the elderly were among the most enthusiastic advocates), and social assistance payments. His party was even able to turn the tables on their rivals and boast that they had lowered welfare costs and subsidies to the poor while improving their standard of living.

Virtuality, with its economic and social benefits to governments, exploded across the globe. No wonder that RLC became an empire seemingly overnight.

Even with all the supposed good it had done, Philip and many other Christians felt that the Virtuals were committing a form of slow suicide- a sin so grievous that the fools had unwittingly condemned their souls to hell.

Virginia was now barking and nipping at Philip's heels, pulling him out of his musings. They had passed the front entrance gate and time was no longer on his side. He had to get back for the school meeting. He smiled at his best girl and whirled the two of them one hundred and eighty degrees... directly into a collision with two Virtuals coming through the gate.

Philip never saw the couple crash through the gate of the Center- only that one of them had run straight into Virginia and fallen over her. The dog yelped in surprise and pain. Philip watched one of the bodies tumble in what seemed to him like slow motion, hitting the concrete face first. Philip leaped to his dog and went to one knee beside her. Virginia, startled and scared from the collision, pressed her body as best she could against him in a bid for shelter.

"Idiots! What the Hell were you thinking, running into us like that?" He looked over at them, face dark with anger. "Did you leave your brains in there?"

A black boy was sprawled to the side of him. A girl was dropping down beside him and grabbing at his shoulders. The boy's hat was on the street in front of them.

"Wil!" the girl cried out. "Oh, shit! Are you ok?"

The boy lay there for a few seconds longer than he should have and Philip began to wonder if he had been hurt. Then he rolled over to face to girl. "What just happened?" he asked breathlessly.

They reminded Philip of scarecrows.

"You tripped over my dog, you freak!"

The girl glared at him. "Listen, mister; we're sorry, but this was obviously an accident. It's my friend who's on the ground so why not try to be a little nicer to us."

"Just get away from me, you abominations!" Philip looked at the boy and pointed ominously. "You are both damned! You've taken the Mark of the Beast."

As if on cue, Virginia began barking.

"Wha... what?" asked the one she had called Wil. He seemed disoriented from the fall.

—

47

"Jesus Christ, you're one of those," the girl spat back. "No wonder you're such an asshole."

"Don't take the Lord's name in vain." Philip was growing even more agitated at these disciples of Satan blaspheming. "You should be ashamed, selling your souls to the demon for false comfort. You need to pray for salvation."

"Look, you son of a bitch, I didn't sell my soul to an...." the girl suddenly clutched at her stomach and screamed.

Philip felt as if a hand was tearing out his own stomach. "What did you do to me?" he gasped.

"Go... back!" whimpered the boy.

Then just as suddenly, it was over. The pain was gone.

Chapter Three

Jim Gillette didn't mind that the President was running late as usual. He was still in the process of organizing the afternoon briefing, and he found the few additional minutes of preparation to be a blessing. In his three years as White House Chief of Staff, he had come to realize that it took a great deal of effort to keep Samuel Craig on schedule. The President tended to linger on specifics, gleaning all the particulars of each subject. The trait could be a double-edged sword. The President was a master of detail and management when the issue was close to his heart, but it also gave him tunnel vision at times. Sometimes, he couldn't see the forest for the trees.

Gillette was happy that his era of public service was coming to an end. He had already told the President that he would be leaving after the election next year. Then it would be some other poor sap for the second term- if a second term materialized.

He busied himself outside the Oval Office, sitting on a somewhat rigid sofa and manipulating the virtual desktop in front of him. He always organized the briefings to begin with anything of urgency or interest on the global scene, then worked his way back to national and regional issues. They ended on legislation and politics. Gillette always ended with those because if he started with them, they wouldn't get on to any other subject. Samuel Hiram Craig was a creature who thrived on politics. The man could either be disarmingly charming and charismatic or brutally ruthless depending on what it took to move his agenda forward. President Craig also had a gift for engineering compromise- a talent Gillette remembered from his childhood as being a political prerequisite. It wasn't in many toolboxes these days.

First, it would be Turkmenistan and then the Argentine famine. The Central African War would follow. Gillette chose to push the row between Israel and everyone else in the Middle East back to number four. Things were relatively stable there if the perpetual brushfires between Sunni and Shia or Israel and everyone else could be classified as stable. For his final global issue, Jim Gillette chose the International Space Program. It would make a good segue into the national issues since the isolationist elements of the party wanted to cut the cord on it altogether.

That would bring him back stateside and to the Florida shoreline efforts, the southwestern drought, the bridge collapse in Pennsylvania. Gillette would use that to move onto Capitol Hill and the infrastructure bill. They would finish with the election and the swing state strategy.

"Mr. Gillette, the President, is ready to see you now," Preet was speaking to him from behind her desk. She was a charming woman in her mid-forties, of Indian descent. She had been with Craig for years, going back to his time as a congressman. She was also a member of the same church as Craig. Gillette always wondered about the two of them, but if something was going on then, they were the most discreet couple he had ever seen. It was probably nothing, except for a longstanding mutual loyalty, but it was in his pay grade to be suspicious of everything.

Gillette touched the face of his Magi-Watch and the virtual desktop in his contact lens disappeared. He rose up, buttoned his suit jacket and walked through the open door. A secret service agent closed it behind him.

The President was sitting in a dark, padded, leather chair with the coffee table before him, a whiskey glass and briefing binders within reach. He looked up and flashed the smile that had won over seven of ten voters.

"Hello Jim," Craig motioned him to the sofa. "Have a seat. You know Jorge Bautista from ADC."

Gillette recognized the Air Defense Corporation lobbyist rising from the opposite sofa. That Bautista was in the Oval Office without his knowledge was irksome. As Chief of Staff he was the President's gatekeeper. That shouldn't have happened. He put on his best smile and shook Bautista's hand. "Hi, Jorge, good to see you again."

"Likewise, Jim. How goes the planet today?" Bautista was second generation money. His father was CEO of Air Defense Corp and had felt there was no better way to advance the family business than to send his second son to Washington. The oldest was being groomed for the real power, taking control of ADC, when the old man kicked. Still, Jorge had power of sorts. ADC threw tens of millions at politicians to secure billion-dollar satellite and drone fighter/bomber contracts… not to mention the even more lucrative maintenance business. Jorge Bautista decided which politician would benefit from that money.

"Well Jorge, I'm afraid that's classified," replied Gillette, only half joking.

50

"It's alright, Jim. Jorge is going to sit in with us for a little bit today." Craig's baritone pulled Gillette's eyes back to the President. "Who knows? Jorge here might just be taking over your job next year when you move on." He looked at Gillette with steely blue-grey eyes. The smile never wavered.

"Of course, Mr. President. In fact, we have Mr. Bautista's birds to thank for the confirmation of substantial troop buildups along the Russian border with Turkmenistan."

"Hmmm. Looks like Ivan might be getting ready to swoop in and *protect* the Karakorum oil fields now that the AOG and CAR are on their heels."

"Yes, sir. This and the genocide in Serdar are going to make it an easy sell for western aid to the Turkmen government."

"If I may interject," Bautista broke in, "the GAF is going to scream bloody hell over any funds or arms going to what is on the surface a Muslim on Muslim war."

Gillette knew that the lobbyist was likely right about that. The *God and America First* faction of the party was heavily isolationist, especially when it came to non-Christian issues. Gillette considered them to be complete whack jobs, but they were the darlings of the base… and deafening for their numbers.

Craig rubbed his chin. "The EU can take the lead on this for now. Let them do the heavy lifting. In the meantime, let's build a case for support. We have intel that NNI has a crew heading for the massacre. Let's see what the base thinks after a week of looking at dead children. How can we be Christians and not help?"

The President turned to Bautista. "Of course, we would need to help the Turkmen government build up its air capabilities now wouldn't we, Jorge? Perhaps you could use your influence to help convince our esteemed members of Congress that this is a prudent move given the region?"

"I am at your disposal, Mr. President," replied the likely future Chief of Staff.

The President stood up, both men instinctively rose with him. "Thank you, Jorge. Your assistance in this matter won't be forgotten. Now, if you don't mind I have to go over some other things with Jim." He held out his hand. Bautista took the cue and, after parting pleasantries, left the office.

Craig picked up his glass and went to the bar caddy. "Let's cut this one short today, Jim." He poured bourbons for himself and Gillette. "I already know that Argentina is starving and Florida is underwater. Where do we stand on the infrastructure bill?" He handed Gillette a glass.

"A bridge collapsed near Harrisburg, Pennsylvania this morning, sir. Three people killed, twenty-one injured." They both sat back down. Gillette didn't really enjoy bourbon; he preferred the smokiness of scotch. When in Rome…

The President leaned back in his chair. There were moments when he didn't look very presidential at all. He was slightly pudgy; his tight black curls now had streaks of gray, and his hair nearly always looked as though it were on the verge of exploding into disarray. How Samuel Craig was able to get away with a mustache was beyond his comprehension. He often thought the president reminded him of a reincarnation of Kurt Vonnegut- appropriate as they both hailed from Indiana.

What he did possess was a razor sharp mind and a voice of persuasion that was blessed by God. The man could communicate ideas like no other. Maybe like Reagan, but none since.

"Well Jim, nothing says the country's infrastructure is falling apart like a bridge falling down and killing people. That should help us with securing the funds for the urban areas, but we still need AgriBus to keep its promise. After all, it has the farmland leases. Those folks said they'd keep the roads and power lines up to date and they've been dragging their feet. That's your old stomping grounds, Mr. Chief of Staff. Maybe you should be putting those feet to the fire. If AgriBus throws in for the rural infrastructure costs, then we can probably shove the bill through."

"I will do what I can, Mr. President but even so, this bill is very dangerous to enact before you are re-elected. Raising taxes on the electorate is not going to make you a lot of friends."

"Jim, one-third of the electorate is boxed and can't vote. Another third doesn't bother to vote most of the time. The last third is Christian and will never vote for anyone who isn't with our party. Of those, only about ten percent are going to feel any pinch and, even though they own most of the country, they still only have one in ten votes. I appr… augh!"

Gillette never heard the president cry out- himself doubling over with the most violent stomach pain he had ever experienced. The pain was too much, and he screamed.

—

Then it ended. Jim Gillette and Samuel Craig looked at each other.

"What the Hell just happened?" asked the President of the United States.

The two men had begun to compose themselves by the time the Secret Service entered the room, in numbers with weapons drawn. Gillette already knew that Jennifer Harling would be on point. She was the lead agent today, and he had seen her briefly in the corridor just before he entered the office.

Samuel Craig held up his hand as if to slow the stampede into his office. "I'm ok. Jenny, do you know what's going on?"

"We may be under attack, Mr. President. We need to move you into the secure area," replied Agent Harling. "Everyone on this floor seems to have suffered a sharp abdominal pain at precisely the same moment."

"Well, that doesn't rule out today's lunch," joked the President. "Let's hope the veal wasn't to die for."

Gillette chuckled, but the attempt at humor went over Harling. "I don't believe we all had the same thing for lunch, sir. We can likely rule out food poisoning. Come with me please, Mr. President."

They proceeded to form a cordon around Craig and walk him quickly out of the Oval Office toward the service elevator at the end of the corridor.

The group had made it halfway down the hallway when Gillette and a few others suddenly stopped. His Magi-Watch had activated on its own. In his contact, a popup read:

"This has been a demonstration of our control over your lives. We reveal ourselves at the United Nations General Assembly 10/27 17:00 GMT. Attempted violence against us will be met with the death of nations."

A voiceover repeated the words in twice in English. The Magi-Watch shut off. The event was over in less than fifteen seconds.

Gillette spoke first. "Mr. President, I don't think we are in any imminent danger."

"I saw it too," nodded Jennifer Harling. "I agree with Mr. Gillette that there may be no immediate threat, but I recommend we continue to a secure area."

"We saw it on the hall monitor," said Craig. "They must have simulcast somehow." He turned to Gillette. "Jim, we need to assemble the NSC or at least as much of it as is in town. Let's see if we can crawl out of the dark."

"To the best of our knowledge, every human being on the planet experienced the same stabbing pain in the abdominal area. The pain lasted for approximately five seconds upon which it promptly subsided with no lasting ill effect. There have been no recurrences, but we are less than ninety minutes since the event. Therefore, we have no way of knowing if this will remain the case," said National Intelligence Director Drew Tillison. "I admit we are speculating about the scope of this event, but anecdotal evidence is indicating that this was a spontaneous global occurrence.

"This was followed immediately by another global event in which an anonymous group was able to usurp control of nearly every media source or communications device to claim responsibility. Also, it would seem, to announce a rendezvous at the UN General Assembly less than thirty-four hours from now."

The President leaned forward and looked around the table. "Ok, who are they and how did they pull this off? And what was the point of giving every man, woman and child on Earth a bad cramp?"

"It's a shot across the bow, Mr. President. Whoever it is, they wanted our attention," observed Louis Ramsey, Chairman of the Joint Chiefs. "We have put the entire national defense grid on high alert against an attack."

"I'm sorry, Mr. President but we just don't know who we are dealing with at this point," said Secretary of Defense Janice Polson. "There is a superabundance of speculation going on in the press but nothing that can be substantiated."

The NID jumped in. "Sir, we run scenarios such as this and look at capabilities on a continuous basis. Our birds at SATCOM detected nothing out of the ordinary with respect to transmissions or unusual activities prior to or during the event. There is no known government or terrorist organization we know of that could pull something like this off. Besides, if this truly was a global event, what nation would put its own populace in peril?"

"Was anyone really in peril?" asked Vice President Chris Cameron. "All we know is that everyone had a brief stomach pain. Since when do terrorists attack us with the equivalent of bad gas? Perhaps we should be getting the CDC to look at this."

"Already on it," said the NID. "We have volunteers undergoing intense screening for unusual pathogens that could have been genetically engineered."

Gillette saw that the President was clearly frustrated. "So we are being attacked by an enemy whose geographic location is unknown, uses tactics we can't defend against, and leaves no trace of its methods."

Chris Cameron spoke up, "Mr. President, I believe we should take a step back for a moment and keep in mind that, whoever is behind this, not one American citizen has died that we know of. It seems to me that anyone who could stage an event such as this... if they wanted people to die that probably would have already happened.

"I would counsel that we continue our efforts to find out who is behind this, and their methodology, but maybe we should also just see what they want. More important, we need your leadership to maintain calm among the people. At this juncture, what else can we do?"

"I have to agree with the Vice President, Sir." Gillette had been silent to this point but felt he needed to move things along. "No one that we know of has been hurt, and we have no visible enemy to strike against. What we *do* have is a terrified populace that we need to calm immediately.

"Mr. President, I would strongly recommend that you address the nation as quickly as possible. We can devote every resource to finding out who is behind this and what their agenda is. We have more than thirty hours to do that. We may not have much time before our own people become panicked mobs. At the moment, that's the greater threat."

Craig nodded. "I would agree with that assessment. Let's get Stuart on it to arrange a snap address with the media outlets. Jim, see if we can get Martinyuk to put something together on the fly- emphasis on our strength, but be reassuring. No one's hurt, nothing is damaged, et cetera. I believe we should shoot for some time in the next sixty minutes."

He stood and the room stood with him. "One more thing, we need to get State in contact with our embassies as quickly as possible. Let's project a message of calm around the world. We don't want anyone lobbing nukes at each other. America needs to be the voice of reason. Let's start networking it. Also, let's get State and the CIA to monitor the messages that everyone else is sending. Maybe they know something we don't. I want to hear about anything that could give us some answers."

55

The room began to clear. Craig moved over to Gillette. "Jim, we need to assume that we'll be blind going into this UN meeting. Let's get Anne North into the loop. She'll be on point, but I want you to find John Harriman and get his ass up there as fast as possible. We may need our hammer. Give him anything he needs and tell him to report only to me."

***

Over the years, as his notoriety within select circles grew, John Harriman had acquired *The Hammer* as his moniker. He felt *The Blade* might have been a more accurate designation- his skill set was most often in the realm of surgical than that of a bludgeon.

At times, people would refer to him as *Craig's Hammer*, a title he didn't particularly appreciate as he had served two other presidents in the same capacity. He also didn't run around assassinating the nation's enemies willy-nilly. More often than not, his job was as a direct observer or negotiator, an extractor. He considered himself a situational specialist, a fixer... so to speak. If things got out of hand or if the president wanted a specific threat reduced, John Harriman's training in covert operations came to the forefront. At forty-two, Harriman had the perfect mix of physical strength, intelligence, and experience.

Still, he was no James Bond. At least not in his own mind.

Harriman was at the farm when the event occurred. He had always referred to it as his *farm*. The land was, in fact, twenty-three acres of densely wooded foothills that ran along a small lake just outside of Cincinnati. For him, the mix of civilization and nature was in harmonious balance. He had all of life's modern amenities in a rustic setting, with great fishing to boot. It was the complete opposite of his childhood in a Queens orphanage- where the fish came in the form of breaded sticks.

When the call came, he was finishing dinner. This evening, not fish but a rosemary chicken with wild, long-grain rice and steamed carrots. He did his best to eat well and make every meal count, never knowing when it might be his last.

The call came in on the secure hardline. Harriman knew it was the White House- no one else used a hardline anymore. Jim Gillette was on the other side.

"Harriman," he answered.

"Security code A," requested Chief of Staff Jim Gillette.

"John the Baptist. Security code B."

"Ragnarok."

"Let's hope not, sir. You want me in New York?"

"United Nations, Mr. Harriman. Officially, you will be the special assistant to Ambassador North. Unofficially, you have the point. The objective is reconnaissance and intelligence. We need to try and get a handle on who and what we are facing. Any edge you can give us. A flight is on standby at Wright-Patterson."

"May I ask, sir, what we do know?"

Gillette's candor was surprising to him. "A brief is waiting for you to review in flight but it is going to be pretty thin and very frightening. We don't even know if this threat is terrestrial in origin. We can extrapolate from the demonstration that if they can give everyone a simultaneous stomachache, then they can probably do much, much worse. At the moment, we are blind... a position the most powerful nation on Earth cannot be in.

"You will report directly to the President. Good luck, Mr. Harriman."

The line went dead.

Harriman put down the receiver and turned to the monitor on the wall. A replay of President Samuel H. Craig's address to the nation filled the screen.

"My friends, there is no cause for concern. Your government has the protection of the lives of American citizens at its forefront. The full might of the United States military, as well as our civilian security forces, are both on high alert. We have the situation under control, and I assure you that there is no cause for panic or concern."

Harriman laughed.

"Well, Mr. President, aren't we full of the finest form of bullshit this evening."

Chapter Four

Grace Williams knew she had to get to New York City and fast. The biggest story of the century, possibly the millennium, was taking place there in less than twenty-four hours. There was no way in Hell she was missing that party.

Hell it might be. It quickly became apparent that the pain everyone had experienced wasn't a new Army of God weapon but instead a global event. The chiefs at NNI had conducted quick and effective negotiations to get her and John Kearney out of Turkmenistan, on to London, and from there to New York. It had taken a great deal of American dollars (which she hoped NNI would have paid anyway in the event of a hostage situation) and acquiescence to a demand, but they had secured safe passage… through Balkanskaya and the Army of God.

It had been determined that it was quicker to go west to the Caspian and Turkmenbashi than it was to try and go back to Ashgabat. Under a white flag, they had been moved up to the front and, with Grace donning a hijab, the two walked into the lines of the Army of God.

There, they boarded a helicopter and within an hour were sitting in a Quonset hut just off of the tarmac of an air force base outside of Turkmenbashi. Waiting- far too long in Grace's opinion, to fulfill the demand and be on their way.

In time, a colonel dressed in fatigues entered the room, smiling. He went directly to Grace and bowed.

"Ms. Williams, it is an honor to host such a famous Western personality. Our Leader has been delayed but is now on his way and will be in our presence within a few moments." Grace picked up a hint of Persian in the accent. The man was likely an Iranian advisor. She was surprised by the brazenness of the Army of God not to hide its complicity with Iran. She hoped that they would assume that she wouldn't pick up on it, being a westerner. The other prospect for such openness left her uneasy. Grace stood and bowed slightly.

"Thank you for your kind words, Colonel… I am sorry, sir. No one has introduced us. Your name is?" she said, trailing off in anticipation.

"Unimportant, Ms. Williams. I am but a servant of the great Mullah Azat Mohamed. In that capacity, I have been instructed to provide you with… ah… instructions. I am so sorry for my English."

"Your English is much better than my Arabic, Colonel," lied Grace. "What instructions are you to give us?"

"The Mullah will begin with a statement. He is not to be interrupted. He will then answer questions from you." The colonel pulled a folded paper from his left breast pocket. "These are the questions."

Ignored to this point, Red Kearney snorted loudly. Grace glanced at him as she reached out to take the paper. She looked at it, then walked over to the big Irishman and handed it to him.

Kearney read the questions, looked up at Grace, and shrugged. "I guess so. I would have probably asked these questions myself. Not NKC for sure."

Grace understood the reference. The questions were innocent enough on the surface but leading nonetheless. Over the years, terrorists and rogue states had become very sophisticated in their dealings with the media. The North Koreans were the exception, still spreading their propaganda with a club- North Korean Clunky.

She had to admit that the questions didn't pull any punches but she thought the first one was history in the making. It also answered the blatant Iranian presence. They were going to let her ask some hard questions as well, especially about the genocide at Serdar.

Grace looked back to the colonel. "We are honored for the opportunity to assist the Mullah in communicating his message to the world."

"Wonderful! Thank you so much," the colonel beamed. The smile was replaced with a more serious look. He spoke in a lower, more hushed tone. "Tell me, what have you heard about the incident from this morning? The pain we all experienced?"

Grace thought she probably knew a lot less than the colonel. They had been in relative isolation at the front. "Colonel, I only know what the network is telling us. It would seem that everyone on the planet felt the same pain at the same time. Everyone who had a media device saw the same message. No one knows who is behind it or what it is all about."

The colonel pursed his lips in thought. "Here, they are saying it was a Zionist trick to scare the faithful into submission and surrender. However, I do not believe that the Jews are capable of such a feat, even with the help of the Americans."

—

"Colonel, I know what the American government is capable of, and this is beyond their reach. I can't think of any government able to do what happened this morning. I can also tell you that Americans were affected just like everyone else."

The colonel's gaze had drifted away from Grace momentarily and out the window to the Caspian Sea in the distance. "I cannot understand it. Still, it was all very frightening, would not you agree?"

Mullah Azat Mohamed, the former Azat Nurali, sat in the makeshift studio in traditional Iranian cleric's robes, waiting for his cue. His people had originally wanted to conduct the interview in Arabic only but Grace had convinced them it would have more impact on the West if Azat, an Oxford alumnus, performed it in English.

Grace, still wearing the hijab, had positioned herself to the left of the leader. A coffee table had been placed between them. On it sat a pitcher of water and two half-filled glasses. Two high-backed office chairs had been provided for their use. Azat Mohamed's chair had been elevated significantly higher than Grace's to enhance the illusion of his size in the camera frame. Behind them stood a white cloth backdrop with the flags of the makeshift state of Balkanskaya and that of Iran in alternating sequence across its front.

Azat Nurali had been a shrewd and charismatic figure in pre-war Turkmenistan. Painting himself as a leader of an oppressed minority had attracted many followers and made him an influential figure within the government. His role in the post-Soviet era had been as a young and ambitious politician who had played his part in maintaining the system even as he rose within it.

One day a decade ago, Azat had stood on a street corner and announced that he was taking up the standard of his oppressed Shia minority. The fact that the Shia were no more or less oppressed than anyone else notwithstanding, that decision was the initial step toward a sectarian, civil war.

Grace had initially assessed Azat from afar as a cynical Machiavellian who was strictly manipulating the situation in a big way to realize his own fiefdom. Now in his presence, Grace wondered if Azat himself actually bought into what he had been selling everyone else all these years. Sure, it was about energy profits, but maybe there was something more bubbling away underneath.

Grace did admit to feeling the center of gravity shift when Azat had first entered the room. He reminded her of a slightly overweight Omar Sharif, an actor from an old movie she had loved in film class, *Lawrence of Arabia*. He moved with speed and ease of purpose. One only had to look in his eyes to see the fire of a fanatic blazing within.

Red had pulled the camera apart, folded it out into a triangular shape and positioned it on a table before them. For him, this was easy work. The online uplink was live, and he didn't have to follow anyone around. Red simply had to frame the shot and press a button on his Virtuwatch to set things rolling. At his discretion, Kearney could use a micro-cam to drop in close-ups of Grace and Azat from different angles.

Grace's right contact had activated, giving her access to both the NNI homepage and uplink page. The interview was to be live-streamed on both the homepage and the Current World News page. She knew that Red could also see both pages and they now began to sync up with the live-stream by viewing the countdown on the uplink page. They were down to thirty seconds.

"Thirty seconds, sir. I will give an introduction and then you can give your statement without interruption. When you are finished, I will begin with the first question."

The mullah nodded in understanding.

John brought his hand up fingers spread. "In five, four…" The rest of the count was silent. His fingers folded to *one* and then pointed at Grace.

"Grace Williams for NNI, the eye of truth. We are streaming from the city of Turkmenbashi on the Caspian Sea in what was formerly western Turkmenistan, now known as the Islamic State of Balkanskaya. We are very fortunate to have been granted an interview with the spiritual and political leader of the Army of God, Mullah Azat Mohamed. The mullah will begin with a statement."

She saw in her HUD that John was pulling the camera over into a closeup of Azat. A seasoned pro, the mullah began on cue.

"We wish to announce to the nations of the world of our intention to request annexation into the Greater Shia Islamic Republic. It is the desire of our people to walk the path of our fellow Shia brothers and sisters of the former southern Iraq in joining with the Islamic Republic of Iran."

The mullah looked directly into the camera. "My friends, our struggle to be free has been victorious! It has been a hard road, with many martyred to Allah, but soon we will all live with our brethren in the one, true way."

"We demand that while this annexation is being considered by the Greater Shia Islamic Republic's legislature, no intervention by any outside powers be allowed. Any attempt to foil our right to self-determination will be met by the wrath of Allah. Make no further incursions into our lands. The European Union, United States, the Russian Federation would be wise not to interfere with our right to exist. Any further aggression by the apostates of the east or by the apostates' abomination will be shattered by the hand of God."

The mullah now turned to Grace. She knew that the *apostates' abomination* was the Sunni Islamic Caliphate, now occupying what was once Syria and northern Iraq. Grace took her cue.

"Mullah Azat, why have you made this monumental decision to seek a union with the Iranians and Iraqis? You have no historical or ethnic connection to them any more than they have to each other."

"We all are brothers united by the one true faith. It does not matter where a person comes from as much as what he believes. We are all brothers and sisters of the one true God and his prophet.

"Our Shia peoples are threatened by infidels and apostates of the abomination on all sides. It is they who wish to keep us divided and apart so that we will be weaker and easier to destroy. It is only by joining that we can find the strength to defend our faith and defy our enemies."

Azat had an incredible voice. It was a calm baritone, full of power. His eyes danced and sparkled with every phrase. Grace understood how he could have influenced so many to follow him.

The Iranians had better be careful, she thought.

"What if the Greater Shia Islamic Republic rejects your request for annexation?"

"I firmly believe that they will not. The GSIR has already recognized our legal right to exist as an independent state-- much in the way that your own United States once recognized the Republics of Texas and California in their struggle to free themselves from Mexico.

62

"The Greater Shia Islamic Republic has been providing us with technical advisors and material in our struggles. We have asked GSIR military forces to enter our state and help us to defend our right to exist. We expect troops to move in to protect our borders within days. Even if the GSIR should decide against annexation, we know that as fellow Shia, we can count on their continued support of our cause."

She decided to throw the roundhouse.

"Mullah Azat, we have just come from the city of Serdar to the east. There, we found evidence of a horrible genocide committed by Army of God troops- allegedly under your direction. More than ten thousand men, women, and children were brutally and systematically slaughtered as your troops retreated from the area. As a man of God, why have you overseen the murder of thousands of innocents and how can you expect the world to react with anything but horror and retaliation to this atrocity? Finally, how can you expect a respected member of the family of nations such as the GSIR to support the legitimacy of any group committing such acts of genocide?"

Azat smiled patronizingly at her.

"Ms. Williams, you and the West have been pawns in a game of misdirection. We condemn the murders of the innocents at Serdar. I would remind you, most of those slaughtered were Shia. We would never kill our brothers and sisters in faith. This terrible crime against humanity was committed by the Turkmen army as it entered the city.

"We denounce this heinous act against Allah and have committed to honor the martyrdom of these innocents by retaking the city and annihilating the apostates who committed this horrible act."

It was the only thing he could say. By claiming that the other side was at fault, Azat could attempt to grab the moral imperative and justify further hostilities against the Turkmen. Now he would be doing it with Iranian troops, whose presence would likely deter western action. The war would be over within weeks. The remainder of Turkmenistan might fall to him as well. It was a masterstroke.

"The government of Turkmenistan claims it can offer proof that the Army of God did, in fact, commit the genocide. If evidence of your complicity is found, will you submit to the International Court of Justice for trial?"

This one was not on the list of questions. It might get Kearney and her stranded- or worse- if Azat decided to take retribution for it.

Smiling smugly, he didn't miss a beat.

"Evidence is easy to manufacture. When we retake the city, we will show the world evidence that the Sunni apostates committed these crimes. Satan uses many tricks to cloud the truth, but Allah is with us in our struggle."

"One final question for you, Mullah Azat. What do you make of the recent world event, in which the entire globe was suddenly seized with pain for a brief moment, and the message that followed?"

Azat hesitated. "We believe that this is a trick of the Zionists and their slaves to scare the followers of Allah and the Prophet into submission. It is nothing. The Jews should know by now that they cannot use fear to defeat us."

"Mullah Azat Mohamed, thank you for your time. With producer John Kearney, I'm Grace Williams."

"And cut," said Red, motioning with his hand.

Grace turned back to Azat and leaned forward in her chair. "Mullah Azat, in the short time we have spoken, I find you to be one of the most interesting persons I have ever met. Thank you for the opportunity to interview you." Grace really couldn't say much else without risk of insult. She knew had just interviewed another in the long parade of humanity's monsters.

"It was a pleasure hosting both yourself and Mr. Kearney," oozed a beaming Azat. "It is I who wish to thank you for your assistance on this historic day. And now, I believe you have a plane to catch."

Grace couldn't get off the ground quickly enough.

***

Wil walked between the rows of corn, admiring the height of his planting. As tall as himself, the stalks were dark green and well cared for. It was almost time for them to turn color and signify the harvest, a time he thoroughly enjoyed. He loved driving the large combine and bringing in the bounty.

Corn wasn't the only crop he had planted. In the southwest corner were fields of soybeans. In the southeast, the sunflowers were in their prime. That field would get the winter wheat; the soybeans he would replace next year with alfalfa for the livestock.

He emerged from the field and turned to face the sun, low on the horizon. The colors of the sky were a magnificent backdrop to his lush, green fields. He could feel the sun's warmth on his face. This was Wil's favorite place. He turned again and headed towards the farmhouse where Rosie and the kids would be. Dinner should be ready soon.

An angel was waiting for him when he came in.

She wasn't his regular angel, that one was tall and blonde, wore a white robe and had wings- the archetypical image that everyone possessed when they thought of an angel. This woman was shorter and biracial; he couldn't tell, but she had a face that seemed to be Eurasian or Polynesian. She had black hair that went past her shoulders and wore a blue tunic that came to the top of her knees- and she was barefoot. He saw no wings on her back.

Even so, Wil instinctively knew she was an angel. She possessed a gentle smile and bright green eyes. A glow seemed to emanate from her; not an actual glow but an otherworldly shimmer outlining her body, as though she was out of sync with the rest of the program. When she spoke to him, he lost all doubt; it was as if she were singing with the most melodious voice.

"Hello, Wil, I'm very happy to meet you finally." The angel lifted her arms as though to take in everything around them. "What a beautiful dream all this is."

"What do you want? Where are Rosie and the boys?"

"Don't be afraid; they are fine. I have sent them somewhere else for now. In Rosie's world, she is having dinner with you at this very moment. I wanted to speak with you alone."

Her eyes and smile were infectious, compelling him to look at her. She motioned to the couch. "Please sit down."

"Do I have a choice?" He slowly dropped onto the worn, floral-pattern couch, staying on the edge of the cushion and leaning forward ever so slightly.

The angel sat down next to him. "Oh Wil! Of course, you do! That is why I am here. I have been watching you for some time now."

"Why would you be watching me?"

"Because you are different from most- special," she said. "Let me ask you something. Are you happy here?"

Wil shrugged, "I guess… this is my favorite world. I like to come here most of all."

The angel took his hand in hers. It was warm, and he felt a calmness envelop his body. "Do you ever ask yourself why you are so happy here in this world?"

He thought for a moment. "I guess it's because I feel like I am doing something with my life. I can feel something positive in here... but it isn't real, I'm not getting anywhere at all. I'm just killing time until I die and join Jesus in Heaven. So... I'm not happy. Who could really be happy here?"

Her face betrayed a melancholy mirroring his own. "You would be surprised. The majority of people who enter here have become bored with the struggle of their lives. These worlds provide for them, if not happiness, then a complacent acceptance. Not long ago, people who were bored and lost would turn to drugs and alcohol as a way to accept themselves. Now they have virtual worlds. This has become their drug of acceptance. Most people who come here go to worlds of sex or violence. They fight wars or jump from airplanes or ski down mountains. They go to the worlds that make them feel alive, but in truth living is the last thing they want. It is too much of a challenge, so they hide in here."

She turned to look at him again, her smile returned. "But you, Wil. You come here, to a world where there is no adrenaline rush, just hard work, and challenges. You come to a place where you can feel as though you are giving something of yourself, accomplishing things, making a difference. That makes you very special, and I am here to help you."

"Help me do what? No one gets out of the box. We're just passing time until we can go to our reward in Heaven, where we can be with God and happy forever."

The angel was silent for a moment. She looked deeply into his eyes.

"What if all there is... is now? What if all you possess is within this life? What if there is no heavenly reward waiting for anyone, just the end of existence? Do you want to spend the time you have, the life you have, in this prison, accomplishing nothing, passing quickly and leaving nothing of yourself? Or would you rather leave this machine and go into the real world, where you can strive to make a difference for yourself, and for others?

"I already know the answer, Wil, and you know it yourself. I will help you to leave here and find great things out there."

—

Wil felt something that had been missing for a long time. He didn't recognize the feeling at first, but the angel had brought it back. It was hope. Still, it sounded too good to be true.

"How do you plan to go about *helping* me?" he asked.

The angel stood up and opened her arm. "The men and women who created this machine did not mean for it to be used as a game or a prison. It was to be a place of teaching and learning. For you, it will once again have such a purpose!"

"That's crazy. I'm no good at school. That's why I'm in here."

She gave him a wry smile. "Did you not teach yourself how to be a farmer?"

"That's different. It's just a world where I get what I want anyway. The crops will grow whether I know anything or not."

She smiled at him in a manner his mother often had. "You are wrong, Wil. You have been doing all of this on your own. If you had made mistakes, the crops wouldn't have grown. Instead, you asked the local farmers for help and learned from them, and you read the books and manuals provided. You used the program to improve yourself- as it was meant to be used."

He looked at her, astounded by what she had just told him. The corn outside that grew so high was his doing! Hope grew stronger.

"Ok, so where do we begin?" he asked.

"We begin with the basics. You must have a foundation in the sciences. Over the next few weeks, you will meet some very important people- Newton, Einstein, Hawking, Darwin- to name a few.

"Every day I will meet you and take you to a special place where you can learn from them and others. When you have learned enough, you will begin to develop more specialized skills."

The angel touched Wil's face. "You must understand a few things. I can accelerate your learning curve, but even so, you will still be here for at least one more year. When you leave this place, it will be with your actual body. That means you have to become physically healthy again. When you are outside this machine you must eat the food, take the supplements, and exercise as much as possible. Do you understand?"

Wil nodded.

"One final thing, Wil. You cannot tell anyone what is happening when you come here. Your caregivers will only see you enter certain programs. They will be unaware that I am taking you to other places. From what they know, these other places don't register in their system. They won't be able to see me either, and you must never mention me to anyone."

"I don't understand. You're an angel."

"Yes, but I am not *their* angel. I am an angel that is not a part of their software. I am unique. No one must know of your training or myself."

"Ok, I get it," Wil said. He thought for a moment, "What about Sonya? I want her to come with us too."

The angel frowned. "I am not sure that she is special like you, Wil. She is unpredictable, and her choice of worlds is not like yours."

"We can talk to her together. She is strong and smart and hates this place as much as I do," Wil replied. He looked at the angel, his voice pleading. "She's better than me in so many ways."

He saw the angel considering it. "Alright, we will go to see her together but if she doesn't cooperate I will have to take her memory of myself and the conversation away. You must never mention anything to her again."

"She'll be fine," Wil insisted. He paused, "There is still something I don't understand. You want me to learn and train, but in the end, I will still have to go out into the real world and try to find work. What are the odds of that happening?"

"No, Wil, you don't understand. You are special, but you aren't the only one who is special. There are thousands just like you whom I am helping. A great change is coming, and all will be needed."

The angel smiled, and her aura brightened the room.

"Something wonderful is about to happen!"

Chapter Five

John Harriman wove his way through the crowded, 46th Street sidewalk and into the United Nations Identification Building. The lobby and its many wickets were chaotic- mostly with media, everyone fighting for a ringside seat at what was soon to take place. Harriman wasn't so sure being in the thick of it was such a great idea, but he didn't have a choice in the matter.

He did a double take at the blonde, Eurasian woman who was standing calmly next to a burly ginger at the center of a small scrum. Instinctively feeling his eyes, the woman glanced at him for an instant before turning back to the crowd. Harriman hoped he'd dodged a bullet. The woman was Grace Williams.

He usually didn't make a mistake like that; it was his business to blend in and be inconspicuous. He was a bit surprised to see her in New York. The last he had heard, she was in Turkmenistan. NNI must have pulled out all the stops to get her here this quickly. Still, he understood their motivation. This could turn out to be the biggest event of the century. They were going to want one of their top correspondents on it-- even if she was on the foreign desk and half a world away on assignment.

After all, he was the best his country had to offer and here he was.

Harriman saw a small entourage moving toward him. Three men and a woman, all dressed in the traditional black suits. As they approached him, one spoke up.

"Colonel, the ambassador is waiting. Please allow us to escort you; we have arranged for all of your site clearances and passes. There are just have a few formalities, sir."

So much for keeping a low profile, mused Harriman to himself. He stole another glance out of the corner of his eye. Grace Williams was staring dead on at him.

"Let's just keep it at Mister," he replied. "Lead on, please."

The group converged on him and began moving towards an exit on the other side of the lobby. They were going to walk right past her. As they approached, Grace Williams broke into a full grin.

"The hero of Sao Paulo," was all she said, coyly, as they passed. It was all she had to say. He was made.

Sort of. Williams didn't know who he was, only what he was. She had seen him once before, in Brazil. He decided he had to nip it in the bud. Harriman stopped, braking to a halt the group with him. "One moment," he said, wheeling back to Williams. She was still grinning. The big ginger wasn't in on the joke. He took a step to move between the two of them.

Harriman threw him an annoyed glance and turned back to her. *My God,* he thought, *what a face!* He was glad he hadn't killed her; she had to be one of the most beautiful women on the planet. No wonder Grace Williams was such a star. He did his best to keep to a monotone as he spoke.

"Ms. Williams, it would be in all of our interests if you were to keep my presence here unannounced."

Grace's smile never broke. "Was it *Colonel* I heard? Well, Colonel, this is a huge story, and I think it may be important for our streamers to get all of the pertinent facts. After all, it is a free country and there is a free press."

"No," countered Harriman, "you are wrong on both counts. Technically, we are not in the United States, and the press is free until we say it isn't. This is a matter of national security, and if you threaten that national security in any way, one quick call can crash the NNI servers within seconds. You'll be reporting to dead air."

The man next to her balled his fist in anger. "You have no legal ri…"

Harriman cut him off. "I don't need one. This could be the biggest crisis in world history. We need to gather intelligence about our enemy- get answers. We can't accidentally tip them off to the fact that they may not be in as much control of the situation as they believe."

"It's ok, John," said Williams, never taking her eyes off Harriman. He gave an ever so slight start at the mention of his name. The big guy moved back a little. Harriman guessed he must be a *John* as well.

Harriman looked directly at Williams. "Look, we've compromised before. Report anything else you want, just don't let it become public that anyone like myself is here."

The journalist became serious, the smile dropping away. "Alright, we'll play for now, but I want something from you."

"Thank you... and that depends. What do you want?"

The smile returned. "Your name."

70

Harriman couldn't help himself, breaking into a smile as he turned back toward the exit. He looked over his shoulder at her.

"Smith," he said. "Agent Smith."

"See ya around, John," replied Grace Williams.

The group crossed the plaza and walked toward the building known as DC1. It was here that the U. S. government maintained its United Nations offices. The State Department was housed separately across the street, but the UN diplomats and support staff were kept on site to provide international accessibility. As they made their way down the corridors, Harriman couldn't help but notice that the carpets needed cleaning and the walls needed paint. The UN had always struggled with funding, but it had usually found ways to keep up the façade. Harriman knew that U. S. funding had dried up over the last decade. America had always maintained a strained relationship with the UN, even in the salad days. The past decade had seen massive cuts to foreign aid in general. He knew that American contributions to the UN had been cut by two-thirds. The EU threw some money in the till, but the Russians and Chinese could care less. Most of the rest of the world paid only lip service to the ideals of Bretton Woods.

Anne North was a career diplomat, an anomaly these days when ambassadorships typically carried a big, juicy, price tag. One of the reasons why she had been assigned the UN gig was precisely because of its nature. The cash cows who lined up for their ambassadorships were ideologically opposed to the United Nations. Sam Craig liked her and had tossed her the bone.

North was a petite woman with graying, shoulder-length hair but Harriman noticed that she had a salesman's confident grip and a strong voice to match. They entered a large conference room- North, Harriman, her chief of staff Logan Li, and CIA station chief Tanya Vespers.

"We've all read the brief on the situation," said Ambassador North after the amenities had been exchanged. "We are essentially blind and on the front lines of God knows what. Colonel Harriman, the President, has expressed to me that you are the point man at this shindig, so I'm curious as to what you've got to say."

Harriman took a deep breath. "Ambassador, at this stage, it's about threat assessment and intelligence gathering. There isn't much else we can do other than to try and find out who or what the perpetrators are and their motivation. We will also determine if they have any potential weaknesses that can be exploited."

"I'm not so sure there is a threat," said Li. "What if all this is some elaborate parlor trick and these guys don't have anything else up their sleeve?"

"That's a valid question, Logan," replied Vespers. "You could be right… or they could be extraterrestrials who can incinerate the planet at the pressing of whatever their version of a button is. Because we don't know, we need to be vigilant and err on the side of caution."

"Thank God they didn't ask to address Congress!" snorted Ambassador North. "Those buffoons would get us all killed, although I must say there's a volatile enough group of flakes in the General Assembly!"

North had segued into an important issue. "Have you established a protocol for addressing… whatever?" asked Harriman.

"The GA will be in session for- whatever," said North. "The GA and the SecGen have all agreed that this is a matter for the Security Council so it will take the lead on dealing with… people, I must say it is somewhat exasperating to keep describing this event as *whatever*!"

"Maybe that's their evil plan, to devolve the population of our planet into vapid, valley girls," deadpanned John Harriman.

Everyone in the room turned to look quizzically at Harriman.

He broke into a grin. "I have found that humor is often the best way to break the tension during a global crisis."

Ambassador North feigned a grimace and continued.

"As I was saying, the Security Council will be charged with deliberating the events and putting together potential options. Secretary General Lemke will represent the Council should it come to that."

"There is another issue, and that's what to do about the media," said Vespers.

Logan Li spoke up, "At the moment, it has been agreed to bar any media from the Hall of the General Assembly. There will be a media blackout until we know what we are dealing with. It's standard operational procedure for us to cordon off an area in the plaza for those with press credentials."

"I agree that there should be a real time media blackout," said Harriman. "Still, it might be a good idea to have a pool reporter in the hall as an observer. I would suggest Grace Williams."

Tanya Vespers frowned. "Why Williams? She's a bit of a wild card, isn't she? She's not exactly a friend of the administration either. Why not Syed Rampur? He has her status, and he's pliable."

"Exactly why we want Williams," countered Harriman. "She has a reputation for integrity that is unblemished. Everyone knows that Rampur is a shill for the administration. That said, I have run across her in the past, and she will cooperate with us in keeping quiet what needs to be kept quiet. With Williams, we get the best of both worlds."

"I will recommend her to the SecGen," said North. What about security-- both here and throughout the city?"

"The UN complex and plazas will be locked down with not only standard security personnel but also American special forces units. All will be coordinated through the UN Security office. American infantry units are in the process of clearing all buildings within a two-block radius of the complex. A cordon will be established within this area that is off limits to the general public. In two hours, if you aren't in here already, you're not getting in," explained Vespers.

"Defense forces are stationed at key points around the city, and we have all approaches covered," added Harriman. "General Kurtz has established a command post in what we have deemed to be a safe distance from ground zero and has the city completely covered with our drones and satellites, not to mention attack jets and helicopters in position over the region's airspace. Naval ships are stationed in and out of the harbor, with a defensive ring of hunter-killer subs protecting the approach. We should have ample warning of anything unusual coming our way. If this is a conventional terror attack, we should at least have a fighting chance to stop them.

"But I don't think that's the case. I wish it were. The truth is that what we are facing is unprecedented in our civilization's history. These folks made the entire planet stand still for a few seconds. We can plan and prepare, but we don't really know for what."

Harriman looked directly at Anne North. "In the end, if something bad does go down, I can't protect you."

Anne North leaned back in her chair, chin resting on her chest. For a moment, the room was thick with silence.

"When I was a little girl, the Soviets shot down a Korean airliner that had wandered into their airspace," she began. "I remember my parents being very frightened because we were on high alert. For a few days, it seemed as though there was going to be a nuclear war and the end of everything.

"When the Sino-Indian conflict began, it looked as though they were going to be the ones to bring about the end. A few years ago, a massive asteroid passed within twenty thousand miles of the Earth. A tiny fraction of a degree difference in a four-billion-year-old orbital arc and we would have been incinerated."

She looked at Harriman. "Whether by God's hand or our own, we are never really safe, John. It's an illusion… it always has been. We have forever been on the edge of extinction. Why should I expect the addition of one man to the City of New York make any difference within the chaos of our existence?

"Don't try to shoulder that burden, Colonel Harriman. Just do your job, and we will too- come what may."

Grace and Red Kearney entered the UN General Assembly Hall media center and looked around. A large, plate glass window dominated the room, offering a view of the entire hall from fifty feet above the floor. The speaker's podium was directly ahead a few hundred feet away.

"Not quite in the action," complained Grace to Red.

Kearney stood in front of several banks of monitors and production equipment, scowling.

"This isn't exactly cutting edge tech either. This stuff looks to be twenty years old." He looked over at Grace, smirking sarcastically. "I love a challenge."

The Irishman sat down at one of the stations and contemplated the board. "This one looks to be the control monitor for all of the stationary cameras in the hall." He paused. "I think this one is the live feed out."

"Which you won't be needing," said Agent John Smith, walking through the door. Kearney glared at him, anger flashing across his face.

Smith smiled. "You don't like me very much do you, Mr. Kearney?"

"Never did like spooks," growled the big man. "They always manage to find a way to get good people killed."

"Agent Smith!" beamed Grace, stepping into his line of sight. "To what do we owe the presence of your company?"

"In fact, Ms. Williams, I believe you owe *me* the very presence of your company," deadpanned the government's man.

Grace gave him a puzzled look.

———

74

"I was able to pull some strings to get you the pool reporter slot."

"Now why would you go and do something like that for us?" asked Kearney.

Harriman looked over Grace Williams' shoulder at him. "Because this way I can keep an eye on you."

He returned his gaze to Grace. "Besides, you did me a favor once. I thought I'd return it. Frankly, you two are as good as they come. Why not Williams and Kearney? There's just one catch..."

"Here it comes," moaned Kearney.

"You can report what you want, say what you want, but you can't do it live."

Grace spoke up. "That doesn't make any sense. Why would you want us to delay the transmission, unless your intent is to vet the facts for public consumption?"

"Ok, let me put it another way. It is not our intent to interfere with your reporting of the facts of the story, but we don't yet know what the story is, do we? We don't know what we're dealing with and the last thing we want is to generate a global panic because of what might be said or done here in the next few hours. For that reason alone, we want to delay your transmission until after the event has taken place, whatever that event may be."

An uneasy silence blanketed the room.

Agent Smith broke it. "Look, I don't want you to go against your ethics. If you don't want to do it, we can get another crew to act as the pool reporter."

Grace didn't appreciate being boxed in and this man had done it to her twice. Even so, she wasn't going to pass up front row seats on what could be one of biggest moments of her lifetime. In human history, for that matter.

"We're in, Agent Smith." She looked over at her partner. Kearney nodded in agreement. 'We're in."

The consensus at the UN had been that since New York was an American city, it would be the responsibility of the American military to protect the UN complex, securing the immediate surroundings and to a lesser extent the city itself. The assignment had fallen to General Alexander Kurtz, a circumstance that John Harriman considered a blessing. The two men were close friends.

75

Kurtz was the United States Army's youngest general, and the fact that he came from a century-old family tradition hadn't hurt his rise. The Kurtz family had distinguished itself in every American war of the twentieth-century; beginning with a great-great-great grandfather who had marched into France with Pershing and had survived being gassed with the 9th Division at Belleau Wood. Successive generations of the line had lead men at Anzio and Pork Chop Hill. The running family joke was that a great-uncle had almost singlehandedly won Vietnam before the politicians stepped in and mucked it up.

Kurtz's father had fought in Gulf 1 and done another two tours in Gulf 2. He returned just before Alex shipped out for Afghanistan as a 2nd Lieutenant, fresh out of The Point.

West Point was where John Harriman had met Alex Kurtz, he as a plebe and Kurtz a yuk. Being a year ahead usually meant little fraternization but both had been solid linebackers for the Black Knights and the team comradeship had quickly evolved into a friendship as well.

No two friends could be more different. Harriman's six-foot frame, dark hair, and nondescript looks were ideal for his future life as a spook. They were no match for Alex Kurtz's square-jawed, blond perfection. A female acquaintance of Harriman's had once compared Kurtz to the visage of an Aryan god.

The only thing more godlike was his charismatic confidence. To Harriman, it was as if seven generations of selective breeding had brought forth the iconic military leader.

Harriman, in contrast, had been blessed with the ability to hide in plain sight. It was one of the reasons why he had elected for Special Operations after graduation.

Kurtz was the product of a large and boisterous military family. Harriman was an orphan, who had been sponsored by the Source Corp conglomerate. He had been selected for his intelligence and athleticism and given every opportunity to excel in his chosen field. The military had seemed a natural fit for him. The orphanage administrators agreed, and his dorm room at the home morphed into one at West Point almost overnight.

The two friends had remained in contact over the years, even so much as Harriman attending Alex Kurtz's wedding and celebrating Kurtz's promotion to general. Kurtz gleamed in the spotlight while Harriman moved in shadows.

In the now, as the two friends stood together in the command center just minutes before who knew what was going to happen, General Alexander Kurtz had no doubt about the chain of command.

Colonel John Harriman was his superior officer.

Harriman was the President's man, and the orders had been clear. He was to observe, advise, and consult. His command was to provide tactical support to Harriman's strategy.

The two men listened politely as one of Kurtz's junior officers explained *The Brain.*

"… as the system taps into the entire metropolitan surveillance network. The Brain then sorts through hundreds of thousands of images and an algorithm helps it to determine and report any anomalies. The system cycles every seven seconds. So, if anything strange is sighted, we will know where almost immediately."

"We also have standard surveillance from orbital satellites, drones, et cetera," interrupted Kurtz. "The navy and air force are out there as well with their data streams integrated into the system."

"Yes sir," confirmed the captain. "We have the city and surrounding area so locked down that we should have a minimum thirty-minute notice in advance of anything unusual."

"Thanks, Bill. Keep us posted," replied Kurtz. The captain turned and blended into the rows of monitors and observers.

The two men moved into Kurtz's makeshift office. The building was a converted warehouse that had been transformed into the eyes and ears of the nation within hours. It was centrally located to quick transport routes but far enough away from the UN to remain functioning if things went south. Kurtz had commandeered the old dispatch office for himself. The rapid move in had foregone cleanliness and the space seemed to be soaked in hydraulic fluid and gear grease. Kurtz smiled and pointed at a filthy chair as he closed the door behind them.

"Make yourself at home, John."

"Thanks, I'll stand. Besides, I have to be getting back. We have maybe an hour until the deadline. I want to make sure I'm at ground zero."

Kurtz's face lost its smile. "What do you plan to do?"

"What I always do, Alex. Blend into the background. I will be one of the security escort personnel." Harriman looked around and opened his arms, palms up. "You have the macros covered. The devil is in the details. If I can get close enough to get something that might let us know who these jokers are, then maybe we can turn it on them."

—

"The devil indeed!" chuckled Kurtz. "God help whoever has to go up against Hammerin' Harriman!"

"Stop that. You know I hate that nickname," countered Harriman.

"I know! Hits too close to home!" Kurtz replied. "Just be careful. We won't screw the pooch on this end," Alex Kurtz held out a hand to his old friend. "You make sure you don't either."

That was about as warm a goodbye between two career military men as Harriman could expect. It was all he needed. At the end of the day, it was about successfully executing the mission. Still, they had been friends long enough to know the sentiment behind the words.

"I'll be all right, General," smiled Harriman as he shook Kurtz's hand. "I'm too goddamn mean to die."

"Don't I know it, Colonel!"

Within forty minutes, John Harriman was discretely standing in the heavily secured United Nations Plaza before the Secretariat Building-- waiting with the rest of the world for what was to come next.

In his earpiece, he heard Alex Kurtz's voice, unusually tense. It set him on edge. "John, I don't know how they managed it, but there is a craft of some sort that just appeared out of nowhere and is hovering over the East River behind the UN.

"And John, you aren't going to believe this, but the damned thing looks just like a flying saucer!"

The object floated over the water, stationary and silent. Harriman got his first glimpse of it rounding the General Assembly building at breakneck speed with several dozen others close behind.

"General, are you reading it now?" asked Harriman into his mic.

"No, John. We only picked it up through visual observation," replied Kurtz. "Maybe what we are seeing is an illusion. A 3D projection of some sort?"

"If it is, then these are the best magicians on the planet," replied Harriman. "It looks pretty solid at one-hundred meters."

Grace and Red Kearney saw it for the first time on the NNI network monitor. Audra Slagle was the correspondent assigned to the outer perimeter. As luck would have it, she had been using the East River as her backdrop when the object appeared suddenly behind her. The pair, who had been absorbed in their preparations, now stopped and gaped at the monitor.

"... and now as you can see, the saucer shaped craft seems to have two outer rings rotating in opposite directions. It's silver, and it's hard to tell from here, but it doesn't appear to be very large, maybe thirty feet from end to end." Slagle was good, but Grace could hear the tension in her voice as she lost control.

"Oh my God! It's moving toward us!"

Harriman could tell who was civilian and who was military when the craft began approaching the UN complex. The civilians were running in the opposite direction.

Probably for the best, he thought. *They're just going to get in the way.*

He determined that the craft was heading toward the gardens behind the General Assembly building and began walking in that direction.

It wasn't a large craft, maybe ten meters across and four meters high. It did look just like the flying saucers out of those timeworn movies he had to watch when he was a kid in Mr. Chaucer's class. He remembered the movie, *The Day the Earth Stood Still*.

"How appropriate," he said to himself.

In the General Assembly media center, Kearney and Williams watched the ship move vertically over the top of the concrete river wall and glide toward the UN gardens, floating just a few feet off of the ground. Seconds later, the monitor screen picture began to break down and snow out.

"See if you can get another feed," she said.

"It looks as though anything close is out," replied Kearney, already on it. After a few more seconds, another view of the craft came onto the monitor. It was very shaky, the vehicle coming in and out of view as the wind blew the camera. "Here's an ABC feed from across the river but it isn't great. I'll keep looking. Any close-by cameras within the complex seem to be out."

"Great! That means we have an exclusive," replied Grace.

John Harriman and the craft made it onto the UN gardens at the same time. It wasn't that big at all, his guess of ten meters from tip to tip looked to be right. It reminded him of a priest's hat- circular, with a brim half a meter thick and flattened at the edges. A half-spherical center that was perhaps seven meters wide and four meters at the apex rotated opposite to the counter-clockwise revolutions of the brim.

The craft made no sound but did kick up a violent disturbance of the flowers around it as it floated a meter above the ground. It moved almost lazily over a small, grassy patch and stopped. A whining noise emanated from it as servomotors began to whir a tripod of flat-footed landing gear toward the ground.

Harriman had been unconsciously walking directly toward the silver craft, providing a detailed description to the command center. At ten meters, he heard the audio cut out. Simultaneously, his skin began to crawl as if he were covered with thousands of ants. A meter closer, the crawling became biting, and his skin felt as if it were on fire. He retreated a few seconds later when he could stand the pain no longer. At ten meters, the fire subsided back into the ant sensation. At twelve, all negative sensations receded.

"Colonel, are you alright?" he could hear Alex Kurtz in his ear. "We saw you fall to the ground and crawl away from the ship."

Harriman couldn't remember falling to his knees or crawling away. "It would seem that it has established a perimeter we are not to cross, General. I would say roughly ten meters. It felt as if I had been bitten everywhere by fire ants once I was inside that perimeter. Do you still have a visual?"

"We do but only from our drones. Anything closer is dead. We lost communication with you at ten meters as well. My expert is telling me that it might be some type of specialized, electromagnetic interference."

"I've never known EM to have that kind of effect on the body, but at this juncture, I wouldn't be inclined to disagree," replied Harriman. He noticed that as the craft had become still, the plaza now began to fill with others. Some were bravely stepping in and out of the EM perimeter with the same result as he had come to moments ago.

"We still can't get a radar read on it either," Kurtz responded. "Uh oh! Do you see that?"

"Yes sir, I do! I would speculate that's a hatch opening."

The hatch was an iris-like opening in the side of the craft. Harriman saw it rotate open to reveal a light so brightly emanating from the interior that no detail could be discerned.

The creature came through the opening and into the light of day, the iris closing as it cleared the exit. It appeared to be humanoid but it was obviously not human. It was wearing a white robe- belted with a purple sash. The robe's hood covered what passed as a head.

It also seemed to be floating. It floated over the brim of the craft and onto the grass in front of the ship.

Then it walked directly to John Harriman.

As it approached, he saw that it had a human face or at least the projection of one. It had a surreal quality, as if it was a three-dimensional copy of a young, Caucasian man, smiling and serene.

By this time, Tanya Vespers and a security contingent had arrived as an escort. Harriman looked at her and motioned for her to remain behind him. When he turned back to the creature, its face was now that of a young, African man. It had closed the gap between them and stopped a few feet from him. The creature shimmered.

"Fear not, John Harriman, for we bring a promise of peace," it said.

"You know my name," Harriman said, startled.

"Of course. We know everyone's name," it said. Its voice was soft and light, layered as though a choir was singing through it. The face had become that of a young, Asian man.

"What should I call you?"

"We are Seraphim. Once, long ago, we were known by some of your kind as Gabriel," it replied with the face of a young, South-Asian man. Its lips didn't move when it spoke. Harriman speculated it wore the faces as a mask.

He took a step back and to the side. "We are to escort you to the General Assembly, Gabriel."

"Please lead on. It is important that we speak to the people of this world." The face had returned to that of the Caucasian man.

Harriman turned back to Vespers and her entourage and gave a nod. They fell into place, surrounding the creature but giving it ample space to move freely within them. Harriman took the rear.

It turned to look at him. "Please do not approach the Orphanum," it sang, pointing toward the craft. "They don't appreciate people the way that others of our kind do. It can be quite protective of itself, as you have already felt firsthand. Can you tell General Kurtz not to put anyone in danger unnecessarily?"

"Did you get that, General?" asked Harriman.

"Loud and clear," replied Kurtz through the earpiece. "We will put a guard around the perimeter to keep away the curious."

"Thank you, General Kurtz," said Gabriel, still facing Harriman. It turned to follow Tanya Vespers up the steps and onto the main plaza of the General Assembly building.

The group's progress was halted momentarily when the creature paused to take in *Non-Violence*, the sculpture of a giant handgun tied into a knot that occupied a corner of the central plaza. After a few moments, it continued across the plaza and through the main entrance of the building.

It knew exactly where it was going.

Grace and John Kearney were able to follow the procession through a live feed stationed on the other side of the street in Ralph Bunche Park. Red recorded a running commentary that Grace was voicing over the images for later use. The group was lost momentarily on camera when it entered the General Assembly building. Kearney cut to a widescreen shot of a packed hall, the world's ambassadors buzzing in anticipation of the unknown to come.

The room grew silent as the creature appeared, moving briskly toward the speaker's podium where Secretary General Helmut Lemke stood, waiting with the representatives of the Security Council. Grace noted that the diminutive American Ambassador Anne North was front and center of that group.

Grace maintained the commentary. "As you can see, the being's face keeps changing. It is hard to see from our vantage point, but the face seems to be reflecting a different image every few seconds."

Kearney hit the cough button. "Uh, Gracie, you should take a look at the monitor."

Grace looked and gasped slightly. "This is the strangest thing! Our cameras cannot pick up the varying faces the creature is emitting inside the hall! On camera, as viewers can now see, white light is emanating from where we are seeing a series of human faces!"

82

Kearney hit the button again. "One more thing- the network says we're live."

Harriman received the news that the media feed was live just as the procession reached the podium steps.

"Of course we are *live* as you say, John Harriman," confirmed the creature, turning to show the Asian face to him. "Did you think you could hide us from the people of your world?"

Harriman sighed. Whatever this dog and pony show turned out to be, it was now becoming apparent that they were not capable of maintaining control of the stage.

Secretary General Lemke and his entourage waited at the top of the podium. Harriman could tell he was terrified but also that several decades of diplomatic experience had kicked in to help the diplomat hold it together. The rest of the Security Council seemed equally uneasy.

The Secretary General bowed and spoke in a strong voice. "On behalf of the diplomatic corps of the United Nations, we welcome and receive you."

"Greetings, Helmut Lemke," sang the choir-like voice of the creature, turning its African face to the Security Council. "Greetings to all of you. With your permission, we will now address the people of your planet."

Lemke hesitated as if weighing the potential consequences of refusing the creature's request. Silently, he took a step towards the podium. Continuing to look at it, he motioned the creature forward. The robed being took its place at the dais.

"We are the Voice of Our Host. In the tradition of the ancients, you may refer to this construct as Seraphim Gabriel," it began. "We are created in your image so that it may be easier for you to engage with us."

"We bring a message to your world from Our Host. All organized hostilities across this planet must cease immediately. There is to be no more war, no more fighting between either nations or factions."

"Furthermore," it continued, "the military assets of all nations are to stand down immediately and be placed under the direct control of the Secretary General and Security Council of the United Nations. You have forty hours to comply. We shall reconvene the General Assembly in forty-eight hours to review the transfer of assets."

A chaotic din began to rise throughout the great hall. Gabriel raised its arms; its voice now roaring over the crowd as if it were a full orchestra.

"Failure to comply shall result in the complete destruction of those who refuse the will of Our Host."

Helmut Lemke was failing to comprehend that Gabriel was about to make him the most powerful human being on the planet. "What you ask is impossible! No nation will give up the right to defend itself!"

Gabriel looked directly at the Secretary General with the same serene chorus of faces and pointed to him.

"Can you defend yourself against Our Host?" it asked. The Secretary General began to gasp and clutch at his chest.

"Can anyone in this hall?" it continued, lifting its robed arms to the assembled diplomats.

As if on cue, Grace suddenly felt a tightness in her chest. Within seconds, it had grown into an elephant sitting on top of her, not allowing her to breath. She looked around in her pain to see that the entire hall seemed to be undergoing collective heart failure.

Gabriel lowered its arms, and the pain subsided immediately. It paused as the room gathered itself.

"Once before, we demonstrated the power of Our Host over your lives and yet you fail to understand. Now we offer a second demonstration." Gabriel looked at Lemke. "Our Host can at a moment's notice end the life of one," it again opened its arms, motioning to the hall, "the lives of hundreds... or of billions.

"In the blink of an eye, Our Host can destroy a city... a nation... or a world. If It must, Our Host is willing to cleanse humanity from this world and begin anew.
We beseech you that the armies of all nations yield to the will of Our Host or the people of those nations that refuse to comply will be destroyed instantly and without mercy. Death will come within a heartbeat. There will be no time to defend yourselves. You must comply... or you will surely die."

The room was without a sound.

Seraphim Gabriel offered a last warning. "We now return to our companion Ophanum, to await the allotted time. We implore that there be no panic amongst the nations nor that any hostile action be committed against us during this period. If either occurs, Our Host will take retribution against this aggression by extinguishing all human life from the planet. What is to come, Our Host does out of Its love for the Children of Man."

Chapter Six

Wil and the angel materialized in the midst of a fierce battle. From what he could tell, it looked to be an ancient war- one from the time of the Romans or Greeks. He couldn't tell.

They were standing on a plain several dozen yards removed from the fighting, toward the center of the battle. Wil could see thousands of soldiers clashing together in a line that seemed to go on for a mile. At the very ends on both sides of the line, he could make out what appeared to be thousands more men on horseback, waiting.

The next thing he noticed was that the line in front of them was moving steadily backward. Soon they would be in the middle of it all. Wil gave the angel a nervous glance.

She smiled back at him.

"Don't worry Wil, we're here, but we aren't really here. No one can see us or hurt us. We aren't a part of the scenario." The angel pointed to a group in front of them. "Aha! Sonya is over there and coming our way. Let's say hello!"

Wil couldn't see anyone that looked even remotely like Sonya in front of him. He guessed that she must be wearing a shell.

Wil and the angel stood together with the slowly retreating soldiers moving through them as if the pair were ghosts. "There she is!" smiled the angel. "Hello, Sonya! I hope you are well!"

Sonya was a bearded man, who looked to be in his late thirties. He wore classical body armor and wielded a curved sword in his right hand, a blocky wooden shield in his left. The man had lost his helmet and was soaked head to toe in a crimson that Wil realized was blood.

"Who're you?" asked the warrior between breaths.

"She's an angel," answered Wil.

"She's not my angel. It can't be time yet; I just got started!" said the man without looking up. He swung the sword low and hacked into the leg of the opponent in front of him. The soldier screamed and staggered, dropping his rectangular shield for just an instant. Sonya's avatar used the slip to drive his sword straight into the throat of the man. Choking on his blood as it spurted from the wound, the unfortunate soldier fell forward and disappeared under the feet of the advancing troops behind him.

"No, Sonya, it isn't time yet. Wil and I have come to pay you a visit and speak with you about a matter that is very important."

"I'm kind of in the middle of something right now," replied the man gruffly. "How about you come back after we've won?"

"It doesn't look like you're winning, girl," laughed Wil. "You seem to be going backward."

"Ha! That just shows you how little you know! It's 216 B. C., and this is the battle of Cannae on the Italian plain. I am the Carthaginian General Hannibal, in the middle of implementing the first classic pincer movement in military history."

"We're engaged in a controlled retreat of the center to draw the Roman army in and collapse its ability to move and fight," Hannibal said, still steadily hacking away with his sword and moving backward slowly.

Sonya's shell looked over them just for a second and pointed with his sword to the mounted horsemen at the edge of their vision. "You see that cavalry massed on the edge of our line? In the next couple of minutes, they are going to begin attacking the flanks and rear of the Roman army. The Romans will be so tightly packed together that they won't be able to fight."

The General ducked a sword and reacted by driving his into the stomach of the assailant. "By the time I am finished here, we will have slaughtered seventy thousand of the Republic's finest soldiers."

"Let's get a look at the real you," said the angel.

Before them, the Carthaginian general morphed into a thin young woman. Still swinging away with the now oversized sword, Sonya's face flared in anger at the transformation.

"Hey! What the hell is wrong with you?" she cried indignantly.

Wil was overwhelmed. "How do you know all this stuff? And why would you get a kick out of slaughtering seventy thousand people?"

The girl dropped her guard and turned to face them. "First of all, I didn't slaughter anyone. Hannibal did two thousand years ago. I like the underdog, and no one was more of a pain in the ass to the mighty Roman Republic than Hannibal.

Second, I used to like to read and watch shows about history. This battle is one of the most important events in military history. Hannibal's tactic is still used by modern armies today. Third… shit!" Sonya staggered as a Roman soldier swiped his sword through her. Realizing that the angel had taken her out of phase with the battle, the girl murmured, "Oh, well," dejectedly dropping her sword and shield. She walked over to where Wil and the angel stood, the battle continuing to take place through them. "Third," she muttered, "I can only be Joan of Arc so many times.

"I've got an idea," said Wil. "Why not be Sonya of Chicago?"

"Because Sonya of Chicago lives in a box and has no future," retorted the young woman.

"Listen to what she has to say," replied Wil. "It doesn't have to be this way. We can have real lives, better lives."

"Bullshit!"

"It's true, Sonya," said the angel. "I was unsure about you because you usually pick destructive or frivolous worlds to live in, but now I see why."

"Yeah, Doc? Whadaya see about me?"

The angel took their hands, and they began to rise into the sky, the ground and the din of the battle falling away from them. Sonya let out a joyful cry and smiled wide-eyed at Wil. He smiled back sheepishly. Heights were not his thing and even though he knew it wasn't real, he instinctively felt his testicles tighten in fear. Sonya was ecstatic. He was happy for her.

"I see that you love adventure and want to do great things in this one life you have," said the angel. She looked down at the carnage below. "You know it yourself, Sonya. Men have always measured themselves with war and gold. It has been that way since the beginning, and it is the path that Mankind still walks to this day.

"Those who created me have decided that it is time for men and women to walk a new path. A way without fear or want… one of peace.

"You have a sharp intellect and great leadership ability, Sonya. You are not alone. There are millions just like you who want a better way. Together, we will make a new world that is prosperous and just for everyone. Your life will be real, and it will possess the great meaning that you so desperately desire."

Sonya was transfixed, something Wil had never seen before.

"This is real, right? The real world, not just another sandbox?" she said finally.

"There is one more thing," continued the angel. "You know Wil loves you. He is coming with us, and he wants you to join him. I did not believe in you, but he did and has convinced me to offer you a place in our new world. He was right to believe in you. Do you trust and believe in him?"

Sonya looked at Wil as if for the first time.

"Lady, say no more. I'm stuck in a metal coffin, and I'm slowly rotting away. Where do I sign up?"

***

Philip Janikowski did what he always did when there was a crisis. He took his family to church.

He wasn't the only one. This crisis had coincided with the mid-week services, and the pews of the *Church of the Children of the One True God* were full.

Of course, no one took the time to actually say that title. They went by *Children of God* or Chogs for short.

Tonight, there were a couple of hundred Children in the church. After the invocation prayer, Pastor Gregson was overseeing a fierce debate about what exactly they had seen on their monitors and tablets this afternoon.

"Perhaps it's the end of days!" exclaimed Michael Garibaldi. "We are seeing the beginning of the fulfillment of prophecy. We will soon be raptured and enjoy eternal life with our Lord and Savior! It is all we could hope for!"

"That's a possibility, Deacon Garibaldi. Still, we should counsel patience and take no rash action until God's will becomes clear," cautioned Pastor Gregson.

"Respectfully, Pastor, what other signs are we waiting for?" replied Garibaldi. "The signs are given. The Trumpeter has returned. Did we not all see the Archangel Gabriel herald the arrival of the Heavenly Host? Is it not written in Revelation that the Host will wreak destruction upon the wicked and prepare our world for the Kingdom of God?"

"Is that really what we saw, Brother Garibaldi?" asked a familiar voice above the murmur of the room. Philip looked to his right to see that Ana Maria Janikowski had climbed onto the pew beside him and was now standing on it, head and shoulders above the congregation, right hand raised for attention.

"It is written that Satan appears to us as an angel of light," his wife continued. "That Angel was nothing but light. It threatened to destroy everyone, sinner and saved alike, in order to get its way."

—

"It called its chariot Ophanum," intruded Olga Karrassos. "These are sacred words. A wheel within a wheel, just as Ezekiel saw when the Heavenly Host appeared to him. How could Satan possess the chariot of Gabriel and the Host? This must be the Angel of God!"

"Is not the Deceiver himself a fallen Seraphim? Perhaps the Ophanum is fallen as well. Many were cast out as demons," replied Philip's wife. "Satan works to confuse us and lead us to perdition. What if we are not snatched away? What if this isn't the end times after all? Do we risk our souls on a deception?"

Ana Maria was a powerful and persuasive sister of the Children, and Philip could feel the room begin to sway to her thinking. Philip decided to throw in his two cents, not something he often did.

"I have to tell you folks, what I saw looked a lot like a spaceship, not a chariot of Heaven," he began. "What if these are aliens trying to conquer our planet without a fight?"

"For aliens, they sure know a great deal of Scripture," countered Olga Karrassos. "What would aliens know about the sacred texts? How could they have knowledge of the angels?"

"I don't know about you folks, but I didn't see a demon or an angel or a chariot. What I saw looked a lot like some kind of a ship and that thing looked like an alien of some sort," said Philip above the din.

The room grew quiet as all eyes turned his way. Some of the looks were not so pleasant, and Philip began to regret that he had spoken up. He looked over at Ana Maria and the kids. Since he had just stuck a pin in her demon theory, the nastiest look came from her. Campbell and Tina seemed frightened. He smiled tightly, hoping to reassure them.

Pastor Gregson threw him a lifeline. "Please continue, Brother Philip. I believe it is important for us to consider all viewpoints, even those of a secular nature."

He had the room and an ally. *Jesus, guide my words*, he prayed silently.

"Look, I don't know what we saw, but I think we can rule some things out if we think about it for a minute," he began. "For one, God wouldn't threaten to kill everyone in the world, at least not the God of the New Covenant. God has promised that the saved shall live on the New Earth as the Kingdom of Heaven. So killing everyone doesn't make any sense to me, and that makes me think this creature that we saw isn't an angel."

Philip paused as heads began nodding in agreement.

"It could be a demon but, on the other hand, since when does a demon need what looked like a flying saucer to get around?" he continued.

"Maybe they are being used as a tool of destruction by Satan?" spoke up one in the crowd. Philip couldn't make out whom it was. His wife nodded silently next to him.

"Could be," he agreed, "but what is more important is that we know they just can't appear and disappear at will. They need a vehicle to travel in. That makes me think they aren't supernatural at all.

"That doesn't mean they aren't dangerous. They can make everyone sick, and we've seen that for ourselves. Now they threaten to kill everyone if we don't surrender to them.

"To me, this sounds like an invasion."

The room exploded with noise and confusion as Philip finished speaking. Above the roar, Michael Garibaldi shouted out to no one in particular, "So what can we do about it?"

Pastor Gregson raised his hands in order to restore order. Instinctively, the crowd fell silent.

He looked at Philip. "I believe that Brother Janikowski has brought a thoughtful and inspired perspective to our discussion. We do not yet have enough evidence of the divine to put our faith in this visitor not do we have enough to support evidence of the Fallen.

"As Brother Philip says, we do have enough evidence of the potential for evil, possibly even directed at the Children of God. Therefore, we should pray for guidance and salvation while preparing for resistance. I now call for a meeting of the Sons of Liberty after the service.

"If the end times truly are at hand, we must be on the side of the Lord in the great strife to come. If we are in fact being invaded by a foreign power, then we must resist in the name of freedom and defeat the evil that befalls us.

"We will overcome and be victorious because the One True God is with us!"

***

Sam Craig was livid.

"Don't even try to feed me that bullshit! You may have had to spout scripture and prophesy to get to Washington, but God didn't suddenly show up in Ralph Bunche Park today!" fumed an unhappy President to the assembled group.

—

91

"Mr. President, please! What if this is the fulfillment of scripture and we are in the end times?" asked Secretary of Religious Freedom James Roberts. "We must prepare for the rapture of souls!"

Jim Gillette closed his eyes so no one could see him roll them in disgust. He had never thought much of the Department of Religious Freedom, but Jim Roberts was dangerous. He wasn't some politician parroting scripture for easy votes. He was a true believer, with the support of millions of like-minded folks. Roberts had been president of the Council of Evangelical Churches of America and a leading televangelist before that. Sam Craig was from a Midwestern state (albeit one that was both rabidly conservative and Christian) and needed Roberts's influence to pull in the South. In return, Craig appointed him Chief Defender of the Faith, which was what the Secretary of the Department of Religious Freedom was perceived to be.

Gillette thought Roberts was a moron. An extremely dangerous man, due to his ability to mobilize masses of followers, but a moron still.

Jim Gillette despaired that in his time, the world had become fixated upon extremes. With Islam rapidly growing into the largest faith and more than three billion Buddhists and Hindus occupying a large part of the globe, Christianity had found itself in a crisis of ambivalence. As the citizenry of Western Europe and North America became secularized, Christians grew more extreme in their dogma- and they organized.

Gillette had been a young man when the evangelical and conservative Christian movements had first taken wing. Initially, politicians paid them little more than lip service. He remembered as a high school student listening to Ronald Reagan parrot the prayer in school and anti-abortion mantras back at the evangelicals. So enchanted were they with The Great Communicator's wooing that they never saw the crossed fingers behind his back.

For years after, the Christian Right threw its vote in with conservatives, who spouted on about family values but did nothing about them once elected.

Then it discovered primaries.

Evangelicals didn't have the numbers to take a general election, but they could use their mass to determine who was going to run. As one moderate politician after another fell to the evangelical sword, others chose to fall in line. No longer was it enough just to say you were with them. Politicians now had to prove it by backing a religious agenda or find themselves flaming out in the next primary election.

Gillette thought the evangelical movement's stroke of genius was in priming an inherent flaw in the American psyche- that everything is a game, us against them, winners and losers. America was a culture that had a hard time seeing shades of gray.

As Jim Gillette had grown older, he saw an alarming number of people opt out of the political process, buying into the argument that the parties were two faces of the same coin. Eventually, that became roughly half the eligible voting public. Those who did vote became swept up in the media driven news cycles that hyped *the Game*. It was red against blue. The networks and their pundits giving the same weight to every argument and idea- no matter how ridiculous upon scrutiny.

There were always going to be those who had perennially voted for one party or the other because of family tradition, patriotism, devotion to the free market, or simply because of a candidate's genetics..

Gillette knew the evangelicals counted on them to not examine candidates or issues too closely, hyping the *Red and Blue* aspect of the game. Slowly and steadily, it got them wins at all levels of government.

Things changed dramatically after '20 when the opposition split apart into a left-leaning faction and a more middle of the road party. By then, world events and the fear created by them had pushed the process far to the right. So far that, from Jim Gillette's perspective, middle of the road Democrats looked like Reagan Republicans. The liberal element seemed downright communist.

For the evangelical right, it was as if the gates of heaven itself had swung wide open. All of the *family values* agendas they had waited so long to implement finally bore fruit. *Christian* prayer returned to schools. The teaching of evolution and the scientific method was legislatively displaced for creationism. Abortion rights were banned once again. The Ten Commandments were placed proudly in the rotundas of capital buildings across the nation.

As AgriBus's long-time operative within the GOP, Jim Gillette had been instructed by his masters to stand aside or support these measures as a way of gaining influence with the Republican National Committee. Even so, he thought these were all small potatoes compared with what was to come next- the Department of Religious Freedom.

The DRF was a knee jerk reaction to a world that most evangelicals either couldn't or didn't care to understand. To a significant degree, the Islamic wars helped to fire the mold. Gillette found the combatants' strategy obvious. The Muslim factions fighting over the ideological future of Islam had a habit of tweaking the nose of the West as a way of mucking up the field. When it was convenient, extremists would attack targets in America and Europe, hoping the West would come storming in, with guns blazing, and backing the other side. They could then win over their own faction's moderates by pointing out that the other side was supported by infidels. It was a tactic that nearly always worked. As a rule, Americans didn't like having their grocery stores blown up.

Over the years, security had become both more restrictive and less effective. Fear and suspicion of immigrants grew despite the fact that many of them were leaving their own countries to escape extremism and that many others were themselves Christian. Stir in the polling numbers that had mainstream Christianity shrinking in size with white America soon to be a minority and Gillette saw smelted metal ready for the mold.

He thought what had been conveniently ignored in the hysteria leading up to the DRF was that other faiths made up less than ten percent of the American population. In fact, the flight from mainstream Christianity had its roots in secularized Christians. In a way, this served to stoke the furnace even hotter. The sole demographic of Christianity expanding on a global scale was that of the evangelicals. Its increasingly extreme view of the world offered simple solutions to complex problems, bringing millions of fearful citizens into the fold.

The act creating the Department of Religious Freedom was justified constitutionally by claiming the religious freedoms of all Americans would be upheld. From the start, it became obvious that it was meant to tip the playing field to the advantage of Christians.

The DRF enforced the social reforms enacted by an increasingly radicalized Congress, but then it went one step further. Those who proclaimed Christianity as their faith began to receive tax breaks, this being justified by requiring funds to tithe in support of their churches. Businesses claiming to be Christian also received tax exemptions. Christians who patronized these businesses received reduced sales tax requirements.

All lower income Christians paid no income tax at all, instead receiving stipends and subsidies to increase their standard of living. This *Faith Subsidy* was politically important and ingenious. Those who chose the box surrendered their voting rights. Christians were dead set against virtuality, seeing it as a tool of Satan. The only other option, subsidizing the faithful in the real world, secured the loyalty of a large following who considered voting a religious obligation.

The DRF effectively became an enforcement arm of the Internal Revenue Service.

Gillette hated everything about it, including those who operated it. He knew that its policies and influence had both dumbed down and nearly bankrupted the nation.

It wasn't that Gillette hated Christianity itself; he was proud to be a practicing Lutheran. It was the evangelicals' strict adherence to outdated dogma that had regressed the nation's position as a world leader in science and technology; with the result being an increasingly ignorant populace. Whoever had played them understood this and knew that millions would be viewing the events at the UN as the beginning of the apocalypse.

Still, he was a political animal, and the Department of Religious Freedom was a tool of their times. One did not refuse the instruments of power. It was his job to help Sam Craig use them.

The President was looking at Roberts coolly. Gillette watched Craig bring his hands off the table tightly, palms down, hands cupped. They swung in Roberts's direction as if he were going to strangle the man.

Instead, he lowered his left hand slightly and turned his right hand to the DRF director with his thumb, index, and middle finger extended. Gillette was reminded of paintings of Christ instructing the apostles- or of the classical statue of Zeus at Olympus. He had seen Craig use it before, as a means to gain a psychological advantage.

"Jim, I think everyone here appreciates your expertise in matters of faith," began the President calmly. "However, in this instance, I believe it would be prudent to at the very least begin by looking beyond the supernatural for our answers."

He turned to the rest of the assembly. "Now, please! Can someone give me an idea of what in God's name we are dealing with here?"

"God!" muttered a sullen Jim Roberts.

Craig flashed him a dark look, and Roberts slid a little deeper into his suit.

"Mr. President," began Drew Tillison, "I believe we are looking at three distinct possibilities. The first is that we are dealing with a highly sophisticated and well-funded terrorist organization. Second, we could be dealing with an enemy state making a play for world domination. The third is that we are dealing with an extraterrestrial attack.".

The room began to hum at the mention of an off-world presence. Craig held up his hands for silence. "Ok, Drew, let's start there. What are the arguments for and against either case?" Gillette saw the Hoosier lawyer emerge from Craig as he grappled with what had been postulated. In the absence of hard facts, he needed at least a rational hypothesis.

The NID continued, "If they are extraterrestrial and I'm not convinced of that, they seem to possess superior technology, especially in their ability to control the immediate health of entire populations. We don't have anything like their ship's electromagnetic shielding and whatever that messenger was…"

"Gabriel," interjected Craig.

"Yes sir, Gabriel. Whatever it was, on the surface it seems to be beyond anything that we can manifest."

"We definitely don't have their ability to inflict pain on a global scale in such a surgical manner," said General Ramsey. "I mean, we can blow up the planet or bring about a plague with bio-weapons, but we can't make everyone on the planet have a simultaneous stomach cramp or seemingly induce the symptoms of a heart attack on a whim and then pull it back. That's way beyond us."

Craig looked towards a man at the end of the table. "Is it really beyond us, Jerry?"

Gerald Sagen, head of the CDC, hesitated momentarily. He kept his gaze down at his notes and without lifting his head replied, "I don't know, Mr. President. We have been examining dozens of healthy individuals affected by the first incident and have come up with nothing unusual in their biology. There is no evidence of virus or a chemically-induced reaction to a marker. We can't find anything in toxicology either. The truth is that in real time this is all happening at a lightning pace. It was thirty-six hours between the first incident and first contact. Now, we are six hours into this second potential crisis, with roughly forty hours remaining and we don't even have a starting point. It might be enough time to come up with a cure or solution in a movie, but in the real world, we just can't react that quickly to something we don't even understand."

"They sure wrap themselves in the Old Testament. All the references to a Heavenly Host and angelic hierarchies," said the Chairman of the Joint Chiefs of Staff. "Pretty smart way to get half of the world back on its heels."

Chris Cameron spoke up, "Mr. President, let's say for a moment that they are extraterrestrial in origin. Bernie's right, they sure know a lot about the Abrahamic religions. Could it be because they were here before in our past? Maybe Gabriel *really is* the Gabriel of the Bible. Have these guys have been around for thousands of years providing guidance to our ancestors?

"What if all the old, wacky speculations about angels being aliens are actually correct?"

"That's blasphemy!" cried out Jim Roberts. "It's not possible!"

"Why not, Jim?" asked the President calmly.

"Our entire social order is based upon the teachings of the Bible and the Bible is the unadulterated word of God. If these things are aliens and were masquerading as angels in our past, then that would mean that everything we believe in is a...!"

Jim Roberts's bombastic staccato ended as he felt the weight of his words. He sank back into his chair, his eyes wide with the fear of knowledge.

The room was awkwardly silent. Gillette knew why. Being an Episcopalian gave his belief system a little bit of wiggle room. He could accept Genesis as allegory and still be in good standing.

For many in the room, they had grown up believing that every single word in the Bible was from God. The world had been created in seven days and Eve did in fact spring from Adam's rib. For *any* verse to be found false or in error called the whole book into question. Gillette almost felt a little sorry for Jim Roberts- almost.

Sam Craig broke the silence. "Ok, that's one possibility. Let's explore the other options. Rogue nation or enemy state?"

"We don't believe it is the Russians or Chinese," said CIA Director Allan Kelly. "We also don't think it was the usual suspects. We've been monitoring and reviewing transmissions from before and after the initial event, and they seem to be just as concerned as we are. If one of those countries did possess the technology to pull this off, they didn't spare their own citizens."

"Besides, another nation doesn't make any sense. Why not simply just come out with the trigger cocked? Also, why force every nation to place their defense forces under the control of the Security Council? We're all members of the Security Council," said Secretary of State Amanda Weinkep.

"That's also why I don't think they are terrorists, at least not in the traditional sense," said Director Kelly. "There is no rationale for what is being asked of us. From a technological standpoint, if they are terrorists, then they have been both off the radar for the years of planning it took and are super-criminals to have the billions it would require to develop tech capabilities that no standing nation has. That's beyond reality; it's Dr. Evil stuff."

President Craig smiled at the archaic reference, then grew serious.

"Folks, what you're telling me is that we are most likely dealing with an extraterrestrial force..." he looked and smiled gently at Jim Roberts, "or God. Either way, we're behind the eight-ball. So what can we do to fight them, if anything? How can we resist? Do we think they really can destroy the nation in seconds?"

"We heard both Colonel Harriman's and Ambassador North's debriefings. I believe they can do what they say," said the Vice-President. "I'm not saying that I believe they are aliens or that we shouldn't try to figure out how they are doing it but at this point, I don't know if it matters. They seem capable of carrying out their threat. I'm not sure we can risk doubting their ability."

"Sir," said Weinkep, "the demand is for all global hostilities to cease and all defense forces to come under the command of the UN Secretary-General and the Security Council. As I mentioned before, that's close to the equivalent of handing the armed forces over to ourselves."

"Mr. President, I wish I could tell you where we could drop a well-placed tactical nuke and end this right now. Unfortunately, we have no target other than what is parked at the UN. We've already been warned attacking that will extinguish humanity," said Ramsey. "Given what we know, as well as what we don't know, I can't recommend it."

"Forty-seven armed conflicts are occurring across the world at this moment. Some are full out wars such as Central Africa. Most are civil wars or sectarian violence," said the Secretary of State. "Mr. President, we have advisors or special operations in thirty-three of them."

The room grew silent, waiting for a response from the President.

"Have them stand down immediately," said Craig. "If you can get them home, or at least in the air by the deadline, then that's a show of good faith. The troops permanently stationed on foreign soil are to pull back to their bases. I don't want a single member of our armed forces to be on the streets of a foreign country when the deadline passes. Do we declare martial law?"

"Homeland Security recommends that we don't, Sir," said Gillette. "The concern is that it might be viewed as a hostile act. So far, the public has been surprisingly calm. People seem to be going about their business. That may change as we get closer to the deadline. Another address to the nation is suggested, Sir."

Craig reached into his breast pocket and pulled out a cigar. He took his time cutting the end, even more time lighting it. Jim Gillette had been around long enough to know that this was the President's way of stretching while he thought things over. Craig took a few more puffs and spoke.

"I will go online and request that Americans be at home with their families when the deadline comes. This is only as a precaution to ensure that no action of the United States can be misinterpreted in any way as aggressive. I will tell our people that we are going to comply with the demand... wait, let's call it a request... for peace.

"Before that, I want State to get the word out to every embassy that we will comply with the request of the creature who calls itself Gabriel, at least for now. We are also urging all other nations to follow suit. I especially want to urge the North Koreans, Iranians, and Congolese to cease their hostilities for the sake of their people."

"I wouldn't worry too much about the Iranians, Mr. President," said Allan Kelly. "Intelligence reports say they're high-tailing it home from Turkmenistan as we speak."

***

Azat Mohamed knew an opportunity when he saw it. He was going to make this one pay off in a big way.

Turkmen forces were pulling back to positions twenty kilometers from the front, leaving several key towns and transport routes available to be taken. What had been lost in months of fighting and possibly, even more, could now be regained in hours. He had to press the advantage- now.

Unfortunately, his Iranian advisors didn't agree. Colonel Yazdi had made it plain and in no uncertain terms that all Iranian military personnel were returning to their homeland... on the double.

"You are a coward, Yazdi!" Azat had goaded. "Now is the time to finish this. The Turkmen are in retreat!"

"No, Azat, they are being prudent and so are we," replied Colonel Yazdi. "You should do the same and order a cease-fire."

"This is no Angel of God! It is a trick of the infidels to strike fear into our hearts. We will not die... Allah is with us!"

Yazdi stared at the Party of God leader. "You don't actually believe that, do you? God is a fifty-caliber machine gun, my friend. He takes shape in the form of an attack helicopter that protects your troops with close air support. Without that God, your men become very ordinary. When this threat is behind us, we will pick up where we left off, none the worse. Besides, you are wrong about the Great Satan. The West is not behind this threat. They are frightened as well. To risk everything for a few kilometers of ground is foolish. We are leaving."

"With the Turkmen army fleeing in fear, I no longer need your help. We will slaughter them as they run," spat Azat.

"Then you are a fool, Azat Nurali, or worse. You are insane to risk the lives of your soldiers and your people," said Yazdi, turning to leave. "They would be wise to kill you."

100

Twenty-four hours later, the Army of God was closing on several Turkmen army units in full retreat. The gains had been easy and glorious; whenever the AG came upon a Turkmen unit, it would lob a mortar into it. The unit would immediately fall back. Using this simple tactic, the AG had made up not only the twenty original kilometers hoped for, but also five more across the front.

As the deadline approached, his soldiers began to waver. Azat Mohamed saw this and approached the commander of the lead unit.

"Why are you hesitating?" he cried. "We have driven them out of our lands. We must push them against the mountains and annihilate them!"

"Imam, the men are afraid. They have heard that as the clock strikes the Angel of God will walk the Earth and destroy all who fight," replied his lieutenant.

"Idiot! *We* are the angels of God! Allah has anointed us as his Earthly sword! He has used a false angel to trick the infidels and given us the means to victory and judgment over them."

As the deadline passed, Azat Mohammed picked up a rocket launcher and shouldering it, aimed at a retreating Turkmen convoy in the distance.

"I will show you," he said to his men, firing upon the unit. It missed, exploding a few meters behind the last vehicle in the Turkmen convoy.

Several seconds passed. Azat smiled.

"See! What did I tell you? Press forward! Allah is with us!"

In the next few seconds, the one who had been Azat Nurali along with four hundred sixty-seven thousand two hundred thirty-two men, women, and children in the province known as Balkanskaya felt a sharp pain pierce their skulls. Grabbing at their heads, they screamed in unison and died.

Chapter Seven

John Harriman stood at the edge of the military cordon and stared at the vehicle parked in the UN gardens, doing his best to determine its origin.

He had to admit that the Ophanum did remind him a great deal of the classic flying saucer design that had dominated stories of alien encounters for hundreds of years. Gabriel, the *construct* as it called itself, had damn well enough seemed otherworldly as well.

"They sure know how to put on a show, don't they?"

Harriman looked over his left shoulder to see Grace Williams standing next to him.

"That they do, Miss Williams. That they do."

"Call me Grace and I'll call you John if that's what it really is. No reason to stand on formalities when the world is about to end."

Harriman smiled. "It's John… and I wouldn't be too concerned about the world ending. I don't think it's their play."

"They sure didn't have any problem keeping their word in Balkanskaya. Reports are coming in of a mass genocide of the Shia. Ships coming into Turkmenbashi are saying that everyone in the city is dead," she said grimly.

"I know. The Turkmen army is reporting that every AG unit fell dead at its position. It would seem that the only thing that saved the Turkmen was that they weren't firing back. The AG was pressing an attack, and these things killed them for it," replied Harriman. "What happened in Balkanskaya is proof that if they wanted to kill us all, they could have done it easily and without warning.

"Just so long as they don't plan to eat us," cracked Grace.

Harriman gave her a long serious look. He shrugged his shoulders and returned his gaze to the craft before them.

"We still really don't know what they are, do we? Like you said, they put on one helluva show with the flying saucers, the androids, and the biblical references. Are they the original angels of the Bible?"

"A little bit of blaspheming from Mr. Smith!"

"I must confess that I'm an atheist, Ms. Williams," said Harriman. "Too much science in my background to be impressed with the magic of the supernatural."

"Magic is a good term for this," said Grace. "Are they extraterrestrials or just extraordinary magicians?"

"If they are magicians, they just killed half a million of their audience," he replied. "But you've got a point." His eyes went back to the machine in the garden. "I'd sure like to get a good look inside that little bastard!"

"Have you eaten?" she asked.

"What?"

"Have you eaten anything this morning? We've got an hour and a half before Gabriel is supposed to come out of his shell," said Grace, thumbing toward the craft. "We're ready to go on our end, and I am sure you're ready to go on yours. Not that there's much you can do about creatures who capable of committing mass murder in the blink of an eye. I'm starving, and I'm asking you if you want to get a quick breakfast with me? You can spare fifteen minutes can't you?"

Harriman didn't know what to think. "I guess I am hungry now that you mention it."

"Stop smiling, Colonel! It's not like it's a date," she laughed, taking Harriman's arm to steer him inside.

"That'll come if we live through the day."

"Monsters! Devils! Your Host has committed a horrible genocide!" cried out the Iranian Ambassador. "You said the Host was interested in peace, but it has killed a half million people. We cannot trust your lies!"

Gabriel turned its attention to the ambassador, the sole person standing in the General Assembly, pointing at the construct in anger. From her perch in the media center, Grace half expected the creature to strike him dead. Instead, it spoke in its singsong voice.

"You are correct, Ambassador Hussein. We have committed a horrible act on this day, but we did not lie. We did as we said we would. The Army of God in Balkanskaya would not end its aggression; therefore, it was exterminated, along with those who supported it. We did not wish to harm anyone, but there must be peace. Those who would shatter the peace are to be destroyed without mercy or hesitation.

"There are no murderers here but you!" replied Ambassador Hussein.

"We have done nothing more than what humanity has been doing to itself since the beginning; we went to war. Simply put, we are more efficient at it than you."

"In the last century, more than two hundred million of your species died from war, political repression, and famine. Almost as many died from disease," replied Gabriel. "This century, if left to itself, humanity is going to double that number. Nearly twenty million souls die each year from war, brutality, and oppression. There are currently forty-seven armed conflicts around the world. Millions of humans are refugees, fleeing war's destruction of their homelands. Those we killed in an instant are still fewer in number than those you yourselves will kill in less than ten days. War is not humanity's only sin. You have created an economic system that rewards a small number with great wealth and comfort while condemning the majority to poverty and slavery. Thousands die daily from the starvation and disease that results from this poverty. You have the ability to end this suffering, yet you do nothing. Humanity has sown the seeds of its ultimate extinction. The solutions are at hand but greed and shortsightedness block its ability to organize itself. It is unable to stop its own demise. We ask you- who are the true monsters? You who kill and enslave nonsensically and indifferently every day or Our Host, who kills once to bring attention to it?.

Gabriel paused then continued speaking to the now silent room, "We have watched and waited. Now, at this time we reveal ourselves to you with our intention sincere. Our Host has come to liberate humanity from itself. We are here to bring you to the crossroads and act as a guide. We are charged with helping your species along the right path until you can know for yourselves that what which is correct. We are not your conquerors. On the contrary, it is our mission to be your protectors, until you are capable of protecting yourself. We will not rule you; you will rule yourselves. We are here to offer up goals and help you to provide the means of achieving them. To find humanity's ultimate destiny, there can be no more place for war and strife in the world. The old way- of destruction in the name of religion, tribe, or nation has ended with the sacrifice of those who refused to abandon it."

Gabriel returned his gaze to the embittered ambassador, "Keep your faiths, and their lost hope will be restored to you. You may love your people and nation without being forced to hate another's. You must now view all of humanity as one. Now comes the time to finally fulfill the promise of Man. We command, in the name of the Host, that all the nations of the world will commit to these United Nations the wealth that until now they have squandered upon war and death. They will turn their annual military budgets and personnel over to the United Nations as a tithe.

"This tithe will now be used as the means to creating a better life for all by finding solutions to the world's ills, the most immediate being the starvation of millions in Africa and South America. We charge you to use what we have provided to end the suffering there. Our Host will continue to charge you with goals that will ultimately end hunger, poverty, and disease on this world. We will challenge you to find ways to stop the process of your destruction and flourish as a race. That which was once used to kill must now be used for life. As we speak, Directors of Our Host are entering every major city in every nation around the world. They are not to be harmed; violence against them will be met with violence against both the perpetrators and their supporters. They will be our hands and your guides."

Gabriel continued, "This construct will remain at the United Nations, as the Voice of Our Host. When no longer required, Our Host will leave your world. There will be no need for us to return. You will live on your own in peace and prosperity.

The Voice of the Host offered a final warning, "No one is to enter Balkanskaya for a period of three years from this day. It will serve as a reminder to all that the wages of the old world are death and extinction. In this new, Promised Land to come, what will have changed is the focus of your intentions. The sword will at last be beaten into a plowshare. Humanity will walk the path toward a better life for all."

"Why did you have to murder so many innocents?" asked Helmut Lemke.

The SG and the Security Council had escorted Gabriel to its private meeting chambers, as requested by the Seraphim.

"The members of this council murder innocents as a matter of course," replied the construct. "Besides, we needed to get your attention."

"Our attention!" cried the Russian ambassador in his native language. "You did not just murder the Shia Turkmen! There were Russian citizens in Balkanskaya. How can you justify killing them!"

"They were supporters of a regime that had recently committed an atrocity upon its own countrymen by killing every single human being in Serdar. They were not innocent," countered Gabriel in Russian. It turned back to the Secretary General.

"Secretary General Helmut Lemke, members of the Security Council, Our Host has given you a great blessing! You have dreamed of solving the world's problems, of bringing peace and prosperity to all. Our Host has now provided you with the means to accomplish these goals."

"The nations will never agree to turn their entire defense budgets over to the UN. That is a fantasy," said Lemke.

"Of course they will," replied the chorus of Gabriel's voice. "There is no longer need for defense because Our Host will provide it. Subsequently, there is no longer a need for armies or defense budgets.

"The nations will provide the means for you to cure their ills or they will be destroyed. That is the lesson of Balkanskaya. There must be peace- as a foundation to advance humanity and prevent its ultimate extinction. Our Host will provide that peace. The armies of the future will be armies of scientists and physicians, engineers, and builders. The armies of war are extinct."

"You have no right to do this!" fumed the French ambassador. "We have a right to free will. We have a right to choose our destinies without interference."

"You still have free will, Andre Sarrazin. You may choose peace through life or peace through death. Either way, there will be peace. Elect for war and aggression, and your nation will be destroyed to the last child," replied the Seraphim.

Anne North now spoke up, her head nodding in agreement. "Gabriel is right; it's the only way this can work. None of us will give up the means to defend ourselves so long as we believe there is the possibility of an outside threat. Take away the threat of war, and there's no need for defense. What country is going to start a fight that would bring about its instant annihilation? It would be national suicide."

"You are correct in your logic, Anne North," said Gabriel. "Those who do not comply will be removed and replaced by those who do. Their wealth and resources will be distributed to others.

106

"There will be monthly allocations of what had been defense budgets into the United Nations' coffers. The personnel that had once been used to take lives can now be used to save lives as representatives of the United Nations. You now have the path to the Promised Land. Ironically, the nations will find that a significant portion of the wealth they contribute will be returned to them so that they may improve the lives of their own people. Your world is quite a mess after all."

"What about these Directors?" asked the British ambassador. "You said they were going into our cities. Will they take over our governments? This is very disturbing. How do we know the Host won't begin to round us up or turn our democracies into police states? We have no way to stop you."

"Our Host has no need or intent for such things," said Gabriel. "We care not about how you choose to rule yourselves as long as the dignity of each human is maintained. Our concern is limited to ending organized aggression and improving the lives of humanity. We will define the goals, and you will work together to find the method for achieving those goals. Long ago, we invited some humans to live as one with us. We have trained their descendants to be Directors. The Directors are here to help provide guidance and maintain the peace at regional and local levels," it said. "It is not their purpose to interfere in your politics or faiths

"I want to know, what are you really?" asked the Chinese ambassador. "You are neither human nor alive. Where do you come from? Are you from another world?"

"We are a construct, created by Our Host, so that It may interact with you in a more efficient manner, Li Xiao Peng."

"Why?" asked Lemke. "Is it because the Host is so much different from us that we would be unable to communicate?"

He paused. "Are you an angel of God?"

"Our Host has always been here, always watching humanity's development," said Gabriel. "There have been times when Our Host has guided that progress."

"Why now?" asked Li. "There has always been war and suffering. Why did the Host not reveal itself when we created nuclear weapons? That would seem an existential crisis requiring intervention."

"It is true that nuclear warfare could destroy humanity, but that is an obvious threat. It is so obvious that your leaders all agree nuclear war is out of the question. The deterrent worked. Our Host had no need to intervene," explained Gabriel.

107

"Circumstances are now different. Humanity has more than war to be concerned with; the actual danger to Mankind resides in the climate of your planet. Changes to the oceans and atmosphere in combination with population growth will soon affect your ability to produce flourishing and reliable food sources. Your economic system is derived from competition over resources as opposed to co-operation. The symptoms of these problems are poverty and disease, war and famine. These changes, long your companions, are so subtle that your leaders have lost their senses. For the first time in your history, you have the ability to control your own future. Those who could lead dither instead, lost in greed and fighting for power. They refuse to believe that the end is much closer than they could ever imagine. This is the most critical moment in your species' existence. Our Host has borne witness to this moment before. Do nothing, and your civilization will collapse. With it vanishes your last opportunity to avoid extinction. It is for this reason that Our Host has elected to intervene. Your species contains great potential to become more. For now, it must be saved from itself. For this purpose, Our Host once again reveals Itself.

An hour later, John Harriman was sitting in Anne North's office listening to her recap when the call came in from the President. It was on the secure hardline, and he had requested they both be in the room.

"Hello, Anne. John. This has been quite an adventure the two of you have had the past few days," Sam Craig said dryly.

"Yes, Mr. President. That might be the understatement of the millennium," cracked Ambassador North, her eyes twinkling.

"I want to thank you both for the excellent work you have both done. Anne, especially what the entire UN staff has done," he began. "Based upon the brief I just read, it would seem that your department is about to get a funding increase."

"Not my idea, Sir," replied North. "Unfortunately, at this stage of the game, I'm not seeing a lot of options. We turn over our defense budgets or risk killing every American on the planet."

"I'm not quite ready to hand over the keys to the kingdom just yet. Although, I can think of some friends of ours in Congress who would jump at the chance to die for God and country. Let's see if we can find an option that doesn't involve either death or capitulation," said the President.

"John, I imagine you're pretty well exhausted right now."

Harriman suddenly realized he was wiped out. He had been catnapping the past few days, something he could do when he was a younger man- popping up recharged and ready to go. Now, it just kept him in a balance between catatonic and collapse.

"I won't lie to you, Mr. President. It has been a difficult few days for everyone involved. I would assume the same for our colleagues in Washington, Sir," he answered.

"Well, I've got good news for you, John. You're going to get some sleep, at least a few hour's worth. There's another favor I have to ask of you, but I'm sorry to say it's going to be neither fun nor easy."

Chapter Eight

Harriman was able to sleep for ten of the fifteen hours to Astrakhan. The route to the city at the mouth of the Volga River had been roundabout. It began with a commercial flight from New York to Berlin so as to not arouse suspicion. The Langley wonks felt that they had to use the Lufthansa flight as a blind to anyone or anything that might have an eye on him in particular. He was grateful that it had given him a chance to catch up on sleep.

In Berlin, a double-blind. Harriman went through customs posing as businessman John Smith. He then checked into a posh Berlin hotel, caught a few more hours of precious sleep and went to a late supper. On his way out of the hotel restaurant, he stopped into the men's room, opened the janitor's closet located there and used a security code on his Magi-Watch to open the false wall leading to the tunnels.

The passages were old- Second World War relics dug by the Nazis that lead to underground bomb shelters. With typical German efficiency, they had elected to link the central shelters to several buildings through a system of tunnels. Harriman used the tunnels to emerge several blocks away. There, a car was waiting to take him to a small airfield. He flew a private jet to the American air base in Stuttgart, alone in his thoughts.

President Craig had made it clear that he wanted Harriman for this mission. Harriman had argued that a Navy Seal team would be better equipped, but Craig would have none of it. He felt that pulling a Seal team would be too obvious a ploy in a new world where no one knew who was watching or even how.

There was another factor- plausible deniability. Harriman's identity, his genetic markers, and physical features had been erased from databases long ago. Technically, he was untraceable.

He knew that capture alive was out of the question- suicide the only option. Potential captors would have a body and nothing more. No one would ever know whom he was, where he came from, where his loyalties lay. He was the perfect spook. On this mission, Sam Craig needed his perfection.

With all this carefully-constructed anonymity, Harriman was troubled by something that had bothered him for three days. How had Gabriel known his name?

In Stuttgart, he picked up the equipment- two sets, one for the Russian and one for himself. A CIA tech instructor utilized a virtuality helmet to download complete instructions on use. Harriman imagined somewhere on a base in Astrakhan his counterpart was getting a similar feed.

Harriman then boarded a Ukrainian cargo transport for the flight to Astrakhan.

Now he found himself inside the equipment, onboard a Russian K-226T search and rescue helicopter and flying over the heart of the Caspian Sea. His Russian partner and a support crew sat next to him in the passenger cabin.

The equipment was something with which he wasn't familiar. The tech manual named it a *PDC Individual Amphibious Stealth Vehicle*. In practical application, it was a very sophisticated wetsuit.

On dry land, the suit itself looked quite typical, with the exception of the headpiece. It was, in fact, two separate pieces. The goggles and re-breather fit over the face much in the manner that a pilot's helmet did, allowing him to speak and providing oxygen. Inside the goggles, a heads up display transmitted both telemetry and suit controls that he could operate either through voice control or by looking directly at the HUD and rapidly blinking twice.

The second piece was composed of a pliable plastic material that formed around the back and sides of the head, fitting over the edges of the front piece. Once in place, it then became rigid. The head was now encased in a self-contained atmosphere separate from the rest of the suit. Fiber-optic connections linked with the suit; transmitting data and commands throughout.

The wetsuit was a technological marvel. An exoskeleton, controlled by micro-servos, provided increased strength and was inlaid into the thermal layer of the inner lining. This lining maintained a default temperature of twenty-three degrees Celsius that could be adjusted by the operator for personal comfort.

The outer shell was comprised of a material that revealed no heat signature or deflection wave larger than that of a fish or small mammal.

The suit became a vehicle when it entered the water. A series of hundreds of micro-tubes, running in parallel down the length of the suit, worked to propel the diver much the same way a squid does; expanding to take in water through the tube and contracting to expel the water in quick, violent bursts. This method allowed the diver to reach speeds of up to thirty kilometers an hour without having to engage in traditional swimming strokes. He could simply glide through the water in the suit, changing direction with slight contortions of the body.

The real genius of the suit was in the power plant, a middle layer that contained a flexible, chemical battery. The storage unit could offer up to twenty hours of electricity under standard conditions. Harriman knew wouldn't be using much of it on the next leg of the mission.

The other piece of equipment was a modified *Personal Diving Vehicle*. The two divers would take the PDV to the rally point and anchor it below the surface. It would then be converted into a transport for their cargo, following a pre-programmed course until it could be recovered. Harriman hoped he and his counterpart would still be alive to accompany it on its trek.

That the U. S. government was willing to hand over such advanced and sophisticated technology to the Russians highlighted the importance placed on the mission. Harriman doubted their counterparts would be giving it back.

The bird taking them to the rendezvous was the most recent version of a tried and true model from the past twenty years. The flight had been smooth and surprisingly quiet; the high-pitched whine of the primary engine barely noticeable inside the passenger compartment. He could tell the bugs had been worked out of the design long ago. It's what the Russians did. They were masters at getting the most out of an idea or concept, as opposed to developing them on their own.

He looked over at the Russian who would be accompanying him.

"Call me Ivan Ivanovich," he had joked when they first met; the Russian equivalent of John Smith.

Ivan sat next to him in an identical suit. Both had their headgear off for the moment. After exchanging amenities, they had ridden most of the journey silent in their thoughts.

A little more than ninety minutes into the flight, the tech suddenly brought a hand up to the side of his helmet as if listening to his headphone. He looked up at the divers and said in Russian, "We have fifteen minutes to drop point. It's time to run through the checklist."

"Understood," replied Harriman, also in Russian.

The three men began their checklist review, verifying operational systems. Ivan put his helmet on first, the re-breather coming to life as the two pieces locked into place. Harriman could barely hear it working.

He locked his own helmet down, and it immediately became operational, the HUD lighting up to give him GPS, compass, vital signs, and suit controls.

"So John Smith, can you hear me clearly?" asked his counterpart.

"Loud and clear, Ivan Ivanovich," he replied. "How about Mother?"

"Mother is listening. Time for you boys to go outside and play," replied a new voice. Harriman assumed it was the trawler captain.

The trawler was their cover story. It was supposedly in distress and in need of assistance, allowing for the dispatch of the K-226T on a rescue mission. It was far enough off the coast to not attract too much attention, and their next actions would look normal to any eyes in the skies.

In reality, the trawler was a Russian intelligence asset. A specialized spy ship that acted as both listening post and staging platform. For this mission, it would serve as the decoy. Harriman and Ivan would drop themselves and the PDV into the water next to the ship. Two similarly dressed divers would leave the trawler through a pressurized hatch in the hold of the ship and re-emerge on the side. They would then re-board the ship and proceed with the *rescue* of the sick crewman, leaving with the helicopter. Anyone watching would see two divers enter the water and two divers return. The K-226T would be back at the base in Astrakhan by nightfall.

Harriman and Ivan would still be in the water at that time, fifty kilometers from the now dead port city of Turkmenbashi, Balkanskaya.

The two men swam toward the city under cover of night, harnessed to each side of the PDV, which performed its task at a brisk clip of thirty kilometers per hour.

The two hours of travel was spent discussing their approach to the harbor, collecting the cargo and transporting it back to the PDV. Harriman was somewhat surprised at how workmanlike Ivan was in his conversation. He never once made mention of the Host or the now altered balance of power in the world. It was better that he hadn't- Harriman wouldn't have volunteered much to him.

They had been forced to adjust the balance of the blow/ballast tank of the PDV to compensate for the lower salinity levels of the Caspian Sea. With only a third of the salt content of a normal ocean, Harriman had to get used to the lack of buoyancy to which he was usually accustomed. They decided a travel depth of eight meters would be enough to blur any optical imaging a satellite (or spaceship) might have surveilling the area. Considering the events of the past two days, they could assume it must be monitored in some way. A moonless night aided their stealth.

As they entered the mouth of the harbor, a bright light passed quickly over them, but didn't stop to linger. It gave them the knowledge that the city was not entirely empty, and that the suits did significantly enhance their ability to avoid detection. At least they did at twenty-five feet below the surface of the Caspian.

The real test came as they closed to within one hundred meters of the docks. They left the PDV anchored to the sea floor and verified the GPS coordinates; having agreed a homing beacon was too great a risk. The two then swam to a docked cargo vessel, slipping along its side until locating a ladder leading from the water to the pier. Ivan went up it first, Harriman waiting for the all clear before proceeding.

The city may have been declared dead, but activity abounded within it. Streetlights glowed all around. At first, Harriman suspected that the power plant's generators were running unsupervised, likely drawing on fuel from yet to be drained storage tanks. It made sense that they could still be fully operational, given that less than forty-eight hours had elapsed since the cull. He rejected that theory when he saw the moving lights. The city wasn't completely dead.

The two men had made it off the pier and were pressed tightly against the wall of a warehouse when the first one came around a corner twenty meters away. Harriman blinked his POV camera on and kept it trained on the subjects.

The first was a humanoid of normal height and build, completely covered from head to toe in what looked like an orange flight suit. It wore boots and had gloves that extended halfway up the forearm. A skintight cowling covered its head. The face was obscured with goggles and a breather mask that flanged into what looked like an elephant's trunk. The trunk ended in a rounded cartridge attached to the suit at the chest.

Floating above the humanoid was what appeared to be a drone aircraft. It was a meter and a half in diameter and a half a meter thick. Three circular components were on either side of a triangular unit, moving independently on their own axis. Harriman guessed the outer, circular units housed fans that gave the drone its lift, pitch, and yaw. The triangular unit in the middle was likely the brain and business end of the drone. A floodlight emanated from it, illuminating the ground directly ahead. He wondered if this was another version of a Director.

The figure halted suddenly and Harriman's heart jumped. It remained motionless for a few seconds, giving Harriman pause that they had been detected. He carried no weapon. Violence against any of these creatures would have tipped off the Host that the quarantine had been broken. He knew the world was not to be put at risk for a single life.

What looked like a lightning bolt erupted from the drone, striking an object just a few feet in front of the humanoid. Something on the ground in front of it caught fire, incinerating almost immediately. The figure and its white drone companion moved out of sight.

Ivan and Harriman both looked at each other. Even though their faces were obscured by the helmets, Harriman had a good idea the Russian's expression mirrored his own.

"They're burning the bodies," said Ivan.

"It's a cleaning crew," said Harriman. They moved silently and slowly up the alleyway, finding an open doorway and slipping into the building next to them. Ivan pointed up, and Harriman nodded. They needed to get more reconnaissance from a better vantage point. Finding a stairwell, the two began climbing steps until they reached the top floor. Harriman opened the fire door, and the two entered a pitch-black office. They stood looking carefully out a window at the plaza below.

There, they saw half a dozen of the humanoid/drone cleanup crews. Some were coming in and out of buildings carrying bodies. Others were incinerating heaps of bodies using the drone's lightning bolts. In the distance, they could see what seemed to be hundreds of lights moving back and forth.

Harriman realized that his mission had become much more challenging- and yet increasingly vital. They had no choice but to succeed.

"I believe the building over there is an apartment block," said Ivan, pointing across the street. "We may be able to find what we need in there. I for one would like to complete this part of our mission and leave as quickly as possible,"

"Agreed. It's close to the water. That should make it easier for us," replied Harriman.

They descended slowly down the stairwell. An exit in the rear of the building put them undetected and next to the waterfront. They wove back and forth through a series of alleyways and buildings devoid of bodies- it looked as if the area had already been cleared. Harriman figured that might be good for them. The cleaning crews would not be so apt to return to these buildings and find them.

Eventually, they were able to find a side entrance to the apartment building and slide inside. The lights were on in the lobby area, and he could see that the building had not yet been cleaned.

They were in luck.

After a brief discussion, they agreed that a plate glass window made the lit lobby far too dangerous for their work. They also had to be aware that a cleaning crew could begin working on this building at any moment. The last thing they could ever do was to walk into one of those. It was to be avoided at all costs.

They found a storeroom on the ground floor that could be used as a staging area and began their trek up the stairwell steps. Fortunately for them, they found what they were looking for on the second floor. Through the open doorway, he saw the target.

The body of a woman had fallen through an apartment door and into the hallway in front of them. Ivan quietly opened the door further and stepped over the dead woman into a family room and kitchen.

On the sofa were the bodies of a man and two children. The man had slumped forward. His torso was over his lap, arms at his sides, head between his knees and facing the floor.

The children, a boy who looked to be ten and a girl who may have been seven or eight, were resting on the arm of the sofa, his body on top of hers. She looked to have already been asleep when death came. The boy had his hands at his head as if trying to stave off a headache. His eyes were open, staring blankly at the television. It was as if he were watching the broadcast from Tehran, still playing softly in the background.

On the floor was a dog, Harriman judged it to be a spaniel of some sort. It was pure black and not large, maybe twenty pounds. It was dead as well. That was important to know, he deduced. Every living thing had died within the kill zone, not only people. Come to think of it, he observed, the room didn't even have flies and they always found their way to the dead, even in October.

The pair went to work, first clearing the woman from the doorway and laying her back into the apartment. Harriman saw that decomposition had begun to accelerate. Rigor mortis was almost entirely absent from her body.

Harriman reached into the pouch at his side and pulled out a body bag, laying it out beside her while Ivan checked the apartment for more bodies.

It wasn't just a standard body bag. This bag was coated with the same stealth material as their suits. The plastic was flexible and thin but incredibly strong. Two carrying handles were sewn into the top and bottom of the bag. He was able to place the woman inside without assistance from Ivan. She was wearing a chador- a garment she wouldn't have had on unless she was on her way out. He could tell from her face she was probably in her late twenties or early thirties. He zipped up the bag and slid it to the side.

Next came the children and the dog. Harriman was no stranger to corpses; he had created his share- many in the goriest of fashion. Children were different. He had never needed to kill a child and wasn't sure if he could, no matter what the mission. With the kids, he had to force himself to stop thinking about what he was doing and simply do it. Once the zipper was closed, he could think of it as just another package for shipment and delivery. It was the only way he could stay focused on the challenges of his work.

Ivan emerged from the recesses of the apartment. "Nothing else here," he said.

"Help me with the male," requested Harriman.

The two grabbed the man on each side and laid him out in the body bag. They were lucky again; the man was slight of build. Harriman estimated he wasn't more than one hundred forty pounds at the most. He also looked to be in his late twenties or early thirties. *Good specimens*, he thought.

They worked in stages, moving the bags one by one through the dimly lit corridor, down the stairwell, and into the storage room by the rear exit. Retrieving the last bag, they had turned off the lights and television in the apartment and locked the door. It would look as if the family had been out when the killings had occurred. That took thirty minutes. Harriman realized they had to get the next stage finished within an hour or they would be swimming back in daylight.

They slowly worked their way back to the pier with the first bag. When they reached the ladder, Ivan attached a line to the bag, and the two men lowered it into the water, securing their end of the line to the ladder. They repeated the process twice more- only once did they have a close call, when a cleaning crew passed within ten meters of their position. They took cover behind a dumpster as the unit stopped and scanned the alleyway before moving on. The men waited another thirty seconds before resuming their transport.

"Your suits work very well, John Smith. Please give my many thanks to the designers," said Ivan. "It would seem that the Host isn't a god after all."

"Well, they definitely aren't the perfection they portray," agreed Harriman. "The better for our side." This mission was as much about intelligence gathering as recovery, and he had a great deal to report. Now, they just had to make it back- alive.

The final trip to the pier went without further interruption. At the ladder, together they lowered the third bag into the water below. Harriman then went down the ladder as Ivan kept watch. Once in the water, Ivan freed the remaining lines from their mooring and dropped them one by one to the waiting Harriman.

Once both men were in the water, they tested the bags for buoyancy. They didn't want them floating on the surface, but then dragging the packages along the rocky bottom was out of the question as well. They didn't have to make much adjustment. The bodies contained just enough gas to counterbalance their weight. The bags floated a few feet beneath the surface of the water.

After a brief conference, the two elected to bring all three bags at once to the PDV. Time was becoming an ever-increasing worry; the last thing they wanted to do was test the stealth of the suits in a daylight setting. The Caspian was not a murky sea; they would be relatively easy to spot from the air.

Securing a line between them at the belt, they attached the three bags to the line. Then they let the suits do the work of bringing them back to the PDV.

The trip was less than one hundred meters, and all he had to do was let the thousands of micro-jets in the suit pull him through the water. Still, he could feel the dead weight of their cargo, and it was a slow journey. He was relieved when they finally reached the PDV and made the transfer.

Activating the PDV, Harriman set the vehicle along its pre-determined course. The PDV lifted itself off of the sea floor and set off at a quick pace, the two divers following a few meters behind it to monitor its progress and ensure that the packages remained secure.

The trek back was long but uneventful- just what every black ops specialist truly desires of a mission. Harriman was glad for it; Ivan kept to himself for the most part. After the past few days' events, Harriman relished the peace he found within the confines of his suit.

A little over three hours out, his sonar detected the trawler. The PDV had found it as well, slowing to position itself under the open airlock beneath the ship. It began to ascend, the bags trailing beneath it like multiple tails as the directional change forced them down.

They waited for the trawler crew to secure the PDV and pull it into the hold before climbing aboard. Harriman was finally able to sit and remove the helmet that had been covering his head for nearly nine hours.

Ivan sat across from him, visibly exhausted. He looked up and smiled.

"See my friend, our two countries can work together in the spirit of co-operation," he said.

"The enemy of my enemy…" Harriman replied.

"Before, this would be the time when we would kill you and throw your body into the ocean," returned Ivan with a serious face.

"Or I would kill all of you," countered Harriman.

Ivan Ivanovich smiled again. "But those days are behind us, for now. What are we to do?"

***

Grace finished the plates and started on the pans. There was a dishwasher, but she was rarely there and often left in a hurry. She had found that the homecoming would usually be to a rancid kitchen and a machine full of forgotten dishes. It was easier to do them by hand after dinner.

Grace rarely had the opportunity to cook for herself, and she missed it. Her mother had been too busy with her career to spend a lot of time in the kitchen. Her father had given her his exemplary culinary skills. He was good at providing a home-cooked meal that was delicious, if not extravagant. He loved cooking simple- chicken tetrazzini, lasagna, meat loaf, rib eye steak, chili, lots of salads.

Tonight, Grace had treated herself to a chicken parmesan in marinara sauce, fettuccini noodles, and a Caesar salad. An Ontario red to wash it down- she used to enjoy the California's until the drought had brought them to near demise. Now they were too damned expensive.

To Grace, it was magnificent. The best meal she had eaten in weeks that had been filled with bland restaurants, fast food, and military rations. She ate alone, enjoying the silence of not being plugged in anywhere. It gave her time to think.

She was standing by the balcony window, looking out over the October night, when she heard the knock at the door.

It took her by surprise. No one knew she was here, except for her parents and a few colleagues. Her mother and father would be out west, and friends would have buzzed at the building entrance. Her neighbors on the floor never visited. Her computer was off, and she didn't have her watch. Grace went to the door and looked through the eyepiece. On the other side stood another surprise. She opened the door.

"Hi," he said, looking very uncomfortable. She smiled at him.

"Mr. Smith. Of all the people in this world, I should have known only you to be able to track me to a condo leased to a random company."

"It's Harriman. My name is John Harriman. I wanted you to know that. It's not a secret I want to keep from you anymore."

Grace could read that he was struggling. He looked her in the eye, and she could see an unease in them. A part of her understood.

"Would you like to come in, Mr. Harriman?" she asked gently. Grace took a step back to pull open the door in invitation.

"I thought we were past that. Please… call me John," he said, stepping through the doorway. He was dressed in a thin brown jacket over a black polo shirt and khaki Dockers. Perfect for a late October night in Manhattan. Grace assumed this was his version of casual. She thought he looked delicious. She noticed the jacket was too thin and tight to hide a gun, but also knew he wouldn't need one if that's what he was here for. For a second, she had a flash of wariness.

It subsided just as quickly. There wouldn't have been any warning if the man was here to kill her. Grace would never have known; she would just be dead.

"I just wanted to say your actual, last name. I'm still Grace," she replied, closing the door behind her.

"Grace," he repeated, looking around. "You have a lovely place. Very nice."

"It's just a flop. I have a few personal things here, but most of this was from the realtor. They staged the place for show and when I got it, I bought the furnishings as well."

She smiled at him and motioned to the sofa. "Honestly, I'm not here enough to care. A few days in, three months out. That's been my life. There's no time to worry about the color of the walls. It always seemed trivial anyway. Can I get you a drink? I have this nice red from the Niagara region you might like."

"I'm not much of a wine drinker, thanks. Do you mind if I have some of that Knob Creek?" he asked pointing at the bottle of bourbon behind her.

"Oh, that's Red's, but I'm sure he won't mind," Grace said. She saw the quizzical look on his face. "It's Kearney's. Come to think of it, he might mind. He's not your biggest fan."

"I see. Are you two…"

"Kearney? Oh no! I learned long ago not to mix business and pleasure. My dad always used to say, 'Gracie, never shit in your mess kit.' Red's like my big brother. He's very protective of me. Not that I need him to be, but it's nice. Besides, he's married with three kids; working on growing a big, Catholic family. You want ice or water?"

"Um, neat please," Harriman replied.

Grace laughed. "In that case, I'll make it a double."

121

She took a short glass from the cabinet and poured the bourbon three-quarters of the way up. Picking up her wine glass, Grace moved over to the sofa and handed him the bourbon before plopping down on the other side, back against the arm and facing him. She slipped her legs into a figure four, left foot curled behind the right knee. He was sitting perpendicular to her with his knees apart, both hands cradling the glass in his lap. For a moment there was silence, Grace looking at John, he staring forward. Then, he turned his face to her.

"I don't know where to start," he said.

"Why not start by taking a sip of your bourbon," she offered.

John took a gulp and swallowed.

"I need to talk to you, not agent to journalist but just person to person."

Grace looked down at the glass in her hand and thought for a second. "OK, but before I agree, I have to ask... are we going to be talking about things I should be reporting on?"

He looked a little startled. "What? No... at least I don't think so. It's more about... some things on my mind. For some reason, I feel as if I've known you all my life... like I can trust you."

"Alright then, off the record, just two people talking about their day at work," nodded Grace, hoping she wouldn't regret her promise.

He paused again as if he was attempting to organize his thoughts. Finally, he said, "I'm lost."

That took a moment to register with her. John Harriman seemed to be one of the most confident men Grace had ever met. It was among the qualities that attracted her to him. Her first thought was that he knew something about the events of the past week that had put him back on his heels. She started mentally kicking herself for her promise to keep the conversation between themselves.

"What do you mean? How are you lost?" asked Grace.

There was a long moment of silence.

"I'm a merchant of death," he began. "I've spent my whole life dispensing it in the service of my country. I've killed on the battlefield, and I've been an assassin. I've always convinced myself that I was doing something morally reprehensible in the service of a greater good. Most of the people I killed were evil... monsters in the worst way."

122

Harriman paused as if to gather his thoughts before continuing, "I'm an orphan. I have no family that I know of and few friends. I never wanted to be close to anyone. I couldn't have relationships anyway. In your world, I'm a ghost. I don't exist within the system. I am the perfect weapon of war and death."

"And now there's no more war," said Grace.

He nodded. "And now… there's no more war, hot or cold. There's no more need for a nation to target assets for assassination because to do so would be too great a risk. What leader is going to send someone like me out to do his dirty work? Is it worth the lives of an entire nation if I'm found out?"

He took another drink from his glass.

"So that's it?" Grace asked. "We aren't going to try and fight them?"

"Fight what? Who are we going to attack? This Host is everywhere… and nowhere. There's no target, no head to cut off. It's not like nuking Beijing- just those damn android archangels and a network of human Directors with their robot halos hovering above them. They seem to be spread out across the globe. No one would dare risk trying to take them out individually, and there's no way to coordinate a simultaneous assault on them all. It would mean the end of everything, or at least of the nation that had made the attempt.

"Not just that," he continued. "Where is the Host? What is it? How to they maintain their surveillance on us? Where is the command and control center? We know what they can do, and that's end life on a mass scale in an instant. As Gabriel said, they had to get our attention and they did that in a big way. I know for a fact that they aren't perfect, but they're shadows. You can't fight shadows and win. We need to get more light on the subject before we can make a move. Maybe then. Maybe, though, the light never comes. Maybe the Host wins out in the end. That makes someone like me a dinosaur."

Grace looked down at her glass, index finger tracing the rim.

"You know, John, it's a funny thing that you came here tonight. I have been thinking about that very same thing. It seems that we share a similar dilemma.

"I was raised in a very secure and loving home, but I'm a child of war. I have spent the better part of my life chasing it, covering it, bringing it into people's homes. I mean… who wants war and conflict to be in the world? But I'm exhilarated by it; not for the death and misfortune it brings to others, but for the life and sense of purpose it brings to me. Officially, I am a foreign correspondent. In reality, I'm a war correspondent. I'm as much a merchant of death as you are-- you deal it, and I deliver it as news of the world," she said, looking up and into his eyes. "So, what does a war correspondent to do when war has finally become extinct?" .

"Extinction," he said. "That's not something I look forward to."

Grace leaned closer and put her hand on his.

"War is extinct, not us. We're just going to have to learn how to put our skills to better use. NNI wants Red and I to head down to Argentina to cover the famine relief effort. The Host has made it a UN priority. It will be interesting to see how this new world order is going to function, if at all."

She paused. "You know, there's going to be a lot of winners and losers shake out of this. I wouldn't want to be a defense contractor, but I can see a lot of money changing hands over food purchases and transport. It could turn out to be the biggest works-project in history. Might be a story angle. The main story is going to get stale pretty quickly if you ask me. So can I ask where you might be off to next, Colonel?"

He hesitated and then smiled. "You can ask, but it's classified. I've got some down time until they figure out what to do with me next. I'm going home for now. I've got a farm in Ohio. It's beautiful there, rolling hills and lots of woodlands, all sitting on a lake."

"It doesn't sound like a farm. Do you grow anything there?" she asked.

"Not really, I just call it that. Maybe you can come and visit sometime. You'd fall in love."

"It might be a while before I can get there, John. As for love," Grace leaned closer and kissed him on the lips.

Harriman was startled and pulled back to look her in the eye. "I… I wasn't coming here to make a move on you, Grace."

"I think you've got it wrong, John. I'm making a move on you," Grace laughed and then quickly feigned indignation. "And what's the problem? Don't you like natural blondes?"

Harriman looked at her, and she saw desire leap into his eyes.

———

"I can't think of anyone on this Earth more stunning than you."

She smiled, her eyes dancing, and she kissed him again. This time it was slower and longer, and he kissed her back.

Grace leaned back and laughed, her eyes bright and animated. "I really am a natural blonde, you know. Wanna see?"

PART TWO:
ONE YEAR AFTER THE ADVENT
OF
THE PEACE

Chapter Nine

Harriman swung the clubhead smoothly through the ball and was rewarded with a familiar metallic *tink*, telling him his shot was solid and true. He and Alex Kurtz both admired the drive as it swiftly ascended into the bright blue sky. The tailwind and backspin gave the ball more lift and distance. It seemed to hang up for an eternity before finally coming to rest three hundred yards away in the middle of the fairway.

Kurtz whistled in admiration. "Johnny boy, I thought for a moment you had achieved escape velocity," he cracked, teeing up his ball. In the relaxed atmosphere of the golf course, Harriman could detect Kurtz's slight Virginia drawl come to the forefront.

Harriman remained silent as Kurtz set up his tee shot. The General displayed classic perfection as he effortlessly drove his ball off the tee and into flight. It settled to rest a few yards in front of Harriman's ball.

"Sandbagging me again I see, you bastard!" laughed Harriman. "Alex, I swear you were born with a club in your hand."

"You aren't too far off, Johnny boy," smiled Kurtz, walking back to place the driver into his bag. Harriman knew it was close to the truth; Alex Kurtz was as close a thing to military royalty as one could get. A great deal of his youth had been spent immersed in the culture of ranking officers. Golf was their passion.

Harriman had picked up the game at West Point and, being a natural athlete, he had quickly become competent. The two men had spent a great deal of their free time during that period on the links, with Kurtz helping Harriman achieve a level eclipsing mere competence. In fact, he was a damn fine golfer, as good as Kurtz these days.

The two men hadn't been in a position to play together as much over the years. Their regular game had resumed with The Peace. The two men met every second and fourth Wednesday at this serene but challenging course north of Washington. Given their history as golfing buddies and the strength of their game, it was the perfect cover.

The two men grabbed their carts and began walking briskly down the hill toward their lies. They always walked, and they always used their own clubs without caddies; carts and rented bags could be bugged, and people had ears. Kurtz went so far as to carry a jammer for potential flies. They were careful as to keep to small talk until they were on the sixth tee, farthest out from the clubhouse and civilization, so as to conceal their real agenda.

"How are things?" began Harriman.

"Same as ever," replied Alex Kurtz. "The Host lets us keep our toys; we just aren't allowed to play with them. Not that I'm complaining about the lack of an armed conflict. Who doesn't want an end to war? I can't quite explain why they haven't disarmed us entirely, but I've got some ideas."

"So do I," nodded Harriman. "I don't think they're capable of it. Besides, so long as they can kill us instantly and at will, there's no need to collect our weapons. As for armed conflict, it would seem that the Host is against large-scale, organized violence, but is much less concerned with it on a small scale. Statistically, violent crime and murder have been on the rise since The Peace. At least where they keep records on that kind of thing."

"That's interesting. Culling the herd?" pondered Kurtz. "Your shot. Looks to be about a hundred yards. Nine iron?"

"Yep," replied Harriman reaching for a club from his bag. "Hope I don't punch it over the green."

"Oh, pulleeez!"

The two men took their approach shots, Kurtz dropping his onto the green and Harriman falling ten yards short. They sheathed their clubs and continued on.

"You mentioned culling the herd earlier, but I'm not convinced that's it," said Harriman as they walked. "I think their control over us is limited. Whether that's because of numbers, or technology, or both, I don't believe the Host is omnipotent. It can't micromanage things, so it isn't going to try. The overall strategy seems to be to force directional change from the top down- with the threat of certain death to those who resist."

"Trickle down theory? Take care of the big things and the little things will take care of themselves? Hmmm… that leaves a lot of holes that we can take advantage of. Initially for intel."

"And later for an insurgency," nodded Harriman. "If something like that were to achieve success, it would have to be grassroots from the ground up. The Directors are all over the top levels. It does mean that we can regain control quickly and easily if we can identify and neutralize their primary weapon."

"Agreed. Have you heard anything from Nick and Nora?" inquired the General.

"No progress to date. In that area, our efforts have proven to be frustrating," replied Harriman. "Nothing out of the UN either, other than resolutions to fund relief efforts for this and that crisis. Now, of course, they have the resources to do something about it. You're still working with Peter Clark?"

"We are. Canadians are good at this kind of thing. They've been doing peacekeeping and running major relief efforts for almost three-quarters of a century. Might as well give the job to people that know what they're doing if you ask me," confirmed Kurtz. "We've been fighting brush wars for so long here and there that we've lost a little bit of the feel for this kind of job.

"I think we'll be quick studies, though. Right now, our biggest capability is in equipment and speed. UN plans the mission, and we provide logistics like transport, engineering, and construction."

"Makes sense. We have all the big toys and we've been putting up bases on the double time for decades," nodded Harriman.

"You know, the Roman army built all the roads in the empire. They had the manpower and skills to get it done fast," said Kurtz. "There's a precedent for this."

"Romans. Now we're all Romans," mused Harriman. "A thousand years of peace."

"Followed by another thousand in the dark," reminded Kurtz. "And the Pax Romana wasn't *that* peaceful if I recall my history correctly. Still, I'm not complaining. Building roads for Africa beats all hell out of bombing it. Your shot."

"Lemke must feel like Jesus with the loaves and fish feeding the five thousand."

"Closer to five billion," joked Kurtz sarcastically.

Harriman pulled a pitching wedge out of his bag and walked over to his ball.

The two remained silent as he lined up the shot and softly stroked the ball high into the air. It landed with a thud and almost no roll, roughly five feet from the cup.

"Damn nice shot! You're too familiar with this course, Johnny boy. I think we might need to change venues next time," complained Alex Kurtz.

Harriman grinned. "You know, you're going to three-putt, and I'm going to win the hole."

"Now, now. In golf, you're only playing against yourself."

"Tell that to all those who didn't win the PGA tour this year," said Harriman grabbing a putter from his bag.

Kurtz stood next to his bag and motioned Harriman to stop.

"If you aren't buying bullets, there's a lot left over for bread," said Kurtz. "Until the bakery runs out of bread."

"It's bad, but it's not that bad… yet," replied Harriman. "Our data from the mega-corps is showing that global food production and reserves are unable to keep up with demand and will collapse sometime in the next decade. That's the *positive* scenario. The weather has to co-operate in order to maximize yields, which is almost never the case these days. After that, it's *Soylent Green* time.

"That's cheerful. Maybe it was lucky getting invaded by benevolent, alien overlords just before everything went to shit. It isn't like we were doing anything to fix the situation. The world was probably a couple of years away from blowing itself to Hell in a nuclear-tipped food fight."

Harriman shook his head. "We don't know what the Host is, much less that they're extraterrestrial. A lot of the technology we've seen from them is just beyond our abilities. It's not hundreds of years away, like you might expect of a species that can travel vast distances of space."

"Unless they're hiding it from us. We still can't find a way inside that damn ship at the UN, and that drives me nuts," said Kurtz. "They don't have to show us much anyway. They've already dropped a pretty big hammer on our heads."

"I'm not saying you're wrong; we just don't know. We *do* know that the Directors are human. We just can't find out where these people came from. They have no prior record of being *anywhere*, no fingerprints, no previous history, nada."

"As if they are the children of abductees who have now been dropped back onto the planet," teased Kurtz. "Still not a believer, I see."

Harriman frowned at his friend. "I will admit that if an alien species did want to impose its will on us, what better way than with our own kind. It's a legitimate tactic that our military has used as well. Anytime we can supplant our troops with the local garrison or militia we do."

Kurtz nodded. "Exactly! We lower our overall exposure to risk and increase the cooperation of the indigenous population by using the local boys and girls. It works well unless their boys have a history of raping and murdering their own people."

"Which isn't the case here," agreed Harriman. "They haven't draped swastikas off the buildings or made scores of people disappear. In reality, it's business as usual in most of the world- for now."

"True, the last year seems to have been about stabilizing hot spots," said Kurtz. "So when does the other shoe drop… or are they here to save our asses after all?"

"It's not our pay grade to speculate. The mission is to restore the sovereignty of the United States by finding a way to neutralize the strategic advantage of the Host."

The two walked onto the green and separated, Harriman to mark his ball and Kurtz to take his shot sixty feet from the hole. Kurtz looked over the green determining the angle of the pitch and thickness of the grass. He stood over the ball and stroked a solid putt. The ball quickly made its way up the green toward its destination. Harriman held his breath for a split second as he saw Kurtz's ball slow to the cup, rimming out and rolling a few inches to the right.

"Wow! Sweet shot, Alex!" he exclaimed.

Kurtz strolled in his most patrician manner to the ball, set up, and tapped it into the cup. He looked at Harriman, all smiles.

"Three putt my ass! Now who's in trouble?" he said.

"I thought in golf you are only playing against yourself?"

"Yeah, that's all bullshit," Kurtz replied, bending to retrieve his ball.

Harriman walked over to replace his marker with the ball and set up the shot.

"Say! When are you going to bring that Grace Williams by to meet Dana and the kids?" asked Kurtz loudly as his friend began his putt.

Harriman stopped, knowing full well Alex Kurtz was using a mind trick to force him to lose focus and blow the shot.

"First of all, you're an asshole," said Harriman quietly as he began his putt a second time. He gently stroked the ball into the cup.

131

"That's one I don't get Johnny boy. I mean, I get it. That is one fine woman you've got there all the way around, but how can the two of you be seeing each other and it not be a problem? She's one of the best foreign correspondents in the world and you..." Kurtz trailed off, shrugging his shoulders; the implication of Harriman's position left unspoken.

"Well, that's easy my friend," replied Harriman, retrieving his ball and looking up at Alex Kurtz with a deadpan face.

"We don't do a lot of talking when we're together."

***

"Do you understand what I am getting at, Wilson?" asked the elderly, bearded man at the chalkboard.

"I... I think so Professor. The finches were the same when they arrived at the islands. Then, when they became isolated on separate islands, each one changed. Eventually, they became so different that they weren't the same species anymore," Wil answered cautiously.

"Exactly, and that is how speciation occurs," smiled Charles Darwin's avatar at Wil's. "Through natural selection."

"So nature chose to change each of the finches to be able to find more food or evade predators," Wil postulated, trying to grasp the concept.

"No, my boy. You've gotten it backward," sighed Darwin. "All the birds started out the same. With each new generation, there are slight variations that naturally occur within offspring. Some of the finches have slightly longer beaks than other finches. Some might be lighter in color. Let's say on our first island the bugs burrow a little deeper into the bark. Our finches with longer beaks will gain an advantage because they will have more to eat than finches with shorter beaks. Our lighter-colored finches are better able to blend into the island's fauna, making it harder for predators to see them.

"As time passes, the finches with longer beaks and lighter color will become more common than finches with darker color and shorter beaks. Nature didn't suddenly decide to make light-colored, long-beaked finches and kill off all the rest. Over time, finches with those traits won out because they were better able to provide food and protection to their offspring. Their children then carried those traits forward into the next generation. Eventually, all that was left on our island were light-colored, long-beaked finches.

132

"Let's now travel to our second island. Here finches that developed shorter beaks and darker colors had an advantage and as time went on all of the finches took on these traits. Over thousands of years, what had been one species of finches evolves into two distinct types that are so different they now can no longer mate for offspring. They have become separate species, distinct from each other and the original species that they evolved from."

Darwin looked at Wil and waited.

"Ok, so this is evolution through natural selection, I understand. Why didn't I learn this in school? They made me learn chemistry and biology," Wil asked.

"Why indeed!" replied Charles Darwin.

"Wilson, you were only taught some biology, not all of it. This," he said pointing to the board, "is the foundation of *all* biological life on earth. You can see evolution everywhere around you! Take the flu virus for example."

"The flu? What does the flu have to do with evolution?" asked Wil.

"Everything! Do you know why there is a new flu shot each year?"

Wil shook his head.

"Because the flu virus changes. Each year we come up with a vaccine based upon the previous year's virus, and it works- on that virus. It is very effective- against that virus," explained Darwin.

"So why do we still get the flu?"

"Excellent question! Why do we still get the flu? On the surface, it should be that no one gets the flu anymore if the vaccine kills all of the original viri it was based upon," replied Darwin. "So what must happen?"

Wil smiled. "Something about the original virus changed. Wait! You said evolution needs a long time to work. How can a flu virus change that fast?"

"I said what we need are many generations before there is speciation. In the case of the flu virus, its entire reason for invading the cells of our body is to use them to produce millions of copies of itself. To do this, it has to replicate thousands of times and when that happens there is a chance for small changes- mutations in the genetic code, to take place. If this happens only once in a hundred thousand copies, then there are still thousands of copies of flu virus that are no longer destroyed by the vaccine.

Darwin finished with a flourish. "Because of evolution, every person who catches this year's strain of flu is, in essence, an incubator of next year's strain as well!"

"Dr. Darwin," said a grinning Wil, "you died over one hundred and fifty years ago! How can you know anything about the genetic code?"

The old man looked straight-faced at his student. "I'm not actually Charles Darwin, Wil. I'm a teaching program that uses his image to help you to understand evolutionary biology."

The avatar winked at him, and Wil's grin grew larger.

Darwin continued, "If you take natural selection and evolution to its logical conclusion, then every living thing on the planet- plants and animals alike- all derive from a single point of origin billions of years in the past."

Wil stopped laughing and became serious. "Professor Darwin, that's why evolution isn't taught in school. Everyone knows that the Earth is only six thousand years old. I mean, you might have had something going with the finches because you were talking thousands of years but billions? That's crazy talk!

"Besides, Genesis says God created the universe and everything at the same time, and in six days, six thousand years ago. That's the way we learned it in school."

Darwin's face sagged. "What has happened? Even in my time, most learned men knew that the Earth was millions of years old. Most accepted some idea of evolution as fact. When did we go back to the dark ages?"

He took Wil by the shirtsleeve. "Come with me, Wilson; there are some people you need to meet."

The two exited the classroom and walked down the hallway to a closed door. Darwin burst through it without knocking. Inside were four men huddled together, speaking loudly amongst themselves and looking intently at a paper that one was holding in his hand. One, a Catholic priest, looked up.

"Hello Charlie!" he exclaimed with a thick accent. "Come in! We are trying to decide on what to have for lunch."

"Gentlemen, may I introduce Wilson Ramirez. Wilson cannot agree with the theory of natural selection because he believes that the universe is only six thousand years old," said a slightly winded Charles Darwin.

"What? Evolution's not a theory; it's an established fact," said the priest. "Where did he get that crazy idea?"

"Brace yourselves, my friends- in school."

"Wilson, is this true?" asked a short, balding man. Wil nodded.

"I don't see what the big deal is," said Wil. "Whether we evolved or not or how old the universe is, it doesn't change anything in my life at this moment."

"Son, it has everything to do with life, the world and how we live in it," retorted a much taller man, with black hair and glasses. "Everything around you works and functions because of scientific theories. Our understanding of the mechanics of evolution has a direct connection to the biological sciences. The medicines we make and food we produce are just two examples."

"Bob's right," said the fourth, an average-looking and slightly balding man with a friendly smile. "Because we strive to understand the laws and mechanics of the universe, we can use those laws to make a better world for ourselves. Equally so, by understanding how the biology of our planet works and where it comes from, we can use that knowledge to improve the quality of everyone's life."

"Well said, Willard," spoke the priest.

"Who are you guys?" asked a somewhat perplexed Wil.

"Where are my manners? Wilson, it is my great honor to introduce to you Dr. Robert Oppenheimer, a great physicist, and father of the atom bo..."

"That damned bomb again!" interrupted the tall man. "I did have a career before and after that, Charles."

Darwin gave him a slightly annoyed glance. "Apologies Robert. I do know what it's like to be misunderstood. After all, I'm known for saying that Mankind descended from monkeys."

"Did you?" asked Wil.

"No," replied a disdainful Darwin. "Shall we move on? This gentleman is Father Georges Lemaitre. He was the first to postulate that the universe was expanding. Therefore, before the beginning of time and space, there was a single point that it came from. He called it the Primeval Atom."

"These days they call my theory *the Big Bang*... and I was proven right, too!" beamed the priest. "Although that sycophant Hubble usually gets all the credit."

"Wilson, meet Willard Libby, inventor of carbon 14 dating, and Dr. Linus Pauling, who discovered DNA."

The two men smiled and bowed slightly.

135

Wil was impressed but undaunted. "Ok, you guys are all some heavy hitters, but there doesn't seem to be any connection between what you're all experts in and evolution. Father, I'm surprised you would even be in the same room as Professor Darwin."

"Why not? In my day, natural selection was accepted as fact. It's very much all connected!" said Father Lemaitre. "Robert, maybe you should go first."

Oppenheimer sighed. "Alright. Everything in the universe is composed of elemental atoms. A water molecule, for example, is made of hydrogen and oxygen. When we add heat and get the water molecules moving quickly, we can break water down and free those elements from each other. It doesn't take a lot of effort to do that. Breaking down atoms is much tougher, but some atoms are easier than others. All atoms eventually break down into other elements, and we can measure that. When half of the original atom is gone, we call it a *half-life*. I worked with uranium, which is a colossal atom as atoms go, and it has parts of itself flying off all the time. Eventually, it becomes lead. When you get a lot of uranium together, the pieces of the atoms fly off and strike other atoms. When that happens, some of the pieces are destroyed, and a lot of energy gets released too."

He looked at the priest. "We knew that would happen because Georges's friend, Albert Einstein, used mathematics to predict it."

"E equals MC squared," nodded Wil.

"Yes. When you get enough uranium together, eventually all of the pieces flying off and striking other pieces takes place more and more frequently. As that happens, large amounts of energy are freed," continued Dr. Oppenheimer.

"And that's why they used it to make the atomic bomb," smirked Linus Pauling. "When the chain reaction gets so fast, it can't be stopped anymore; it reaches critical mass and causes an explosion that is as powerful as a small sun."

Oppenheimer shot him a nasty look. "Or, when it is controlled properly, it can provide limitless power to cities by heating water into steam to drive electrical turbines. And we saved the lives of millions of people on both sides with those bombs, Linus."

"Gentlemen, please! There's no need to be defensive, Dr. Oppenheimer. All science is amoral in its understanding," said Charles Darwin gently.

"I understand what you said, Dr. Oppenheimer, but what has this got to do with evolution or the age of the Earth?"

"Perhaps I can help with that," piped up Libby. "You see, Wilson, one of the elements we can measure is carbon 14. We know that it has a half-life of roughly six thousand years…"

Wil interrupted him, "Guys, please call me Wil. Nobody calls me Wilson unless I'm in trouble. Six thousand years is how old the Earth is supposed to be, right? So how does this carbon 14 disprove it?"

"I'm sorry… Wil," said Libby. "Well, all life that has ever been on the planet is comprised primarily of carbon, and some of that carbon is carbon 14. When alive, the carbon 14 in a body is exchanged and replaced, so the amount within it remains pretty steady. When something dies, that replacement and exchange cycle stops and the carbon 14 begins to breakdown and becomes nitrogen 14. By measuring the ratio of remaining carbon 14 to carbon 12, which has a much slower rate of decay, we can determine how old something is."

Darwin spoke up, "We can take anything that was once alive, charcoal from a fire or a sample of bone. Using this method, we have determined that life has been around for much longer than six thousand years."

"It's very accurate up to fifty thousand years, and then there isn't enough carbon 14 left to get a good read," said Libby.

Wil contemplated what the men had said. "Let's say I can go along with fifty thousand years. That still isn't millions or even *billions* of years. So, is that enough time for a monkey to become a man?"

"I'm being misquoted! Monkeys did not become men, but both descended from a common ancestor," corrected Darwin. "No, natural selection at our level of development is too slow for speciation within fifty thousand years."

"That's ok, though," said Oppenheimer, "because other radioactive elements are found all over the planet and even in the rock. They have much longer half-lives that we can measure as well. Potassium, for example, and even uranium 235 can be measured. It has a half-life of four point five billion years."

"That's how we can look at fossils in rock formations and determine how old they are," said Libby. "We find fossils of dinosaurs that go back as far as two hundred million years, sea life that goes back hundreds of millions of years more. Life itself probably began around three billion years ago."

"*Probably…* so this is all just a guess," snorted Wil. "The Bible is sure about six thousand years, and it isn't a guess."

137

"That's the difference between a dogmatic religious idea and the scientific method," replied Father Lemaitre. "When science gets something wrong, it can change the answer. It has to. Before I came up with the Big Bang and expanding universe theories, most astronomers and physicists believed in a steady state universe- that it had always been here and always would be. It took some time before my theory could be proven through observation…"

"By Edwin Hubble," interjected Oppenheimer.

"Yes… by Hubble," replied Father Lemaitre flatly, "but it *was* proven. Using the speed of light as a constant, as postulated by my good friend, Dr. Einstein, much later we were able to measure the size of the universe, its rate of expansion…"

"Known as Hubble's constant," said a smiling Linus Pauling.

Lemaitre scowled at Pauling's interjection. "You should be thankful at this moment that I am a priest… by measuring its rate of expansion, we can determine that the universe began as a quantum singularity approximately fourteen and a half billion years ago."

For a moment, there was silence. Finally, Wil spoke, "I can't even imagine a billion years… so you're all telling me that people have been around for millions of years?"

"More like one hundred seventy thousand years," said Linus Pauling. "Around twenty-five years ago, a way was developed to use mitochondrial DNA- that is the DNA of the mother, to determine how long our species of human has been around."

"What? How many *species* of humans have there been?"

"Lots, going back close to five million years. The last ones that weren't Homo Sapiens disappeared around twenty thousand years ago," replied Pauling.

"With genetic evidence of only slight intermixing between Neanderthal and Homo Sapiens," added Charles Darwin.

"True, so far as we know," agreed Pauling. "By looking at the mother's DNA from various populations around the globe, we were able to use the mutations to go back to a single female in Africa roughly one hundred seventy thousand years ago."

"Then there really was an Eve, so to speak," said Father Lemaitre.

"Yes, at least a mitochondrial one," clarified Linus Pauling.

Wil slumped into one of the classroom chairs.

"If everything that you're telling me is true…"

"And it is!" declared Willard Libby.

"...then everything I've believed all my life is a lie. The Bible isn't really God's word, and we aren't very special, are we? We're just another animal that has had enough time to evolve from bacteria. There probably isn't a God at all, is there?"

"Wil, I devoted myself to the service of both the Church and scientific pursuit. If I spent so much of my life in search of truth, why would I spend the other part of my life serving a lie? I am very proud to be a child of Christ, our Lord and Savior," said Father Georges Lemaitre.

"In my mind, there's nothing about my theories on the Big Bang or cosmic expansion that denies God or his Son at all, and the Church agrees. What you need to understand is that the New Testament borrows from the Old and that some of the oldest stories of the Old Testament were made up by people who were trying their best to explain the world around them. Genesis is one of those stories."

"Think about it for a moment, Wil," said Willard Libby. "If Adam and Eve were the first people and Cain and Abel their first children, then who did Cain marry after he was banished... and what about the mark of Cain? If he was one of the first four people on Earth, then why did he need a special mark to protect him from other men? And he lives in a city! Where did that come from?"

"I guess that doesn't make much sense when you think about it," said Wil.

"The ancient world was full of creation myths. The Roman creation stories are almost exactly like the one in the Bible," said Robert Oppenheimer.

"And every ancient society in the Mediterranean and the Middle East has an identical flood story," added Linus Pauling.

"So this means that all of you still believe in Christianity and the resurrection after death?" asked Wil.

"Of course not!" snorted Robert Oppenheimer. "I'm an atheist. The concept of a supreme being, especially the God of the Bible and Qur'an is silly. It doesn't make any sense at all that this version of God would be real; given the vastness of the universe, with its hundreds of billions of stars, and the sheer luck of our existence on this little, insignificant rock, one of trillions. There has to be other life; the odds are simply too high. Why would the creator of the universe be so fixated on Jerusalem?"

139

"I don't believe in a God either," said Pauling. "Our circumstance for existence was just too random in chance for it to have been an intelligent designer. We were an asteroid strike away from never getting beyond lemurs. It would be the descendants of dinosaurs having this conversation.   "We've proven that with the laws of the universe. There doesn't need to be a God to set things in motion.

"As for life after death. If there is no supernatural creator needed, there's probably also no need for an afterlife either. As with all life, when we die, our consciousness dies with us. What we are ceases to exist."

Wil looked at Charles Darwin.

"I am agnostic, my boy. I know too much about how we became what we are to believe in the Judeo-Christian God. It seems to me that the gods of all ancient cultures and their religions are just too tribal and limited to be real," he said. "A personal god who protects me from harm and gives me things because I worship him is out of the question.

"Still, I hold out the possibility that there is a divine creator and that it used the laws of the universe and natural selection to make us what we are today. I wouldn't dare to postulate on a reason as to why. Perhaps there is an afterlife. Perhaps omnipotence is a throne of loneliness."

"I prefer to keep my views to myself," said Willard Libby.

"I still believe in the Trinity and the promise of resurrection and everlasting life with our Lord and Savior," reiterated Father Lemaitre.

"Doesn't the thought of not existing scare you two?" asked Wil of the atheists. "It terrifies me!"

"Sometimes… but it can also be liberating. Knowing that there is no afterlife means you don't have to follow a lot of silly, dogmatic rules designed to keep you in your place," said Oppenheimer. "It makes you want to get the most out of every day of your life because it's all there is. It makes me want to be the best I can be right now."

"Understanding how precious our lives are has taught me to respect all life. I can't look at someone who is different from me as less than I am. That's what the corruption of religious ideas can lead to. It's easy to kill another person if you can't think of him as human and it's almost impossible to kill another person when you do," said Pauling.

"True faith in God and belief in the values of Christ's teachings can lead us to the same conclusion and actions," countered Father Lemaitre.

"I don't know what I should believe," said Wil.

"You can believe in truth, found through the pursuit of the scientific method for now," said the priest smiling. "I have always found it to be as much the revealed truth of our Lord as I do the teachings and sacrifice of his Son."

"God or no God, you have free will to choose what you believe. No one can take that from you," said Charles Darwin.

"What we need to choose now is our lunch," said Libby.

"So," he said, rubbing his hands together, "pizza or sushi?"

***

Red finished setting up the suite and motioned for Grace to come over. She turned to the UNOCHA representative thirty feet away and waved for her. The rep nodded and continued to speak with the Director briefly before breaking off and heading over to Kearney.

Who Grace wanted to get to was the Director, but they never gave interviews, not even to her. They weren't terribly excited about being photographed or caught on video, but from time to time it happened. This one, who went by Andre, had been gracious enough to remain in the background of the shot, smiling and playing with the children who were here at the camp. His halo floated just above his head, making him the perfect prop.

It wasn't that Ella Vargas was a bad interview. Over the past year, she had been a regular contact, beginning with their very first stint of coverage on the Argentine famine relief efforts. The UN and the Host always took great pains to hire locally and she had been a school administrator before the famine. Most of the work had been performed by either the Argentine military- which now found itself effectively out of a job- or by contractors who oversaw the proper distribution not only of adequate food and medicines, but also the construction of temporary shelters and infrastructures required for the operation of relief camps. Today, Vargas had something to be happy about.

"Ola, Grace. Senor Kearney. I am pleased to see the both of you once again. I understand you have been traveling through the camps the past few weeks. They are good news, si?" she beamed.

141

"Si, senora, splendid," replied Grace, beaming back as the two women exchanged hugs and kisses. Ella had come a long way from the gaunt, hopeless figure they had interviewed the first time. Grace knew this woman did have several hundred thousand reasons to smile, in all the saved lives of her people.

"Ola Ella, can you just move a little bit to your left. Good. Now stand up straight and keep that beautiful smile," said Red with a smile of his own.

"Ok, we know you want to make the big announcement, and we are going, beginning with that," said Grace to her interviewee. "Then we want to talk about why- all the progress that has been made, everyone that has been involved, including Andre. Then we'll wrap it up with what's going to happen from here. Are we good? Ok, and don't be nervous because this isn't going to stream live. You can make a mistake or I can make a mistake, and we'll just do it again or fix it later. Ready?"

She turned to look at the tablet, and Ella Vargas mirrored her. Kearney with his hand up began a five count.

"In five, four, three…" he mouthed the remaining two numbers and pointed at the women.

"We've had Ella Vargas on the stream a number of times over the past year. As we prepare our last reports from this fascinating land that is Argentina, we are pleased to have her join us once again," Grace began. "You may remember that Ella is the head of the United Nations Office for the Coordination of Humanitarian Affairs here in Argentina. Her primary responsibility has been to help oversee the nation's famine relief efforts. Ella, it's wonderful to be back with you once again."

"Thank you, Grace," smiled Ella. "I'm so happy that you decided to come back and visit Argentina. We always enjoy you being here."

"I understand you have something a little more important to be happy about."

"That's true, Grace. In the past month, no one in our country has died as a result of starvation or famine-related illnesses such as cholera," replied Ella. "Because of this and other factors relating to the coordinated relief efforts between the Argentine government and the UN, we have decided to officially declare that the famine has ended."

Grace gave her best look of happy surprise. "Ella, this is fantastic news! You've done some incredible work here since we first met last year. Congratulations!"

"Thank you, Grace, but this has been the very hard work of thousands of people and many relief organizations. We need to thank AgriBus for providing the food required to feed the millions of starving people and Pharmacon for donating the medicines we needed to get many of the diseases our people were suffering from under control. There's also the Argentine government and peacekeeping forces who were able to build and maintain the refugee camps and quickly get the food, water, and medicine to people who needed it. I also want to thank Director Andre of the Host. Without his help in getting all the groups to work together efficiently there would still be children dying," said Vargas sincerely.

"That's Director Andre behind us, I believe."

"Yes," nodded Ella Vargas. "He loves being around the children, and they like him a lot, too. He likes to tell them jokes and make them laugh."

"Really? We learn something new about the Host every day, don't we?" added Grace. "So, Ella, what happens with your country now?"

"Well, for a little while longer, we will keep the refugee camps open to provide the population some stability, but soon everyone will be able to go back to their homes. We will continue to ensure that adequate food, water, and medicine will be distributed in the towns and villages but we want everyone to return to a normal life. We've even heard that many of the families who left Argentina for our neighboring countries during the famine are beginning to come home."

"Ella Vargas, we are so overjoyed to see how in one short year Argentina has risen from its terrible crisis to become whole again. Thank you so much for sharing this incredible news with us."

"It was truly my pleasure, Grace. Please come and see us again soon. We'll make dinner for you," said Ella pleasantly.

"Oh I can't wait!" laughed Grace.

"And… we're done," said Red after a few seconds. "I'm going to get some B-roll and then we can pack it in.

"Ella, that was perfect! You're becoming quite good at this. Have you thought about a future in journalism here in Argentina?" asked the still smiling Grace.

"I am flattered, Grace, but you make it so easy for me," replied Ella. "In truth, now that the crisis is over, I want to go back to teaching. It is what I love the most in the world."

"Then you should do what you love, Ella. Via con Deus, my friend."

143

"And you. I should hope to see the both of you again very soon under even better circumstance," replied Ella.

Grace continued smiling as Ella Vargas left and made her way back to Director Andre of the Host.

"Oh, Red!" she said through the smile. "I'm so goddamned bored!"

***

The tribal elders were still angry and muttering amongst themselves when their leader spoke over the din.

"We thank you for the school and for everything you have built to make our lives better," he said. "The boys of our village will attend the school, but the girls cannot."

"It is not a matter of choice, Mullah Hakem," replied Director Abdul-Khabir. "All children in the village will attend the school for education, both male and female."

"It is forbidden for the girls to do this. The Qu'ran states this plainly. You are asking us to go against God."

"It is not in the Qu'ran that a female is forbidden from education. The Prophet states that a woman may be outside of the home for the purpose of education," said the Director.

"There are many forms of education," replied the Mullah dryly.

The Director was silent, his halo rising slightly. The two stared at each other. The Mullah broke the silence.

"You said that you would not interfere with our ways, yet here you are, forcing us to go against God!"

"The Host will not interfere with your ways so long as those ways respect the rights of all. There is no part of the Qu'ran that restricts the education of women. There are old ways that treated women as property to be owned, bartered, bought, and sold. These ways are wrong and will be swept away in the new world to come. Everyone will have the same basic human rights. This is the teaching of the Prophet. The right to knowledge is among those."

"You are a demon! Satan come to destroy us!" spat Mullah Hakem. "We will fight you. In the name of God, we will resist."

"Then you will die quickly. There will be no fight, or do you forget what Our Host is capable of?" replied the Director.

The Mullah clutched his chest, gasping. He doubled over as the remaining elders fell silent, watching in wide-eyed horror.

The Director made a show of it. The Mullah fell to his knees, gasping and clawing for a good fifteen seconds. Hakem looked up in anger at the Director as the pain subsided.

"I will return in the morning and escort the children… all of the children, to school for the first day. Then I will return to Kandahar, and from time to time the teachers will report to me their progress. I have matters other than this to attend to but if I must return here, I will. This is your final warning. If you do not comply, you will all die."

"It is better to die in the service of God, fighting his enemies, than to bend to the will of Satan. Paradise will be our reward," replied the Mullah, attempting to regain his breath.

"If that is your choice then Paradise awaits," said the Director. "Better for all if the old ways are swept aside with a single stroke than be left to fester. You will all die, but the children will remain, the girls will be educated in school, and the Promised Land will be upon us at last."

Chapter Ten

Norman Borlaug was intrigued- at least his avatar was.

The father of modern agriculture and Nobel laureate had become a regular visitor to Wil's farm. The two would walk the fields of wheat together, talking about crop production techniques and Borlaug's Green Revolution that had saved a billion people from starvation.

They also discussed in great detail *The Ceiling*.

Wil had spent the past year at the feet of giants. He learned biological evolution from Charles Darwin, general physics from Isaac Newton, general relativity from Albert Einstein, and quantum theory from Max Plank. Gustav Senn had taught him about the effect of light on plant cells, but Borlaug was his favorite. Borlaug had confronted the problem of a world on the brink of mass starvation and had figured out how to feed it. He had ingeniously used strains of genetically modified wheat that, when given large quantities of fertilizer and water, could grow quickly and provide three times the yield per acre of common wheat. He inspired Wil to do something important, too.

Borlaug's work had fed a growing world population for more than half a century, but even Norman Borlaug knew and preached that there was a limit to his revolution. He had predicted that world crop yields would top out in the early 2000's. Eventually, the population would catch up and surpass his brilliance. The food supply would collapse, and billions would again face starvation.

Borlaug was off by forty years. AgriBus and the other food cartels had been able to stave off the inevitable with enhanced, genetically modified crops that used less water and improved nutrients to feed them. Crop yields had made incremental gains, even in the face of increasingly unpredictable weather patterns. Still, over the past decade food production had leveled off with negligible increases. *Borlaug's Ceiling* had been reached.

On this trip, Wil and Borlaug sat in the kitchen of Wil's farmhouse, with the older man staring at a hand drawing Wil had made. It was well done. Wil had been painstaking in his rendering.

"I think it will work," said Wil.

"I believe you're right," replied Norman Borlaug. "If it does, we can quintuple food production worldwide. This is so simple." He looked up from the drawing at Wil. "We need to speak with the angel."

146

In the next instant, she was before them, her smile seemingly eternal. She seemed genuinely pleased to see Wil.

"Hello, Wil. Hello, Norman. How can I help?" she asked.

"Wil has an idea that we need to build and test in this virtual space," said Norman. "I think this would be a fantastic project for some of our engineering students to help with."

"Excellent!" said the ever-cheerful angel. "Wil, what has our Nobel laureate so excited?"

Wil pointed to the drawing on the table. "I was thinking about flower boxes and came up with this. Flower boxes are a controlled environment for the most part. We determine what goes in them, how much water and nutrient they receive, even how much light they get for photosynthesis. What if we could build massive versions of flower boxes for crop growth and what if we could stack them five levels high?"

Borlaug broke in. "We could grow between five and twenty times the amount of food on the same plot!"

"Intriguing but wouldn't you still require five times the amount of soil and water?" asked the angel. "There would also be an issue with getting enough light to the majority of your crops."

"Wil believes he has potentially resolved those issues," answered Dr. Norman Borlaug's avatar. He turned to the young man. "Go ahead and tell our friend your idea."

"Well," began Wil, "You have to go back and understand that agriculture today is a lot like agriculture was five thousand years ago. We plow the land to create seed rows. Then we flood the area from time to time with large amounts of water. We've always fertilized the crop in some manner, whether it was burying a fish next to a cornstalk or spreading manure across a field. We have also always genetically altered plant strains, usually through selecting the traits we want and continuously improving those characteristics over several years.

"Dr. Bolaug's big breakthrough was to use specially selected dwarf strains that grew faster and had a higher yield per acre than prior strains. Even so, his techniques were heavily dependent upon field flooding, with large amounts of both fertilizer and water. Now, that has become a huge problem for us. We've destroyed aquatic systems with algae blooms from fertilizer runoff. This removes all the oxygen from water and kills fish stocks.".

Wil looked sheepishly at his mentor. "I'm sorry, Doctor."

"It's quite alright, Wilson. I was a product of my time," replied the Doctor. "Besides, I told them it wouldn't last. They didn't want to listen. Keep going."

"Yes, sir. In truth, modern farming underutilizes available land because only about a fifth of the soil is actually involved in plant growth and development. The soil around the plant that is not a part of the root system is wasted. The same could be said for the water and fertilizer that is randomly applied to this soil. Perhaps twenty percent of the water and nutrients applied to a field ends up feeding the plant."

"This building isn't just stacking fields on top of each other," he continued. "It is an entirely controlled system. For starters, soil is distributed in channels between walkways. These channels mimic the traditional plow rows. There's enough soil to support the plant's root system, but none is wasted. By doing this, we can take the soil from an acre and distribute it evenly over all five levels of the building. The walkways provide access to the plants and contain the guts of the supply systems. Each plant will use the drip hose systems that were experimented with and then abandoned in India a few decades ago. They will run a hose to each plant to feed from individually."

"If they were abandoned then, why will they work now?" asked the angel.

"The application method was flawed," replied Borlaug. "This time, the distribution of water and nutrients will be strictly controlled."

"That's right," added Wil. "When it rains, that water will be collected into reservoirs located in the building for later use. The supply of water and nutrients required by the plant will be monitored and distributed by a combination of sensors and computers. It will provide maximum plant yield with no waste of resources."

"And because these buildings are closed systems, there is no more widespread environmental damage from runoff," added Norman Borlaug. "We also minimize crop loss from floods or storms."

The angel did not speak immediately, and Wil knew that she was running something through her program. She was, after all, an AI.

Finally, she spoke, "How do you solve the photosynthesis issue? Obviously, the field on top of the building is getting direct sunlight but what about the other four levels? They must be quite dark in most places."

Wil pointed at the drawing again. "You see this? It's a system of mirrors designed to guide sunlight to more mirrors stationed above the plants on each level, using reflection. Light doesn't lose its properties- we can see the light from stars that was emitted thirteen billion years ago. The mirror system will run the length and depth of the building on all four sides. By setting the mirrors at various angles, we can guide sunlight to each plant."

"The building is also capable of using a combination of solar, wind, and battery storage to operate the drip pumps, as well as a network of bulbs that can efficiently provide artificial light," added Dr. Borlaug, staring at the drawing. "We can use a controlled, agricultural environment such as this to simultaneously grow corn and wheat on two levels, tomatoes and carrots on another, soybeans and canola on two more. That's just an example of course. You can pick any combination of crops.

"And depending on where we are at, we could turn over crops three or four times a year using genetically modified, fast-growth strains," added Wil. "That's another advantage; we can grow crops anywhere with these boxes. All that land in California that is no longer arable can become a garden again!"

"So, you can see that we need to get going on a prototype," said Borlaug, looking up from the drawing at the angel. "We need to test this project in virtuality and work out its actual potential before we can take it into the real world. To do that, we need a couple of project engineers and an architect or two."

"Agreed," said the angel. She looked at Wil. "You are slated to leave this facility in thirty-nine days and take your place with Our Host."

"I know," acknowledged Wil. "I'm supposed to help with a relief operation in the Central African Republic. Still, I think we can do this. If we can get the engineering and architectural plans together quickly, then we can create the building in virtuality within moments. Then we can accelerate the simulation to collect the data we need. We could get years of real world information within a month."

"I will arrange for you to meet with your engineers and architect when you return tomorrow," said the angel. "For now, Dr. Borlaug and I have to leave. The others will soon be here to take you back."

With that, Wil found himself alone in the kitchen.

"They seem very excited about it," he said to Sonya later on.

149

"Of course they're excited. You may have just figured out a better way to feed the world," said Sonya, a bit breathless. She held the weight to her chest and finished the set of abdominal crunches while he anchored her feet.

"Your turn," she heaved as she finished. They switched positions. Wil could easily hold Sonya's feet down with his hands, but the much smaller woman had to sit on his feet and lock her legs around his calves to anchor him.

Wil grinned at her as he came up for the first crunch. "I wish your legs were wrapped around my back."

Sonya leaned forward and kissed him. "Soon enough, my love. We'll be out of here in a few weeks more and then I can have my way with you."

It was a dilemma for them that the building didn't have any private rooms. No one ever expected to need them; people lived and slept in the coffins and left them for eight hours in order to fulfill their legal requirement. Who would have thought that two Virtuals would actually want to be alone with each other in reality?

They would have tried the fitness room, but for the security cameras, they didn't want to put on a show for anyone else. Still, at times it was frustrating, particularly since they had begun to regain their strength- their bodies recovering from the box.

The two had maintained a strict regimen of solid food and supplements twice daily- one meal when they came out and another before they returned- and their first eight hours in the box were programmed for an actual sleep mode. That meant eight hours in virtuality then eight, in reality, spent eating, working out, and getting medical attention.

The practice had paid off. Wil was still thin, but now a sinew of hard muscle covered his wiry frame. Sonya had regained her figure and filled out into an athletic body. Eight months in, Wil had looked at her one day and realized that she no longer resembled a malnourished child but instead a beautiful, young woman. She had smiled at him with a mouthful of dental implants and it was lovely to behold.

Surprisingly, the staff didn't bat an eye at their change in behavior. It happened from time to time that a Virtual would want to rejoin the real world. To them, Wil and Sonya were in the one percent.

They weren't alone in their transformation. There were others but not as many as might be expected, perhaps a dozen in total. They formed a small band of brothers and sisters, giving each other knowing looks as they passed in the corridors or shared the fitness room. Nothing was ever said in the real world, although from time to time some would come together in a virtual classroom. Over time, they all began to find their calling for when they would join the service of the Host.

Sonya's was easy. She was a natural leader and an organizer of the highest order. Wil had watched Sonya time and again in virtual classrooms, using her cognitive skills to find solutions to problems or motivating those better suited to find the answers for her. They had both put in for the Central African Republic as their first posting. There was a tremendous poverty that required the building of roads, communication systems, schools, power stations, and agriculture. Wil would be part of an Ag team. Sonya would be a project team manager.

That was what they hoped, at least. There were no guarantees they would get that posting or even be together. After all this time, working so hard, they couldn't imagine being pulled apart.

"Maybe we can meet in one of the erotica worlds later today," Sonya said to Wil later as they finished their second meal.

He thought about it for a moment and cringed. "I'm sorry, I can't. Others are coming to help me with the plans to construct the Flowerbox. I don't know how long it will take us."

She just smiled at him. "I see duty calls. Oh well, your loss."

"I'm sorry. Maybe I can put it off a day."

Sonya grew serious. "No! Didn't you just tell me you're under the gun to get this thing off the ground? This is way too important to you- to everyone maybe. Stay on focus."

The coy smile returned. "Don't worry. I'll find something to keep me busy!"

He felt a twinge of jealousy. "You know I hate that, even if it is in the box."

"You, sir, have a dirty mind. I'm going to spend the day with Nicolo Machiavelli. Might as well learn at the feet of a master!"

Wil was having his first cup of virtual coffee from the virtual pot in his virtual farmhouse when the knock came at his virtual door.

He opened it to find a virtual crowd; at least for his farm it was a crowd. Before him was the angel, Dr. Borlaug, and three others- two men and a woman. All were roughly his age or at least their avatars were. He assumed that this was what they actually looked like in reality. He had long ago dropped other forms for that of his own.

Wil invited them in, and the strangers in the group introduced themselves to him on their way to the kitchen table. They moved the condiments and fruit bowl onto the counter. The one named Baaz pulled a rolled up sheet of plastic out of his satchel and laid it out flat on the table. He waved his hand over it, and Wil's Flowerbox stack appeared in three dimensions on top of the sheet.

"Based on your drawing, I was able to layout this design," he began. "It's close to concept, with a few necessary modifications. For example, we have to allow for a separate, underground control center in order to take advantage of the entire perimeter of the structure with respect to light collection and maximization of growth space.

Baaz looked at Wil. "You wouldn't want to be in the actual structure for long anyway, at least not during the day. You would eventually go blind from the light."

He waved his hand over a section of the building, and it enlarged. Baaz then put his hands together over the image and brought them apart. A section split away.

"We can build the structure with the newest carbon-based materials. This gives us incredible strength but keeps the overall structure light. It also allows us to put most of the operational requirements of the building within its walls. Here, you can see the water collection and recovery systems, liquid nutrient storage tanks, and the corresponding pump and delivery systems."

He waved again. "Pop the top and you can follow the systems all the way to each plant. All of it buried below the catwalks."

"We've been able to estimate the energy requirements of the structure," chimed in the one named Caitlin. "To accommodate the planetary movement in relation to the sun, we've made the mirrors more mobile. A computer will track the sun and use servomotors to continuously adjust the mirrors for maximum efficiency."

"We've also been able to incorporate a mirror that will convert itself into a solar collector for a portion of its use," said the one named Eric. "There will be negligible effect on the plants; it will be as if the sun was to go behind a cloud for a moment. The energy collected between that, and the wind turbines should be more than enough to provide eighty percent of the energy usage to start. We can tweak the model to try for one hundred percent eventually."

"We may be able to close off some of the lower levels and use them as traditional greenhouses during the winter in harsher climates," said Caitlin. "We can lay solar collectors and wind turbines over the top of the structure to acquire more energy to power light and heating systems. At least a couple of the levels could be utilized year round."

Eric looked up from the plans for a moment and at Wil. "This is unbelievable! I'm twenty-four years old and working on a project that will change everything we know about food production! Who gets to do that?"

"You do, Eric," replied the angel.

Sonya appeared in the farmhouse kitchen and knew something was different. Outside was a slow, continuous flickering of light and dark, as if a strobe was going on and off. There was a high-pitched whine in her ears, not painful but slightly annoying. She looked out the window and tried to get her mind around the image she was watching. It was time to find Wil.

Sonya didn't have to look for long. She saw him on back porch, looking out at the fields, except that the fields were no longer there. Instead, there stood a grid of massive buildings that reminded her of parking garages. Above them, the sun rose and set within seconds.

Wil heard the porch door open and turned to see Sonya coming through. They walked toward each other with huge smiles and embraced. She let go of him and turned back to the scene before them.

"I know in my mind that this is a simulation but it leaves you a little woozy," she began.

Wil nodded. "Yeah, it does disorient at first. Eventually, you get used to it. The simulation gives us roughly two months' worth of data within a half hour. That's about as fast as we can go because there are so many variables at work. Rainstorms are insane, you get soaked and dry off within seconds!"

"So this is the Flowerbox," she said after a moment. "Looks more like a bunch of ugly office buildings."

"The acronym the engineers gave to it is ESCAPE. It stands for Ecologically Self-Contained Agricultural Production Environment," he answered. "I like Flowerbox a lot better. Wanna see how it works? Angel, please bring us in sync with the ESCAPE simulation."

The sun and clouds ground to a halt in the sky above them. The high-pitched whine suddenly became the sounds of the outdoors- birds singing and the wind blowing through trees.

"Come on, I'll show you around," he said, starting for the closest building. Sonya fell into step beside him, striding quickly to match the distance of Wil's longer gait.

As they made their way to the closest structure in the field, Sonya began to pick up details very distinct from that of an ordinary building. Wil stopped for a moment and pointed at the array of mirrors surrounding the structure on all sides. To Sonya, they looked to be tilted at all angles in helter-skelter fashion.

"It begins with the mirrors and wind turbines. You can't see the turbines around the perimeter of the complex because of the angle. When the wind is blowing, they're part of the energy collectors needed to run the operations.

"What you can see are the mirror collectors," he continued. "They're computer-controlled panels that adjust to the movement of the sun through the sky. Those that have direct access to sunlight alternate between being a solar collector for the battery stores and acting as a mirror to reflect the light to the other panels. That light is then reflected to the crops growing on each level for photosynthesis."

They started for the closest building again. As they neared, Sonya could feel the heat emanating from it. Getting closer, she could see that the lower-floor wall held a large set of double doors. Their destination, however, was the standard size door next to them. They entered a landing, surrounded by a massive service elevator on one side and a stairwell on the other. Wil opened the stairwell door and beckoned Sonya to follow. To her surprise, they went down instead of up.

"Ok, I'm confused. Aren't all the crops upstairs?" she asked.

"That they are, oh curious one," he replied lightly. "But what makes it all go is in the basement!"

They came out of the stairwell into a large area broken up by thin support columns. The service elevator shaft was still in front of them, but now she could make out electrical equipment and storage tanks. Pipes of all sizes snaked up the columns and across the ceiling. They walked together out toward the middle of the room.

154

"You see that wall?" asked Wil, nodding to the twelve-foot high mélange of various colored cubes that ran the length of the building. "Those are storage batteries. They're actually more like millions of micro-capacitors. Unlike a conventional battery that needs time to recharge, these guys charge as fast as they discharge. It means that very little of the energy generated by the collectors is wasted."

He looked at her and smiled. "At least that's what the engineers tell me."

"I get it," she nodded. "These are micro-batteries, all strung together in a series. They release their charges in sequence, and the flow of electricity is constant. They can also be filled with a small electrical charge, and since not much is being put into them, they fill up faster. If they charge in sequence, then the load input is continuous as well."

"You've got it! You see the big generators just in front of the capacitors? They're emergency power for the building systems. Over here are the storage tanks. They hold both water and liquid nutrients for the plants. They feed into these pumps that disperse it throughout the levels."

Sonya motioned at one of the tanks. "Why is that one connected to the ceiling?"

"Because every drop of water that comes out of the clouds or the tanks that's not utilized by the plants is recycled, using gravity," He replied. "We're kind of taking a page out of the earth's ecosystem. This is the equivalent of an underground cistern that collects runoff as it makes its way through the soil and onto the bedrock. Let's go over here."

Wil began walking towards a door that was close to the stairwell. As they entered, she saw two men and two women seated at workstations that formed a square. In front of them was the 3D model of the building and above that a 3D model of the entire complex of buildings. Each of them was focused intently on the models and their virtual screens. They greeted Wil with smiles and waves.

"Hey guys," he waved back. "we're going to suit up and tour number one. Is that alright."

"No problem," replied one of the women. "Do you want us to dial anything back?"

"No, I want my girlfriend to see the whole system as it is," he said. "We won't be more than an hour at most. Come this way, Sonya," said Wil, motioning her through another door at the end of the room.

"AI's?" she asked.

"Technicians in training."

The next one, she figured, was some sort of a clean room. It was white and contained a dozen or more of what looked like space suits and helmets. Sonya gave him a puzzled look.

"Yeah, I know. They look like space suits and they kind of are. They're environmental suits," he answered. "There isn't anything dangerous up there, but it can get really hot. You can go blind as well if you're in some of the rooms for too long, unprotected."

"These suits keep you at a delightful seventy-two degrees and give you command control of the systems on each floor. Look around and find one that fits you."

They helped each other with the suits, boots, helmets, and gloves. Sonya couldn't tell any difference in the temperature, but she did notice how snug the suit was to her body. It hadn't gone on that way, but now it felt less like clothing and more like a second skin.

They went back the way they came in, toward the service elevator. Wil hit the call button. They heard the clanking and whirring of motors as the large platform began its downward trek.

"This elevator is so big because sometimes we have to get specialized equipment onto a level. We keep all that stuff in a separate building. They take care of the entire complex," Wil explained as they waited.

"That's why you need the large doors into the building," surmised Sonya. "To bring the equipment in and out."

"Yeah," he acknowledged. "In the old days, farmers didn't have the money to buy equipment for themselves so that they would form co-operatives. Everyone would pitch in and help to buy the things they needed, like tractors and harvesters. Then they would share them and help each other get in the plantings and harvests.

"It's a really good idea because you save on the cost of equipment. So I adapted it for the Flowerboxes."

The elevator hit bottom and Wil opened the fence gate to let them onto it. He closed the gate and pressed a button. The elevator, for all its size, moved smoothly upward.

"So then, the idea is to run these places without the need for people and lots of equipment?" asked Sonya.

"Not at all. It's just that the backbreaking stuff is being handled with automation. You'll see that for yourself on the walk, but this place is super hi-tech. With every complex of buildings, you need system monitors and technicians to service equipment. Plus, you have all of the people who will be support staff. People bringing in the nutrients and in some cases water. People who will be transporting the crops-not to mention those who will be building the complexes. Those making the materials to build them. Those making the fertilizers... well, you can see where we're going. These Flowerboxes are going to put tens of millions of people to work around the world."

As they reached the next level, Sonya's visor went into night vision mode, and her view suddenly tinted greenish-yellow.

"This is the blinding light?" she asked sarcastically.

Wil laughed. "We were able to get five growing levels out of the buildings, but the two lowest ones never see real or reflected light. We couldn't make it work. Right now they're in sleep mode. When night comes, and the other levels are asleep, these will be lit up so bright that your eyes wouldn't be able to take it. I'll show you what it looks like. Andrea, can you light up level four please?"

Sonya waited a few seconds. "Nothing happened."

Wil smiled again. "That's because we're on level five, silly girl. Come on."

They stepped out onto a landing that seemed to ring the floor. It extended for hundreds of feet in each direction. Everywhere she could see, row upon row of plants were growing in between small walkways of what looked to be black glass.

"We put the crops that perform best with artificial light on the lower levels," said Wil. "These are two varieties of lettuce. Let's go up and look at the tomatoes."

They rode up to the next level and into a brilliant, white light. Sonya's visor darkened almost immediately. She glanced at Wil; his visor was so dark that she could no longer see his face. He looked like one of those astronauts on the moon she had seen from old photographs.

"Wow! What a difference!" she exclaimed.

"It gets really bright, to help accelerate plant growth. These tomatoes are genetically modified to grow from seed to harvest in forty-five days. For that to happen, we need a lot of intense light for eighteen hours per day and the right water to nutrient mix. A robot harvester travels these walkways once per day and picks the fruit ready for harvest."

157

"The ceilings in here are very low," Sonya observed. "Midget farmers?"

"They prefer to be called little people," Wil shot back. "And no, it's just a utilization of space. The plants in the lower levels are all bushes, and so you don't require a space more than eight feet high to get the job done. If people didn't have to walk through you could probably even do it with less..." he drifted away for a moment, Sonya could tell he was thinking.

"I need to talk to the engineers about that," he said. Then, turning back to Sonya, "Here, take a look at this."

They walked toward the plants. As she got closer, Sonya could see that the tomatoes were planted in twos and that the plants ran in rows several hundred feet in length. Every fifty feet, a walkway, cut the row, she assumed so that one didn't have to walk the length of the building to get to a spot in the field. Only it wasn't a field; to her, it was more like a series of dirt troughs a couple of feet wide sitting between the walkways, which themselves didn't seem much wider than a foot.

Wil stepped onto one of the walkways, took a few strides out and turned around to face Sonya, who was still on the outer ring platform. Dropping, he motioned for her to do the same. He placed his right hand on the side of the walkway just a few inches below the top of the platform.

"There's a latch on your left," he said to her. "Can you lift it straight up?"

Sonya reached out to her left, mirroring Wil, and found the latch. Together they lifted up, and the top of the walkway swiveled ninety degrees and came to a rest. Inside were a series of wires, conduits, tubes, and pipes.

"Remember the tanks in the basement?" he asked. "You see the blue tubing? That's the conduit for the water and nutrient mix. A line runs from the tube to each plant. The pumps in the basement get the mix up to each level and then the actual distribution to each plant is performed by micro-pumps."

He looked up. "In the old days, we would just flood a field and waste most of the water. We can't afford to do that anymore. This way the plants get exactly what they need to grow- no more and no less."

Inwardly, Sonya couldn't think of a more boring subject than farming, but she could tell that Wil was genuinely excited by what he was doing and she knew it was a game changer. She had to admit to herself- all of this high-tech agriculture was pretty amazing.

158

Wil dropped the walkway back into place and stood up, walking to her. He put his hands on her shoulders and gave them a light squeeze. Even though she couldn't see his face, Sonya knew he was smiling as he looked at her.

"Come on," he said as they turned back to the elevator. "The really amazing stuff is above us."

Her visor darkened again as the elevator revealed the third floor. It was here that Wil's original idea had taken hold. Two walls of the building were bright, even through the visor, and it was then that she noticed that the walls weren't actually walls. They were large mirrors, positioned along the side of the building. Sunlight was reflecting off them and onto mirror arrays located on the ceiling.

"What do you think?" he asked her, almost leaping from the elevator platform.

"I think I am very lucky to be in love with such a brilliant man," she answered, taking in the sight before her.

"You're very fortunate to be in that suit. It's incredibly hot in here," replied Wil, letting her compliment pass. He opened his arms as if to embrace the field before him. "These are soybeans. You can see that the sunlight is bouncing off of those mirrors outside the building and onto the ones above the field. They then reflect the light onto the plants for photosynthesis. It's a pretty simple concept."

"It's amazing," said Sonya, genuinely impressed with Wil's work. "This is going to replace growing food in fields?"

"Probably not," he replied. "Where it makes sense, there are still going to be cornfields, although this method of supplying water and fertilizer could be used there to reduce runoff and pollution. I can see these going into places where the land or resources can't support farming anymore. So many parts of the world are deserts now. There isn't any water, but there is a lot of sunlight. That can provide all the energy you would need for both the plants and the buildings. There are places on Earth that have never supported farming. They would be perfect for Flowerboxes. You would have to truck in the water and nutrients from time to time but, with the recycling systems, the water usage is not nearly what you might think it would be."

"Do you have Flowerboxes in the desert?" she inquired.

"We do. There are ten of these simulations in operation, in some pretty hot and dry places. Some pretty miserable places too. We had a few glitches to start off. The great thing about the accelerated worlds is that you can get a year's worth of data really quick and fix the problems just as quickly."

He motioned back to the elevator. "One more thing to show you."

They skipped over the second floor but as it went by she saw golden rows of wheat.

"Are you ready for harvest?"

"We actually harvest five times a year. That's the edge we get with the Flowerboxes. We don't have to rely on the growing cycles that the Earth provides. We can make our own. With the GMO's... sorry, the genetically-modified organisms... the plants here are all adapted to rapid growth. We can turn over these fields every few months. Here we are, end of the line!"

The two had arrived at the roof of the building. As the elevator rose and locked in place, Sonya beheld a sea of green, capped in gold. It was corn. Row upon row of corn, shoulder high to her as they approached.

"It's beautiful, but I thought it would be taller. You always see it that way in the movies. People coming out of it or walking through it and it's seven feet tall," she said.

"Normally it is," he agreed. "This is a dwarf species that has been developed to use less water and mature faster. You can take your helmet off now that we're on top. It's not so hot up here with the breeze."

The hot wind that hit her face when she lifted off the helmet made Sonya think twice. The suit, which had been sheltering her at seventy-two degrees, suddenly became stifling. She gave Wil a puzzled look.

"I guess it's a little warmer up here than you're used to," he said sheepishly. "Angel, can you remove the environmental suits from our bodies, please?"

"If it was that easy to get them on and off, why did we have to go through the trouble of putting them on?" she demanded after the suit disappeared.

Wil looked at her and grinned. "Because then you wouldn't have gotten the full Flowerbox experience. Now for the grand finale!"

He turned and spread his arms before her in presentation. In front of her was not just this building but the entire complex. She could now see the wind turbine towers spaced around the buildings. Positioned above the roof on each side was an array of solar collectors. A retaining wall extended around the perimeter of the roof. As far as she could see were the rooftop fields, the wind turbines, and the collectors.

"There are exactly one hundred Flowerboxes on this site. They are set up on a ten by ten grid and take up just under one square mile," said Wil. "But they produce twenty times the product that you can get from conventional farming of this same area with roughly equal use of resources."

"And this works?" she asked.

"It does in the simulations," said Wil. "We've tried to take into account all the variables, but you really can't know until you build one in the real world. I'm not sure if that will actually happen, but at least I got to get it out of my head and see it like this."

Something buzzed past Sonya's face, startling her. She instinctively swatted at it. Wil laughed.

"Sonya, it's ok. It won't bother you. Angel, please freeze the ESCAPE program."

Everything stopped at once, including the breeze. Virtuals get used to stepping in and out of worlds, but Sonya still found it especially surreal. Wil nodded toward the field. She turned to look.

In the air were dozens of black dots suspended over the corn. She looked at the one closest to her. It looked like a silver and black bee.

"They're pollinators," said Wil. "They were developed by a woman boxed outside of Paris. They're a replacement for bees since we don't have enough of them anymore. The Flowerbox was a great chance for her to try out the design."

"Wilson Ramirez, you are one amazing person to do all of this! How can they not want to at least try it outside?"

"Look, first of all, this wasn't all me. There were a lot of people involved in putting this together. I just had the concept," he replied. "There were engineers and architects, agricultural experts, biologists, AI experts... the woman who came up with these... more than I can mention.

"To me, that's what makes it so exciting- that so many people can come together to create this place. I remember my grandfather had some great ideas. He even built some of them to prove they could work and he couldn't get anyone to pay attention to him. It made him pretty bitter about his life... in the end.

"Nothing is guaranteed, so I'm not going to get my hopes up," he finished. "In a few days, we are off to Africa and a better life."

The day before they were to leave, Wil took one final walk of the farm, this time alone.

He didn't go to the Flowerbox program but chose instead to walk the wheat fields. The program was synced to the outside world, and in this one, the wheat was waist high and golden, ready for the harvest. Wil felt sad that he wouldn't be around to see it come in.

The soil beneath his boots was just right, hard-packed and dry but not cracked and dusty- that would have betrayed a lack of rain. The combine would have an easy run of these fields this year, he thought.

Wil pulled his jacket tighter against the fall chill and came out of the field onto his back yard. He could see the pumpkins in the garden- big ones blazing fire-engine orange in the setting sun. The kids would have some astounding jack-o-lanterns this year, he imagined. After all, Halloween was not far away. He wondered if he would ever have *real* kids…

As he walked toward the house, Wil saw a woman open the back porch door. It set him sideways for a moment- he should be alone in here today. He knew it wasn't Sonya; he was to meet up with her later. His virtual farm family was not in this run so it couldn't be his wife. It had to be…

He saw the shimmer and knew it was her. The angel had come to say goodbye.

A second figure came onto the back porch. As he walked faster toward them, he could make out that she was a dark-haired, middle-aged woman. She looked to be about his mother's age. She was dressed casually and smiling.

"I'm going to miss you very much, Angel," said Wil when he got to within speaking distance. "You saved my life."

"You saved your own life, Wil," replied the angel, ever-smiling. "Perhaps we will not be apart for long. Virtuality was designed to be a construct for learning and experimentation. We will likely meet again, sooner than you think."

She turned and motioned to her companion. "There is someone who wishes to meet you."

"Hello Wilson, I'm Gloria Mooney," said the woman cheerfully as she held out her hand.

"Please call me Wil. Only my girlfriend calls me Wilson and that's usually when she's making a point," replied Wil as he shook Gloria Mooney's hand. "Nice to meet you, Ms. Mooney. Are you a Virtual or an AI?"

"This is my avatar. Right now, my body is at a facility in Kansas City, Missouri," said Mooney.

"Tough times out that way, Ms. Mooney. Hot and dry," Wil replied.

"Yes, they are, but we're holding our own," she nodded. "Wil, I'm with AgriBus. My title is Chief of Operations but what that really means is that it's my job to get the planting and harvest in on time."

Wil's eyes widened. "Wow! Ok, well... you're a very important person!"

Mooney laughed. "I don't know about that, but I do like to think of myself as a farmer who tends to a lot of fields. If it's ok with you, I'd like to take a look at the ESCAPE system that you've modeled.

"We've been monitoring your data results, and they look very promising. I wanted to get a first-hand look at the facility in operation. Do you mind walking me through that program? I'd love to see it through the eyes of the young man who conceived it."

Wil couldn't believe what he was hearing, even though it was what he had dreamt about.

"I'd love to, Ms. Mooney," he said, beaming. "We have to hurry, though. I have only a few hours left in the box today and tomorrow I'm leaving for the Central African Republic as part of an Ag team."

Mooney's smile faded. "About that. I think there might be a change of plans. We'd like to offer you a job. You would oversee the prototype ESCAPE complex that we'd like to build outside of Kansas City. If it is successful, we would then fast track the building of thousands of ESCAPE's worldwide."

Wil was flabbergasted. Then he had a thought, and his smile faded.

"What about Sonya?" he asked. "We're supposed to stay together."

"You still can," replied Gloria Mooney. "We'll give her a job, too. How does that sound?"

"Great, only..." he trailed off.

"What's wrong, Wil?" asked the angel.

"It's just that I thought we would be working in the service of the Host."

Gloria Mooney laughed. "You are, Wil! You are!"

163

Chapter Eleven

"It's waiting for you, Mr. President."

Sam Craig looked up from his desk. "Tell it to make an appointment."

"Sir, I'm afraid it doesn't work that way," said Jim Gillette.

"Goddammit, Jim! I'm the fucking President of the United States!" bellowed Craig. "I should at least be able to control my schedule."

"I'm very sorry, Sir," apologized Gillette as the creature slid past him and through the doorway.

"Greetings, Samuel Craig! We hope to find you in good health!" sang the creature.

"Go fuck yourself, you miserable shitbag! And, it's *President* Samuel Craig, for your information."

"We apologize that we are unable to comply with your request. Our creator did not equip us for such a task, President Samuel Craig," sang the chorus that was Michael's voice.

That the Seraphim tolerated Craig's increasingly nasty taunts had at first made Gillette ponder as to why it didn't strike him dead. He had arrived at two conclusions: the first being that there was no need because there was no threat. As the months under The Peace slid by, Samuel Craig had grown to realize that he was a lame duck at best and a puppet at worst. Craig's tirades and slurs at the creature had mirrored his increasing impotence. The Seraphim tolerated it as a symbol of the supremacy of the Host. If Craig had greeted it waving a shotgun, there was no doubt in Gillette's mind that he would fall stone dead in an instant- but that wasn't Sam Craig's style.

Gillette had another rationale that he thought was closer to the truth. The insults hurled upon it by Craig were meant to anger and belittle humans. Michael wasn't human. It may have a human name for human convenience, but the Seraphim possessed nothing else remotely human- including emotions such as pride or anger. To Michael, Sam Craig's slurs were probably nothing more than infantile babbling.

Even so, the United States and Sam Craig had rated a Seraphim. Only three nations and the UN had one of those. Everyone else had a Director. Gillette humorously imagined the President of France to be extremely pissed off by that slight.

"We bring you news of a significant development. Our Host has enjoined us to notify the various world leaders prior to its announcement at the United Nations General Assembly."

Craig stood up and walked over to the bar, a journey he had been taking earlier and earlier in the days since the advent of The Peace. Gillette sighed and looked at his feet.

"Well huzzah for me! What is it that you are going to do to my country now that neither the executive nor the legislative have any authority to accept or reject?"

"As of January first, approximately two point five months from today, the world will eliminate national currencies in favor of a single, global currency," replied Michael the Seraphim nonchalantly.

"Oh, shit!" said Gillette.

"What? Jesus! You're going to kill the banks! They make a shit ton of money from currency fluctuations and trading," laughed Craig sarcastically. "I can see a lot of my old donors jumping out of windows after you drop that bomb. Not that I need them anymore."

"Michael, why would the Host be concerned with having a single currency worldwide?" asked Gillette. "I would think that this aspect of our economic system would be unimportant to it."

"Quite the contrary, James Gillette. The multiple-currency system is highly inefficient and has the effect of wasting billions of dollars in funds that could be used more constructively. Instead, large percentages of those funds are siphoned away from where they are needed," answered the Seraphim.

"Those are called commissions, you... twat!" spat Samuel Craig, hammering back his drink. "You're going to instantly annihilate an entire industry that is a founding pillar of the global economy."

"It would seem to be an industry whose sole purpose is to line the pockets of a chosen few while offering no meaningful benefit to the general population," retorted Michael.

"Well, we have a lot of those these days," responded the President dryly.

"Not for much longer," replied the construct. It turned again to Gillette. "The introduction of the Global Credit will also assist the United Nations' implementation of the international minimum wage standard."

Craig dropped his glass.

"What! Gaaaa! No!" he sputtered. "You can't do that!"

165

"The entire, modern concept of laissez-faire capitalism is drawn upon the idea that a global economy can continuously move to find the cheapest source of labor and resources," explained Gillette, somewhat less calmly than before. "It benefits the consumer by providing the lowest cost products and services while increasing profits for the shareholders."

"Yes, but at the long term cost of reducing the overall size of the market base. Those who are producers must also be in a position to be consumers as well. This is less and less the case on your world," countered the Seraphim. "It has resulted in horrendous disparities between both people and nations. This can no longer be an acceptable condition for the long-term survival of civilization. Eventually, the economically-disparaged will destroy the plutocracy and all else as well."

"You're not aliens. You're Communists!" exclaimed a wide-eyed President Craig. He looked at Gillette. "Maybe the Russians or North Koreans have been behind this the entire time."

"Doubtful, Mr. President," said Gillette. "We know for a fact the North Koreans almost assassinated Kim because he wanted to launch his missiles at Japan. The Russians are as unhappy as we are, Sir."

"Well, we know it couldn't be the Chinese," snapped Craig.

"Do you not see, Samuel Craig? In equalizing the labor market globally, the ability to produce products and services at a local level once again becomes viable. There is no need to buy Chinese steel because it can once again be produced in Gary or Pittsburgh for the same price. Additionally, less energy is required for transport.

"More local jobs will mean less need for migration solely for the purpose of economic survival. The cost of goods will rise only by a small increment, but the community will thrive and prosper," Michael said.

"This is going to lead to decentralization and the destruction of the mega-corps," said Craig.

"Mr. President, it may not affect ownership so much as diffuse the concentration of specific industries. Stelco can still control half the world's steel production. It will do so from a hundred facilities strategically placed to service specific regions, as opposed to three massive ones."

"Correct, James Gillette," said Michael. "President Samuel Craig, the announcement will come on Friday morning at the United Nations. Your ambassador is being briefed simultaneously. We thank you for your time."

The two men waited a few minutes after the creature left before speaking. No one had any idea what earshot was for a Seraphim.

"What the Hell are you doing agreeing with that thing, Jim?" shot Craig.

"Sam," began Gillette, dropping the formalities with an old friend, "not everything that the Host has done is detrimental. They *have* stabilized the world refugee crisis, stopped the famines, and let's not forget they ended war."

"The sovereignty of the United States is at risk, for all of the so-called good they do. We need to find a way to end their grip on our nation," countered Craig. "Let's hope Harriman's teams are making progress. I don't know how much longer I can kiss that thing's ass."

***

John Harriman rang the doorbell and took a step back, looking warily over at Grace. She gave him her perfect, movie-star smile and squeezed his hand.

"Relax, they're gonna love you," she beamed.

"I'm ok," he lied. Grace always seemed to find his soft spot. First, it was her looks and her smile. The things she would say to him could knock him off balance the way no other person on Earth could.

Now, Grace had talked him into meeting the parents.

They had agreed on San Francisco as one of their three-day getaways; a promise made when they began their affair. No matter where they were in the world, every three to four weeks, the two would rendezvous for no less than three days. Ideally, they would spend the time at his farm, away from the eyes of the world. Occasionally, they would meet at her place in New York. Harriman did spend a great deal of time in the city in his de facto role as *detective in chief*. At times, schedules wouldn't permit the luxury of going home. They would rent a room in a city halfway between the two of them: once in Milan, another time in Panama City, a third in Tokyo.

167

The weekends were exhilarating, primarily because the demand of their schedules kept it fresh. In the past year, they had only physically been together for a little more than the equivalent of a month. The rest of the time was devoted to careers and the nightly call. They couldn't get enough of each other and, though the sex was incredible, what they enjoyed most was how naturally comfortable it all was. They spent most of their time immersed within each other. Cooking meals, taking long walks, or holding each other in bed while discussing life, the universe, and their place in it.

John knew that Grace was making a commitment of sorts when she asked him out to the Bay area. It couldn't be easy for Grace to take that chance. John realized if he wanted to be with her that he couldn't let her down. They met up at the airport, rented a car, gave the auto-drive her parents' address, and made their way down I-280 to Menlo Park. They made love in the back seat- the windows blacked out so passing cars wouldn't get a peek. It was a frenzied coupling, their hunger for each after weeks apart created a burning desire within them. Their circumstance and fire were so intense that they only managed to get partially undressed before she climbed onto him for release.

In the passing afterglow, as they dressed and straightened themselves, John could see that Grace was visibly excited in anticipation of seeing her parents again.

"Don't worry, John. They're gonna love you. I know it," she had assured him in the car. "You guys are going to get along so well. How can you not, since I love you all?"

Bringing them to this landing at this moment- waiting. One impatiently, the other with some trepidation, for the front door to open.

It didn't.

After a few moments and more rings, Grace checked the handle, only to find it locked.

"Maybe they're out," said John.

"Nope. The car is here," she replied. "I know where they are."

Grace bolted around the side of the house dragging John with her. She burst through the side yard gate and bounded down the flagstone pathway, rounding the corner to the backyard and the sounds of pool splashes. John followed behind Grace and came upon a stone-terraced, faux pond with a woman swimming across it. He looked up to see a silver-haired man in swimming trunks, sitting at a standard issue patio table, and staring at an old style iPad, drink in hand.

"Hey, you guys! Did you forget?" Grace said loudly with feigned indignity. "We've been ringing the bell for an hour."

"Hello, Lambchop!" said the man, standing to greet them. He was tall, John figured him at around six foot three, in good shape, and looked to be in late middle-age, probably close to seventy. He saw from which side of the family Grace had inherited her stature.

The woman touched the side of the pool and stood up to see them. John could see she was of Korean heritage and close in age to the man. She still had her looks. Good genes and some nano-work, he speculated.

"Gracie! Is it one already? I'm so sorry, honey. We lost track of time," she said. She flashed the million-dollar smile that Grace threw around so effortlessly and another piece of the puzzle fit into place. Father's frame, mother's great looks.

"Are you John?" the woman asked, climbing out of the pool and reaching for a towel. "Well I guess you have to be, don't you? Sorry we didn't get the door but it's a fantastically warm day! I wanted to get a swim in before we can't anymore."

She walked toward them with her hand extended to him. "Anyway, I knew our daughter the investigative reporter would track us down. I'm Nan and that old fart over there is Bill. Have you two had lunch yet?"

Bill Williams was hugging his daughter, exchanging greetings and smiles. Still clutching Grace, he extended his hand to John.

"Hello, John. Pleasure to meet you. William Williams at your service," he said with a light English accent. "Yes, it's true. My parents hated me and decided to burden me with the joke that would last a lifetime."

"Oh, Dad! Don't feed John that bullshit!" fired back Grace, smacking him lightly on the chest with her free hand. She looked at John. "It's an old family tradition that goes back a couple of hundred years. The firstborn son is always named William."

"I think it's a great name," said John, smiling back and shaking his hand.

"Even though we didn't have a son, we kept the tradition alive with Gracie," said Bill Williams. "That's why we named her Grace William Williams."

Still shaking her father's hand, John glanced quizzically at Grace.

"You took the hook again," she laughed. "My middle name is Evelyn. Which, by the way, is an old family name as well. On my father's side."

"Well it wouldn't be on your mother's," laughed Bill.

"My family's been here over a hundred years, you foreigner!" snapped Nan Williams, heading for the house. "Gracie, did you two eat yet?"

"No, we waited. What's for lunch?" asked Grace. "And how did you manage to keep your pool in a drought? Why aren't you two in jail?"

"Special exemption. It's part of a climate project I'm engaged in," said her father, winking. "Anyway, it's a saltwater pool. Lots of that around, too much."

Later, over lunch that consisted of a mixed salad of fruits and greens, topped with grilled chicken, and accompanied by white wine, the four got to know each other's business a little better.

Bill Williams was a climate scientist. Nancy Williams held a doctorate in physics. Both were tenured and taught just a few minutes away at Stanford. As with most academics, the classroom obligations would be set aside to devote more time to research projects. At the moment, Grace's father was immersed in a study of the changes occurring in Northern California and the Pacific Northwest.

"There's not really much of a drought left to speak of in this part of the region," he said over the glass of rare, California white. "In fact, it's getting to be too wet up here. What's left of our wine industry that wasn't decimated by a lack of rain is going to rot on the vines here in the north from too much rain."

"Are things getting better in the south? What about LA?" asked John, knowing from his intelligence reports what the response would be.

"It's still dreadful down there," replied the older man. "Los Angeles and the Southwest, in general, have lost a great deal of the population base because it can't be viably supported."

"The entertainment industry is gone," said Nan. "It's all moved up to Vancouver and Toronto. Just too expensive to try and operate when it's always ninety-five degrees Fahrenheit, and you have to truck in water to survive. LA is a ghost town compared to the way it was when we first came here. Those that could get out did and of those that couldn't, half are boxed."

"There is a pipeline project in the works that the government has announced," said Bill.

"Which government," cracked Nan dryly, "ours or the shadow government of the Host?"

"My dear, we hardly even notice them. If you didn't know better, you'd never know they were around," chastised her husband. "John, you're in government. How much has this Host negatively impacted upon what you do?"

John's cover story was that he worked for the General Accounting Office in Washington. He and Grace had agreed it sounded better than special operative and occasional assassin for the President. Grace had presented John as a mid-level bureaucrat whom she had met while on an assignment in Washington.

"Oh... well," he began, "There has been a difference in the way things get done these days. It moves at a much quicker pace. I wouldn't be surprised if your pipeline gets funded and built in half the standard time."

"I want my election back," said Nan determinedly. "They had no constitutional right to cancel the federal election. How are we supposed to get rid of that clown Craig if we can't vote him out of office? Assassinate him?"

Grace smiled pleasantly at John. He returned it.

"Mom, you've known John for less than an hour, and you're already talking politics. Please don't scare him off."

"Oh, I don't think we have to worry about that," chortled Bill Williams. He looked at John. "You must be very special, young man. Grace has brought boys for us to meet before but it's been a very long time since the last one."

Nan Williams refused to let it drop. "I don't trust them. They said that they weren't going to change the way we govern ourselves and then they cancel the election. What do they take away from us next? It's a shit show!"

"Things seem to be getting better overall. Look at our situation. We have all the funding we could ever ask for," countered her husband. "Research projects that we could never get through before are being rubber stamped within a week of their presentations."

"Mussolini made the trains run on time," snorted Nan Williams. "It doesn't mean that the Fascists were nice guys. They haven't rubber stamped *every* project, for your information. I happen to know that they killed Teshvir Nawali's proposal."

"What was his project about?" asked Harriman curiously.

171

"He's a nanotechnologist," she answered. I don't know what the actual project was, but it was dead on arrival. Grace, we see your reports from these crisis spots. How much of it is real and how much is made up? What do they keep you from showing us?"

Grace put down her fork. "Honestly, they don't interfere with us at all. What we are sending out in our podcasts is exactly what we are seeing. They seem to be dedicating their manpower and resources to the worst of the world's human crisis. Even then, the role of the Host seems to be more about throwing out a problem and then observing us while we come up with a solution. They don't fix the problem themselves or shower us with any new technology that might make things easier.

"They've never censored anything we've put out and you know we've pointed out some big screw-ups from time to time. But most of those are usually related to logistics or corruption at the local level.

"Since The Peace, I've only seen one person killed by the Host, and that was because he was caught skimming funds. Even then, they just dismissed him from the job. He came back with a gun and tried to shoot the Director that was observing the project. The Director just looked at him, and the poor idiot fell dead before he could get off a shot. No one else was killed, not in the region or the village or even the guy's family. It's like they knew he was acting out on his own and they chose to end it with him.

"Mom, I don't know if the Host is ultimately good or bad," concluded Grace, "but if they are bad, they're doing a masterful job of hiding it."

***

Philip and Campbell rounded the corner and spotted Michael Garibaldi sitting on the street bench across from City Hall. He was nondescript for a Chicagoan- Cubs ballcap and sunglasses, blue windbreaker, jeans, and Reeboks. He made no acknowledgment as they approached and sat down next to him. For all anybody knew, they were waiting for a bus.

"Greetings Janikowskis," said Garibaldi in a low tone, still looking straight ahead. "How are my fellow Sons today? I'm lookin' forward to the two of you takin' over. The demon has been exceptionally boring today. Went into the Hall about four hours ago and hasn't come out yet."

"That's pretty much how it always goes with this one," replied Philip while looking at Campbell. "From what I understand of the reports, our boy won't leave until well after six. Angela will be taking over long before that... and it's not a demon, Mike. I recall you initially claiming they were angels."

"I've changed my mind, brother Philip. We'll know who's right about that soon enough," said Mike Garibaldi rising from the bench. "Have fun, Campbell."

Campbell nodded his head as if he agreed with something his father had said. They had gone over procedures on several occasions, just the two of them, and at the Liberty meetings in the church basement. He had trained for months with the other Young Defenders. Last week, Campbell had turned eighteen and taken the oath and pledge that made him a full-fledged Son of Liberty.

This morning, Philip woke him and told him he would be missing his classes, something never before condoned or even considered. Today they would be conducting surveillance upon a Director.

"We want to understand their movement patterns. We always try to keep track of them, because one day we will move against the Host and take back our freedom from these aliens," his father had explained.

Campbell didn't feel any less free than he had before The Peace. Truth be told, the only real change in his life was that he could attend Northwestern and his family didn't have to pay for it. The government had subsidized his entire education so long as he kept his GPA over 2.75.

His father had disapproved of the subsidy. "Another step in our march to communism," grumbled Philip. Even so, Campbell noticed that his family hadn't turned the money down. Someone else would have taken it anyway so Campbell might as well use it for himself, his father had rationalized.

Campbell wasn't going to rock the boat. The Sons thought that the Host and its minions, the Directors, were a threat to the American way of life. That was good enough for him.

As they walked to City Hall, Philip had filled him in on the Director they were monitoring. There were several in the city and they each seemed to have a specific area of interest. Some were embedded with the police, others with various city departments. This one was at City Hall, presumably in the Mayor's office. That made it very relevant and its monitoring a little tricky.

173

The City Hall building itself was a decrepit, eleven-story structure that was over one hundred twenty years old, but it only took up a portion of the block. Over the years, a complex of government buildings had risen on the grounds, including a separate Mayor's office and the headquarters of the Chicago Fire Department. The monitors had to position themselves at various stations in the plaza to keep watch on all of the buildings. Today, they had positioned themselves between the Mayor's office and City Hall in the plaza facing Clark and Randolph Streets. They would then work around the plaza complex over toward Washington and LaSalle Streets before moving back to their original position.

The Sons were careful to rotate monitors so that they weren't easily discerned by anyone who might be watching. That meant relying on the reports of previous monitors to learn their quarry's movement patterns and activities. They had also gone with short shifts, partly to avoid suspicion and partly because of the practicality of people having to work.

Philip had told Campbell that this particular Director entered the building at eight in the morning and left at six in the evening. They were to be finished with their surveillance by four. There were eyes inside the buildings in the form of loyal janitors. They weren't of the Children of God but were patriots. Philip and Campbell's job was to observe the entrances to the buildings within the plaza.

"This will be a good first patrol for you," Philip had said to his son. "It's going to be pretty boring, but you'll get some experience in moving around."

The two had just moved to the next bench when the Director came out of the plaza entrance of City Hall, moving gracefully down the steps and onto the pedway toward Randolph Street.

The two monitors were taken completely by surprise.

"Oh boy!" exclaimed Philip. "C'mon, we've got to go!"

It was the first time Campbell had ever seen a Director in the flesh. He had seen videos of them, but it wasn't the same. The Director was dressed in a purple robe with a white sash at the waist. That made it look distinct enough in the City of Chicago on an October day, but what really set it off was the golden halo that floated over its head. To Campbell, the orb looked just like the saucer shapes that floated over the heads of Christ and the Apostles in the pictures scattered throughout his Bible.

"A demon's trick. The work of Satan," Michael Garibaldi would have said. A lot of the Children of God would have agreed with him.

The halo, which had been roughly half a foot over the Director's head when it left the building, now rose high into the air. Campbell figured it to be hovering about six feet over the creature. In a way, it acted as a beacon for them; they stayed half a block behind as it blended into the crowd and disappeared from view.

"Send a message to Angela that we're on the move," commanded Philip. "Give her your GPS access so that she can track us. Then catch up with me on Clark."

Campbell slowed to access his Magi-Watch and text Angela what had happened.

The party's moved. Don't know where yet. Follow me at V6T7479C to find out where the fun begins- Cam.

Campbell then sped up, made the turn onto Clark- and came to a dead stop. The street was busy with foot traffic but the beacon that had guided he and his father was nowhere to be seen. His father was missing as well.

"Hello. You seem to be following me. Is there some way I can be of assistance?" came a pleasant baritone from behind him... directly behind him.

Campbell froze. His body flushed with adrenaline, his heart raced and he wanted to run, but he couldn't move. Slowly, he turned to face the enemy, mouth dry with fear.

The Director looked like a young man, maybe in his early twenties. It had shaggy brown hair, and it was smiling serenely at Campbell. The golden halo was just a few inches above its head, now looking more like Ezekiel's wheel within a wheel, spinning in opposite directions and humming quietly.

The creature stuck out its hand, causing the young Son of Liberty to shrink back slightly.

"Hi there!" the creature said pleasantly. Campbell could only stare wide-eyed. After a moment he spoke.

"Are... are you a demon?" he asked.

"No," the Director replied. "I'm a Timothy."

"You look like a human," said Campbell, growing slightly bolder. He hadn't been struck dead, at least not yet, and he counted that as a good thing.

"It's because I am a human," said the Director.

"But you've got that thing over your head."

"Yes, the *halo* as most people call it. We call it an *interface*," replied Timothy. "It keeps me connected to Our Host and Its servants but until I chose to serve, I was once just like you. Now I'm both human… and something more as well."

The Director looked around. "I sometimes go over to that café and have an ice tea and a pastrami sandwich. They make great pastrami. Would you like to join me, Campbell Janikowski? You can ask me more questions if you like. Most people are afraid of me because of…"

Timothy pointed at himself with both hands, moving them up and down the length of his torso, acknowledging his strange appearance. Then he pointed skyward.

"…and that. I eat alone a lot."

"You have to eat?" asked Campbell. "Hey, wait! How do you know my name?" he asked, once again feeling somewhat fearful.

"Of course I have to eat," laughed Director Timothy. "We've already established I'm a human being… and Our Host told me who you were."

"How is that possible? Does the Host use magic?"

"If facial recognition software is magic, then I guess so," replied the Director. "Hey! You know what is magical? The pastrami at Eddies! C'mon."

Campbell hesitated, "I don't know. I'm kind of waiting for someone."

"Your father will be along presently," said the Director. "He's not far away. Three blocks north of here and beginning to double back for you. He should be here in twenty or thirty minutes."

The two stood silently for a moment as Campbell turned everything over in his mind.

"Cam. My friends call me Cam," said Campbell finally.

"Tim," said the Director holding out his hand in greeting.

This time, Campbell accepted it.

***

176

Rajalingham Patel sat at his desk and took a bite out of the chicken salad sandwich his wife had packed for him that day. He hated chicken salad. Probably as much because he had it for lunch three times a week as for the simple fact that her recipe was atrocious. Despite that, he very much loved his wife and didn't want to hurt her feelings with the cold, hard truth.

He had learned the trick of putting thick-cut, ruffled potato chips between the bread and the spread. It had the dual effect of heavily salting the sandwich and giving it a crispiness that the soggy bread desperately needed. It made the mess tolerable.

Raja had tried to get his colleagues to trade their own lunches with him but, after a few times through the lineup, everyone had grown wise and now politely refused. Many of them were in love with her butter chicken and would longingly ask to swap that meal with whatever surprise they might have on that day. Then, it would be Raja's turn to politely refuse to part with the delight. Mahika made one Hell of a butter chicken, and he would have savored its aroma and flavors every day if she would only grace him with it. Mahika was from a very wealthy family in Mumbai and chicken salad was her way of trying to be more... American. Raja understood her need to fit in and suffered in silence.

He would love to be able to grab a burger or perhaps order a couple of pizzas to share with the rest of the lab. It was hard to get delivery three hundred feet below the surface of the West Texas desert, and to a place only a few dozen people knew existed. It did make for an interesting commute from Lubbock though.

Thus, the daily brown-bag lunch, usually containing his beautiful, young wife's horrendous chicken salad sandwiches.

Today, as he munched on, Raja was doing what he had been doing every day for more than a year, looking at the latest tests results from his wards- Nick, Nora, and Asta.

It was a reference lost on his colleagues. After all, the *Thin Man* movies were made a century prior, and hardly anyone watched anything that wasn't virtual anymore, much less in black and white on a flat screen. Raja's grandfather had introduced him to what the old man had affectionately named *the classics*. Movies from the golden age of a Hollywood that no longer physically existed. Made and forgotten before Grandpa had even been born.

Raja grew up being spoon fed an appreciation for Bogart and Bacall, Grant and Hepburn, Gable and Crawford, Astaire and Rogers. They were all strangely delightful and so different from today. While Grandpa had fawned over *Casablanca* and *Bringing Up Baby*, Raja had fallen for *The Maltese Falcon* and *The Big Sleep*. His favorite detective series was *The Thin Man*, featuring William Powell and Myrna Loy as Nick and Nora Charles.

Bogart as Sam Spade was the tough guy whose heart was in the right place. Nick Charles was a borderline cad who drank way too much and seemed to live off his wife's money- all the while flirting with any dame who expressed an interest. Nora also enjoyed the party life and all that went with it. The couple foreswore children in favor of her Wire-Haired Airedale dog, Asta, at least in the first few movies of the series.

Raja always thought the couple deliciously decadent in their adventures, just slightly inside of both social norms and the law.

What seemed to be Nick and Nora Charles's sole redeeming factor was their ability to solve complicated murder cases. Unlike many of their screen peers, Raja found their approach was both impeccably rational and plausible to boot. Nick and Nora Charles were the reason Raja had become a forensic pathologist. It was only fitting to christen his most challenging case in their honor.

When Raja saw the data, he almost bit his tongue in the excitement. The mystery wasn't completely solved, but at least now there was a murder weapon. He had the *what*. The next question was... *how*? Still, Raja knew he needed to verify that what he was looking at was true.

"Val," he called out. A woman in the next area, who had been keenly peering at the holographic projection of a DNA sequence, jerked her head towards his office door with a start. She rose from the workstation and went to his door.

"You saw the results," she said to him from the doorway.

"Can you get Peter to run them again? We need to duplicate the test before we can break out the champagne," Raja said matter-of-factly, trying to maintain at least the veneer of control. What he really wanted to do was jump up on the table and dance.

Val's smile morphed into a full-blown, ear-to-ear grin.

"I thought you'd want that so we ran it again last hour. We've got a verified positive. File's in your queue if you want to take another look," she added.

Raja pulled up the file on his workstation and squinted at the numbers.

"Oh gods! It only took a year of our lives to find it," he moaned sarcastically.

"It might have taken another year if you hadn't had an epiphany, boss," she replied. "Looks like the first round is on you. Maybe the first three rounds. We're all really thirsty!"

"Run it one more time," requested Raja. "If it comes back positive, I'm on the horn to Smith. Then we'll party and *he* can buy all the rounds!"

***

The Director was prompt, arriving just fifteen minutes before the school bell was to ring. He came with only a government-issued driver for the SUV. His halo floated a few meters above the car, keeping pace. He had no need for any other escort.

In the previous months, when the Directors had begun to change the old ways, some warlords resisted. Sometimes it would be a sniper shot. Other times, an IED planted by the side of the road. Nothing had worked, bullets would be deflected away, and the Director always seemed to sense the presence of the explosive and avoid it altogether. Inevitably, the would-be assassin would be found dead at his vantage point. A visit later by the Director to the warlord would result in the instant death of all within his compound. No quarter was given for man, woman, or child.

It became apparent that an attempt to cause physical harm to a Director would result in the extinction of the perpetrator's entire, extended family. Quickly, the assassination attempts ceased.

Director Abdul-Khabir exited the SUV and walked to the center of the village, where it seemed the entire population had come out to greet him. Out in front of all were a few dozen children of various ages, both boys and girls. They were dressed in their best and brightest colors. A quick scan of the crowd by his interface and the Director smiled, knowing that he would not have to make any negative examples on this day. It pleased him.

"Greetings my friends! Peace be with you, Mullah Hakem. Our Host pays you the greatest of respect," Director Abdul-Khabir said, looking directly at the old man and bowing slightly. The Mullah said nothing but the Director saw the hatred in his eyes. He turned his attention to the children.

"My, don't we all look fabulous today! Are you all ready to begin a great adventure?" He paused, waiting for the loud affirmation from the collected children. Taking the hand of a boy and girl in each of his, he led the group to the newly-minted school building. The journey was only fifty meters, the children laughing, gabbing, and giggling as they fell into step.

Director Abdul-Khabir led the children through the open door and into the hallway. Though the village was small, in deference to tradition, boys and girls would be segregated into separate teaching areas. A male teacher would educate the boys, a female for the girls.

A stone-faced man waited at the classroom door on the right. "Come now, boys with me. We must begin soon," he said sternly.

No one was at the door on the left.

"I will take you in to meet your teacher," he said smiling at the girls.

The school was small but state of the art. Each child's desk doubled as a computer terminal with a heads-up display. There was no internet service yet, but the Director had been assured that the project to get it into the area villages was only a few weeks from completion.

At the head of the classroom, the teacher stood in front of her desk, smiling nervously. Abdul-Khabir smiled back reassuringly; he knew she must be very anxious on this day. Standing next to her was a girl, perhaps ten years of age and dressed brightly in red robes. She was smiling happily and holding flowers.

"Peace be with you, Director. We are honored by your presence," began the woman. "Fawzia was so excited for this day that she came to school early."

"I have a gift for you," said the little girl.

"Come, little one. On behalf of Our Host, I would be honored to accept your gift," replied the Director.

When the girl was three meters away, the interface picked up the C-4. The villagers had done a masterful job of shielding it beneath the girl's robe. The interface immediately dropped into defensive mode, a bell-shaped shield of ionic energy enveloped both it and the Director. He hesitated to kill the girl, scanning her for a detonator. There was still hope- if he could find and neutralize it no one would have to die.

"I'm sorry," said the teacher, tears running down her cheeks. He looked up to see her press her thumb down on the button in her hand.

Under the shield, Abdul-Khabir watched as the girl came apart in a fireball, her smiling head flying toward the ceiling. Disembodied arms, still holding the flowers, struck the shield chest high.

Even protected, Abdul-Khabir felt the concussion of the blast against his body. Horrified, he saw the entire room disappear in hellfire. The teacher disintegrated in the flames as her body was blown backward into the wall.

The Director turned to look at the children only to find that their bodies were on fire and being thrown about the room. Some went helter-skelter through the few windows in the room. Others were crushed by their desks, the blast concussion sending their pieces toward the walls.

In a split second it was over. The room smoldered on, small fires throughout adding to the smoke. He realized the fires were being fed by what remained of the children. In the other classroom, he could hear the screams of the boys.

The interface told him it no longer had enough power to maintain the shield. He had to get out now or he would choke to death in the smoke as soon as the shield dropped. Abdul-Khabir asked it if there was enough remaining to terminate the villagers.

The building collapsed on top of him.

This time there was no shield. The Director felt the crush of the cinderblocks as the wall fell onto his unprotected body.

Lying under the rubble, the Director knew he should be in agonizing pain, but he could feel nothing. He surmised his spinal cord had been damaged. He realized he could no longer breathe under the weight of the rubble.

Through the collapsed rubble of the wall, he could see the SUV. His driver slumped over the wheel. The Director could see a bright red stain on the right side of his head where the bullet had exited the skull.

Abdul-Khabir tried to reach out to the interface, but he could no longer feel its presence in his mind. He looked up at the sliver of blue sky peeking through the blocks pinning his head and thought to it: *Engage command thirty-six... self-destruct.*

At that moment, they should have died as they had lived-together. The interface using his implant to set off a brain aneurism that would kill him and then the internal phosphorus charge that would turn it into a shapeless clump of composites.

Nothing happened.

Abdul-Khabir heard the shouts around him and could sense the villagers climbing about the rubble. The block pinning his head was lifted, and he could make out the face of the man holding it. It was the Mullah Hakem. He was smiling.

"Go back to Hell now, demon."

The last thing the Director saw before the block crushed his skull was a villager next to the Mullah jumping excitedly, arms above his head.

"God is Great! God is Great!" the man was shouting.

In his hands, he held the interface.

Chapter Twelve

"I have to leave. I'm sorry," said John. "I don't have to go far. I can be back by tomorrow morning."

He saw Grace try to hide her disappointment from him. "Ooh! Can I tag along? Maybe something of interest to the general public?"

He cocked his head at her. "Maybe of interest, but not for your public to see. Honestly, I don't know what's up. They just told me to get to the airport asap."

That was only a half-truth. John did know that there had been a breakthrough with Nick and Nora Charles. He just didn't yet know the details.

It was one of the uncomfortable balances of their relationship. Because of who and what Grace was, there were a number of things Harriman knew that he couldn't share with her. She had grudgingly accepted this, and as a general rule, they didn't talk about work. In a gesture of thanks, from time to time he did his best to slip her a lead that wouldn't jeopardize the security of his mission.

This wasn't one of those times. Anything to do with Nick and Nora was definitely not for public consumption.

He took her in his arms, and they kissed with passion and forlorn. Parting was always painful, and this time they had barely spent a full day together. Grace spoke first.

"John, you don't have to try and kill yourself to get back here. It'll be Sunday, and I'm scheduled to fly out at six anyway. We can make up for it another time," she said, smiling wistfully.

"If I can, I'll get back. I promise. I would move the Earth itself for a few extra hours with you," he said.

"John Harriman! You are quite the romantic!" teased Grace. "Either way, it's ok. It's been a while since I've seen my folks and I don't mind spending some time with them. I'm sure they have lots to talk about… like when they're going to get some grandchildren from me."

John lustily looked her up and down.

"Tell them you're hard at work on it."

Grace laughed. "You don't know my folks well enough yet. That wouldn't phase them a bit. They'd probably supply the fertility drugs and keep track of my ovulation cycle. You aren't safe here!"

"But we aren't married. It would be scandalous for them," he joked.

———

"Married, smarried. They don't care about the conventions of the day. You're just donating a superior gene pool to their cause. If you close the door, I can probably get that donation from you in under fifteen minutes," she winked.

They kissed again, and he thought that he could be persuaded to stick around for another hour.

"Where are your parents?" he asked sheepishly.

"Probably downstairs waiting for us to make some noise," she said, showing him her annoyance at his hesitation. "Honestly, John, I'm thirty-seven years old, not seventeen. God knows they sure embarrassed the Hell out of me enough when I was a kid! Close the damn door."

"Where are you going next?" asked John, eyes closed but seeming sincerely interested.

She snuggled closer to him and draped her hand over his chest, eyes closed, taking his scent into her nostrils.

"Who knows? Kearney is already in CAR getting some backstory in place, but I'm not sure if they're going to pair us up." Grace opened her eyes to view his profile before her. She sat up on her side.

"Who cares anyway? It's always the same story. Plague, famine, war-torn, but now, crisis averted! Move along! Nothing to see here, people. Coming soon! The Promised Land, courtesy of our benevolent Host. Ugh!"

She rolled over on her back beside him in frustration. "I can see why Lucifer chose Hell. Heaven is fucking boring. I might just take a break and start a family after all."

John opened his eyes and stared at the ceiling. "Millions of people not dying or living in fear and poverty isn't such a bad thing, Gracie."

"I realize that. I just feel as if I'm assigned to cover this perpetual church social," Grace replied. "Hey! Aren't you the guy who's supposed to find a way to get rid of them?"

John looked at her. "I'm supposed to try and take away the gun they have pointed at our collective heads. That doesn't mean I don't appreciate what they would *seem* to be about. I don't buy into the pseudo-religious façade, but we aren't committing murder on a mass scale anymore. Telling people good news that brings hope for the future isn't a bad thing either. Besides, we're a long, long way from Utopia. Our world is in a heap of trouble.".

Grace leaned closer into him until their faces were almost touching.

"You know something!" she whispered. "Tell me!"

"I know that the Earth is getting hotter, the polar ice caps continue to shrink, the coastlines will all be gone in a hundred years, and we get more and more superstorms all the time."

Grace leaned back, pouting. "Everyone knows these things. Covering climate change just makes me a glorified weathergirl. From what I hear, now that the famines have been put down the next big thing on the UN's agenda is reversing climate change."

He turned his head to look at her. "Reversing global warming is going to take decades. We may not have that much time."

Grace's eyes narrowed. "What do you mean?"

"I mean that climate change has had a significant impact in one critical area: food production," said John. "We have less and less arable land because of too much or too little rain and heat."

"The droughts have been out there in plain sight for years," Grace replied. "That's nothing new. Besides, food stocks are being kept in balance with need. I see the reports."

He sat up and leaned over her. "You see the doctored reports. The truth is we have nine billion people to feed and growing, but the desalination of the oceans is killing off fish populations and the places on land where we can produce food are getting smaller and smaller. What the UN and the Host have been doing for the past year is a band aid. In ten years or less, global food production is going to collapse and then much of humanity is either going to starve or resort to cannibalism."

"How do you know this?"

"Because I've read the real reports. The Ag mega-corps don't have to release their actual numbers to the public, but they do have to give them to the UN..." he replied.

"...and they have to give them to the world's governments," finished Grace. "That means the Host knows."

"*Some* of the world's governments... and yes, the Host knows. Not sure what they're going to do about it or if they plan to do anything. Maybe culling the herd, as a friend of mine would say, is the plan. Maybe you can find out," said John. "You want a big story? There's a big story for you, but you didn't hear it from me. I can't give you any of the data directly, but if you look close enough in the right places, you can find it.

"How's that for a lead?"

Grace kissed him.

"I guess I'll put off having those kids for a while longer."

***

Philip was still trying to come to grips with his son blowing their cover.

"Dad, there was nothing to be blown," insisted his son. "Tim knew he was being watched. He says all the Directors understand that they're being watched all the time. He says the CIA watches him the most and a couple of other groups too."

Once Philip realized he had lost contact with the Director, he doubled back to find his son and try to regroup. As he rounded the corner back to Clark Street, Philip once again picked up the bobbing of the Director's halo above the foot traffic. The surveillance back on, he crossed the street and slowly approached the creature's position until he could get a clearer view. What he saw almost made his heart stop.

Sitting at a table in front of Eddie's Deli was the Director- with Campbell sitting across from it. They were each eating a sandwich and talking. The creature was very animated, making bold strokes and jabs at the air with its arms. His son looked on, Campbell's apparent fascination punctuated from time to time by the occasional grin or laugh. Then he would say something to the Director, and the entire cycle would begin again as the creature responded.

Suddenly, the Director's body noticeably stiffened. It was silent for a few seconds before rising, shaking his son's hand, and departing back toward City Hall. Then it turned and waved at *him* before disappearing around the corner. Philip's knees went weak.

"Let's go over it one more time," said Ana Maria Janikowski. "Everything that the demon told you. We need to find a way to make this look like a win before the Sons."

"I told you, mother, he's not a demon. He's human, and his name is Timothy," corrected Campbell.

"Campbell Andrew, are you stupid? Of course, it's going to present itself as normal. Do you think it is going to come to you with batwings and horns and a pitchfork tail saying, '*I am a devil from the depths of Hell! Let's grab a pastrami for lunch*'?

"The evil one will come disguised as an angel of light, halo and all," chided his mother disdainfully.

"He calls his halo an Interface. He says it's how he keeps in contact with the Host," said her son quietly, his eyes downcast.

186

"Sounds very high tech to me, maybe some kind of app or electronic device," interjected Philip. He was growing fatigued at his wife's insistence that the Host and its minions were Satanic in nature. He found them much more threatening as a race of alien invaders bent on enslaving humanity, and felt giving them a supernatural mantle clouded the real danger of the Host.

"Satan would use our familiarity with certain modern words and phrases to gain the upper hand," countered his wife. Philip shrugged at her in silent resignation. As tired as he was of her superstition, he was even more sick of arguing about it with her.

"What else did you talk about?" she asked forcefully.

"He said he had volunteered to become a Director and that the interface allows him to be in contact with the other Directors and with the Host. He can know a lot of things too, without having to study them. It's like having the internet in your head. Tim said it protects him because it can look at people or things and tell him if he's in danger. He said that the Host has always been here and that the Directors are part of the Host too. He said they're here to try and make the world better for everyone."

The young man looked up at his parents. "We talked about the Bears. He says he loves football… and baseball too. He says even though he's always connected to the Host, he's alone a lot. That's why he asked me to have lunch with him. He says people are afraid of him and stay away from him and that he understands why but that it still sucks to always eat alone. He told me some funny stories.

"Then Tim stopped talking and stood up and said he had to take care of something important," continued Campbell. "That's when he shook my hand, said it was nice to meet me, and to have lunch with him anytime. Oh! And then he waved at Dad as he was leaving."

Ana Maria gave Philip a look of disdain over his apparent incompetence. He got that a lot from her. He felt his face get hot. She turned her attention back to their son.

"Wait, you left that out before. The demon told you to come and have lunch with him again?" she asked, studying her son's face as he answered.

"Yeah, sorry about that. He did," said Campbell nonchalantly. "I get the impression he's really lonely in a lot of ways, even with all those other people in his head."

She turned to her husband. "That's the break we needed."
"What?"

Ana Maria began working out the scenario in her head. Philip could see the wheels turning as she put together a strategy for saving face with the Sons of Liberty.

"That's how we'll sell it. It was very unfortunate that our surveillance was discovered, but now we have something even better. We have an in with one of the Directors, and it wants to stay in touch!"

She continued, "Campbell is our mole. He can befriend the creature and gather intelligence about the Host and what it is, what it plans to do. More important, we can find out what its weaknesses are and exploit them in order to destroy the Host itself.

"God has blessed us! In the most backhanded of manners but all the same this is a great blessing!"

Philip was less enthusiastic. "Ana, I don't know about this at all. I mean, whatever a Director is, we all agree that it is very dangerous. This is our son we are talking about. I don't want to expose him to any potential harm."

"I don't mind," interjected his son softly.

Ana Maria ignored him and turned her face upward to her husband. Philip could see the disregard for him hidden behind the thin smile she presented. "This is a great opportunity for him. He will be doing the Lord's work. God will protect him. Perhaps you should have more faith."

Opportunity for you is more like it, thought Philip, but he kept his silence, staring at her with hard eyes. He struggled to find a way to express the anger he felt over his wife's willingness to potentially sacrifice their son, expressly to improve her standing within the Children of God.

"Let someone else become the contact," he said to her through clenched teeth.

"God chose him," she replied icily.

"I really don't mind doing it," repeated Campbell.

Ana Maria swept her hands toward her son.

"See! He wants to serve the Lord in this way! How can we deny His will?"
She went back to strategizing. "We can present the idea to the Sons after tomorrow's service. They'll see the Lord's hand in it as well."

"I will not go along with this," said Philip firmly.

"You will not only go along with it; you will present it to the leadership," she replied coldly. "Don't forget; you made this mess that I'm trying to clean up."

She had him. He looked at his son, his face anguished.

The boy smiled weakly at him. "Dad it's ok. Tim is very nice. I'll be fine."

Philip wasn't so sure.

***

Sonya sat in the reception area staring at the closed office door, waiting. On her last day in the coffin, the angel had come to her and explained that there had been a change of plans. They weren't going to Africa after all because of Wil. Now, they were going to Kansas.

After they had signed themselves out of the care of RCI, the pair walked outside to find several men in suits standing in the courtyard. Wasting no time, the men had quickly shuffled them into one of a number of black SUV's and sped away.

Sonya had been hoping to find a hotel room. Instead, she found herself at the Chicago offices of AgriBus. They had split her and Wil off from each other, something she wasn't at all happy about. Four men had brought her up to this office, where she had now been sitting in an uncomfortable, metal-frame chair for the past fifteen minutes. Although she kept her demeanor cool and collected, on the inside she was growing increasingly anxious.

The door opened, and an African-American man of solid build with graying hair stepped through it. He looked directly at her and smiled warmly.

"So, you're Sonya! I am very happy to meet you. My name is Herm Wallace. Please come inside," he said, motioning with his arm for her to go through the door.

At this point, she didn't see any other choice.

It was a boardroom. A large, long, lightly-stained wood table was at its center, surrounded by a number of plush red chairs.

"Please take a seat. I know that this has been a disruption of your intended plans and one way or another, we will have you on your way very soon," said Wallace pleasantly.

"Why am I here?" Sonya asked brusquely as she sat.

"You're here because of your boyfriend, Sonya. You're here because of Wil," replied Wallace. He didn't sit in a chair, choosing instead to lean against the table next to her, arms crossed. He towered over her.

"What have you done with him?" she demanded.

189

"What we have done is make him into a significant person within our corporation. Trust me, he is more than safe and well attended. He's preparing for the journey to Kansas. You are here with me to determine if you're going to accompany him. Do you want to go with him? After all, this isn't what you thought you would be doing, is it?"

Sonya looked at him without expression, but her eyes betrayed her annoyance with his question.

"No," she said flatly, "it isn't. I was supposed to be heading up an Ag crew in…"

"…the Central African Republic. I know," he interrupted. He was quiet for a moment, studying her intently.

"Sonya, as you progressed through your training, did you notice it became a little less focused on the operational and a bit more intense on the physical?"

Sonya was even more annoyed that Herm Wallace knew what her training inside the box had been. She continued to stare at him coolly.

"I did," she replied. "It became a lot more… martial."

His smile faded. "Why do you think that happened?"

"I assumed it was part of my physical fitness training for when I left the box," she said. "After all, Virtuality was once used primarily for education and training. I'll retain the skill sets through the muscle memory patterns that have been imprinted on my brain. So long as I am physically capable of performing the skills, I'll be able to perform them in the real world just as easily as the virtual one."

"So you *can* put more than one sentence together at a time," smirked Wallace. "You're correct, but that training isn't standard for Ag team leaders. I changed your teaching program a few months ago."

Sonya's stony face now broke into surprise. "You? How do you know me? Why'd you do that?"

"I guess you need to understand who I am," said Wallace. "You see, Sonya, I'm the chief of security for the North American division of AgriBus."

Sonya frowned, "You grow crops. Why does that need security?"

Wallace laughed. "You'd be surprised. Our business has a lot of need for security. We maintain strict control over the land we plant to make sure that nothing bad happens to it, such as sabotage from our competition. Plus, we don't just grow food. We do a lot of research and development on new food types, genetically modified organisms and the like. That area of business is the future of our entire corporation and its profitability. It's a huge target for espionage and intellectual property theft. We spend billions of dollars every year on security, and we employ thousands of people to maintain it. That's where you come in."

"You want me to be a security guard?" she asked.

"No, I want you to be a bodyguard," answered Wallace. "Specifically, I want you to be your boyfriend's bodyguard. Who better to watch over him than the woman who loves him?"

"Why does Wil need a bodyguard? He wants to be a farmer," she queried. "Who would want to hurt Wil?"

"Wil isn't a farmer; he's the architect of what is potentially a revolution in agriculture. His concept, if it works and it looks promising, is going to sweep away five thousand years of methodology almost overnight," said Herm Wallace, raising his voice for effect. "There are going to be a lot of losers when this new technology takes off, a lot of companies that will find themselves obsolete. Just think, if you're a company that makes farm implements and you suddenly find there isn't a need for implements anymore."

Sonya quickly understood. "His life is in a great deal of danger. People are going to try to kill him."

Wallace nodded. "Very likely."

She looked up at him, "Don't you already have everything you need to make the Flowerboxes without Wil? Everything has already been done in the simulations. Why do you even care what happens to him?"

"Two reasons. First, someone could kidnap Wil and get enough information out of him to be able to duplicate the technology. We've spent much time and money developing that technology through Wil and, as the intellectual property of AgriBus, it's worth trillions in production and licensing fees," explained Wallace.

"Ok, not to sound cold but why not just kill us? Then your *intellectual property* is safe."

Wallace looked her squarely in the eye. "You're right. We explored that option. Once we had the data from the simulations, Wil could have simply been the victim of an accident at RCI."

191

He uncrossed his arms and put his hands on his thighs, leaning forward.

"Which brings us to the second reason. What if your boyfriend is the next Edison? What if he is one of those people who possesses not one game changer but dozens or even hundreds of ideas; ideas that could be worth trillions of dollars to companies like AgriBus and our sister companies in other fields? Sonya, Wilson Ramirez isn't a liability to be eliminated. He's an asset to be protected at all costs!"

"So it's about money," she said.

"My dear, it's always about money," said Wallace. "It's just that, in this case, it's also about the life of your boyfriend."

Sonya sat up a little straighter in the chair. "So you want me to go out to Kansas with Wil and oversee security?"

Wallace laughed.

"Of course not! You aren't even twenty-four yet. There's no way anybody in their right mind is going to turn over a multi-million-dollar R&D operation to someone with no experience at all.

"No, I have several trusted personnel who will maintain a twenty-four-hour vigil over the test site," he continued. "You'll need to have five levels of clearance just to get in or out. We've even been able to arrange for the satellites to go dark when they pass overhead."

"So why do you need me?" she asked, a little puzzled.

"Because spies are excellent at what they do. So are assassins. Security is made to be breeched. It happens all the time. When I said you are to be his bodyguard, I meant every second of every day. You won't let him out of your sight when he is on the grounds. You'll be with him at night... in the same bed, I'm assuming. Who could ask for a better bodyguard?"

"How do you know I'm even capable of doing something like this?" she asked.

Herm Wallace leaned back and braced his hands on the edge of the table.

"You P-tested well. You're bright, quick to assess a situation for what it is. Not afraid to think outside of the box, no pun intended. You have an intense loyalty to your asset. Besides..."

Williams right fist flew off the table towards Sonya's face.

In one continuous motion, she kicked out of the chair and caught his hand with both of hers. Using his forward motion against him, Sonya pulled Wallace's hand over her shoulder as she turned her body away from the blow. Using her hip as a lever, Sonya threw the much larger man over her shoulder and face up onto the floor.

Now having the advantage, Sonya pulled back her right fist with lightning quickness and prepared to strike.

"Whoa! Whoa! Whoa!" said Wallace.

"Ok, you're hired."

***

"Nanites!" exclaimed Raja Patel.

Harriman gave him a quizzical look. "I thought you had ruled them out."

They were standing over the body of *Nora*, the woman Harriman and Ivan Ivanovich had recovered from Balkanskaya more than a year ago. She was naked and lying on a sliding, metal, morgue table extending from the large refrigeration unit. The corpse had been thoroughly autopsied. Various long incisions had been made throughout it. Her head had been shaven, and the top of the skull had been removed with a handheld circular saw, exposing the brain.

"Mr. Smith, looking for buckyballs or nanotubes or biological machines when you have no idea what their size or properties are is like looking for the proverbial needle in a haystack," said Patel defensively. "It's like looking for a golf ball in space when you have no idea what specifically you're looking for."

There was a moment of silence as Patel looked at Harriman bright-eyed, basking in the satisfaction of his accomplishment.

Harriman finally broke the silence. "Dr. Patel, I can't read your mind, and I have to report your findings to the President."

"Oh! Yes!" began Raja. "Well, how much do you understand about nanotechnology?"

"What most people know, I guess. The big use seems to be in healthcare."

"It's a huge field of study! I spent a month of constant research just getting up to speed on it," beamed Raj Patel. "There are all kinds of aspects to nanotechnology. There are biological aspects, electronic aspects, molecular assemblers, nanorobotics, mechanosynthesis, fullerenes…"

"Dr. Patel," interrupted Harriman, thrusting his hands out above Nora, palms up, as if to say: *get on with it.*

"You have to understand; it's a massive field in some ways. In others it really hasn't made the progress we thought it was going to thirty years ago," continued Patel. "It's kind of like people thinking we'd be living on the moon by the millennium. Things just got in the way, and we never made it."

"Maybe we did," said Harriman, straight-faced.

193

Raja Patel's eyes grew even larger. "Really! Oh… you're just pulling my leg aren't you?"

He moved on. "We do use simple applications of nanotech, primarily in medicine and healthcare. For example, we can design RNA sequences that will attach themselves to cancer cells and attract toxins to those specific cells. Other sequences can repair chromosomes within a cell and extend the cell's life. That's how we can give middle-aged women a facelift without using a scalpel nowadays and why people live to be one hundred."

"… And?"

"Well, we also have specific molecules that attach themselves to cholesterol cells and make them less sticky. The cholesterol cells detach from each other and arterial walls, passing out of the body as waste. It's saved millions of lives."

He paused and pointed at the corpse. "Nora suffered not one but seventeen, separate, cerebral aneurisms. Eventually, the walls of several blood vessels exploded, and she died instantly. Nick and Asta died the same way. So I started thinking… if we have nanites, that can clear arteries…"

"…then we can have nanites that will destroy arteries," finished Harriman.

"That's right, Mr. Smith!" said Raja Patel. "So, for the past six months, we have spent our time looking for the golf ball in outer space."

"I don't get it. If you knew what you were looking for, then why has it taken so long to find?" Harriman's eyes narrowed. "Why didn't you tell me about this, six months ago?"

Patel put up his hands. "Hang on. This was incredibly complicated! For one thing, nanotech manufacturers use a system of markers within the nanites, so that they can be identified and tracked. The Host didn't happen to offer us this courtesy. We had to postulate what the nanites could potentially be made of and then search for them. And we didn't tell anyone because it was just one hypothesis among many that we were investigating. We could have easily been wrong.

"So how did you find them?" asked Harriman.

"We knew the areas of failure, and we began to look for something that wouldn't typically be found in the blood or tissue. What we discovered was pretty amazing. There was a distinct, carbon-based fullerene embedded into the wall of the blood vessel in each location where an aneurism occurred. However, there was a problem."

"A problem?"

"A problem that we couldn't get past for a long time. There just weren't enough of these particular fullerenes to do the job," continued Patel. "For example, that little pill a person takes to clean out his arteries contains literally billions of nanites. We were finding thousands. Not only that but the nanite was inert. It had attached itself to the blood vessel lining, but it wasn't doing anything else. So I got thinking, what if it wasn't meant to do anything else? What if it was a beacon? That's when we figured it out."

Dr. Patel paused. Harriman assumed for dramatic effect.

"It *was* a beacon! It was being used to attract other nanites to those locations and cause the aneurisms. So I did some more research, and we came up with a general idea of what these nanites might be comprised of. Then, we started looking through all the blood and tissue samples. We kept finding random, carbon-based nanotubes. Eventually, we found seventeen, separate nanite-types, but just not enough of any one type to cause the catastrophic damage we were seeing in Nick and Nora's brain."

Harriman jumped in, "What if you didn't have enough of one type of nanite, but you did have enough of them collectively?"

Patel smiled.

"Outstanding, Mr. Smith! I have to say you made the connection long before any of us did! Of course, you had my guidance getting there. Come over here."

Dr. Patel slid the metal table back into the refrigerator, and the two men moved over to one of the workstations in the lab. Patel stood in front of the bowl-shaped 3D imaging system in and spoke.

"Samantha," he said, "please run scenario four one two."

"Running scenario four one two, Dr. Patel," replied the feminine voice of the computer. An image appeared before the men.

"So here we have our blood vessel lining. There's our embedded nanotube. When triggered, four more types of the nanites begin to clump together and form this nanomechanism. They draw energy from the body's heat and start to rotate. Here's the cool part-the nanomechanisms are drawn to the beacons and begin to bore into the vessel's wall. It keeps going until it breaks through the wall and, poof!" Raja Patel put his hands to his head and made an exploding motion. "You fall dead from an aneurism. As the body temperature cools, the nanomechanism disintegrates, and the nanites drift their separate ways!"

As the scenario's animation ended, Patel looked at Harriman seriously.

"Here's the thing, Mr. Smith. This technology is way past anything we're capable of. Maybe in another couple of decades, but no one on the planet can build a nanomechanism that bores through blood vessels… at least not that we know of."

"You said you had found seventeen nanite-types," pointed out Harriman. "Here, there are only five."

"That's because the nanites are specifically designed for the attack required. Remember, the first attack was aimed at the walls of the small intestine. Same concept- bore a hole through the wall of the upper GI tract, but using a different beacon and four new nanite types to form a slightly different nanomechanism," explained Patel. The two men began walking toward his office in the center of the lab.

"The easiest one to do is the heart attack," he said as they entered the office. "That one only uses three nanite types and a beacon to create what's known as a *utility fog*. When they throw the trigger, one of the nanites attaches itself to the beacon embedded in the arterial lining. A different nanite attaches itself to the first one and a third attaches to the second. Billions of these guys all clump together until the artery is blocked and the blood stops flowing. Boom! A massive coronary."

"Doctor, this is excellent news," said Harriman. "By knowing how the weapon works, we now have the potential to neutralize it and regain control of the situation. What's the trigger?"

Raja Patel leaned back in his chair, frowning.

"I'm afraid we don't know. I mean, we don't know *precisely*. We are assuming that the beacon attracts the other nanites through vibration. That's how we have done it in the simulation. If we carried forward that thinking out to its obvious conclusion, it would point to a radio frequency as the trigger. That's a whole other can of worms. We have been playing around with various RF and electro-magnetic frequencies but we've got bupkus."

Harriman thought for a moment. "Alright, we know what the nanites are and how to find them. Why not bypass the trigger and find a way to flush them out of our bodies? Wouldn't that neutralize the threat?"

Patel shook his head. "You have to understand; the nanites are ubiquitous. The Host probably used a seeding program to introduce them into the environment. To have so completely penetrated our bodies they have to be everywhere. I would guess if you were to take air and water samples, you would find these little buggers. If they're in the air and water, that means they're in the food chain as well. That explains why the dog died. Even if you could isolate yourself and find a way to flush them from your body, they would likely be back in sufficient quantities to kill you in a matter of days... maybe within hours."

Raja Patel leaned forward in his chair and put his arms on his desk.

"There's another problem," he said in a low tone. "Remember how I told you we had discovered seventeen types of nanites?"

"Yes."

"We've only found uses for fourteen of them. We don't know why the other three are there."

Harriman sat up straight in his chair.

"There's another weapon."

Patel nodded. "Most likely, and another beacon which we have yet to find. Hell, we may not. The only reason we found these was because we could zero in on the targeted areas. Just doing that took us six months.

"Mr. Smith, we don't even know if we've found all the nanites," he said. "I'm afraid the Host still has the upper hand for now, but it's a start."

Patel glanced at the clock on the wall behind Harriman.

"Oh, it's three o'clock already. Looks like a late lunch today," he said smiling. "Would you care to join me, Mr. Smith? I have chicken salad."

***

Grace was outside by the pool when her Magi-Watch went off. She had been expecting her story editor, Kate Nolin, to hand off Grace's next assignment in the Central African Republic. Instead, she saw the face of Net News International's Chief of Operations, Kevin Grant.

"Wow! I guess I rate a gold star today," she joked at the image.

"Hi, Grace. Can you get to somewhere private? We want to send you an upload of something we just received," replied Grant, ignoring her attempt at humor.

"Sure thing," she said moving into the house and toward her bedroom. "Send it to my pad. So, I guess something a little bigger than CAR is up."

"You'll see."

Grace closed the bedroom door and sat down at the small desk that occupied a corner of the room. On it was her private server. She looked at it and, once her identity had been verified, it opened into the space above the tablet.

Grace went to the upload. She watched it closely, in silence.

"Where did you get this?" she finally asked, skeptically.

Kevin Grant was guarded. "I can't say, Grace. We've been told it was shot about fifty kilometers south of Kandahar."

"Pretty poor quality. Probably a watch, or even an old smartphone," she replied, watching it again. "That would lend itself to authenticity if I were trying to hoax someone. Is that a halo he's holding? That's a halo!"

"That's why we haven't streamed this over the network yet. We aren't going to until we can determine if it's real," said Grant. "There's no way in Hell we're going to risk pissing off either the Afghan or U. S. governments by falling for a prank video."

"Not sure how the Host will react to this either. They may not play so nice afterward," she added.

"We can contemplate that later. Right now, we need to get you over there and recover the recording device so we can authenticate it and figure out if we've got the biggest story of the year," said Grant. "Kearney is in the CAR, but we're going to try and get him out of there to hook up with you in Kandahar... once we find him that is."

"You're sending me to Afghanistan to pick up a camera," cracked Grace.

"And to do the story... if you want it," said Grant. His face in the image grew deadly serious. "You're probably right about how the Host might react. If you think it's too much of a risk, there's no shame in backing out. I don't even know if I want to make the call on this one. It'll be your face the world will see, if and when we break this bad boy. They may not play nice with you anymore either, Grace."

"It's not every day a Director gets blown up," responded Grace. "I'd better be your first choice."

"We would only send our best. Be careful. Tara will book you a flight."

"Don't bother. I'll take care of it myself."

Grant looked surprised. "You sure? All right then. We are forwarding the information about both our network contact and the source contact. Check in when you arrive. Good hunting."

"Thanks."

Grace waited a few minutes before making the call, weighing the options in her mind fully before taking action. She decided there was no choice.

Harriman's image appeared before her.

"John, you need to get back here now. There's something you need to see."

Chapter Thirteen

"I was here with the Rangers as a second Louie back in fifteen," said Harriman over the din of the plane's engine. "It was my first posting out of West Point. Put in eighteen months here. Been back on an operation here and there since then. I sure as Hell don't miss it. The Pashtun were crazy bastards back then, too. It wouldn't surprise me if they took a run at a Director. Some things don't change, I guess."

"It never changes, not here," nodded Grace. "That's the way they want it, and it's a waste of time to try and make them into anything else. I remember when the Americans finally gave up and bugged out in twenty-two. Twenty years they were here and as soon as the last boots were off the ground, everything they had done went to shit. Taliban took the south and the Tajiks, Uzbeks, and Hazara warlords split up the rest.

"Not the first time. Alexander the Great was stopped here. So were the Brits and Russians. You can occupy this land, but you can't control it," replied Harriman. "Now comes the Host."

"Maybe this is where they get stopped," said Grace.

John Harriman looked at her. "I wouldn't bet on it."

"I'm not so sure, John. Killing off God isn't an easy thing, and the Pashtun are fanatical about their brand of Islam," she countered.

Her hunch to involve John had paid off, at the very least in speedy transport. They had been able to cut precious hours from their journey. Even so, it had still taken sixteen hours to fly directly into Kabul and another two to arrange with the local Tajik militia for a small plane to make the run to Kandahar. Their crossing the international dateline had transformed the Monday into Tuesday morning. A great deal of time had passed since the incident on the video had occurred. Grace estimated it to be as much as three or four days. She would have half expected to find Pashtun-controlled Afghanistan devoid of life had it not been for an old-fashioned phone call.

While John had wrangled the plane, Grace had taken the time to find the local NNI contact in Kabul. She was hoping for more than she got from him. The Tajiks and Pashtun had brokered an uneasy truce in the years before The Peace, but there wasn't lots of traffic or trade between them. She had wanted him to accompany them. Being a Tajik, he would have no part of it.

What he did give Grace were clothes to make her presentable to the Pashtun and the name of the villager who had first contacted him about the video. That would be Pason Mashal from Dawo, a small town roughly thirty minutes south of Kandahar heading toward the border with Pakistan. Then he gave her one final courtesy- he called Pason Mashal and arranged for a meeting at the airport in Kandahar.

Well, there's still life in Kandahar, Grace thought as she watched her contact make the call. She wondered why.

Even with a plane, the trip south through the tail end of the Hindu Kush had taken more than four hours. As the mountains subsided, the airport came into sight. Grace had a sudden thought.

"How's your Pashto?" she asked John.

"Actually, quite good," he replied in Pashto. Up to this point, they had been able to conduct their business in English. The cosmopolitan citizens of Kabul were relatively fluent as a result of two decades of the American presence. The northern tribes were so open-minded about modern amenities and contact with non-Muslims that the prudish Pashtun considered them backslidden.

"Oh. Aren't you full of surprises? I'm afraid mine's not so great. My Farsi is slightly better. My Arabic is good!" she said in Arabic, hoping to stump him.

"It's the language of Islam. We could probably use that," said John Harriman in the same tongue. "Hold on."

He contacted the airport control tower and was directed to the smaller of two airstrips. He brought the plane in smoothly, touching down and taxiing toward a small hangar. John looked over at her and smiled. Grace realized at that moment that she knew almost nothing about her lover.

The plane came to a stop in front of the hangar where three maintenance personnel waited. The couple unbuckled from their seats, popping open the plane's doors on either side. Once out of the plane, Grace rearranged the firaq partug and chador. She used to be envious of how western men could get away with western clothing. After more than a dozen years of being dropped into parts of the world that were more or less misogynous, Grace chalked it up to the job. She knew that tweaking the nose of the locals wouldn't win her any friends or get her the story she was seeking. In some places, it could get one downright dead. Kandahar was a relatively relaxed city of half a million souls by Pashtun standards. The outer villages were another story entirely.

Grace reached into the cargo area behind the seats and pulled out their gear while John went to speak with the maintenance crew. They were traveling light; Grace had a duffel bag containing a change of clothes and a travel kit. She had brought her recording suite in a metal suitcase. John's baggage was similar with the exception of him having two metal cases, one more of a long lockbox. She had a pretty good idea of its contents.

She looked up to see John finishing his conversation with the crew, who were nodding animatedly as he spoke. One pointed toward a building a few hundred yards away- the main terminal. Harriman reached into his pocket and pulled out a wad of bills; she could see they were American dollars. He handed several to one of the crew.

John returned and picked up his gear, slinging the duffel over his shoulder and grabbing a metal case in each hand. He nodded toward the building.

"Crew says that the private charter terminal is over there. They're going to fuel up the plane and find us a car. By the way, you wear it well," he said looking her up and down. Grace smiled at him. John returned it and made a sweeping motion with his hand in the direction of the building, "Shall we, my princess?"

They passed through the terminal door and into a large room ringed by offices. Grace had been to Kandahar on assignment before, but she had always used the commercial wing of the terminal. There, an array of regional carriers had boarding gates. Even though the airport was small, she had remembered that terminal to be a relatively bustling one. This area was sparse by comparison. A few men loitered in the large room; others were scattered here and there in the surrounding offices.

"I'm going to make the call," she said to John taking out her earpiece. They moved over to one of the more deserted corners of the room and she dialed the number on her Magi-Watch. As the connection was made, Grace's HUD displayed the message: *Not Image Compatible*. She wasn't surprised.

"Hello," said a disembodied voice from the watch. It was a man, speaking in Pashto.

"Pason Mashal?" inquired Grace in broken Pashto. "Peace be with you. My name is Grace Williams. Do you speak Arabic?"

"I have been waiting for you," said the voice as it switched to Arabic. Grace let out a small sigh of relief and nodded to John. "Where are you?"

"I am in the private charter area," she replied. "I would like to meet with you."

"I know where it is. Do not move. I will be there in five minutes," said the voice. The connection went dead.

Grace looked up at John. "He's coming to us."

John looked around. "I'm going to sit over there. Don't want to spook him and I can cover you from there. Back's against the wall and I have a view of the entire room. I want you to stay within ten meters, ok?"

A few minutes passed before two men entered the room, walking briskly. They stopped when they saw Grace. One, the younger of the two, stayed back as the older man, bearded and looking to be in his late forties, made his way over to her.

He stopped in front of her. "You are Grace Williams?"

She nodded respectfully.

The man didn't move, inspecting her. After a few seconds, he said, "I am Pason Mashal. Peace be with you."

"Peace be with you, Pason Mashal. It is a great honor to meet you. I have come a great distance, to look at the original video you made of the Director and the equipment you used to make it," said Grace.

Pason Mashal grinned at her showing off brown-stained teeth. "Tabaan said your people did not believe that we had killed the demon. You want to see if it's a forgery."

He fished into his coat pocket, looking down. Out of the corner of her eye, she saw John tense. She glanced at him and shook her head slightly to let him know she wasn't in danger. By this time, Pason Mashal had found the object of his search and was pulling it from his pocket. It was an old Android phone- by the looks of it, she guessed it had to be at least two decades old. She wondered how the man could even find a working battery for it.

Pason Mashal looked at the screen of the phone and with his index finger began scrolling on its face. After a few seconds, he stopped scrolling and made pressing motions. He turned the screen to face her. On it was a still image from the video.

"Here, see for yourself," he said smugly, pressing the video to life.

Grace watched as what looked to be a Director lead several children into a concrete block building. Seconds later the side windows flashed, followed by fire and smoke pouring from them.

———

Grace looked up at him. "The children died?" She already knew the answer having seen the video a dozen times.

"They died in the service of God, fighting the demon," replied Pason Mashal nonchalantly. "Now they live forever in Paradise. We should all be so blessed."

Part of the building collapsed. A man ran into the scene toward an SUV in the foreground, gun in hand, and fired a shot into the car. The perspective of the video changed as the camera began moving forward quickly. Several men started climbing onto the rubble looking for survivors, succeeding only in pulling out body parts. On the other side of the building, men were escorting children out of a doorway that had remained standing.

By now men were jumping excitedly on the rubble. One man had picked up a gold disk and was holding it over his head shouting. Grace saw an older man pick up a concrete block. It had been concealing the head of the Director. The man threw the block back down onto the head of the Director, and she saw the blood and brains as it was crushed.

The video continued as women now began entering the frame screaming and tugging at the remains of the children. Grace watched as several men pulled the lifeless body of the Director out of the rubble, tie a rope around one of its feet and begin dragging it up and down the dusty street. A small crowd formed, its members spitting on and kicking the Director's corpse. Behind the body came the man with the halo, holding it over his head with both hands.

Grace pointed to the halo. "Do you still have this?"

"The horn of the demon. Yes, it hangs next to its rotting corpse as a symbol of our victory."

"I have a friend who is very interested in seeing it up close. He also wants to force out the demons, and he would like to meet you," she probed.

"Is he the one with the money?" asked the man.

"What?" she asked, puzzled.

"Is he the one with the money?" repeated Pason Mashal. "I am here to sell the phone. I want fifty thousand American dollars… in cash. If he wishes to buy the demon's horn that will take a lot more. The fifty thousand is just for me. He will have to pay the entire village since everyone helped to kill it."

Grace motioned for John to come over. He stood up and made his way over, taking a semi-circular path so as to keep the second man in view.

"John, this is Pason Mashal," she said, stepping to the side so that the two men could stand face to face.

Harriman held out his hand. "Smith. John Smith."

The Pashtun took his hand warily. "Of course you are."

"John, he wants to sell his phone for fifty thousand dollars, cash…"

"Done," said Harriman.

Grace continued, now understanding the endgame. "The demon's horn is in Pason Mashal's village, and it is for sale as well."

Harriman continued to look unblinking at Mashal. "I have one million American dollars in cash with me. It is yours for the phone, the horn, and the demon's body."

Pason Mashal took a step backward, grinning.

"I believe that is enough to convince our village elders to part with the trophies of our triumph!" he said happily.

"I was with the Taliban fighting the American occupiers in Helmand province in fifteen," said Pason Mashal gleefully as he piloted the SUV down the highway. He looked over his shoulder at Harriman in the rear passenger seat.

"Many of my friends and family were martyred to Paradise by the infidels. I sent a lot of Americans to Hell myself back then. It was the most exciting time of my life… until last week."

"I was in Helmand and Kandahar in fifteen and sixteen. You were probably shooting at me!" exclaimed Harriman.

"So that's why you speak passable Pashto," nodded the Afghan.

"Yes, I was a Ranger. It was required for us to understand the language."

"Now, here we are twenty years later, sworn enemies yet united by our hatred of an even greater enemy," said the Taliban.

"You know the old saying," grinned Harriman.

"Yeah, yeah, yeah. That's an Arab saying. Now, *they're* crazy! Hundreds of them came here to fight. We used to send them out first," said Pason Mashal disdainfully.

It was decided that the three would take the rental with the Afghan driving. The other man, who turned out to be his oldest son, was driving the vehicle in front of them. Grace understood why. If they hit an IED or were ambushed, Pason Mashal would die along with the two of them.

occupying the front passenger seat. It had almost been a deal breaker. Pason Mashal felt having to sit beside a woman, especially an infidel, to be demeaning. Harriman stood firm on it and in the end the Afghan had chosen a minor humiliation over losing a million large. Grace figured that Pason Mashal could rub a lot of salve on his bruised pride with that kind of loot.

Mashal had made up for it by completely ignoring her existence. He had kept up a conversation with Harriman for most of the last forty minutes as they sped across the plains of Kandahar province. He had not even looked in her direction. Not that she cared, they had been prattling on in Pashto the entire time. From what she picked up, they were mostly telling each other war stories.

"A few years ago, I probably would have just killed you and taken the money for myself," continued Pason Mashal. "I would find another high bidder and do it again."

He turned to look at Harriman over his shoulder, again showing off his mouthful of brown-stained teeth.

"Maybe you should be afraid that I'll do that anyway... shoot you, hang you next to the demon, and take your money."

Harriman grinned back. "You could do that, but then the case contains not only the money but enough explosive charge to destroy both it and you as well. When I get what I want safely back to Kandahar, only then will I give you the encryption code. Kill us, and you get nothing. I will offer a word of advice to an old enemy. You need to leave your village now and not return. All of you. Take the money I am giving you and start new lives somewhere else, perhaps in Helmand. The Host will not allow this event to go unpunished. Leave now, or you will all die soon."

Pason Mashal laughed harshly. "Ha! It has been more than three days since we destroyed the demon! Do you see this Host? They are weak and soft, like the Americans... and the Russians before them! I heard about Balkanskaya and what happened there. They are lies! The Host fears us. That's why they haven't returned. We know how to kill them!"

Harriman's eyes narrowed, and his face hardened.

"Pason Mashal, I was in Balkanskaya after the Cull. It was not a lie. I saw for myself; everyone was dead."

Even with her limited Pashto, Grace could make out what Harriman had just said. She looked back at John, and he met her eyes. She saw that it was true. John had never told her, never mentioned that he had witnessed the genocide in Balkanskaya... until now.

Eventually, a dark speck appeared in the mid-afternoon sun, slowly morphing into what Grace assumed to be the village of Dawo. As they drew closer, Grace saw the body of the Director hanging from a tall post that had been driven into the plain beside the road. The villagers had hung it upside down. His robe, still belted at the waist, had fallen over his arms, exposing his naked lower body. The clothing stopped just short of covering what was left of his head. Grace could see that the Director's genitals had been cut off and shoved into his mouth. Crows were picking at the wound. They had made short work of the eyes. The fly-covered body was beginning to blacken and bloat even in the cool, late October sun. Lying on the ground below the Director's head was the halo.

Grace looked at the Director and then stared hard at Pason Mashal. Acknowledging her for the first time since they had left the airport in Kandahar, he shrugged his shoulders.

"We couldn't hang it in the village," he said seriously in Arabic. "That would be a sanitation risk."

"Stop here, I want to grab the horn, and Grace wants to take some video of the demon," commanded Harriman. Pason Mashal complied and pulled off the road several meters beyond the display as the car in front continued into the village. The three exited the SUV.

Grace went to the cargo door of the vehicle and grabbed the case containing her production suite. She snapped it open, first reaching for the paper mask and bottle of cinnamon as Harriman looked on. Grace offered Harriman another mask from her stock, but he lifted his hand in refusal, tilting his head toward the Afghan behind them. Much as he probably would have loved to accept her offer, Grace knew that Harriman didn't want to look weak in front of the other man.

Grace took her tablet from the case and turned it on. She shut the metal case and closed the cargo door. Then she walked the short distance to where the Director's corpse was hanging.

She was going to start shooting when Harriman suddenly held up his hand.
"Grace! Wait!"

She lowered the suite. Harriman took a deep breath, walked up to the Director's body and knelt, picking up the halo with both hands. He stood up and moved away in a quickstep.

207

"No one needs to know that this exists," he said to her as he expelled the air from his lungs. He took another breath. "You can have anything else, but we can't let it get out we have one of these in our possession. Agreed?"

Grace nodded her acceptance. She spent the next few minutes detailing the Director's displayed corpse. When she was finished, they got back into the SUV and headed into the village, stopping once more in front of the burned-out rubble of the school for more videography of the site. Harriman had put the halo into a burlap bag he had found in the back of the SUV and tucked it in with the baggage. Then they continued on.

Pason Mashal drove a few hundred yards further down the road and stopped in front of a well-tended house. They exited the vehicle to find a group of older men sitting in the courtyard.

Their driver strutted around the front of the car and toward the gate of the yard, motioning for the two of them to follow. They hung back as he stopped in front of the man in the center of the group and bowed in respect. A brief conversation followed at which the seated man nodded and motioned for the couple to approach.

Pason Mashal made the introductions, speaking in Arabic for Grace's benefit. "It is my honor to present to you the Mullah Hakem, mastermind of the defeat of the demon! The Mullah has heard your generous offer and had accepted it on behalf of the people of our village."

"Peace be with you, Mullah Hakem. You honor us," said Harriman as he bowed. Grace knew to remain silent for now.

"You are giving us the blessing," replied the Mullah. "We grow tired of the stench from the demon's putrid corpse. You are removing garbage from our sight, and we don't have to waste good soil to bury it. That you would bestow us with your generosity for the privilege of taking away this refuse is a further blessing upon us.".

"Mullah, my companion is a journalist from the West. She would like the opportunity to speak with the villagers about the attack on the demon. She would be taking video of their accounts. May we have your permission to do so?" asked Harriman.

The elders leaned forward to confer. After a few moments, Mullah Hakem spoke, "She has our permission. She may also speak with the women, but she is forbidden from using their images."

John looked at Grace, and she bowed before the elders, turning to leave. They heard a scream in the distance. First one, then more, accompanied by shouting and running footsteps. In the courtyard, the men began to rise, looking for the source of the commotion.

John and Grace already knew.

"I hope we don't die before I can get the chance to tell you how much in love I am with you," he said to her earnestly. "I guess I'd better do it now."

"I love you too but… why aren't we dead yet?" she wondered aloud.

They went to the SUV, Grace grabbing the production suite out of the front seat and ran toward the south edge of the village. Rounding a corner, they stopped dead in their tracks.

"This is bad," said John.

Just beyond the village was parked an Orphanum and several large, black, boxlike vehicles. Harriman had never seen those before, but he had seen what was exiting them… in Turkmenbashi. The two backed up and ducked behind an old truck.

"What the hell are those? I've never seen them before," asked Grace as she lifted the recorder to her face.

"I have. In Balkanskaya last year. They're a cleaning crew."

"What? Oh, shit!" she lowered the suite and looked at him. "When were you in Balkanskaya?"

"If we live through this, I'll tell you, but I don't like our odds at the moment. These guys with the elephant masks were using those drones floating over their heads to remove the bodies after the Cull."

"How were they doing that?"

He looked at her straight-faced.

"They were disintegrating them with what looked like lightning bolts," he said dryly. "If they came from the south, then they're probably out of Pakistan. Maybe they haven't made it to the other side of the village yet. We can get to the SUV and get out of here."

An RPG suddenly came flying toward the Orphanum from somewhere to the right of them. Ten meters from the machine, it changed direction and disappeared from their sight. A Cleaner turned in the direction that the grenade was fired from and discharged a lightning bolt from its drone.

"Ok," said Grace. "I'm convinced. Let's go."

They did their best to work themselves unnoticed over to the other side of the village. As they crept through the alleys, the truth of their predicament became apparent- he village was surrounded. When they finally strayed into the path of two Cleaners, all they could do was raise their hands in surrender. They were escorted into the village center.

Standing next to two Directors was a Seraphim, its back to them. It turned and drifted over.

"You are John Harriman," sang the creature plainly.

"Gabriel?" asked Harriman.

"Not Gabriel," corrected Grace. "The faces are slightly different. This is another one."

"You are correct, Grace Williams. We are Malak."

"I've never seen or heard of you, Malak," said Harriman.

"That is because we sit at the Left Hand of Our Host," Malak replied. "Only once before have we been sent into this world recently. In Balkanskaya."

"You're the angel of death," said Grace.

"Not of your death, Grace Williams, nor yours, John Harriman," responded the Seraphim. "You had no hand in the murder of Our Servant. For you, justice dictates you continue living."

It pointed to the growing crowd of villagers sitting and kneeling on the ground before them.

"As for them, the justice of Our Host is to end their lives. Our Host has stayed its Left Hand and delayed in exacting justice. It had contemplated terminating the lives of all the Pashtun tribes. Instead, justice is to be carried out only on these villagers, those who committed the atrocity against the Servant of Our Host."

"There are at least two hundred people here. Many of them had nothing to do with killing your Director," pleaded Grace. "Let the innocent go."

"The innocent will be spared," said Malak. "Those under the age of twelve will be taken in by Our Host and trained in our ways. They will become part of the next generation of Directors for your world. The loss of Our Servant will have been repaid tenfold. Look for yourself; there are no children here.

"Among the rest, none are innocent. The elders conspired, the men executed the conspiracy, the youth defiled the body of Our Servant...

"The women..." interrupted Grace.

210

"The women sacrificed their children. They are the most abhorrent beasts of all," retorted Malak.

"Then we may leave?" asked Harriman.

"You may live. You cannot yet leave."

Grace broke in. "You can't just kill these people. You won't be able to hide this. You're committing mass murder. It's evil."

"The evil is before you. We are eradicating it," sang Malak. "The old ways must be swept away if there is to be a fulfillment of the Promised Land for humanity."

"The world will learn of this. I'll tell them!" she snapped.

"We insist you tell the world. That is why you cannot leave," replied the construct.

"What?"

"We want the world to understand the wages of evil are death. The lesson must be taught. You are to be the instrument of its delivery, Grace Williams."

Malak turned to face the villagers.

"There is a video recording of the death of Our Servant," it said in Pashto. "Who among you has this recording? Whoever among you tells us may go free."

Several hands in the crowd pointed to Pason Mashal. He sat expressionless.

"You see? Evil is without honor. It will always put itself over all else."

Two Directors grabbed him by the arms and pulled him out of the crowd. They threw him down in front of Malak.

"You made the recording of the death of Our Servant?" asked the Seraphim.

Pason Mashal was defiant. "Yes. Soon I hope to have a recording of your death, Satan."

"You are mistaken. We are Malak. The Left Hand of Our Host. Please provide the recording device."

"Go back to Hell!"

A Director searched the man and, retrieving the phone, presented it to the Seraphim.

"Take the device, Grace Williams," it said. "You are to present this evidence of their crime against Our Host to the world. It must be shown in its entirety. Now begin recording the events about to take place."

"I won't," said Grace.

"It does not matter. We will do it for you if you like. You will still present this event to the planet. You know you must. It is inevitable."

Knowing that Malak was right, Grace lifted the suite and began recording.

A Director brought forward Mullah Hakem.

"You are the one who planned the death of Our Servant."

"I brought down the demon," spat the old man, glaring at the Seraphim.

"Then you are also responsible for the murder of your children," responded Malak.

"They are warriors of God," replied Mullah Hakem. "They have been rewarded with eternal life in Paradise."

"Then blessed is this day, for very soon you shall be joining them… but not before watching everyone else reunited with them before you. You will be the last to die."

Malak pointed to Pason Mashal. "For attempting to profit from your atrocity, you will be the first to die."

A lightning bolt from one of the drones struck Pason Mashal. His clothing caught fire, and he screamed as his skin began to blacken from the flames. He writhed uncontrollably from the pain. Another bolt struck him, and he screamed again. Cries went up from the villagers and panic swept through them as they sensed what was about to happen.

Grace lowered the recording suite and looked at Malak.

"This is an atrocity! If they must die, why not quickly as the people of Balkanskaya died?"

Malak replied, "Those humans were killing each other, Our Host chose a quick and merciful death for them. These humans killed a Servant of Our Host. In addition, they murdered their own future, their children, in the commission of their crime. This was the atrocity. For both reasons, they will die slowly and with as much pain as can be inflicted. The villagers will burn, and the village will be razed to the ground. Nothing will remain of this community and its people. It will be erased from history, except as an example of the demise of the old ways of your world. Such is the fate of any who would attack a Servant of Our Host."

Over the next several hours, Grace recorded the burning of every villager. Mullah Hakem wept as he watched his people die. At last, it was his turn.

Then began the systematic destruction of the village. Every home, the mosque, the shops, everything, was burned and bulldozed. Once flattened, Malak didn't stop there; all the rubble was crushed and dispersed throughout the plain. When they left, the only things remaining were the ruins of the collapsed school building and their SUV.

Then the Cherubim, the Directors, and Malak boarded their transports and headed south- back to Islamabad.

The two climbed into the SUV and, shell-shocked, began the trip back to Kandahar.

Fifteen minutes in, Harriman finally spoke.

"Why didn't they ask us for the halo?"

Grace perked up. "I... I don't know. Maybe they don't think it still exists. Maybe it has a self-destruct mechanism. Maybe they're using it to track our movements. Maybe they don't care that we have it. Who the Hell knows?"

Harriman nodded driving into the dusk.

"So, we're in love," said Grace.

They didn't speak again until their plane touched down in Kabul.

Chapter Fourteen

"Cubbies are looking pretty good so far," said Timothy in between bites of his sandwich. "We should go take in a game before the June swoon sets in."

Cam nodded at the suggestion as he swallowed. "Freeman's on fire right now. He's got a thirteen-game hitting streak. Might be their year."

Timothy turned sardonic. "These are the Cubs we're talking about, Cam. It's May… don't be planning any parades yet."

Cam looked up into the sky peeking between buildings and took in the sun's warmth.

"We've got God on our side this year. I can feel it."

"Really? You think God abandoned the other thirty-three teams and their fans this season?" countered the Director.

Cam cast his eyes onto the halo bobbing above his friend's head.

"Are you always connected to that thing? Don't you ever have any time to yourself?"

Timothy gave him a puzzled look. "I have time to myself right now. After all, we have lunch a couple of times a week, and I just invited you to go watch a ballgame. That's time to myself. I can probably get us a VIP box as well. After all, I know the mayor."

Cam leaned forward in his chair, putting his forearms on the table. He looked directly into Timothy's face.

"You know what I mean," he replied. "Is the Host always in your head? How does it keep you from going crazy?"

The Director looked away and pursed his lips, searching for words.

"You have to understand," he began, "it's not like there are thousands of voices in my head all talking at once. That probably would drive me crazy. It's more like I'm plugged into a computer that is continuously giving me status reports and I'm doing the same for it."

His face brightened. "It's as if there's a news stream always on in the background. When the interface runs across something it finds important, it gives me an alert. It helps me to find things I need as well. It's a massive database that I can access instantly with my mind.

"When Our Host has instructions for me, it breaks in to tell me. Same with other Directors or with the Seraphim. If they want to contact me, then the interface lets me know. Then it acts as the transmitter of both their thoughts and mine so that we can communicate with each other."

Cam was surprised. "You can talk with Gabriel?"

"Sure, although it is more like telepathy than actual talking," replied the Director. "That would look weird, imagine me just standing there talking to air."

"What about when you sleep?" asked Cam.

"When I sleep, it is always there, monitoring my wellbeing. It never sleeps, but there's a program in my implant that turns the volume down... so to speak. It's the same program that allows me to remain an individual and keep all the voices from talking at once. It's how I can still be me and not go crazy.

"The interface does a lot of other things for me as well. It keeps me updated with my environment, points out potential threats... you were one of those... and it shields me from harm," he continued.

"It couldn't protect one of you from harm," Cam said darkly. "He died, and the interface couldn't stop it."

Timothy grew wistful. "That's true, and we all felt him die. It was an awful feeling. We were touched by his sacrifice. It helped to remind others that we really are people. We've just made a commitment to serve Our Host."

Cam grew bolder. "Tim, I know you serve the Host, and I know that the Host will be able to hear what I say but... I'm scared of it. Look what it did to all those people in Afghanistan. They were burned alive, men and women alike, even some teenagers. What kind of a monster is capable of that? You can see why so many people want the Host to go away.

"Cam, those people murdered their children. They blew up their little girls in an effort to cling to the old world of hatred and ignorance. You saw the video. What kind of creatures would kill their own flesh and blood in such a manner?" asked Timothy calmly. "Those old practices of violence and pointless death must be purged from the Earth if we are to move forward as a species."

"Some people want to go back to the way it was before the Host. They say we aren't free anymore," Cam shot back.

215

"Are people starving to death anymore? That's what was happening to millions before Our Host arrived. What about the mass murder of hundreds of thousands every year through wars between nations and factions? That's what was happening before The Peace. More important, all the resources that were used to make war are now going to build schools and roads and create jobs for people. If it weren't for the changes Our Host has brought to the world, would you be able to go to Northwestern?"

The Director looked at his guest with a sharp gaze that Campbell felt was piercing his very soul. "Let's be completely rational for a moment... what innocent person has been hurt by Our Host in the past year and a half? Have you ever heard of Our Host killing anyone at random?"

"I... I don't know. I guess not. Not that we are aware of anyway."

"What about just for the fun of it?" continued Timothy. "Or simply for the sake of killing, without reason or purpose?"

Cam shrugged and shook his head sheepishly.

Timothy went on. "Our Host knows that the Children of God and the Sons of Freedom hate It and speak out against It. Have any of the members of your church suddenly disappeared? Has anyone come to take away their right to express themselves and their feelings? Has anyone come in to shut down your father's business?"

Inside, Campbell was shocked that the Host was aware of both the Children and the Sons. He did his best to hide his shock, without success. The Director's eyes gleamed knowingly as he sipped his tea. He put the cup down and smiled at his companion.

"What? You think we don't know?" said Timothy with a smirk. "The old ways will die hard, Cam, whether because of misguided religious belief, or political ideology, or money, or just plain hatred and fear. There are national governments that do everything in their power to try and subvert The Peace. For every government, there are a hundred other groups who want to do the same. Our Host is more than aware of those who want It gone. You ready?"

Open-mouthed, Campbell could only nod. The Director rose from the table and motioned for the young man to follow him. The two began to walk toward City Hall.

Cam spoke next. "If the Host knows about all of these groups conspiring against it, then why doesn't it just wipe them all out and be done with them? It obviously has no problem killing… we've seen that."

"Because talk is cheap. Lots of people talk about doing something, even something evil. In reality, very few people ever act upon it," replied the Director, eyes focused on the street before him. "It would be unethical to destroy everyone who objects. For one thing, people change, and we hold out the hope that those who hate Our Host now will eventually come to see the good It has brought to the world. Besides, these groups can't really hurt Our Host. Even those people in Afghanistan- all they succeeded in doing was killing another human being.

"Our Host has always been here, and It will remain until we have fulfilled the Promised Land. That Director was one of thousands. Think of us as individual cells of the body. One cell can die but, when it does, that doesn't affect the other cells. They keep on going, doing their jobs.".

They had reached the steps of City Hall and began to climb. Timothy stopped and turned to look directly at Cam.

"Let's say your Sons of Liberty were to succeed in killing me. No, no, hold on. Ok, I'm now dead, but you didn't hurt Our Host. I belong to Our Host, and I serve It, but I'm just Timothy- one Director out of thousands," he said. "You look for the head to cut off but there is no head. Our Host isn't like that."

"Why are you telling me this?" asked Campbell.

"Because you need to understand how Our Host is perpetual and infinite… and what would happen if you did succeed in killing me? That would have been an act of violence against Our Host. In retribution, and as a warning to others, the Left Hand would kill every man, woman, and child of the Children of God, wiping them from existence forever. Not because it wants to kill but because the only language that those who live in the past understand is death and annihilation."

Timothy's gaze intensified. "Let me put it in a way you can better relate to. Just as the Israelites had to live in the wilderness for forty years, so those who cling to the old ways of hatred and violence must either change or purge themselves before the rest of humanity can move into the Promised Land. That's a message you can take back to your people. For your sake, I hope that they choose change over death."

217

Campbell had never seen Timothy look so serious and it set a chill into him despite the warm, spring sunshine. Finally, the Director broke the tension.

"So you want to try and take in a game on Thursday? Mexico City's in town."

***

"Let me get this straight. You're going to do what and where?" asked President Samuel Craig.

"Our Host, in conjunction with the United Nations General Assembly, has decided to move ahead with elections on the North American continent within the next twelve months," repeated Michael.

Craig put up his hand. "There's that phrase again- *North American continent*. Are the Canadians and Mexicans having elections as well?"

The Seraphim had requested to meet one-on-one with the American President. Craig was trying to understand why.

"Yes," came the simple reply.

"So the United States, Canada, and Mexico are all going to have simultaneous elections on the same day?" probed Craig.

"Not exactly. The sixteen new regional governments that will make up the North American continent will be holding simultaneous elections," explained Michael, in that ingratiating, singsong-calmness Craig despised so much. Sam Craig could feel his blood begin to boil and the vein in his forehead start to throb… again. He managed a cold smile.

"What makes you think that I am going to allow you clowns to break up the greatest nation the world has ever seen? America had been a symbol of liberty and prosperity for more than two and a half centuries. Your precious Host can't just arbitrarily decide to break an entire country into pieces. We are a unified nation," he said through clenched teeth.

"That isn't quite the case, as the demographic and political models reveal," replied the Seraphim. "Our analysis has shown that there are sixteen different socio-economic and political regions upon the continent. Parts or all of nine regions occupy what is currently the United States."

"Really," Craig said sarcastically, "and just what are these regions going to be?"

The construct raised its left hand, and a projection of the continent appeared in front of the President. With its right hand, it began pointing out the new regional structures.

"As you can see, there will be North Atlantic, Eastern, and Southern Atlantic regions along the coastlines. The current Great Lakes states and Ontario will comprise another region, with the southern states to the Mississippi River making up the fifth region.

"Here are Arctic, Rocky Mountain, Plains, and Southwest Regions," it continued. "You can see that the Southwest region will take in Mexico and the two areas south of it. Finally, Northern California, Washington, and Oregon will join with British Columbia and Alaska into the Pacific Northwest region. Southern California will comprise a region with Baja California."

Michael fell silent as Craig continued to study the map. It was a long silence. Finally, Craig spoke in a low tone, doing his best to control the anger he felt.

"I know why you're doing this. As a unified nation, we pose the greatest potential threat to you. As the greatest nation on earth, only America has the power to stop the Host from world domination. If you break up the country, then you reduce the threat," he said.

"The Chinese and Russians might disagree with your assertion of the greatest nation, but to a point your assessment is correct," said Michael.

Sam Craig was caught off guard. "What? You mean you admit it?"

"As we stated, to a point you are correct. However, the threat is not to Our Host but other nations. As your history has proven, those countries with larger land mass and greater access to both natural resources and human capital have tended to dominance over their smaller neighbors. Inevitably, the larger powers will clash with each other as they attempt to extend their influence and control over resources. The usual result is war. At times, the conflict is global. By reducing the geographic size of political units, access to capital and resources is also reduced, limiting the ability to make war on others."

It continued. "Conversely, the adverse effects of warfare upon the population, as well as economic and political structures of the society, increase exponentially. The net result is that it is much more of a burden for a small nation to wage war than it is for a large one."

"Then you aren't just gerrymandering the United States," queried Craig. "You're breaking up the Russians, the Chinese, and the Indians as well?"

"In fact, the entire globe will undergo an administrative restructuring, primarily along ethnic or tribal divisions. In some instances, such as with the North American continent, the groups are based on socio-economic factors."

"I don't understand. Why would the Host care about politically restructuring the world to avert war when it has made war impossible?"

"The concern of Our Host is with the survival and advancement of your species," came the calm, singsong reply. "However, Our Host is a temporary caretaker. Its ultimate goal is to assist humanity in achieving the level of maturity required to face the challenges of the future."

"Our Host is not here to solve the problems of your world. More to act as an aid for humanity in learning how to resolve problems on its own peacefully. A major cause of global strife has been the suppression of one ethnic group by another due to the conjoining of various groups. This has been aided by the imposition of nonsensical political boundaries. Our Host will now remove these artificial constructs and return the variants of humanity to their natural boundaries. In doing so, the need for one group to dominate another for political advantage is significantly reduced," explained Michael.

Craig made the long, familiar walk over to the bar and began filling a short glass with ice. "I see… and how is this going to work logistically? There have to be close to a thousand of these tribes and ethnic groups around the world that you want to, um, liberate?"

"Not quite, Samuel Craig. The exact number of new regions will be seven hundred sixty-five."

"Aha! So that's how you plan to take away our power! You're only going to give us nine seats out of almost eight hundred," snapped Craig. "America will be at the mercy of the rest of the world! That isn't fair at all."

"If you would prefer to have one vote instead of nine, we will review your request," said Michael's chorus matter-of-factly. "However, we do not see the strategic advantage to reducing the voting strength of the North American continent by eighty-eight point nine percent."

"Hang on, now!" blustered Craig quickly. "I don't want to reduce our voting strength. I want to increase it."

The faces of Michael changed again.

"It is the intention of Our Host to give North America just such strength in the General Assembly. Each regional government will receive one representative in the GA, proportional for every ten million citizens. Those regions whose populations fail to reach the minimum requirement will be represented by a limited number of at-large representatives. Their representation will be equal to all others in the newly-created Senate, but diminished in the General Assembly."

"By this measure, North America will possess fifty-six representatives, the twenty-four regions of the former Russian Federation will possess only fourteen. China's sixty regional governments will share two hundred forty-two representatives and, as you already know from your CIA's analysis of the Chinese, they will very rarely be voting as a bloc," said Michael. "As you can see, if North America votes as a bloc, it will exert significant influence in the General Assembly. Additionally, the United Nations Executive Council will contain at least one representative from each continent."

The construct continued, "Our Host wishes to point out that should you stand for election in your native Great Lakes region, the likelihood of your successful election to the General Assembly or Senate would be close to one hundred percent. A man with your name and reputation would most assuredly become a member of the Executive Council and perhaps even Secretary General."

Craig had been sipping his drink as Michael explained the future of global politics to him. Now the President leaned up against his desk and set what was left of the bourbon on it. He pulled at his mustache and rubbed his chin, deep in thought.

He looked over at Michael in frustration. Sam Craig had made it to the top of the political mountain through his uncanny ability to read the intentions of others. Being able to pick up on the facial tics and body language of his fellow students had paid his college tuition-through weekend poker tournaments on frat row. After graduation, he had used his gift to sniff out the bluffs of his rivals... as well as their desires and needs. It had made Craig a merciless politician during elections, but a pragmatic facilitator in practice, earning him respect on both sides of the aisle. Samuel H. Craig got things done. Despite the growing, dogmatic rhetoric of the parties, he was able to walk the tightrope without falling.

He now understood why this meeting had been a one-on-one. If a human being were to have just made the statement that the Seraphim had made, he would have sworn that the fix was in. Craig was pretty sure he had just been offered at the very least a position of importance in the new world order, possibly even its leadership. Then again, if a human being had made that statement, he would have been able to study the eyes and facial features, the inflections of the voice, the mannerisms of movement to confirm his beliefs.

Now, as he leaned on his desk studying the construct Michael, he was at a loss. How does one read the body language or voice inflections of an artificial intelligence? Sam Craig decided to go fishing.

"The American people will never go for it. There'll be blood in the streets," he began. "Especially considering that one-third of the country believes that this nation has been ordained by God to lead the world. They already believe that the Book of Revelation warns against a world government, controlled by Satan through the Anti-Christ. Your Host is about to confirm all their suspicions, and on a silver platter at that."

"We agree that there will be… fallout… from some factions but our analysis indicates that the transition will be much smoother than you fear," replied Michael. "There have been active secessionist movements in both the Southwest and Pacific Northwest for decades. The Great Lakes states have much more in common with Ontario than they do with the southern or eastern states. Politically, the northeastern seaboard has more to regain as a separate region than it does remaining as marginalized states in your union."

"There's still the problem of the evangelicals- especially the God and America First folks," retorted Craig, setting the hook.

"It will be up to you to show them that the new path is, in fact, an extension of American idealism and the adoption of its political structure on a global scale. America will have delivered the Promised Land to the world."

Selling that idea was going to be very tough but the potential reward could definitely be worth making an effort. *Besides*, he thought, *what other choice do I have*? Turning to gaze out of the oval office window, Samuel Hiram Craig felt a twinge of sadness for the end of the American empire. Then again, all empires eventually fall… or are transformed.

"I'm the last American president," he said quietly.

"Or the first Secretary General of a new, united Earth," sang Michael.

***

"It took us four months to get inside it," Dr. Ali Naji said to John Harriman. "Couldn't penetrate the shell with x-rays and we were concerned that ultrasound might set off a booby trap. We finally decided to drill a small hole in the top of it and explore inside with an orthoscope."

"I see that eventually, you got it open," said Harriman as he examined the disassembled interface on the table before them.

"We did, but we had to be careful not to damage any of the components inside. There was also the ongoing concern that we were going to inadvertently engage its defensive or self-destruct mechanisms," replied the project manager. "Eventually, we were able to locate the production seam from the inside and used a micro-saw to cut it and get it open. Once we got inside, we were able to find some amazing technology!"

"Ok, so what have you got?"

Dr. Naji paused, thinking of the best way to begin.

"Well, basically it's just a drone. An incredibly sophisticated one but nevertheless, it's a drone."

He pointed at the outer casing. "These triple fans provide the lift, pitch, and yaw. The leading edge and inner wheel rotate in opposite directions and act as a gyro for balance. That's what gives it that *wheel within a wheel* look. Pretty smart."

Dr. Naji picked up the top shell and handed it to Harriman. "You see how light it is, Mr. Smith? Even with all of the components in place, it doesn't weigh much more than a kilo. One point three kilos to be exact... and that's not paint. The entire shell, including the fan blade screens, is composed of a material that is naturally golden in color."

"I remember being surprised by how light it was in my hands when I picked it up," recalled Harriman, turning the cowling over in his hands in examination. He looked up at Ali Naji. "So what's it made of?"

"We don't know, exactly."

Harriman looked up quizzically.

Dr. Naji waved his hand over the components strewn across the table. "Don't get me wrong; there's nothing before you composed of anything you couldn't find right here on Earth. The molecular structure of the shell is derived from a complex carbon. It also can draw energy from sunlight just like a solar panel. However, there's also a parallel power system that seems to be able to draw wirelessly from the electrical grid. The fuel cell is like nothing I've ever seen. It's minuscule but has been harnessed with a series of power converters. It can simultaneously operate the internal functions of the unit on micro-amps or generate thousands of volts to power the protective shielding. Don't even get me started on how that works but we think it's some kind of ionization or plasma trapped between electromagnetic fields. It's going to take years to reverse engineer all the secrets this little bastard holds."

He shrugged. "Then, there's some relatively simple stuff. The RF transmitter they use is nothing special. We decided not to try and fire it up though for fear that it might tip off the Host to our game. There's also a phosphorus packet inside the unit that looks to be part of a self-destruct component. If that had worked, we'd have a big clump of nothing. I think there wasn't enough power left in the unit to activate it. The fuel cell is completely drained. But now… we go from the mundane to the miraculous!"

Dr. Naji reached onto the table and with his gloved hand picked up a small, bland-looking cube. Harriman guessed it to be roughly an inch in size.

"Do you know what this is?" Ali Naji asked, eyelids narrowing as he held the object before Harriman. "This is the CPU, the brain of the drone. Here's the miraculous part- best as we can tell, I'm holding a God's honest DNA-based computer."

The researcher paused to let the statement sink in. Harriman considered himself up to date on much of the latest technology, but on this news, he was lost.

"I'm sorry Al, I've never heard of a DNA computer before."

"That's because we stopped seriously working on them around fifteen years ago and put our efforts into quantum computers. We haven't really gotten as far as we'd hoped on those either. At the time, DNA computers just seemed too far out for us to make them practical. Somehow, whoever created this motherfucker figured out how to get around a lot of problems that stumped our best minds- to the point that we threw in the towel."

"Theoretically, this two-centimeter cube can perform up to twenty-trillion computations at a time," he continued. "To put that into perspective, this little guy is capable of running calculations in seconds that conventional computers take hours or even days to complete. If this is what we think it is, it can perform those twenty-trillion calculations in parallel- as opposed to linearly. In other words, while a standard computer goes from one calculation to the next, this machine is doing all twenty-trillion at the same moment in time. What you see before you is the fastest and most powerful computer ever built!" exclaimed Ali Naji.

Harriman could see the fascination and awe in his eyes as he gazed at the nondescript, gray cube.

Dr. Naji set the CPU back down onto the table and looked up at Harriman. "That little cube makes everything the Host does possible. Imagine thousands of them all working in concert with each other. Artificial intelligence becomes a reality. It also gives them the ability to control practically every network system on the planet and... beyond it."

"So what are you saying, Al? Is this technology so far past us that it's extraterrestrial?" asked Harriman.

"That's just it! It's more advanced than anything we have now, but we aren't talking hundreds of years here. If anything, with some effort a lot of this technology could be had within a decade or two. Whoever is behind this just got a little bit further ahead of us. Not much further, but enough to gain an edge. The research we've been doing on their nanites would confirm that as well. We could easily be in the same place within ten to twenty years."

"Whoever, as in human beings? Another country?"

Dr. Naji nodded. "Whoever as in- definitely human. For one thing, our initial analysis of the computer has revealed the DNA molecules to be terrestrial in origin and specifically human."

"That doesn't necessarily mean we aren't dealing with an alien intelligence," countered Harriman. "It just might mean that they have used the resources most readily available to them. It would seem to me that DNA would be a nearly infinite and inexpensive resource."

"True but then you aren't taking into account the technology itself. As I said, it's only a few decades beyond us at most. Wouldn't aliens who could cross vast distances of space be at least *hundreds* of years ahead of us... or even thousands? Their technology would seem like magic!"

Ali Naji grinned. "That's not why I called you, though. Take a look at this." He turned to the desktop display behind them and waved his hand over the console. The heads up display came online. In front of them was a three-dimensional representation of one of the drone components. "This is the inner housing of one of the fan motors," said Naji. He waved over the console again, and the 3D image zoomed to what Harriman assumed must have been an almost microscopic point on the part. What he saw made him catch his breath.

"That's alphanumeric."

"It certainly is! What would the odds be of extraterrestrials using both the Roman alphabet and the Arabic numeral system?"

"It looks like a part or serial number," said Harriman. He turned to Naji, perplexed. "After all this, why would they make such a sloppy mistake?"

"Who knows? Hubris? Their confidence that the self-destruct mechanism was a hundred percent fail-safe and that this unit would burn into an unrecognizable blob? That's my hypothesis, although bear in mind it took an electron microscope to find this," said Dr. Naji. "We've cross-checked the numbers, and nothing concrete came up in the database. They weren't *that* sloppy."

"Oh," said Harriman, "so we have another dead end?"

Dr. Naji couldn't stop grinning. "No, they were just sloppy enough. We began to look at the font they used to print the serial number, and it turns out to be somewhat unique. In fact, it happens to be the same type of font used by Air Defense Corporation to code its parts."

"Holy shit! You mean to tell me that ADC is the Host?"

Ali Naji waved his hand over the console and the image disappeared. "Not exactly, Agent Smith. ADC is probably more than capable of building the drone, but there are no subsidiaries we know of that are engaged in any fuel cell research or biotechnology," he said. "They would need significant help in those areas."

Harriman frowned. "We're talking a collaborative effort here. A cabal."

"So to speak. I prefer to think of it as a team effort with some pretty heavy hitters in the lineup," replied Dr. Naji.

"Who else knows about this?" asked Harriman.

Ali Naji cocked his head over his shoulder "You and I… the kids here in the lab I've kept compartmentalized. They haven't put it all together."

"I need you to prepare a report for the President, everything we have on this to date. I need it before I leave," said Harriman.

"Already done."

Harriman gave Ali Naji a hard stare, his face showing no emotion. He saw the man suddenly become uneasy. Harriman thought he detected a shiver from the research scientist.

"I need you to remove all data from the computers and load it onto a secure, portable, memory core with an encryption code that only the two of us have. Make the code complete gobbledygook, something that can't be guessed. Put the halo and the data somewhere safe where only you can access it. I want nothing of this left in your lab's database. We no longer know who can be trusted and I'm not going to take any chances that we get hacked and whacked. Do you understand?"

Naji nodded, coming to grips with the gravity of the situation. "I'm not so sure I want to know anything about this now, Agent Smith."

"I'm not so sure I want to either," agreed John Harriman. "Kind of wish it *had* been aliens."

Chapter Fifteen

"Welcome to NNI's *Livestream Today*. Our guest is the Seraphim Gabriel, Voice of the Host. Gabriel, thank you for being here with us today."

"Thank you, Grace Williams. We are honored to be with you."

"I have to tell you, Gabriel, in all the time I have known you, I have never seen you seated. I wasn't even sure you could sit in a chair. This is an NNI exclusive." Grace laughed as she engaged the construct.

"As you can see for yourself, we are quite capable of utilizing a chair. It is rarely required, but we have chosen such a position in an effort to put you more at ease during our discussion. It would have been uncomfortable for you to stand and look up for the entire duration of the interview."

"It certainly would have! Grace laughed again and continued. "Thank you for your consideration! Gabriel, I understand that you have an important announcement to make. What is it that you wish to tell the people of Earth?"

"In conjunction with the United Nations' recent vote for global reorganization, it has been decided that English will become the universal language of your world."

"Really. What does *universal language* mean, exactly?"

"Everyone has their mother tongue. Additionally, English will become the universal language of communication. It will be taught as a second language in school so that communication between the various peoples of your world can take place without difficulty."

"I see. Why was English selected as the new method of universal communication between people? Frankly, Gabriel, if the universal language were based on the number of people speaking it, I would have assumed we would all be learning Mandarin."

"In fact, English is currently spoken by five out of ten humans on Earth. It has long been the method of communication for business. Often those who have entirely different first languages can resort to English as a common denominator. English has evolved to replace French as the primary tool for communication with respect to diplomacy. For the everyday person, English is what they hear when viewing entertainment or communicating with others via your Internet. Since almost half of the individuals in the world already speak English, logic would dictate that it is easier to teach the other half English as well than to try and educate all to another new language."

"Who decided this for us? I don't recall a UNGA vote on this subject."

"No, it was a decision made by the United Nations newly-formed Executive Council, based upon the recommendation of Our Host. The council felt that there was no need to call a General Assembly vote based upon the apparent rationale of Our Host's proposal."

"Well, Gabriel, as an artificial intelligence, I guess we should just trust that your logic is better suited for making such a monumental decision than us li'l ol' flawed humans, no matter how we might feel about it."

"We would agree with your assessment."

"Gabriel, when the Host first appeared and established The Peace, you said at the United Nations that humanity would make its own decisions. You said, here, I believe I have the exact quote: *we will not rule you, you will rule yourselves.* I've noticed over the past year that more often than not the Host is making critical decisions about the future of humanity- without too much consultation from humans. You made that promise to our world as the Voice of the Host, and I assume on its behalf. What happened to that pledge?"

"We are unclear about the intent of your question. Each and every decision that has been made about the future of your species has been arrived at democratically through the United Nations General Assembly."

"Based upon the recommendations of the Host."

"From time to time, yes."

"Then it really isn't democratic, is it?"

"Please explain your logic, Grace Williams. In matters of politics, Our Host has always deferred to the vote of both the United Nations General Assembly as well as national and local legislatures, so long as the fundamental rights of all human beings are respected in the execution of those decisions."

"I guess the Host would know all about executions. Did those national legislatures all happily agree to vote themselves out of existence?"

"They agreed to abide by the decisions made through their duly-appointed representatives at the United Nations General Assembly."

"So that decision was a democratic one?"

"Yes, it was."

"Based on the recommendation of the Host."

"Yes."

"But it really wasn't democratic because all those who are casting a vote have a gun pointed at their head, don't they?"

"No weapons are permitted within any legislature, Grace Williams."

"Yes, we all know that, Gabriel. But figuratively, we all have a gun pointed at our heads, don't we? After all, the Host possesses the power to end our lives at any moment at its discretion. If I'm one of the UN reps and I've got that gun pointed at my head, then I'm pretty much going to vote for the Host's *recommendations* too, aren't I? It doesn't matter what the actual recommendations are; I'm voting with the Host because I want to keep living."

"This is an incorrect assessment, Grace Williams. Our Host has never harmed a member of the legislature for voting against a recommendation, nor anyone else as well for expressing a contrary opinion. Every person who lives has a right to an opinion, including negative views of Our Host, without the fear of reprisal. In your personal observations as a journalist, you have shown the world the good works and lives saved from efforts attributable to those who have followed the recommendations of Our Host. There is no more war. There is no more starvation. Soon economic prosperity will be the right of all as opposed to the privilege of a few. These rights are guaranteed."

"I see. Exactly which rights have the Host granted to us?"

"The foundation of all law with respect to the rights of human beings is not derived from Our Host but from humanity itself. It can be found in the United Nations' Universal Declaration of Human Rights. All recommendations of Our Host are in fact derived from its interpretation."

"That's interesting. How does the adoption of English as a world language fall under the UN Universal Declaration of Human Rights? That would seem to be quite a unique interpretation."

"It is based upon the paragraph four wording within the preamble."

"The preamble?"

"Yes. *Whereas it is essential to promote the development of friendly relations between the nations...* A primary aspect of developing friendly relations is through improvement in communication skills. Human history has recorded numerous instances in which a mistranslation of words has resulted in negative consequences. A common language can help to reduce the misinterpretation of words and ideas and thus promote friendly relations between nations."

"Just so I don't misinterpret your words- what you are telling me is that every single recommendation of the Host is based upon the Universal Declaration of Human Rights?"

"You are correct. For example, the recent decision to implement a global minimum wage has its basis in Article Twenty-Three, paragraphs two and three; as well as Article Twenty-Five, paragraph one. Paraphrased, both establish that every person has a right to a living wage to ensure that the human dignity of their family may be maintained. Also, that every person has a right to an equal wage for equal work."

"And where is the planned breakup of nation states mentioned?"

"Article Twenty-Eight. *Everyone is entitled to a social and international order in which the rights and freedoms set forth in this Declaration can be fully realized.* A valid case may also be made within Article Fifteen, in which nationalities are upheld. Additionally, within Article Twenty-One... *guaranteeing individuals the right to participate in government.*"

"I'm not sure I understand why the current political structure was deemed by the Host to be detrimental to the democratic process?"

"The new United Nations political structure will have a bicameral legislature in which one house will be based upon political region and another based on population size. Not dividing the larger nation-states into smaller units would have meant some populations would be underrepresented in one of the legislatures and overrepresented in the other. The new system will provide equal weight to all who vote."

"Why not, say, give China more votes in one of the houses? Doesn't that achieve the same effect?"

"The electors from China might be coerced by their government to vote as a single bloc, which would reduce the impact of smaller nations with only a single vote. Grace Williams, this system has a proven record of success. It is very similar to the political structure that the European Union adopted decades ago and there has been increasing political and economic stability in the years hence."

"Well, Gabriel, it would seem that once again the Host has everything worked out for us. Would you say that the Host is committed to the full realization of the Universal Declaration of Human Rights?"

"Of course. This document was created by your species in order to establish a standard for the protection of the political, economic, and civil liberties of individual humans. It is the ideal to which your kind strives. Our Host seeks only to help humanity fulfill the promise it sees within itself."

"Why then did the Host so callously violate Article Five, which prevents torture or cruel, inhumane, and degrading punishment? Or Article Three, which establishes that all persons have a right to life?

"For that matter, the Host violated Article Ten when it elected to murder the more than two hundred individuals of the village of Dawa in Afghanistan only a few months ago. There was no trial or tribunal to judge their guilt or innocence… only their deaths. Your Host's Angel of Death violated all three of these articles when it brutally and cruelly tortured them and took the lives of men, women, and children by burning them alive."

"Simply put, Grace Williams, the United Nations Universal Declaration of Human Rights is a *human* construct. Our Host is not human."

"That's a good segue. Just *what is* the Host anyway?"

"We are of the Host. We speak for the Host."

"Yes, but what *is* the Host? Many people think that you are the angels of God. Are you?"

"Of which God do you speak? Your world has so many."

"That's not an answer, is it? That's more of a deflection. Do you know the correct one? Is there a correct one? Please tell us!"

"We have always been with you."

"What does that mean? Are you an alien race that watches over us? Are we some kind of experiment you're running? Why the Hell does the Host even care about what happens on this little planet, in the middle of nowhere?"

"It is our purpose to help guide you in your development as a species."

"Why, Gabriel? What gives the Host any right to interfere with our development? And if you have been here all the time guiding us, then why have you done such a poor job of it until now?"

"Because now is the time that humanity needs us the most, in order to survive as a species."

"You know what I know, Gabriel? I have been around the servants of the Host as much as any other person, and I know nothing about you. No one does. You want us to trust your judgment, but we don't know what you are or where you come from. We have no idea what you really want from us. For all we know, you could be raising us as cattle to be slaughtered when the moment comes. We could be an army of slaves."

"There is no more slavery."

"I disagree. We are all slaves of the Host. We live in fear for our lives because we have seen the Host murder hundreds of thousands for the sins of a few."

"It was unfortunate but necessary to facilitate such a purge as a means of establishing peace for all. Those who died had been warned of the consequences of their actions. They refused to comply, and Our Host had no choice but to initiate The Purge. For your species to survive and ultimately thrive, the old ways must be driven out."

"So really, what you're implying is that as long as we are collectively moving down the path set by the Host, there is nothing to fear. That doesn't sound like free will to me. I can't see a Promised Land, as you all love to say, without the inclusion of free will. I see slavery, a gilded slavery perhaps, but nevertheless we are slaves."

"You are dissenting at this moment, Grace Williams. You have expressed a negative opinion of Our Host, and although it is an irrational opinion, no harm has befallen you. You are free to say what you like and live as you like- so long as you do not commit an act of violence against Our Host."

233

"True but when does that all change?"

"It never will."

"You say that, but what happens when the Host suddenly decides my negative opinion constitutes an act of violence against it? Do I disappear? Do you immolate me as a warning to others who might speak out? Will you force them to watch me die in the horrible agony of fire the way I was compelled to watch your brother Malak burn alive more than two hundred human beings?"

"This will never happen. Also, Malak isn't our broth…"

"It already has happened, though, hasn't it? When the Host chose to eliminate the Army of God in Balkanskaya, it murdered almost half a million innocent men, women, and children simply for the sin of living in the wrong place. Some of those villagers in Kandahar did kill your Director last Fall- but not all of them. Your Angel of Death again killed everyone… men, women, and children."

"That is an incorrect statement. No children were punished at Dawo, only adults."

"Gabriel, there are very few human cultures that would consider a fourteen-year-old boy to be an adult. Maybe that's the problem with the Host- without being human, it can't be *humane*. There's no conception of mercy or forgiveness, only some warped, twisted sense of justice."

"If we may respond… To your first assertion, we agree, very few cultures consider fourteen-year-olds to be adults. One exception would be the Pashtun tribes of Afghanistan. The teens who were subject to the justice of Our Host were willing participants in the murder of Our Servant. Concerning your latter point, Our Host had decreed that any act of violence against It would be punished by the destruction of both the antagonists and their nation as well. By this measure, the sixty Pashtun tribes of Afghanistan and Pakistan were subject to the penalty of having their culture and descendants removed from humanity's future. Instead, Our Host stayed the punishment of an entire people and elected to punish only the perpetrators and their bloodlines. Two hundred were sacrificed so that sixty million could live. Is this not an act of mercy?"

"Then, if these people had to die, why not give them a humane end? Why make them suffer a horrific and agonizing death by fire? At least the deaths in Balkanskaya were quick. The villagers of Dawo were forced to watch their loved ones die in a most sadistic manner; with the hopelessness of knowing that they would be the next to be burned alive. Can you imagine what that does to a person's soul? I guess you aren't capable of that are you, Gabriel, since you don't have a soul yourself. You're just a machine, aren't you?"

"It is true that the intention of Our Host was for the deaths of the antagonists in Dawa to be as merciless and painful as possible- as a warning to all not to commit violence against Our Host."

"That's interesting, Gabriel, because that is exactly the same strategy used by our kind throughout history to keep our own slaves in line. I guess you've been paying attention. I'm afraid we're out of time. Thank you, Gabriel, for enlightening us a little more about the true nature of the Host. I'm Grace Williams... in need of a shower."

Red Kearney was incredulous. "What the Hell was that all about? Jesus! I'm all for sticking it to the man but Gracie, c'mon! You're gonna get us fired."

"We will be asking for NNI to do just that," glowered one of the UN handlers assigned to the construct. "You had no right to attack Gabriel in such a mean-spirited manner. There was no journalistic objectivism at all. This was obviously a hatch..."

"There will be no such retribution on our part," interrupted the Seraphim. "John Kearney, have no fear for your livelihood. Grace Williams is within her rights.

"It is our wish to converse with Grace Williams privately. We respectfully request all others to please leave the room."

Along with Red Kearney were the outraged handler and three other assistants. Rebuffed and red-faced, the handler and his entourage picked up their belongings and exited the studio. Kearney hesitated, looking for a sign from Grace. She ignored him, continuing to fix her stare at some point in front of her.

"Please do not be concerned, John Kearney. We assure you that no harm will come to Grace Williams," spoke Gabriel. Taking a final look at his partner, Red turned and left the studio, closing the door behind him.

For a few seconds, there was dead silence. Grace looked up, head turning slowly to face the construct. "It doesn't matter."

"What doesn't matter?"

"Your kindnesses," she replied. "You could be heralding the second coming of Christ and I would still despise you for what you did to me."

"You went to Dawa looking for a story. Our Host gave you a story for the ages."

Grace grimaced.

"That's a devil's bargain."

"Although we are not human, we do understand your sadness and frustration. What you witnessed was horrific, but Our Host needed an impartial observer to stand witness to the punishment of the aggressors. There had to be a testament to your world. For your sacrifice, Our Host will always be in your debt."

"I don't want to be owed a debt. I want to stop seeing their faces. I want to stop hearing the screams." Grace shuddered. "I've seen people die, lots of people, but I have never seen anything as heinous as what I saw that day in Dawa. I know what some of them were and they deserved to die... but not all of them. Not in such a brutal and inhumane way. For that, I can never forgive your Host."

"Is it not better to treat an infection as opposed to allowing it to grow and risk the death of the patient?"

Grace glowered at the Seraphim. "You can't compare human lives to gangrene! It isn't the same."

"It is exactly the same from the perspective of Our Host. Nine billion humans reside on this planet. The actions of a few hundred cannot be allowed to fester into thousands or millions. The survival of your species is at risk. There is too much at stake to allow a few to take focus and resources away from what is important."

"Ok, I get that but why not just kill them and be done with it? Why make some sick show of it?" asked Grace.

"You already know the answer, Grace Williams, having spent much of your life documenting the worst that humanity is capable of. There will always be those who take advantage, those who will put themselves over all others. There will always be monsters," answered Gabriel. "Unfortunately, the only effective deterrent is fear of death. For some, even that isn't enough to stop them. So the threat that their death will be as slow and painful as possible keeps the monsters among your kind at bay."

"I'm not so sure anymore that you aren't the monsters."

"Grace Williams, you know that Our Host is here to save humankind, not to destroy it," sang Gabriel's ever-changing faces. "It is an unfortunate fact that some will never learn to respect life. It is our obligation to the long term future of your species to cull them."

"We've muddled through before and not needed your help, bad guys and all," Grace retorted. "There have been many dark ages in our history. Why is this moment in time so special as to require your so called guidance? Why not just leave us alone to figure it out for ourselves again? I would think that would make us both better and stronger."

"Two great dangers are converging that threaten the existence of your species. The first is changes in the Earth's climate; with weather patterns that will reduce global land mass and with it arable land. These changes have also had a devastating impact on aquatic life through desalination of the oceans. By our estimate, within seventy years your planet will have lost its polar ice caps, and with them much of its current coastlines, yet more than half of the remaining land will become a desert. There are regions currently inhabited by billions of humans that will become untenable to life."

Gabriel continued, "For decades, many of your leaders have known the truth but lacked the will or ability to work together for change. Others have denied that a crisis even exists. Their inaction has led humanity toward a precipice. Even so, a small population of your species could survive this event and continue. However, there is an even graver and more immediate threat that will bring about the downfall of Man and his eventual extinction."

"John told me. We're going to run out of food."

"Within seven to ten years, agricultural production across the globe will collapse," affirmed Gabriel. "Base food-chain species such as plankton are close to extinction. With their demise, ninety-percent of aquatic species will disappear as well. Combine this with unpredictable weather, extreme droughts in some regions, too much rain in others and global food production becomes unstable. Our models predict a reduction in global food stocks of more than seventy-percent."

"People... entire nations, will starve," said Grace. "The have-nots will go to war against the haves for what is left."

"We are afraid *the haves,* as you put it, will not have much to take, but your conclusion is correct," said Gabriel. "Nations will choose war for resources over famine. Within the first year, four billion humans will die. As nation states disintegrate, mass migrations will roam the planet, consuming everything in their path. When there is nothing left to consume, humans will consume each other."

"It will be the end of civilization."

"It will be a mass extinction event, unprecedented in your planet's history. It will be the end of everything.

"It is for this reason that Our Host has returned. Trillions in credits will need to be invested to affect the changes to climate and agriculture that will bring about the redemption of humanity. The current, global, socio-political structure is ill-suited for the task ahead. A restructuring had to take place for the war ahead."

"War?"

"Against extinction."

Grace frowned. "I don't understand. I mean, you've said before that the Host is here to save us from ourselves. Why didn't you mention any of this while we were live-streaming? Why keep the real danger hidden from the public?"

"Simply put, to prevent panic and chaos. Our Host maintains control over the worst elements of humanity through fear of death. What if death was certain and close at hand?"

Grace thought for a moment. Finally, she spoke, "Everything you say is logical and rational. I understand how dire the situation is, but your Host has a soullessness in how it goes about its business, and I'm afraid of it. I don't trust the Host. I will never be able to forgive the Host for Dawa. When this war is over, I will fight for you to leave us to ourselves."

"There will be a day when the presence of Our Host will no longer be required. On that day, the Seraphim, the Orphanum, the Directors, and the Cherubim will leave humanity to continue its evolution without assistance. On the last day, Our Host will reveal Itself and depart. In the meantime, there is something we wish to show you. Something wonderful."

***

238

Wil stared into the blackness that was the ceiling above him, unable to sleep. It was the bed- he had spent more than two years of his life sleeping in a metal coffin eighteen hours a day. The softness of the queen-size mattress felt wrong to him. He could hear Sonya next to him, snoring lightly. Wil smiled in the knowledge that she wasn't having any problems with sleep. Sonya never did.

In a way, the blackness was comforting to him. It reminded him of the box just after they closed the lid and before the worlds of Virtuality took hold. Wil liked to pretend it was a blackboard and he would fill it with the ideas that inhabited his mind.

Tonight was different; he was just plain restless. His Virtuwatch told him that it was one twenty-five. That meant he had another five and a half hours before breakfast. Still another hour before his shift began. Wil sighed.

"Lights, night, dim," he whispered into the watch. The room brightened to a soft red glow, giving Wil just enough light to make out the features in the bedroom. Gently, so as not to wake Sonya, Wil slid out of their bed and quietly into his clothes. Padding lightly through the small living room, he reached the door to the corridor and cracked it open. He could see that the hallway was also bathed in red. With a final command to extinguish the room lights, Wil went into the corridor, closing the door quietly behind him.

Wil had never been on a submarine, not even in Virtuality, but the red lighting of the hallway made him feel as if he was. Windows would have been welcomed, even simulated ones. He made a mental note to speak with the design team about it. Windows weren't practical thirty feet below ground but here he was- in the middle of the Kansas prairie- and he couldn't even enjoy the moon and stars from his bedroom. It made him feel like he was still boxed. Wil decided to head topside.

Standing in the elevator, he knew that whoever was on station security would have seen him and be monitoring his whereabouts. He hoped it was Adam. He would at least give Wil a chance to enjoy the night air. Some of them were just bastards- they would call the patrol to intercept him right away. Even worse, some of them would wake Sonya, and he felt awful that they would take away the rest of her night. Unlike him, once she was up, Sonya could never manage to get back to sleep again. Wil decided to be quick about it. He would be outside on the deck for a few minutes, and after some fresh air, he would go back to bed and sleep like a baby.

Not that Wil didn't both understand and agree with the placement of the farm's living quarters underground. Given the brutal summer heat, the propensity for high winds, and the occasional tornado, it made a tremendous amount of sense for both the safety of personnel and energy savings. The underground was a constant temperature, much like a cave. In the summer, it would be a refreshing respite from the near triple digit numbers above ground. In the winter, a little extra energy redirected gave it a cocoon-like warmth against the bitter Kansas winter. He and Sonya had just experienced their first one of those and Wil secretly hoped it would be their last.

Exiting the elevator and stepping into the garage, a late spring heat slapped Wil in the face. The concrete structure had yet to fully cool, even five hours after nightfall. Tapping into the insect-repellant screen on the Virtuwatch, Wil made his way through the small door beside the massive steel doors of the garage and walked onto the tarmac outside. Out in the open, the light breeze was much cooler, and he slowly drew the fresh air into his lungs.

Looking up, Wil viewed a sight that he could never have known in Chicago. Winding before him across the black sky ran a white river composed of billions of stars- the Milky Way. He thought it was the most spectacular thing in all of God's Creation. Wil stood in the middle of the tarmac; head tilted back in wondrous awe. He was so absorbed that it took him a few minutes to notice that he wasn't alone. A figure was silhouetted against one of the Flowerboxes in the starlight. Security had been alerted before he had even reached the surface. His spirits drooped, and he waited as the figure approached in the faint light.

"Hi," came a woman's voice. It wasn't security after all. The figure materialized into Mickey Haines, one of the tech supervisors.

"Hi, Mickey," greeted Wil. "I thought I was the only vampire around here."

She laughed. "More of a werewolf myself. I came out here to howl at the moon. To my surprise, there isn't one."

Mickey Haines was about as opposite from Sonya as one could get. Sonya was short in stature, with long brown hair, and who filled out a powerful, well-built body now that she was out of the box. Mickey Haines was a tall, wiry, pageboy brunette who looked as though she should be running marathons. Wil guessed Mickey was probably only a few inches shorter than he was, maybe around five-feet, ten-inches. She wore glasses, unusual these days but, to Wil, it made her look intelligent. He noticed that she didn't carry any of the implants that he and the others from the box had. She was probably straight out of college, maybe a year or two older than him. She came up next to him and smiled.

"They told me you were one for wandering the grounds at night. Me, too… I guess we just pick different times to do it. Still, it's nice to see you outside of the control room. I imagine you do have other interests." Mickey was close enough that he could smell her perfume. He guessed it must be laced with pheromones because he suddenly had trouble concentrating on anything but her.

Wil took a step back and pointed up at the night sky. "I have to admit I love the stars. I could look at them all night. The breeze is pretty nice too. It's nice to feel a real wind on my face again."

"Oh, that's right. You're a Virtual… or you were," she said haltingly.

"It's true. Sonya and I both were," he replied. "I got the idea for the Flowerbox in there. It's a great tool when used as it was meant to be. Unfortunately, too many use it the wrong way."

"Sonya, your bodyguard… wife?" she pried.

"Not my wife. Girlfriend is an apt description… and yes, bodyguard. One of many, too many. Kind of drives me crazy after a while. There's always a guard on duty. Sometimes I just want to be alone."

Mickey's smile faded. "Oh, um, I'm sorry! I didn't mean to bother you. I'll be on my way."

"No, please stay. I didn't mean it like that. It's always security that I'm surrounded by. I wasn't referring to you. It's just they never leave me alone. To be honest, they'll probably be out here after me in a minute or two." Wil didn't want to hurt this woman's feelings, even if he did want to be alone. "Here, let me show you the best way to take in the show."

Wil sat down on the tarmac, lay on his back, and put his hands behind his head. "Ground's a little hard, but the view is tremendous!"

Mickey Haines didn't hesitate. She dropped down next to him, mimicking his improvised pillow, and leaving a small space between them.

"Oh my!" she whispered.

"Yeah, that's how I get too. The universe is so unfathomably vast, and here we are just blown away by the view of a single spiral galaxy-- one of billions. Kind of makes you feel insignificant."

"I wouldn't say that if I were you," she replied, continuing to gaze at the sight above her.

"Huh?" Wil turned his head to look at her, puzzled.

"Wil Ramirez, you are very significant. Everybody knows that. You're the mind that conceived this place; you did all of the beta testing. You made it happen, and we all know what ESCAPE means for the future of agriculture. You're a genius!" Mickey exclaimed brightly. "I'm just thrilled to be able to say I got to work with you."

Wil grinned and shook his head, "I'm not a genius. I'm just someone who had an idea. Lots of people helped to make it real."

"Yeah but what an idea... and it works! Three harvests already without a hitch! The Company says you're its greatest living asset," said Mickey. "You can write your ticket, Wil. Anything you want it can be yours. Anything... or anyone."

For Wil, it became uncomfortably quiet as Mickey Haines looked longingly at him, waiting for the next move.

"What's up, Mickey? Better not be my boyfriend." Sonya's face and torso broke into their view, towering over them.

"Oh, um... hi Sonya," stammered Mickey. "Wil was just showing me the stars."

"So long as he wasn't showing you anything else."

Wil grinned up at Sonya. "Hi honey, I'm sorry they woke you to come get me."

"From the looks of things, I'll bet you are," she snapped. She turned to the other woman. "You know, Mickey, when Wil was in the box, he couldn't stay away from those threesome sex programs. He just loved getting two girls on him at once. Then he would make me, and the other girl do each other while he watched. Maybe he's decided to try one on for real. Whadaya think? You game, girl?"

Mickey Haines sat up, a look of terror on her face.

"I really should be getting to bed. I've got the early shift. Goodnight."

Wil lifted himself into a reclining position on one elbow as he and Sonya watched the other woman run for the garage. As the door closed behind her, Sonya lightly kicked Wil.

"Hey! I think you scared the shit out of her, by the way."

She bent down over him, frowning. "You woke me up leaving our apartment. I called Adam and told him not to worry, that I'd be up to get you. I thought I'd come out to be with you and look what I found you doing!"

Wil reached up and pulled his girlfriend down to him.

"Watching the stars."

"Wil, goddammit! That bitch was making a play for you!"

"I know."

"You know?"

"Yeah… but I wasn't going to let anything happen."

Sonya was now lying beside Wil. She leaned forward, pouting slightly. "You know, if you want her, I'm not going to stop you. It's not like we're married or anything."

"Maybe we should be. That might get you to stop me. After all, I do love you. When are you going to admit you love me, too? After I screw Mickey Haines?"

Sonya's eyes narrowed. "I do love you, you sonofabitch, but that doesn't mean I'm not going to keep you safe. There's something I don't like about that woman. Something not right."

Wil laughed. "Yeah, like she wants to fuck me. Sonya, I just proposed to you. Will you marry me?"

"Yes."

He stood up and reached to help her up as well. "In that case, let's get out of the sight of these cameras and get home. You aren't going back to sleep anytime soon. Might as well make the best of it!"

He kissed her, and they walked back towards the garage arm in arm.

"You know, if you really want a threesome with her, I would go along with it," said Sonya coyly.

"Stop it! I don't want to have a threesome with Mickey Haines."

"Maybe I do," smiled Sonya.

"Jeez, Sonya! Can we wait until after we're married for the kinky sex?"

***

Philip bent to take the leash off of Virginia; they had stopped on the sidewalk a few hundred feet before his house so that she could have a chance to run to the front door. It wasn't much, but it at least gave his girl an opportunity to get a quick sprint in for exercise purposes. The dog sat waiting for his command, twitching in anticipation of what was to come.

Philip unsnapped the leash. "Ok, 'Ginnie, go home!" Virginia was off in a flash toward the front door, making low growls all the way. He smiled, imagining that, in her mind, she must be on some dusty, Aussie ranch, bringing in the cattle. Sometimes he thought they might both be happier back in Iowa.

The dog made it to the front porch of the house within seconds, sat and looked at Philip, waiting for him to catch up. Philip ambled up the steps and opened the storm door. Virginia stood up and snorted excitedly as he reached for the front entrance doorknob. When he cracked it open, Virginia did something unusual; she burst past him and pushed the door open, barking loud and low.

"We must have guests," he surmised, closing the door behind him. He could smell the fresh coffee. Coffee at this hour either meant dinner or visitors. Philip couldn't detect any other odors that might betray a meal being prepared.

The barking stopped as Virginia ran into the kitchen. Philip could hear muffled voices, including that of Ana Maria, and a couple of male voices. One was Pastor Gregson, laughing and greeting Virginia as an old friend. The other voice was distinctively familiar, but he still couldn't recognize it as a fellow CHOG. He decided to follow the dog and solve the mystery.

When he did make it into the kitchen a few seconds later, Philip was taken by surprise. Sitting at the table next to his wife was Representative Elvis Ansen- United States Congressman and a leading voice in the God and America First faction of the party, smiling easily as Ana Maria gushed over him. In two other chairs sat Pastor Gregson and a woman that Philip didn't know or recognize as famous in the manner the congressman was.

The group's attention had been focused on the dog as she had been slipping between everyone's collective legs beneath the table; now all eyes turned to Philip as he entered fully into the room.

The men rose to greet him. Elvis Ansen stuck out his hand in the most engaging way. Philip accepted it blindly.

"Hi! Elvis Ansen. You must be Mr. Janikowski," said Ansen smoothly as he pumped Philip's hand. "Ana Maria has been telling me all about you."

I'll bet, thought Philip derisively.

"Philip. It is an honor to meet you, Congressman Ansen," he said. Philip truly was honored. Elvis Ansen wasn't his district representative. He wasn't even an Illinois representative; Ansen was from Tennessee, and he was a very prominent member of Congress. Philip looked at Pastor Gregson. "Hello, Pastor. Who's your friend?"

"I'm a friend of the Congressman. Jennifer Harling," said the woman, rising to greet him. Philip saw that she was almost as tall as he was and had a very firm handshake.

"Nice to meet you,' replied Philip politely. Everyone returned to their respective chairs as Philip slid into the closest empty one. Ana Maria poured him a coffee from the carafe in the center of the table. Philip admired how she could keep up appearances; affecting the disposition of subservient spouse to outsiders.

"Dear Congressman Ansen and Ms. Harling are very interested in your adventures with the demon Timothy as part of the Sons of Liberty," she began.

Philip laughed. "It's not me so much. Director Timothy seems to have become friends with Ca...." He drifted off into silence, noticing the intent stares of those at the table.

"That's right, Brother Janikowski," chimed in Pastor Gregson. "As you know, the Sons have been passing on our intelligence gathering to our allies within the government. In particular, that information has been going to the God and America First faction of the party."

Philip remained silent.

Congressman Ansen picked up the baton. "Philip, I have a very influential presence in the GAF, as you may be aware. Ms. Harling here is with the Secret Service but is also loyal to the GAF. She has been keeping tabs on the events taking place inside the White House over the past year and has been coordinating intelligence reports from loyal units around the country."

"Congressman, I support the GAF," replied Philip tentatively, "and I am flattered you enjoy our reports. It's not every day that the leader of the GAF *and* a member of the Secret Service pays a visit to our home. In fact, this is a first. I assume there is a reason why?"

"There is," replied Agent Harling. "For the most part, the Directors pretty much keep to themselves in their interactions with normal people. Every once in a while, we will hear a report of friendships being taken up between Directors and Normals. The other examples of this are not usually with the Normal being a true believer in our Lord and Savior Jesus Christ. In fact, most of the time, Directors seem to choose atheists… or groups of children… to interact with."

Elvis Ansen jumped in. "Now, finally we catch a break; Director Timothy has developed a personal relationship with your son, and it seems to be, if not with the blessing of at least without interference from the Host."

"Alright, Timothy and Campbell are… friends. Campbell has been very forthcoming on providing information about the Host and the Directors. He has done his part. He is a true Son of Liberty and a faithful member of the Children of God," said Philip.

"It's true; Campbell has been most helpful, and we trust him completely. I think you may misunderstand our intentions," responded the Congressman. His face grew serious as he leaned in to speak. "This *friendship* between your son and the demon has presented us with an opportunity to end the occupation and restore America to its rightful place: as a Christian nation, leading the world and preparing for the Kingdom of Heaven."

Philip grew stone-faced, suspecting what was to come next.

"Husband, they've developed a weapon," said Ana Maria, putting her hand over his. "They want Campbell to deliver the weapon."

Philip stared darkly at their guests. "Yeah? What kind of a weapon would that be? We've already seen what happens when one Director dies. What kind of weapon stops an enemy no one can see or locate? What kind of weapon is so effective that you would be willing to risk killing four hundred million people; of which my children, *our children,* would be a part… or maybe their just counting on only getting my son killed when it all goes to shit?"

"Philip!" cried Ana Maria pulling back, embarrassed by his vulgarity.

"Brother Janokowski, please!" said Pastor Gregson, making a calming motion with his hands; as if to hold back Philip's anger from the others. "You know I have supported and lifted you up in the past with both the Children and the Sons. No one wants to see any harm come to Campbell. Just listen to what they have to say."

Congressman Ansen jumped in, "Philip, it's true that no one wants to see anyone hurt, especially your son. But the cards have been played just as was predicted in the Revelation; the Evil One has shown his hand. Our great nation is to be dismantled, and the one-world government of the Antichrist is upon us! Agent Harling will confirm with you that, just as was predicted, President Craig has fallen under the spell of the whore of Babylon. He is no longer with us and works with the Antichrist for a reward of gold and power. Sam Craig can no longer be trusted, and we have to take up the Lord's cause for ourselves. We have been caught up in the war between Heaven and Hell… just as prophesized. Our time is at hand; God has compelled us all to choose a side. Which side will you choose, Brother Philip?"

The room grew quiet except for the noise of the oven fan. Philip took a sip from his coffee cup and nodded.

"Smart people, a lot smarter than any of us, believe that we don't need to see the Host or even know where it is to destroy it," began Harling. "We know this from what has been learned through Campbell and others. These people believe that the Host isn't a single individual, but functions as a collective hive mind."

"Hive mind?" asked Philip. "You mean like bees?"

"Yes. The hierarchy of the Seraphim, Orphanum, and Directors…. and the warrior Cherubim who destroyed that village are all connected through various interfaces. The Archangels and Orphanum are machines and were constructed with the interface. The Cherubim could be either organic or machine, but we know there is a connection of some sort because they have to use it to operate the weapons that float above them. The Directors, though, we know them to be human. Your son's Director Timothy confirmed that he had been surgically altered with an implant that allows him to be in communication with the entire Host network."

The agent went on, "Our people have created a virus that will disrupt this connection between these different units of the Host. The virus will use the Host's own wireless network, traveling simultaneously to each unit and cutting them off from being able to communicate with the others…"

"… or their halos," said Congressman Ansen, taking up the explanation. "Cutting them off from the Host means they are no longer able to carry out its orders. Cutting them off from their halos and interface weapons renders them harmless. We can then destroy them one-by-one without fear of reprisal. We can rid our world of Satan's servants and take back our nation's freedom!"

247

Ana Maria reached out to take Philip's hand. "We are soldiers of the Lord God and his Son, Jesus Christ. It is our obligation to do His bidding and fight Satan's minions. If we die in His name and are saved, a reward of eternal life and happiness awaits us in Heaven."

Philip wasn't yet convinced. "You mentioned that the Host is organized like a beehive. Every hive has a queen. Maybe a queen that controls the ability to do to America what they did to those Muslims when all this started? So we cut off the worker bees; that doesn't mean we all still won't die at the hand of the Host."

"That is a valid point, Philip, but when all the drones are dead, the queen becomes powerless. She has to start over and rebuild the hive," countered Ansen. "Once the virus is uploaded into its network, the Host… Satan… will become just as disoriented and powerless as his demons. He will have no choice but to crawl back into Hell for another thousand years as the Bible reveals to us."

"We will be helping to fulfill prophecy. All glory is to God!" said his wife, lifting her hands and face heavenward, eyes closed in ecstasy. The heads at the table swiveled to watch her momentarily.

"If you have this virus already, why not just upload it to the Host? Why do you need us…Campbell?" asked Philip, continuing to look at Ana Maria.

The Secret Service agent frowned. "It's not that easy. In fact, we've tried a few times but failed. The Host has built in a number of guards against just such an attack from a wireless transmission. We think our best opportunity for success is through physically introducing the virus into a Director. We've created an organic package that contains the virus within its DNA sequence. Once inside the body of the Director, the virus will begin to replicate and seek out the Director's interface implant. At that point, it will transmit itself to the interface and every other interface in the entire network."

"Then it will proceed to scramble their brains," smiled Congressman Ansen.

"So what you really need is for someone to deliver your… package. That's where our son comes in."

Jennifer Harling nodded. "Yes, we need to have your son get the package inside the body of Director Timothy. It has been refined into a gel capsule containing millions of viral units. Your son says that Timothy has a penchant for hot tea. The easiest way would be to dissolve the capsule into the tea."

Elvis Ansen presented a bright-eyed smile. "The virus, we call it *Babel*. I find it fitting that the Devil's corruption of Our Lord's angelic hierarchy so as to confuse the ignorant will end with God's confusion of Satan's evil nation; just as He did at Babylon so long ago!"

"Philip, it is important that we have your blessing to proceed with the plan. Do you wish us to pray with you for the Lord's guidance?" asked Pastor Gregson. All eyes now turned to Philip.

Philip sat quietly for a few moments; head bowed in silent thought. He looked up.

"Would you like to meet our son?" he asked quietly.

Ana-Maria jumped out of her chair and, moving to the kitchen's entrance, called out loudly up the stairs beyond.

"Campbell! Come downstairs, please! There are some people here who want to meet you."

Philip heard his son's stirrings in his room and quiet descent of the stairs. His mother hugged him as Campbell entered the kitchen.

To Jennifer Harling, he looked much younger than the nineteen years reported to her. He was blonde with a close-cropped cut, tall but slight of frame and clean-shaven; she wasn't sure this man-child was capable of even growing a beard. The young man looked at the group wide-eyed and a little bit fearfully. Harling felt a twinge of guilt for the danger she was sending Campbell into. She knew he probably wouldn't live through the mission. She rose with Representative Ansen to greet the boy.

Ana Maria turned to the group, her arm still draped around Campbell's waist, "My love, I want you to meet Congressman Ansen and Agent Harling. They are here because of you. Something wonderful is about to happen! God has anointed you to be the point of His divine spear in the war against Satan!"

Chapter Sixteen

With no technician allowed off the complex for the duration of the year-long trial, the Company had provided various forms of entertainment for their diversion. Among these was a bank of Vrtuality interface units installed within the recreational area.

Wil and Sonya had decided to utilize them for a day trip to the Smokey Mountains in Tennessee. It was, in fact, a compromise; Sonya had wanted to climb one of the Rockies in Wyoming, but Wil knew that unless he cheated his virtual skill settings, he would not be able to keep up. Since they had a standing rule to enter the box only as themselves, Sonya had graciously but grudgingly accepted a hike along the Appalachian Trail to the Chimneytops. Her only insistence was to take the long way- along the Road Prong River Trail to the Chimneytop Trail and up the mile-high mountain's backside.

Wil found the hike challenging but by no means impossible. They took in the dank coolness of the forest floor along the river- the sun fighting to peek through the tree canopy and light their way. Eventually, they reached the incline trail, and the temperature began to climb in conjunction with the humidity levels. After a few hours hiking, they had arrived at the end of the trail, resting momentarily at the foot of the highest capstone before continuing the climb along naked rock face to the summit.

Sonya was the first to make it; reaching out her hand to give Wil some help. Together in the warm breeze, the two held hands and stood, looking out over the green carpet of the Sugarlands Valley from the rooftop of the Smokies.

"I've never seen anything like it. It's marvelous!" declared Wil.

"Me neither. Sure beats the hell out of flat, hot, dry Kansas," agreed Sonya. She looked up at Wil. "Come here, you."

The couple embraced and held a deep kiss for as long as they could. Laughing, Sonya broke away from Wil and reaching into her backpack, pulled out a large blanket. From the size of it, Wil could tell that Sonya must have fudged the program; there should have been no way for something that size to fit into such a tiny space.

"Hey! What do you have in mind?" he asked with mock wariness.

"What do you think?" she replied, spreading the blanket onto the rock. "Give me your sleeping bag. It's not every day we're on top of a mountain. I want to make the most of it."

Wil smiled as he unshouldered his pack. "We can't do that. I mean, we're on top of a mountain in the middle of the day… and it's rock- which is hard."

Sonya stopped and gave him a look of disbelief. "Wilson Ramirez, who are you going to embarrass? The mosquitoes? And don't worry big boy, I'll do all the work if you like. You can lay quietly on the nice, soft sleeping bag, so you don't bruise. Now get over here and let's see if we can get something else as hard as this rock."

Wil found he had no choice but to happily comply.

"Do you miss it," she asked him later, "being in the box?"

He squeezed her tighter and smiled. "Some things, I do."

She punched him. "I don't mean the sex. You can get the same in the real world. I mean, do you miss *it*?"

Wil stayed quiet for a moment.

"I don't miss having to be in it all the time. I think the real world and what we are trying to do is obviously much more rewarding than anything the box can offer. On the other hand, I do miss what it could let me do with my mind. To be able to take the ideas in my head and turn them into something that I can see and feel and tinker with. I miss that a lot."

"I think the real world is so much better when you have a reason to be in it," nodded Sonya. "Even so, sometimes reality can be downright boring."

He looked at her. "Well, that's pretty obvious for a thrill junkie like you! Maybe you should think about doing something other than babysit me. Something that makes you feel like you're doing what you want with your life."

Sonya gave him an anxious look. "I can't do that. For one thing, I don't want to be without you. For another, what about ESCAPE?"

"I don't think I'll be needed much longer for the Flowerboxes," Wil replied. "Once we prove that it is a viable system, it becomes a cookie cutter for the engineers and Ag specialists. We won't be needing money with the royalties I'll get from the licensing fees and production.

"That means I can follow you around and be your bodyguard!" he reasoned. "Besides, I want to work on some other things that I can't get out of my head. What do you want to do?"

"I don't know. Maybe the space program. I hear that they're going to revive it. Or the marine exploration project. That would be interesting."

"Wow!" he said, "reach for the sky- literally! Well, if that's what you want, why not apply for a position with one of those programs? We might have some influence to pull a few strings if the Flowerboxes are a winner. Whatever you decide, understand this; you were there for me when I needed you. Now it's my turn to be there for you."

They finished the day trip hiking back down the mountain under a canvas of brilliant reds and oranges, courtesy of the setting sun.

"It's been like this all week," said Blake to Wil. "The readings are showing that we're within optimal parameters."

"So why then is everything dying?" pondered Wil. "What have the Caretaker samples been like?"

"They check out fine," replied Kyung. "We've gone through the light and heat settings, water fertilizer mix ratios, soil, and plant biotics. You name it, and we've looked at it."

Blake spoke up, "Maybe it's blight."

Kyung shook her head. "I'm not so sure. Maybe across one crop strain or even within one unit, but we have what is becoming a catastrophic failure taking shape throughout the entire planting and in every unit. That's a system issue."

The two looked up from the readout monitor and turned to stare at Wil. He shrugged his shoulders.

"Could be blight, but I have to admit I'm leaning toward Ky on this at the moment. There might be a flaw in the system."

Blake was persistent. "Ok but I think we should at least double check the plant samples for something biological just the same. We've had three successful harvests. Why would the system suddenly develop a glitch?"

"Catastrophic systems failure and loss of the entire crop cycle is *not* a glitch. Maybe there was always fatal flaw hidden in ESCAPE that simply didn't show itself until now," responded Kyung.

"When was the last time a human being went in and took samples from the units?" asked Wil.

"Not since the second cycle. There wasn't a need to. The Caretakers have been operating without incident since we worked the bugs out in the shakedown," answered Blake.

"That's what I thought. Maybe it's time we had a look for ourselves. I'm going to ask the SD to authorize a couple of crews to suit up and go into the units for sample collection."

"Whoa! There are one hundred units with five floors each! That's the whole point of having the Caretaker 'bots. Doing it by hand will take forever. The crops will be dead before we can finish," protested Blake.

"I realize that. I don't think we need to have complete coverage at this point. Whatever the problem is will show up throughout the units. Let's say two crews, collecting from five units each. That will give us a ten percent sample size of the entire facility," said Wil. "Get Mickey Haines to oversee the crews. That's her area of expertise."

"Ok, what are we looking for?" asked Kyung.

"Anything and everything," replied Wil. "Mixture ratios, temperature settings, O2 and CO2 levels, invasive fungi, bacteria, viruses. These GMO's are just as experimental as the Flowerboxes are. Maybe something's gone wrong within their DNA to cause them to fail."

"I guess we had better dust off the lab, then. It sounds like the techs are gonna get their hands dirty if we aren't going to trust the Caretakers anymore," said Kyung.

"I never said we shouldn't trust the Caretakers. What we need to do is verify their results," countered Wil. "We'll do the initial evaluations, but I'm going to request that the SD forward an identical set of samples to Kansas City as well."

Blake grinned. "You're going to ask White to potentially cut his own throat and let AgriBus know that their baby is going into the shitter? Good luck!"

Wil kept a straight face. "That's what the site director is supposed to do in these situations. Getting on this now and getting some outside assistance may be just what is needed to find the problem and fix it. Then the boss is going to look pretty smart to the company. Might even get a promotion."

"What about Director Allison?" asked Kyung, referring to the onsite representative of the Host. "When do we let her in on all this?"

"Ky, for all we know the Host is *already* in on this," said Blake sarcastically. The three exchanged looks of consternation.

Wil broke the silence, "Tell Haines to pick her crews and get them ready. I'll go see White."

Half an hour later, Wil was in his apartment laying out the situation to his future wife.

"You realize the implication of this," said Sonya.

"I do. If the test samples match those of the Caretakers, we have a biological problem. Something is either attacking the crops, or they are failing from a genetic defect. If the testing is out of whack with the results of the Caretakers we have a major software failure," he added..

"There's a third possibility," offered Sonya, "and that's sabotage."

Wil gave her a puzzled look.

"Oh, Wil! I love you, but you're so goddamn naïve! Did it ever occur to you that not everyone in this world wants ESCAPE to work?"

"Why wouldn't they? It's going to make food cheaper and more plentiful."

Sonya threw up her hands. "Exactly! AgriBus stands to make trillions from this project, but that also means others are going to *lose* trillions. They're going to lose control of food production and distribution. There's a lot of money and power at stake here, Wil. Why do you think security at this complex is so tight? Why do you think everything going on here is being kept secret? Why do you think someone's watching you twenty-four seven? If a spy were to discredit the project or steal the operational plans for this place… or take you… then they gain, and AgriBus loses."

Wil took in Sonya's words. "Ok, if that's the case then who can we trust?" he asked. "I need to collect the samples myself, without anyone else knowing about it. Then we need to get them off to Kansas City."

Sonya thought for a minute. "Does it matter when you collect the samples?"

"Not really."

"I'm going to put in a call to Mr. Wallace. Maybe he can have the security schedule changed so that we can get Rand Morris and myself on the board overnight. Then you could come and go as you please, so long as you stayed away from the perimeter walls. We could use a private comlink and tell you when it's clear to move from building to building. That way you can get the samples and data you need."

"Is Morris ok?" asked Wil.

"I trust him as much as anyone. Besides, we've sparred together in workouts. If there is trouble, I can take him," replied his bodyguard with a smile. "How much time do we have to make this happen?"

"The crop degradation is beginning to accelerate. Maybe a week before we experience a significant loss of production and two before complete failure."

Sonya nodded. "Then we'd better get our asses in gear. I'll contact Herm Wallace today. Tomorrow's Friday and we get the shift schedules for the coming week. How much time to analyze?"

"Some things I can do myself," answered Wil. "Light and heat readings, feed mixtures, are all easy enough to read. The biological and genetic stuff requires fairly detailed lab analysis."

"Three days then, it's probably the best we can do," said Sonya. "I'm sorry we'll be cutting it so close, Wil, but if it is sabotage then losing the crop is just collateral damage. We'll still be able to prove it wasn't a problem with the Flowerboxes."

Wil gave Sonya an anxious look. "What if it's not sabotage?"

The Sunday shifts were set up on the eights- the morning shift began at eight o'clock, second shift at four, and third at midnight. Security contained the greatest number of personnel within the compound, working in tandem with automated sentinels to physically patrol the grounds. All was in conjunction with state of the art heat and motion sensors to track movement. Crews were trained on all related tasks and equipment and were rotated on a regular basis to maintain sharp skill sets and prevent the onset of complacency.

Three eight-person crews were assigned to ESCAPE. Half the crew worked with three sentinels each to maintain perimeter wall security and clear gate traffic in and out. A fifth guard and four interior sentinels patrolled the grounds in between the buildings. Two guards monitored the sensor and camera systems from the control board in the primary security office. An eighth member was the *float*, giving the other crewmembers a day off or filling in if someone became ill. Sonya was the supervisor of Gold Crew, answering to the site's Chief of Security, Ilya Bankhead.

Provided the Company's the habit of changing up routines, no one gave the schedule a second thought that Gold Crew had the midnight to eight shift when it posted Friday. As the crew leader, Sonya could set the individual assignments- putting herself and her second, Rand Morris, on the board for Sunday and Wednesday. Together with Wil, they made their arrangements and did their best to keep themselves occupied through a long, tense weekend.

"We aren't seeing anything outside of the operational parameters," said Lise Marin. She was the chief lab tech who had conducted the testing of the samples. "I'm sorry, Wil, but these samples are indicating that there could be a biological cause for the crop failure."

Wil frowned as the group reviewed the data on the desktop HUD. He looked at Mickey Haines. "You're sure there was nothing unusual when you went into the units?"

"Not at all. All the temp and light readings were normal. So were the atmospheric readings. We took plant, soil, and food mix samples from each floor of ten arbitrary units just as you specified," she replied. "I oversaw the collection and labeling myself."

Site Director White had been leaning on a desk with crossed arms, listening to the exchange between his techs as they analyzed their results. Now he spoke up, "I know that we wanted to handle this internally, but I don't think we have any choice but to get KC in here for a complete top-to-bottom sweep of the system."

Blake Whitman protested. "Alan, please wait until the biological tests come back in the morning. Let's show them that we could find the problem on our own. If you call in Kansas City, our careers are effectively over."

"Look Blake… everyone, I know that you are all young and a little bit apprehensive about appearances, but I've been around a lot longer than all of you, and I can assure you AgriBus doesn't operate that way," replied the SD. "R and D projects run into problems and failures all the time. No one loses their head over something like this. Besides, we've had some success with ESCAPE. No matter what happens here, you will all have a shiny diamond to show off on your resumes as you move through the Company."

"That may be true, sir, but it isn't the same as bringing a project of this size from cradle to completion. We'll be superstars if we can pull it off, you too, sir," retorted Blake.

"I have an obligation to the Company first," responded White. He looked at the long faces around him. "Ok, I'll wait for the bio-tests to come back in the morning but if they're clean, Kansas City is in here on Tuesday."

Wil left the gathering with an uneasy feeling. He agreed with SD White that Kansas City should get new people in to go through the entire project and find the cause of the impending failure. What he wasn't sure about was the validity of the on-site testing itself. Originally, he had thought about finding a way to get his own test samples into the hands of the Kansas City lab. That could be as early as Tuesday if everything went according to plan. Still, who could he trust, even inside the highest levels of the Company itself? If Sonya was right and there were outside forces willing to pay millions of credits to disrupt or discredit the ESCAPE project, then where would that stop? Who couldn't be bought?

At that moment, Wil made a decision.

He took the stairwell down a level and walked into the office of Director Allison, closing the door behind him. The representative of the Host was sitting behind a desk in her robe, halo floating roughly a foot above her head. She was motionless; her eyes were open, but her arms were folded and resting on the desktop. From Wil's point of view, she looked to be in a trance.

As he closed the door, the humanity returned to her face as the Director turned her head and smiled at him pleasantly. "Hello, Wilson. Our Host has been expecting you."

"It has?" Wil had met the Director formally and ran into her a few times in the corridors or control rooms, but they had never engaged in a conversation with each other. It seemed to him that Allison pretty much kept to herself, coordinating with SD White and spending most of her time in this office. He was never really sure if the *all-knowing* mantle that the Directors portrayed was actual fact or merely an act meant to impress and awe Normals. Like most people, the Directors creeped him out, and Wil had been reluctant to engage with her one-on-one. Still, the Director was the Host's representative. Now Wil felt he had no choice but to confide in one of the few entities he thought he could trust- the Host.

"Yes, circumstances would logically dictate that you need our help," replied the Director matter-of-factly. "According to Site Director White, the ESCAPE project has run into a potentially fatal wall. As its creator, you would be immune from the temptation to discredit it for financial gain. Perhaps only Sonya might be as single-minded due to her loyalty to you."

"You need the help of Our Host because you aren't sure who you can count on anymore," continued the Director. "Our Host also has an active interest in the success of ESCAPE. Therefore, be assured that we will assist you in any way within our means."

Wil took a good look at the woman before him, sizing her up. He knew from seeing her in the past that she was reasonably tall, the robe belied a figure, but she had a pleasant enough face below long, straight, brown hair that fell between her shoulder blades. Today, as in most of the times he had seen her, it was pulled back into a ponytail. Off the top, Wil figured Director Allison to be just slightly younger than himself... maybe early twenties. He took a deep breath and threw the dice.

"I want to know if you have the ability to analyze some samples for me… from the Flowerboxes."

"Hadn't you had already done that last week?" asked the Director.

"Yeah, well I'm not sure I believe that the test results are correct," countered Wil.

"The crop tests have not returned yet. It could be that a parasitic organism is responsible for the failure."

"I don't think it's blight. Blight wouldn't usually jump across to affect every plant species the way this has," said Wil. "I believe that it might be something else."

Allison's face went blank again momentarily as if she was somewhere else. Just as quickly her smile returned.

"You believe that someone has been tampering with the test samples."

Wil nodded, "I suspect it."

"Using the lab, we would be able to test a new batch of samples. Do you have them?" she asked.

"Not yet but I will sometime around three in the morning."

The Director nodded at him knowingly.

"That would be an ideal time to utilize the lab facilities without notice by other personnel. What about security?"

"I've got it covered. Sonya will be on the main board for the overnight shift. We can come and go as we please. How long will it take you to get test results?"

"If you are looking for incorrect food/water mixes, or biotic imbalances in the soil, that can be accomplished within ninety minutes," answered Allison.

———

"Fine. I'll see you in the lab at three o'clock, give or take a few minutes."

The Director stood and extended her hand from beneath her robe. "Good luck, Wilson Ramirez."

"What we need is some good science," Wil replied as he took the Director's offering.

Even enveloped in the environmental suit, Wil knew something was off as soon as the elevator opened. The room was exceptionally bright, so much so that he instinctively thought he could feel the heat through his suit. He reached into his sample bag to fish out a temperature gauge. It read one hundred four degrees, almost twenty degrees more than the optimal setting. Sometimes controlling the climate was a challenge late in the hot Kansas summer, when temperatures often did exceed one hundred degrees, but it was the middle of the night... in June.

Wil went on with the sample collection; taking atmospheric readings first with the vacuum collector, followed by soil and food/water drip gatherings. He moved as quickly as he was capable of, needing to cover at least one more floor inside this building and the floors of two more buildings as well.

On the second floor that Wil visited, the temperature was also at one hundred four degrees. He could see the soybean plants wilting in the heat, brown spotting on the edge of the leaves.

In the second building his suspicions were confirmed- a temperature of one hundred four degrees. It still wasn't enough for the catastrophe he was visually observing; genetically modified harvest crops could withstand both high and low-temperature extremes for lengthy periods and survive. Wil had to find the other catalyst. He kept collecting his samples.

The third building threw him into doubt about his hypothesis; the temperature was seventy-five degrees, roughly the same as the night air outside the building. By 1:30 AM, the sun's heating of the structure would have dissipated, and this should have been the expected result. Again, Wil collected his samples and decided he needed to see one more building, skipping the fourth for the fifth in the row. Over the secure com-link, he informed Sonya of his intention

"Alright, I'll redirect the sentinels. You should have a clear path but let's move it. We need to wrap this up... and keep your com-link on just in case," she admonished.

"Sorry, I've got to check out a hunch. It shouldn't take long."

When he reached the third level of the Flowerbox, Wil felt a sense of disappointment; everything was normal with the room temperature at seventy-eight degrees. He collected his samples and was heading back toward the elevator when the room suddenly brightened. Reaching for the temperature gauge in his kit, Wil took it out and checked the reading. It was eighty-two degrees and rising rapidly. Time to head back.

He practically ran from the Flowerbox back to the parking garage and its adjoining crew lockers to stow the environmental suit. Wil then picked up the sample bag and made his way down the stairwell to the lab level, Sonya giving him the all clear through his com-link before proceeding into the corridor. Waiting inside the lab was the Director Allison.

"Run the drip samples first," he said handing her the bag. "It doesn't matter from which building. I'll bet that the fertilizer/water ratios are way out of whack and I'll double down that every sample will be the same."

"That should only take fifteen minutes," replied the Director. "It is a relatively simple test to perform."

"I'll wait."

"I'm coming through the door so don't panic," he heard through his com-link.

"Your bodyguard is coming in," said the Director almost at the same moment as she fiddled through the bag, pulling out the drip samples.

Sonya opened the door quietly and slipped inside. Wil's first urge was to run over and hug her, but the Director's presence caused him to hesitate.

Allison looked up from the lab table and nodded at him. "Aren't you going to give your girlfriend a kiss and hug?"

Wil smiled and walked briskly to embrace Sonya. He nodded over at the Director. "She knew you were coming in before you even told me!"

"Of course she did," said Sonya. "She's Host."

She pulled away from him to arm's length. "Ok, what do we know so far?"

"I have one more place to go to, and then I'll be sure. C'mon."

The two left the lab together and walked up a level to the control room. The night shift was always two techs, and tonight it was Holly Gwinn and Roberto Alejandro. They were focused intently on a three-dimensional board game projecting from a tablet on one of the tables. Wil assumed that they had been occupied by it most of their shift.

"Hi guys!" said Wil loudly. He winked at Sonya as the two startled technicians jumped up.

"Hi, boss!" rasped Roberto excitedly. "We were just on a break."

"Sure. I'm just out taking a walk with the old ball and chain," Wil replied jokingly. Sonya glared at him in mock anger. "I have a little bit of insomnia tonight and Sonya was kind enough to let me try and walk it off. How's everything going this evening? Any excitement?"

"No, no, nothing much happening," said Holly nervously. "The Flowerboxes are all reporting normal."

Wil walked over to the control station for the last building he had been in and waved up the readings. The temperature on all levels read seventy-four degrees. He pulled up the fuel cell levels and energy readings. Everything was normal for 3 AM, at least on the board. That confirmed it for him.

He gave a glance to Sonya and then looked over to the two lab techs standing anxiously a few feet away. He smiled at them.

"Well, I guess you two had better get back to your game. Third shift sure does suck, doesn't it? We'll be on our way. Maybe now I can sleep."

"Thanks, Wil. Good night...um, morning," said Holly Gwinn.

As Wil and Sonya left the room, he could see the sighs of relief from the techs out of the corner of his eye.

"What was that all about?" asked Sonya. Wil put a finger to his lips. They made their way quickly back to the lab. Director Allison was waiting at the open door when they arrived. She motioned them inside.

"You were correct in your assumption Wilson," she began. The first two test samples show an eighty-five/fifteen ratio."

"Is that good or bad?" asked Sonya.

"It's bad," said Wil. "You see, the fertilizer we feed into the drip is primarily a nitrogen and potassium mixture that promotes rapid and healthy growth for the GMO's, but the drip should contain no more than fifteen percent fertilizer to water. This mixture is more than five times the proper mix."

"So the plants are dying of gluttony?"

"Not exactly," said Director Allison. "Too much nitrogen and potassium and not enough water causes a buildup of salts and alkaloids in the plant leaves and damages the roots, causing even less water to be brought into it. The plant dies of thirst."

"Just to move things along, the plants are being exposed to high temperatures for extended periods of time. The readings I got in two of the four buildings were over one hundred four degrees," said Wil. "In the last building, I actually caught the temperature beginning to cycle up.

"Those high temperatures would cause the plants to want to hydrate, and in doing so, they would pull in even more of the poisonous mixture into the soil from the drip. It's why the plants have degenerated so quickly."

"Clever but you said only two of the buildings had high temperatures," said Sonya. "Why not fry all the plants in all the buildings at once?"

"That would be to limit the energy drain on the complex's fuel cells. By limiting the temperature increases to a specific number of buildings, one could achieve the desired effect without being detected," speculated the Director. "At least not right away; even with regular solar and wind replacement, there is going to be a leaching of the energy stores. Eventually, over a period of weeks, the cells would drain out very early in the daily cycle."

"That's true, but not before the crops are long dead. Probably no one would ever even look. A couple of days offline with the Flowerboxes secured for investigation and the cells would be back at one hundred percent without anyone ever knowing what had happened," countered Wil. "So, here's the question: Why did all of the previous samples test normal?"

"I'd love to say it's that Haines bitch, but the truth is it could be Lise Marin or anyone," sneered Sonya. "For that matter, why are the board readouts within parameters when we know that those buildings are baking?"

"It would seem that we have a saboteur in our midst," said the Director, "but who could it be?"

———

"It's got to be someone with access to the software and the ability to change it with some pretty sophisticated algorithms," replied Sonya. "If you're getting normal reads on the boards while all hell is breaking lose outside, then somebody is messing with the program and doing a pretty good job of it."

"Let's call in the IT guys and start looking for viruses or glitches that shouldn't be there. We should be able to find it and fix it pretty quickly now that we know what is going on," said Wil.

The Director gave him a look. "That might not be as easy as you think, Wilson. For one thing, code writers have a tendency to cheat the program. They enter shortcuts not in the original code to increase speed and efficiency. Only looking for code that is not part of the original blueprint could send us down a thousand blind alleys.

"There's probably a kill switch incorporated," added Sonya. "If the clowns who did this realize that we're onto them, then they may just fry the entire system."

"Ok, then we have to keep this between us, but then we also need to get some help from Kansas City. We can't just sit and do nothing," said Wil glumly.

"Don't worry about Kansas City. I have a secure channel to Herm Wallace. I'm going to call him asap. This place should be crawling with Company security by 8 AM."

"Our Host believes that, with access to the programming computers, we can very quickly run a sweep and find the virus," said Director Allison. "We should be able to neutralize any threat to the ESCAPE software and return control of the system to AgriBus."

"How can you do that?" asked Sonya warily.

"Our Host can mobilize vast computational power, beginning with thousands of Directors around the world."

"Won't that defeat the purpose of keeping the Flowerboxes a secret?"

Director Allison looked at Sonya with a straight face. "Who do you think has been behind this project from the moment Wilson conceived it in virtuality?"

Sonya thought for a moment. "Well, then I guess we all had better get busy. Come on, Wil."

Wil put up his hand. "There's one other thing I need to do, and then I promise I'll be right along."

Sonya hesitated. "What's so damned important? We're very likely in danger, and I'd like you to be secure with me."

"I need to give Director Allison the access key algorithm that will open up the system for the Host to search. It's in the safe; only SD White and I can open it. I promise I'll be right along. Ten minutes."

"Go then. I wish I had a gun to give you."

"You know I'm a lover, not a fighter," he said, smiling reassuringly. "I'll be okay.

The three left with Sonya heading back to their apartment; Wil and the Director to the primary mainframe room.

Once inside, Wil opened the safe, utilizing DNA recognition software in combination with a voice and retinal match. He reached inside and found the key storage device, handing it to the Director. She held it momentarily and gave it back to him.

"Thank you. Our Host has obtained the key. We will now remain and access your mainframe. Go back to Sonya and go nowhere else."

Wil left the room and headed for the elevator. It opened to reveal Mickey Haines. Wil felt a rush of adrenaline as he realized his danger. Mickey was holding a gun on him.

"Hi, Wil."

"Feeling the noose tighten, Mickey?" Wil tried to hide his fear.

"You're the last piece to be collected," Haines replied with a smirk. She took a step back, "Come on in. We're going on a trip."

Wil took a step into the elevator. Mickey Haines had already pressed the button for the ground level. The doors closed and the elevator began its trek upward.

"You know, Sonya's crew is on security tonight, and they can see everything that is happening. You aren't going to get very far."

Mickey laughed. "Oh, come on, Wil! Give me some credit for being a professional. I'm afraid Rand has a bullet in his head. Well, it passed through his head- probably isn't in there anymore. I was hoping to find your dear, sweet Sonya there too, but I missed her. Too bad, I kinda owe her. So you see, there's not really anyone watching us."

"There are the perimeter guards and the sentinels."

"A little, self-directed EMP takes out your sentinels and some significant, well-placed dollars… oops! I mean credits these days, can buy you a guard or two. I mean, do you know what those poor guys make a year? A couple hundred thousand credits can give a girl lots of influence."

The elevator door opened into the parking garage area. The woman motioned with the gun for Wil to step out first.

"You switched the samples."

"Oh, that was easy. I had a couple of clean sets ready to go when the moment came. It was so sweet of you to trust me with the collection; made things a lot easier."

"You're pretty amazing!" he said to her as they began walking toward the exit door. "To be able to single-handedly sabotage this entire complex and almost get away with it."

"Oh, honey! That's just a little bit of dog and pony show to keep everyone off balance," she replied. "I'm surprised it took this long for you to figure it out. When White told everyone that we had to call in Kansas City, that was my cue to get outta town. No, my employer could care less if this complex succeeds or not. They just don't want to have to pay the licensing fees and royalties for the operational plans and software. Cheaper to steal them and set their own versions up. The patent suits will be tied up in the courts for decades."

He stopped and turned to face her as they reached the door, "You wouldn't be able to get access to that information without the key. There're only two people who could give it to you, and I don't think Alan White is in with you."

She grinned at him. "You're right about that but you know it's amazing what a blowjob and fuck can get you, especially one you can keep on video forever. And Alan is a happily-married man. Well, at least he was. Now he's dead ~~now~~ too. Shame, he had such a nice dick."

"You blackmailed him."

"You know what they say, Wil. Happy wife, happy life. He was extremely co-operative and even kept it quiet when everything started to fall apart, at least until the very end. Well, what else could he do? He said he loved her; but I can be very persuasive, now can't I? Let's keep walking.".

Wil pushed open the door, and they stepped out onto the tarmac. He could see the first hint of daybreak in the eastern sky.

"You didn't get far with me," he countered. "So who are you working for?"

"The same people you'll be working for soon. Happy Time Foods Corporation."

"HTF? The Chinese?"

"They also have a significant market share in India as well," sniffed Mickey Haines. "You'll like them, Wil. I mean, after all, it doesn't matter who you work for as long as the Flowerboxes get built, and you and I get paid. Turn right here. We're going to the north gatehouse. I have some friends waiting there."

265

They made the turn onto the lanes between the buildings. Wil slowed his pace slightly, trying to buy time. He was scared, really scared, but he knew he had to keep Mickey talking and look for a way out.

"So why do they need me? They already have what they need with you, don't they?

"Let's just say you're their insurance policy."

Wil stopped walking and turned to face her again.

"What if I say no? What if I refuse to go any further with you? I'm valuable to them, right?"

Mickey Haines stopped smiling and aimed the gun at Wil's chest. "I'm afraid you're not that valuable, Wil. You're the jewel in the crown but not the crown itself. If you don't want to come with me, then I have orders to kill you. Your choice. Fun with me or food for the worms. I'm ambivalent about it myself."

Wil saw the shadow briefly, darting between the buildings behind his captor. He did his best to keep his eyes on Mickey Haines. He raised his hands in mock surrender.

"Ok, I get it. Sounds like a pretty easy decision." Wil saw the shadow rapidly growing closer. He did his best to stay focused on Mickey but it was too late; she had seen his eyes stray. Face hardening, eyes narrowing, Haines instinctively began to drop into a defensive position and turn to meet the threat. She wasn't quick enough.

Sonya kicked at the gun arm as it swiveled. Haines cried out in pain as the gun flew out of her hand and disappeared into the darkness. She turned with the momentum of the blow to get space between herself and her attacker. Sonya landed on her left foot and used her body's momentum to attempt a finishing roundhouse with her right leg. She missed. The two women paused momentarily, sizing each other up.

"Well, well, little girl. I missed you earlier," sneered Mickey.

"Here I am, bitch. I thought I made it clear to leave my boyfriend alone."

"But he's so cute! Besides, when I'm finished, you won't be around to enjoy him anymore! Maybe I'll make him my boytoy," taunted Mickey.

She began to move slowly to the right. Sonya mirrored the movement. The taller woman feigned an attack to the left and swept right with a kick to Sonya's head. Sonya dropped to the tarmac with a kick of her own that took out Mickey's pivot foot. She fell to the ground, rolling back into a defensive position as Sonya recovered her own balance.

Mickey Haines gave her a toothy grin. "Not bad, but you know how this is going to end. You might be faster, but I'm bigger and stronger. Eventually, I'm going to wear you down and then I'm going to kill you… or you can let me walk away and live."

"We'll see who's going to walk away," snapped Sonya. "You wanna leave? Gotta go through me."

Wil watched in stunned silence and amazement for the few seconds that the two women had sparred in front of him. Mickey Haines was right; she had at least four inches and thirty pounds on his bodyguard, and she looked to be just as competent a martial artist. Wil knew he had to do something or he and Sonya might both be dead. Taking a deep breath, he ran.

With the noise of the two scuffling women in his ears, Wil ran toward the area where he had seen the gun fly off into the gloom. He kept playing the scene out in his mind; trying to project a trajectory from Haines's hand to the tarmac. When he was close to where he felt the gun might have landed, Wil fell to his hands and knees, and searched desperately for the weapon. He felt around in all directions in front of him, and after a few moments, his left hand slid beneath the cold metal of the pistol. His heart jumped into his throat as he lost contact; the force of his hand had inadvertently pushed the gun away. It was another second of panic before Wil grasped the barrel.

Making sure not to touch the hammer, Wil picked the gun up by the barrel with his left hand and slid the handle into his right. Finger off the trigger, he ran back to the standoff.

The two women were circling again, looking for an advantage. Wil could tell that both were tiring but didn't think fatigue would benefit the smaller Sonya. He had to do something to help her.

Wil's first instinct was to announce that he had the gun and demand that the two stand down, but he immediately thought it would be a mistake. He was horribly incompetent with weapons of any sort and was so reluctant to hurt another human being that he wasn't sure he could bring himself to shoot Mickey Haines even if she attacked him. She could end up with the gun again.

Wil's other instinct had been to overcome his reluctance and simply shoot her in the knee or shoulder to stop the fight, but the two women were moving fast and occasionally charging one another. He might hit Sonya by accident.

There was possibly another way.

Walking briskly toward the antagonists, Wil raised the gun above his head and fired two shots into the air. A startled Mickey Haines glanced in Wil's direction, trying to locate the source of the noise.

It was all the opening Sonya needed. She pounced- driving the full weight of her body onto Mickey's left knee. The blow was so forceful that Wil thought he saw the leg bend backward. Haines screamed and fell. On the way down, Sonya landed a right and left combination with lightning speed on her opponent's face. Mickey Haines dropped to the tarmac and lay still.

Sonya stood over her quarry like a champion fighter.

"Let's see if you ever walk again, you piece of shit!"

Wil broke in, "Do you think you can come over here and take this gun away from me before I hurt someone?"

Sonya looked up and ran to Wil, wrapping her arms around him in a bear hug. Will kept his gun hand above his head and returned the hug with his left arm.

"Uh, honey? The gun. It makes me nervous."

"Oh. Ok, take your finger off the trigger and bring it down to your side but aim towards the building as you do it."

Wil complied. When the barrel was facing the ground, his bodyguard gently slid the gun from his hand and engaged the safety. She set it on the ground beside them and resumed her bear hug. As she did, the complex's floodlights came on, and the alarm sounded. The brilliant light momentarily blinded Wil.

"Oh, my God! I was sick that I had lost you!" she moaned. She pulled away and looked him in the eye. "Thank you for distracting her. I don't know how much longer I could have kept her here."

"I was sick that you had lost me too. How did you know I was out here?"

"When you didn't get back right away, I went to security," she explained. Her face grew solemn. "I found Rand. She killed him."

"I know. I'm sorry."

"Me too. I saw the two of you in the parking garage and figured that she must be trying to get you offsite. I waited until you were outside and then went after you. I didn't want to set off the alarm because I was afraid if Mickey knew that she was caught, she might just kill you."

"I almost got you killed," he said painfully. "I tried not to let on that you were behind us but she saw me look at you. I'm so sorry, Sonya!"

His girlfriend's eyes sparkled in the bright light, and she winked at him, "Wil, I was counting on you giving me away! I'm not sure I could have taken her and even if I had tried, she had the gun pointed at you. If you hadn't glanced at me, Mickey would never have turned the gun away from you. We'd probably both be dead right now!"

"So you were counting on me to screw it up?"

Sonya bent down and picked up the pistol.

"Let's just say things worked out fine for the good guys. C'mon. Let's get you back."

Wil looked at the motionless Mickey Haines, "What about her?"

Sonya laughed, "If the bitch wakes up… and isn't screaming in pain, it'll take her about three hours to crawl out of here. I shattered her kneecap; she's not gonna walk again for a long, long time."

The two began walking back to the parking garage arm in arm.

"I think maybe you should teach me how to use a gun," said Wil.

"Well, it's my opinion that you're off to a damn fine start!"

Over the next few days, the ESCAPE complex was a beehive of activity as the Company operatives from AgriBus's Kansas City headquarters descended upon it. Security Chief Wallace brought several details of guards with him to lock down the facility and replace those who had been lost.

The death toll had been tough for them to accept. In addition to Rand Morris and Site Director Alan White, three others in Sonya's Gold crew had been murdered. That their killers had been the other members of that same crew was especially painful; everyone involved with the program found the betrayals disheartening.

Director Allison and the Host needed only a few hours to isolate and destroy the computer virus that Mickey Haines had deposited into the mainframe. The Flowerbox operating systems were returned to normal. A massive flushing of the soil within each unit removed the salts and PH imbalances that had been set in motion by the sabotage. Most of the crops were able to right themselves. The ESCAPE project was saved.

Mickey Haines was never seen or heard from again- at least not by Wil or Sonya. Herm Wallace had mentioned, "a deep hole she would never be able to crawl out of." They didn't care to know anything more- Sonya figured that Mickey Haines would pay dearly for her betrayal and crimes for many years to come. She recalled the stories about Virtuality prisons.

One morning, a few weeks after the excitement, Director Allison entered the control room where Wil and several other members of the technical crews were monitoring the recovery process.

"Wilson, your presence is required," she said cryptically.

Wil smiled. "Director Allison, please don't call me Wilson. Nobody calls me Wilson."

Wil couldn't believe what happened next; the Director smiled back at him. "That might be changing. Come."

The two made their way up onto the tarmac outside where Herm Wallace and Sonya were waiting. The two had been deep in conversation but turned to greet them.

"So what's the deal?" asked Wil.

"We have some VIP's coming in, and they want to meet you," said Wallace.

Wil looked at Allison. "Why are you here? You're normally a hermit."

The representative of the Host smiled at him a second time. "It's a big day for Directors as well."

Wil could hear the distant thumping of the helicopter's blades, slowly getting louder as it approached them. Within a minute, it was hovering above the helipad on the tarmac; the wash from its blades blowing the thin coating of Kansas dust from the asphalt as it settled down. It landed a few hundred feet from the welcoming party.

Once the engines had cut, the side doors opened, and Wil saw some figures scramble out. From their demeanor, he assumed they must be the handlers and underlings. They set the ladder in place and stepped back ready to assist.

Out of the helicopter stepped a robed figure. Wil immediately understood why Director Allison had accompanied them.

"That's a Seraphim," he said to her.

"That is Gabriel, Voice of Our Host," she replied. "They have come to see you and ESCAPE."

From the reaction of the handlers, he could tell that the next person out of the vehicle was important as well. He was a big, red-headed man, carrying a briefcase as he stepped out and onto the tarmac.

The last person out was a woman. For a second, just a second, Wil caught his breath.

"That's my Angel," he gasped to himself.

He realized he was wrong almost immediately. This woman was blonde; his angel had been a brunette, but from this distance, they looked almost like identical twins. The group collected itself and then began to move toward them, the Seraphim Gabriel taking the lead.

Director Allison stepped out to escort them. Wil stepped closer to Sonya and quietly took her hand to squeeze it. She kept her eyes forward but smiled knowingly.

Wil had never seen a Seraphim up close before, only from the Internet. In the v-streams, a white light emanated from where the face should have been. Now that he was standing a few yards away from one he could see what had been reported; the archangel had a human face, it looked kind of strange from this distance, but it was definitely human. He turned his head to see Sonya's reaction, but she was focused on the group. When he looked back, Wil was startled to see a different face under the hood of the robe.

"Did you see that?" he asked his companions.

"See what?" asked Herm Wallace.

"Its face changed! Look there it goes again!"

"Looks the same to me," replied Sonya.

"Ok, it was the face of an Asian, and now it's a black... man, I think."

"Looks like a white guy to me," said Wallace, glancing over at Wil. He looked back at the approaching party. "Oh! I see what you mean. Neat trick!"

"Don't you think the woman looks like your angel? Except for the hair," said Sonya.

"Yeah! I thought it was just me," said Wil.

They grew quiet as the party reached them, the Seraphim standing directly before him. Wil suddenly found that he was nervous.

271

Director Allison made the introductions. "Seraphim Gabriel, this is AgriBus' Chief of Security Herman Wallace, Project Security Sonya Anderson and..."

"Wilson Ramirez, the creator of ESCAPE," broke in Gabriel. To Wil, it was as though a choir was singing. "We are honored to meet all of you. Our Host wishes to thank you for your valuable work. With the successful testing of the ESCAPE project, humanity has now found a way to provide itself with a stable food supply for centuries to come."

Wil cringed. "There were a lot of people involved in putting ESCAPE together, Seraphim Gabriel. I think we are all happy that the project has turned out so well."

"This may be true Wilson Ramirez, but it was your mind that conceived of ESCAPE. In the Promised Land that humanity is building, there is no greater tool than the creative vision of the mind. You are a testament to that," insisted Gabriel. It turned to the woman. Wil was finally able to see her up close. She did look like his Angel. The woman smiled and extended her hand.

"Hi, Wil. It's nice to meet you. I'm Grace Williams."

Chapter Seventeen

"Those sonsabitches!" exclaimed Sam Craig, grinning broadly. "Those sonsabitches!"

John Harriman thought that the President was taking the news very well, figuring Craig was happy because at least they now knew that the threat was terrestrial. A human enemy could be defeated.

He and Jim Gillette exchanged glances as Craig chortled.

Craig laughed again. "Those bastards sure put it over on us, didn't they? Hell, I almost made Jorge Bautista my chief of staff! Wouldn't that have been a pisser, Jim? Replacing you with one of these Host fuckers? Well, fun time's over, kiddies… let's go kill them all and end it.".

Jim Gillette cleared his throat. Harriman spoke first.

"Mr. President, I would urge caution moving forward. There are still some mitigating factors that prevent us from taking action against those behind the Host."

"Yes, Sir. For one thing, we don't know the full extent of the conspiracy. We still aren't sure who all the players are yet, only that Air Defense Corporation is involved in some way," added the Chief of Staff.

The President's smile faded. "What? You mean there are more of these clowns than just the ones at ADC?"

"It can't just be ADC, Sir," responded Harriman. "From a technological and financial standpoint, they aren't capable of what we've seen from them. Very likely there are a number of other conspirators from many areas of specialization. We know that nanotechnology is involved and that the software to link all of the various pieces together must come from somewhere else. Their ability to control all means of media transmission confirms that a mega-corp from that field must also be involved."

"It looks to be some kind of conspiracy of the mega-corps. What we are unsure of is which ones," said Gillette.

"You mean to tell me that the Illuminati are real? Because that's what it sounds like," said President Craig darkly.

"Oh, I don't know about that," countered Jim Gillette hastily, "but this is a highly sophisticated attempt at giving the impression of something akin to that legend. I mean, look at their utilization of Abrahamic religious references and mythology; it's designed to instill fear and awe into two-thirds of the world's population. A lot of people believe we are dealing with angels of God."

Harriman attempted to redirect the conversation. "There's another consideration too, Sir- a practical one. Whoever the Host turns out to be, they still have their finger on the trigger. We could go storming into the offices of ADC or even drop tactical nukes on all its facilities, but that doesn't mean another of the conspirators somewhere else won't give the order to activate the nanites we all carry."

"Effectively wiping out the entire population of the United States," added Gillette.

Samuel Craig rubbed his chin for a moment, taking it all in. "Ok, let's look at this another way. At least we have a place to start. We can begin covert surveillance of ADC, looking for evidence of links to others and build the investigation out from there.".

"Yes, Sir. I might add that since we now know that the nanites are terrestrial, we can begin to search for a point of origin," added Harriman.

"How do you propose to do that? I think we all agree that until we are ready to make a move, this whole business has to remain on the QT, even with our allies."

"The molecular structures of the various nanites are unique," responded Harriman. "I would recommend that the EPA and FDA review existing samples from as many of the manufacturing and production facilities around the country as they can. They could look for these specific molecular signatures without having to know why they are looking for them. The EPA database is the easiest place to begin, but I would also examine all new test samples as they come in. Eventually, we are going to start finding matches and more of the conspirators will be revealed over time." .

"Time. I wonder… how much time do we have?" pondered the President. "Eventually, our window of opportunity for taking them down is going to close. Once the global reorganization takes place, any chance we had to get rid of the Host will disappear. We simply won't have the resources to do it as separate regions."

"That brings us to our final subject: If the Host is a cabal of mega-corps, then who can we trust? Our own government and many others around the world are filled with the former employees of these very same companies," said Gillette.

Harriman nodded in agreement. "It's true, sir. ADC alone has hundreds of former and existing employees scattered throughout the DOD. It's been that way ever since subcontracting began to take hold throughout the bureaucracy. There are probably spies for the Host everywhere, even in the White House."

Sam Craig took a long look at his chief of staff.

Jim Gillette laughed nervously. "Mr. President, in all of the years I was with AgriBus, I never heard even a peep about anything like this. If they are involved in some way, I was never in the loop."

"Let's hope so, Jimbo. Treason is still a capital offense."

Gillette shifted in his chair. His gaze fixed upon the older man; Craig smiled at him disarmingly, showing a full set of teeth. Harriman couldn't help but be reminded of a shark to the kill.

The President continued, "Still- it does present one hell of a problem. Who *can* we trust? We need to have a degree of revelation to conduct effective investigations, but what if we are unwittingly keeping the enemy updated on our progress? If we do decide to act, which of our military units and commanders will remain loyal? Who *isn't* the enemy?"

"The researchers in Section R are sworn to secrecy. Besides, that program is so compartmentalized that only Dr. Naji knows the full extent of our investigation," said Harriman.

"From a tactical perspective, I would trust General Kurtz implicitly," he continued. "Alex Kurtz's family has been removed from the corporate world for generations. They're military people loyal to the defense of the United States. Kurtz hasn't been co-opted, and I believe he is the man capable of planning and implementing a response when the time comes. I would stake my life on it."

"You'll be staking all of our lives on it, John," responded Craig. "Ok, we'll bring in Kurtz. Who else?"

"I believe that my old unit can be trusted for... more covert operations. They have proven their loyalty time and again over the years and are the best at their game."

"Have any of them developed corporate ties over the years? That could be a red flag," Gillette pointed out.

"I can update their background checks to see if there may have been any outside work done, but I believe that they have remained in the employ of the Company."

"If they check out, bring them up to speed. Everyone else is considered need to know," said the President. "Well fellers, I figure we've got less than twelve months to bring these rats to ground. That year is going to go by pretty fast. Time's a wastin'!"

As Harriman and Gillette left the Oval Office, they heard President Samuel H. Craig exclaim once more to no one in particular, "Sonsabitches!"

...

***

"The Aztecs are a good team. They lead the NL West. Plus, we had to go up against Tamberlain, and he's their ace," said Cam.

Timothy wasn't consoled. "I know, but I really thought we had a chance when Mexico City put Stanton out there in the seventh. I thought we would get to him."

The two men continued to walk up North Clark towards Grace Street where Timothy lived. After games, they would stroll up to the intersection and then part ways with Timothy going home and Cam taking the bus up to Oak Park.

"Where did you get such a love for the Cubs?" asked Cam. "I mean, I was born here. You're…"

"Not born here? It's true that I'm not a native Chicagoan, but we are encouraged to assimilate the customs of the local population in order to gain acceptance," explained Tim. "It turns out that I really love to watch sports. I get into them all… da Bears, and da Bulls, and da Blackhawks."

Cam laughed at Tim's affectation of a Chicago accent. "That's pretty good!"

"Thanks! It's a work in progress. Of all the sports, I love watching baseball the most. It is the most fascinating of games, not like any other. There's no clock, only twenty-seven opportunities to fail for each team. Where else can you fail twenty-six times and still be the hero on your twenty-seventh chance?"

Cam had heard the *baseball is like life* sermon before, but never an insight such as Tim had just made. That was one of the things Cam liked about Tim- he put a fresh eye on an old world.

"Well tonight we were the goat on the twenty-seventh opportunity," he joked.

276

"Yeah... that happens too, more often than not," agreed Tim, "but that's why it's so much fun to watch!"

"Where are you from, Tim?" asked Cam.

The Director hesitated. "I... I don't really know. It's one of the things they do to you when you pledge yourself to the service of Our Host. The past is removed from us so as to provide a clean slate for the future."

Timothy stopped walking and turned to face Cam, smirking.

"Is this one of those questions your little group wants to know about?"

Cam grew indignant. "No Tim, it's one of those questions I wanted to know about."

For the first time since they had met, Cam saw the Director caught off kilter.

"I'm sorry Cam. I spend my entire life on guard from everyone. I'm not used to honesty, unless it's from you. Even then, I know that you get pushed hard a lot by your people for information. That's why I try to give you things that I think will make you look good, but not hurt Our Host or myself."

The two continued walking on in silence. Cam felt sorry for his friend; Tim always seemed so full of energy about life and the future. Cam thought he was smart and witty; that's why he liked the Director. In his mind, they would have been friends anyway, Host or no Host. Cam did know what it was like to be always on edge, always holding something back from the world. Growing up as one of the Children of God, Cam could understand being forever suspicious of the motives of others; the Children were practically baptized in a glowering paranoia over non-believers. He guessed that was why Tim had chosen him as a friend; in a way, they were both very much alike despite being from enemy camps.

A few minutes later they reached the intersection with Grace Street.

Cam turned to shake the Director's hand. "Thanks again, Tim. The game was good, the seats were great, and the food was fantastic as always. I hope you had fun, too."

Tim smiled wanly. "Yeah, too bad our poor Cubbies lost." He was silent for a moment. "Hey, you want to see where I live? It's just right over there."

Cam's heart jumped, but he didn't quite know why.

"You won't get in trouble for it?"

Tim looked puzzled. "No, why should I?"

277

"Well, isn't it kind of... secret?"

"You mean like a Batcave? No, it's just a place where I shower, eat, and kill some time at when I'm not working," Tim leaned forward and put his hand to the side of his face as if sharing a confidence. He said in a mock whisper, "Laser beams are guarding the entrances, though. Keep zapping the neighbor's cat."

Cam smiled broadly. "Yeah, right."

Tim turned and began walking up Grace Street. "No, seriously, there are laser beams. Don't worry; the interface will shut them off for us. You coming? Consider it reconnaissance."

Cam knew he couldn't stay long; the bus up to Oak Park would be at least an hour's journey, and he had a nine o'clock class in the morning. If he did at least bring something new back to his parents, it might delay their intent on having him deliver Babel. He had kept insisting to them and the others that Tim's ever-vigilant halo made it almost impossible to put into the Director's food. Anyway, he didn't really want to hurt Tim or the Host for that matter. Cam liked this new world... at least so far. What wasn't to like? He was able to go to Northwestern for free, his dad's business was booming, and he was best friends with a really important member of the Host who could get tickets to anything. Life was pretty good.

Still, his folks and everyone else kept insisting that he find a way to *deliver the package*. He even thought a couple of times about telling Tim of the conspiracy, but decided against it out of fear for his family's lives.

Screw them, thought Cam as he followed Tim up the street.

He remained a few steps behind the Director as they made their way along the sidewalk, finally coming to a nondescript bungalow with white siding. It had a small yard in front surrounded by a white picket fence. To Cam, it looked like every other house on the block. Tim opened the gate and stepped through. As they approached the front door, Cam could hear the deadbolts unlock; the most unusual feature of the residence so far. Usually, that required a retinal scan or voice match command. Tim had said the halo would disarm the security system; it must control the door locks as well.

The door opened on its own before them. Cam saw Tim's halo drop to just a few inches over his head as the Director went through the doorway. He followed Tim through the entrance into a small, already lit room. It looked just like any other family room with a couch, easy chair, and coffee table in the center. A few paintings decorated the walls, but Cam noticed there were no photographs or portraits. Just off the room to the right, he saw a kitchen through a half wall with a bar counter top. The kitchen was small too. He guessed that a bedroom and bath were behind the other doors in the room.

Tim turned and spread his arms in presentation. "Well? All the comforts of home! I guess they figure we don't need much. Sorry about not having a monitor; there's always one in my head if I want to watch vids or browse. You want water or juice? I've got orange and grape."

Then Cam saw something he never thought he'd ever see- the halo left its perch over Tim's head. It floated over to a position above a table in the corner of the room and began to descend. Cam watched it settle into a device on the table and come to rest. He figured the device must be important- some kind of a carriage or charging station for it. The two pieces looked as though they fit together.

Tim grinned at the look of shock on Cam's face.

"Did you really think it floated over me while I slept?"

"But I thought it was always protecting you?" asked Cam.

"It always is. Right now the defensive mechanisms built into the house are taking its place," responded his friend. "Don't worry; I'm perfectly safe. So you want juice? A snack? I might have cheese and crackers if you like."

"Grape is fine, thanks. Tim, why don't all of you… the Directors, stay together in one place? It would seem like you would all want that."

"Safety protocols again. Our Host doesn't want us all in one place; it would be too easy for a potential threat to try and take us all out at once. So we're scattered around the city," replied Tim as he opened the refrigerator door and reached inside. He pulled out a container and sat it on the bar counter. He opened the cabinet door and pulled out two plastic cups.

Cam looked over at the Halo in its resting place. "So even like that, it's still on? Is it still in your head, telling you things?"

Tim walked over and handed Cam one of the cups. "It can be if I want it to be."

279

Then Tim reached up and gently touched Cam's cheek. "But it isn't right now."

Cam looked into Tim's eyes and saw his need. He felt it too; he had felt it for so long now, but was afraid and ashamed. It was a deep, hidden shame that had always been with him, now overcome by his desire for Timothy- the most wonderful person in his world.

"How did you know?" he asked.

"To me, it was obvious," said Timothy, leaning forward to kiss Cam.

Later, they lay in each other's arms on Timothy's small bed. Cam looked at his lover and thought he had never seen a more beautiful creature, like a morning star in the heavens.

Then he remembered something... the Morning Star. *Lucifer* was the Morning Star; the most beautiful creature in all of God's creation.

"I have to get going," he said, slipping away from Tim and out of bed. "I have classes in the morning."

"I wish you could stay longer," said Tim lazily.

"I have to know... are you allowed to do this? Because I am most definitely not. If anyone in the Church found out about this, I would be driven out," said Cam.

"Sex? We aren't restricted. Our Host realizes that human beings have needs. Most of the time the Directors stay within themselves for it because to go outside becomes... complicated. Marriage is out; in a way we are married to Our Host the same way a nun is married to the Church," replied the Director. He looked up at Cam who was dressing hastily.

"Oh, you mean sex between men. No, it isn't a sin, but we don't think in those terms. So long as your actions are not harming others or yourself, it is not condemned." He rose out of bed and walked over to Cam, who by this time had his shoes on and was turning to leave.

"Hey!" said Timothy. He reached out and took both of Cam's hands, looking him in the eye. "I've never been happier."

"Neither have I," lied Campbell.

He cried silently during the bus ride home; red-faced and wiping tears away as the other riders stared at him in silence.

The house was dark when Campbell made it inside, everyone already in bed. Looking at his watch, he realized it was almost two.

The crying became sobs, drowned out by running water, as he tried to wash away his sin and shame in the shower.

Before he crawled into bed, Campbell fell to his knees and begged God for forgiveness. He couldn't sleep.

In the morning, he came downstairs for breakfast. His father had already left for a job. His mother gave him coffee and a kiss as he sat at the kitchen table.

Campbell kept his eyes fixed on the scalding hot mug, holding it tightly in his hands- praying that the pain would be another small penance for his sin.

"I've found a way to deliver Babel," he murmured, head down, eyes fixed on the vapor rising from the mug between his palms.

Ana Maria sat down next to him and touched his forearm. "You have? That's wonderful! All glory be to God! How?"

"There's a time of the day when the demon isn't connected to its halo."

"Demon? I thought you weren't convinced."

Campbell looked up at his mother with hateful, dead eyes.

"I know he is the Evil One, he revealed it to me. They are all demons, Mother. We have to cast them back into the Lake of Fire."

Ana Maria stood up and laid one hand on top of her son's head, the other hand palm up to the ceiling. With closed eyes and upturned face, she cried out, "May God give you the strength and will to strike at the Devil and defeat Him. You will be anointed as a soldier of the Lord; fighting the Evil One in the service of our Lord and Savior, Jesus Christ!"

***

Dr. Ali Naji ran the test again and again and again. In every case, it worked to perfection... which made him very anxious. At first, he wasn't sure whether to proclaim his findings to the world or to keep them to himself and tell no one. He settled on a compromise.

It took a day to organize his plan; he would need only a few hours to execute it. Those moments came on the Friday of the July Fourth holiday. Everyone would clear out for the long weekend, and the lab would be empty.

Naji waited for the last of his colleagues to bid him a pleasant weekend and then waited half an hour more. Occasionally, he would look up from the busy work he was distracting himself with to stare at the safe in the corner. Soon, he would need to open it and reveal its contents and their meaning. The thought made him sick to his stomach with fear. Finally, Ali Naji decided it was time to enact the plan. He opened the safe and placed the contents on one of the lab tables, instructed the central computer to turn on the lab cameras that were used for documentation, and began talking.

He looked at the labcam. "Hello, my friend. I hope that you are well. There's a project I have been working on recently that I believe is of vital importance to the safety and future of our planet. A significant aspect of this project falls within your area of research and will be of great interest to you.

"Unfortunately, that's not the reason I am leaving this information with you. What you are about to learn is very dangerous, and unlike me, you have no other immediate family to put in peril. As for myself, I believe that no matter where I may turn in the next few days, my life and that of my family are forfeit. Please forgive me, Tesh. This research can't be lost, and I have no one else I can trust to keep it out of the shadows."

Ali Naji began with the discoveries at the Lubbock facility. He went into detail discussing the nanites used by the Host to subjugate humankind, what each set's function was, and the mysterious fourth set; still unknown in its purpose.

He devoted more than fifteen minutes to explaining the interface and the discovery of the Air Defense Corporation serial number buried within it. He did his best to be thorough, interspersing images of the serial number taken through electron microscopes. Then he dropped the bombshell.

"Recently, my investigation into the characteristics of the nanites has revealed a breakthrough in understanding the process by which they are set into action. Seventeen separate types of nanites have been discovered to date. These nanites have been seen to break down into four distinct groupings or families. Each family performs a unique task. When activated, we believe the various members of each family of nanites seek out and cluster around a single nanite that embeds into a specific area of the body. We call it the Beacon, as its sole function is to call out to the other nanites in its family group to gravitate to it.".

282

The scientist waved his hand and activated a display screen over one of the lab tables. He directed the lab cams to record the simulation he was preparing to run.

"Recently, I stumbled upon the trigger frequency of one of the Beacons by accident. Note that it is vibrating in harmonic synchronization with the trigger frequency. However, the other nanites that comprise group one remain in a dormant state. I am speculating that each type of nanite reacts when subjected to an electromagnetic frequency meant specifically for it. I am now putting up for viewing a sample of nanites from the Beacon's family group, used to cause intense abdominal pain. I believe that as its trigger frequencies are activated, each particular nanite group will synchronize with those frequencies. If we could find these frequencies and their fluctuation patterns the nanites would then link up in family groupings. I am also assuming that there must be some mechanism utilized as a security measure to prevent the accidental activation of the weapon."

Naji sighed and continued, "If I am correct, the nanites should begin to react to this EM pattern fluctuation by gravitating towards the Beacon. Each member of the family links up with the others, creating a molecular machine that acts as a micro-boring tool. The synchronous vibrations, in conjunction with the frequencies, causes this newly-formed molecular structure to rotate. Still attracted to the Beacon embedded in the stomach lining, these molecular machines begin burrowing through the soft tissue in an attempt to unite with it."

"With thousands of these molecule-size machines simultaneously driving towards their Beacon nanites, the result would be an intense, stabbing pain in the abdominal area. Allowed to continue for any length of time the stomach ulcerates in hundreds of places, causing a slow and painful death," stated Naji matter-of-factly. "My colleagues in Lubbock have suggested that the cooling of the body causes the molecular machines to lose energy and dissipate. I believe it is the cessation of broadcasting the associated frequencies; within seconds the machines would cease to function and decouple; the nanites drifting away in random directions. In a human body, they would continue to inhabit the cardiovascular system in a dormant state."

Dr. Naji ended the simulation and faced the camera, his face grave.

"We attempted to find the specific frequency for each nanite with limited success. The nanites would activate individually from time to time but wouldn't combine into molecular machines. I believe the fail safe factor is in effect. At this stage of the research, I shut down the project. I have passed on what I refer to as the machines' frequency chords to you. These groupings of frequencies from time to time will cause the different nanites to activate. Tesh, you may wish to pursue the research and find the fail-safe, but I strongly caution against it for your own safety."

"For my purposes, I have gone far enough. The Beacons are activated by an ultra-low frequency wave. I am going to report to the President that the evidence strongly suggests these ULF's are likely being generated by our own defense satellites, typically used for communication with deep water submarines. It would be the only way that the Host could simultaneously blanket the planet or target a specific region. What the President decides to do with this information is out of my hands. In the end, I'm just a university researcher in a low-security lab, a place where no one would ever think to look for the key to the doomsday device. I want nothing more to do with this. Maybe if I stop now, my family might be spared."

Naji sighed again. "What I am not going to do is hand over the frequency chords to this or any other government. What we have found is the ultimate weapon. At the time of this recording, only those behind the Host and I know the frequency chords. Once the failsafe is discovered, whoever possesses this information would have the ability to control or kill a single life... or all life on the planet. While I am ethically against anyone possessing this power, at least those behind the Host have demonstrated some restraint and benevolence. I don't believe any government on the planet, given the opportunity to become the supreme superpower, could ever be as disciplined."

He picked up a small cube on the table and held it up for the camera.

"This is the CPU for the interface unit. Somewhere in the software of this cube lies the key to the failsafe. I am going to hide it and then send to you not only my collected research but also the location of the cube. It is too dangerous to fall into the wrong hands, but too important a piece of engineering to destroy. It must stay safe and hidden for now. When the time is right, you can retrieve it. Finally, I need a favor. I don't believe that I will live much longer, but if something happens to my family, I want you to take the information on this storage device and make it public knowledge. The world needs to know the source of the threat. The Host must be exposed for what it is."

***

"It's amazing! You must be very proud of what you have accomplished here, Mr. Ramirez!"

The young man grinned sheepishly. "We are. So many people have worked very hard to make this possible and prove that it is a viable alternative to current agricultural methods."

"I understand that just last year you and several other members of your team were in RLC's virtual living centers," Grace continued as Wil Ramirez nodded. "This must be quite a change. How are you adjusting to our everyday world?"

The young man thought for a second, and the smile faded. "For me, I'm fine with it; I prefer being the best that I can be and contribute to improving people's lives… but I also very much appreciated a lot of what virtuality offered in helping me to do that. I came up with the idea for ESCAPE in virtuality, and we were able to pull the best minds together and run all the simulations there before we even turned over a shovel here. Virtuality was able to give us a pretty good idea that we could be successful. As a lifestyle, I think it is a bad idea, but as a tool for teaching or testing ideas, there's nothing better. I'm even thinking about going back in soon so I can work on some other things!"

Grace's face flashed surprise. "Really? Improvements on your Flowerboxes?"

"No. I'm not needed here anymore. The whole point of these systems is that they are cookie cutters- they can be duplicated easily. I've been doing some thinking about gravity lately, and I want to test out some ideas I have."

"Wilson Ramirez, thanks to you and everyone here at ESCAPE for giving us a tour of the future of agriculture. All the best to you!" smiled Grace.

The grin returned. "Thank you. It was nice to meet you."

Red Kearney signaled cut as the ESCAPE crew that had been standing behind them in the shot broke into applause and excited chatter. Ramirez smiled and shook hands as the group encircled him. The young woman who had met her group when they arrived walked over to Grace and Red. She stuck out her hand.

"I don't think Wil knows who you are, Ms. Williams, but I'm a huge fan. I think I've watched all of your podcasts ever since I was little," she said with an ear-to-ear smile.

"Thank you. Call me Grace," said the journalist taking her hand. "You're... Sonya, right? Mr. Ramirez's bodyguard from what I've been told."

"I am assigned to him, but it's been pretty quiet," sniffed the younger woman. "After all, we are in the middle of the Kansas plain."

The grip was firm and strong. Grace could tell that this girl probably packed one hell of a punch. She hadn't counted on it being a verbal one.

"You know-- we've seen you before... in the box. You were our angel."

"I beg your pardon?"

"Well, not exactly you, but close. Her hair was black, and she was shorter, but she had your face," replied Sonya. "The hair threw me, but now that I've seen you up close, I think you must have been who they had in mind when they made her. I'm sorry, the angel is kind of like the VR interface when you are in the box. Except your angel was special- RLC didn't know about her. She would appear after we were inside and take us to different worlds away from the RLC ones. That's how Wil and I learned so much so quickly, because of you... I mean her. We figured out later she must be part of the Host. Funny, after all of those podcasts, I never made the connection until now. Still, it makes sense, you being with them and all."

"This is fascinating," answered Grace, smile locked in place. "Tell me more about my doppelganger."

"So this is how you plan to feed the world," said Grace over the engine's whine. The helicopter's increasing altitude pulled their view of the ESCAPE complex back into a series of squares within squares.

"It is a significant contribution," sang Gabriel. "It will also help humanity in making vital inroads against global warming and help to cool the oceans."

"How's that?" asked Kearney not looking up from the pan shot he was taking of ESCAPE out of the helicopter's window.

"One of the most significant benefits of ESCAPE as a self-contained operating system is its ability to be placed almost anywhere on the planet," replied the construct.

"Which means you can now grow food in places that were unsustainable in the past," said Grace "Places with rocky terrain or deserts, for example."

"Yes, or brownfields left unusable by old industrial methods."

"Ok but what has that got to do with the oceans?" snorted Kearney gruffly.

"Humanity no longer has to remove vast areas of trees for agricultural pursuits," replied Gabriel. "In the past, more than seventy percent of arable land mass was covered with trees. Today, it is twelve percent. Deforestation in the pursuit of feeding humanity has, in fact, caused a further degradation of the ability to produce food."

"You're going to reforest the planet," said Grace, "which is going to create a large carbon sink to draw CO2 out of the atmosphere and cool the planet. That will also cool the oceans."

"This is the expectation. It is one of many solutions being implemented to address the crisis."

"I see two problems with your grand plan, Gabriel," interjected Red Kearney. He had now put away the production suite and turned to face his companions. "First of all, I know something about forestry; I did some time as a conservation volunteer out west during the big burn of twenty-one. It can take up to a century to bring a forest back to what it was before it was destroyed. Second, let's say that you did manage to get ocean temperatures and currents back to pre-industrial levels. That still isn't going to bring back the whales or the fish or the land and bird species that we've lost over the past half century. You're just going to have immense pine forests full of blackbirds and rabbits."

"These are valid concerns, John Kearney," sang the Seraphim. "We must first remind you that Our Host does not view a century as an exceptionally long moment in the passage of time. Also, this is only one aspect of the overall approach to restoring the planet's climate to pre-industrial levels. However, the proposal is to reforest slightly more than fifty percent of the planet and to accomplish this with tree species that have been genetically modified for rapid maturation. Full potential as a carbon capture mechanism can be realized within fifty years."

"So we aren't going to see limitless seas of forests in the plains," said Grace.

"There never were. There will be large areas filled with what Wilson Ramirez calls his Flowerboxes. What will be restored are the former global weather patterns that will make the Great Plains as wet as they once were, and restore ice to the poles."

Gabriel continued, "As for species recovery, Our Host has been maintaining the DNA and, in some cases, frozen embryos of thousands of recently extinct or endangered species across the entire range of this planet's plant, insect, and animal kingdoms. While this project is secondary to protection of the food supply and counteracting the effects of global warming, it will eventually occur. Within a century, your planet will be a very different and much better place to live."

"Sounds like we're all going to be city folk from now on," said Kearney.

"John will be disappointed. He loves that farm," said Grace playfully.

"There will be no restrictions on movement," countered Gabriel. "For the most part, people may live where they wish. In fact, what John Kearney says is true; almost eighty percent of humans already live in urban zones."

Red and Grace smiled at the construct's misunderstanding of their attempt at humor.

"To think this all began with that kid's idea," said Red.

"To think that if the world hadn't changed that kid would either already be dead or well on his way, rotting in one of those boxes," replied Grace. "What the world almost missed out on."

"It is one of the reasons Our Host will eventually be recommending elimination of the RLC centers as a means of dealing with the impoverished and unwanted," sang Gabriel. "We never know where the next great mind will reveal itself if given the opportunity."

Grace suddenly grew bellicose. "Speaking of the virtual living centers, Gabriel- our friends back there told a story about being aided and guided inside virtuality by a special angel... an angel that looks just like me."

"They spoke the truth," replied the Seraphim nonchalantly. "Our Host scouted and selected individuals who displayed an aptitude for the creative process inside the RLC virtualities. Wilson Ramirez was one of those prospects and was initiated into an education and training program that would allow him to properly develop his potential."

"That still doesn't explain why the Host used my image as its interface. You have no legal right to do so without obtaining my permission," snapped Grace.

"Our analysis of prospective avatars revealed that you possess an overall rating of ninety-three percent in the area of trustworthiness and empathy. Much of it has to do with your facial characteristics and demeanor. While there are noticeable differences between the avatar and the real Grace Williams, the avatar does bear an obvious similarity in order to instill a sense of goodwill in its interactions with others."

"That's very flattering, but this is also my bitch with the Host. Sometimes your well-intended actions trample all over an individual's rights and freedoms. The Host should have asked for my permission before using my image to promote its agenda. If you were a corporation, I'd have a pretty good case for copyright infringement."

"No harm was ever intended. If you desire, some form of financial compensation can be made to you."

"That's not the point. You're offering restitution after the fact. It should never have happened in the first place."

Red Kearney raised a hand. "Did you happen to use my image anywhere? I'm very willing to receive financial compensation."

"No, John Kearney."

"Shit!" Red dropped his hand and leaned back against his seat.

"Our Host does wish to present you both with a gift of respect." Gabriel's arms had been folded across its torso and partially hidden by its robes the entire journey. Now it drew something out from under the robe. Grace saw that it was a wooden jewelry box of the highest craftsmanship. With its free hand, Gabriel reached to open the box. As she saw the bony composite that was its hand, Grace was reminded of the Seraphim's mechanistic nature. It was, after all, a machine, artificial intelligence was driving it- the construct of others. Sometimes, in dealing with Gabriel, that could be lost on one.

The cherry wood box opened to reveal two pendants on chains of gold laying on a white satin bed. They were not small, looking to be around two inches in diameter, the pendants were like nothing she had ever seen before. A golden isosceles triangle pointed downward to a second, identical triangle pointing up. The two triangles intersected at their points to form a rectangle shape; filling the shape was a large diamond. The work was encased in a blue, translucent material edged in gold and forming a perfect circle. From the golden edging sprang a small ring at the top through which the finely made chain ran.

"It's incredible," said Grace, restraining herself from touching it.

Red Kearney had leaned forward in his seat for a better look. "Wow! Finally bringing something home the wife will appreciate."

"This is the symbol of Our Host's love for and devotion to Humanity," sang Gabriel. "This is to be the sign of the Covenant between Our Host and all life on this world. Our Host will never forsake your people and together we will create a land of peace, prosperity, and eternal promise."

"The Promised Land," said Grace quietly under the whine of the engine.

"Yes," replied Gabriel, "the Promised Land. It is yours to take."

Chapter Eighteen

Anne North looked up from the pad containing the brief. "Is this true? Has it been confirmed?"

Harriman nodded. "That ADC is part of a corporate conspiracy behind the Host... yes. I've seen the evidence with my own eyes. You are now part of a select group that includes only the President, Jim Gillette, Dr. Naji, General Kurtz, and myself. No one else knows... outside of the Host itself. As for ADC satellites broadcasting trigger frequencies; that is Dr. Naji's educated guess."

North leaned back into the padded leather chair; her diminutive frame enveloped in its girth. If not for the years on her face, Harriman thought her almost childlike in stature, silhouetted against it.

"That's a pretty big leap of faith without proof of evidence," she said grimly. "So why have I been honored with membership in your little club?"

"The President is concerned that we may be running out of time to act upon this information. That soon, there may not be any way to neutralize the control exercised by the cabal," said Alexander Kurtz. "Even coordinating a formulated plan of attack could take months. The President feels we should initiate that process by contacting the Russians and the Chinese."

"And do what?"

"We want to explore the possibility of using their space-based defense systems to neutralize the ADC satellite network. Apparently, our systems have been compromised; perhaps theirs haven't," explained Harriman.

"ADC also has a huge presence in satellite communications technology through its international subsidiaries. Those would have to be neutralized as well," added Kurtz.

"Gentlemen, this is a very dangerous play on so many levels," countered Ambassador North. "For one thing, we don't know if we can even trust the Russians or the Chinese. What if they knock out the systems over their territories and leave the ones over the United States in place? What about global communications? We might be initiating a new Dark Age- knocking out the very technology that keeps our world running.

"What if we're wrong and the Host is using an entirely different method for triggering its weapons? Then we're all dead. Are you sure the President has authorized this? It doesn't seem well thought out for Sam Craig."

Harriman and Kurtz exchanged a sideways glance.

"May I speak freely, Madam Ambassador?" asked Harriman. Anne North nodded. "In my recent contacts with President Craig, there seems to be a desperation in his effort not to have his legacy be that of the last American president."

Anne North leaned forward, elbows on the table before her, chin resting in folded hands. She said nothing for what to Harriman seemed a long time, lost in thought. Finally, she looked at Kurtz.

"General, does this plan have a hope in Hell of success?"

Alex Kurtz grimaced. "If we are right about the trigger mechanism, then yes." He nodded towards Harriman, "We do believe that it's the only delivery method that makes sense, something that could be both global and simultaneous. The rub is if the Russians and Chinese have their oligarchs inside the Host. Then they may be just as helpless as we are if their defense systems have been compromised by their contractors."

"That's a huge red flag, General."

"There's possibly a way to find that out," said Harriman. "A few months ago, we began utilizing EPA test data in an attempt to determine the origin of the nanites. We now know that at least some of the particles are turning up in food products from the Wella Cola Corporation, Handle Brewing, and Novel Foods."

"That doesn't get you very far in your conspiracy theory, Colonel," smiled Anne North. "Those three companies are among the last of the independents. They have been doggedly determined to stay that way. The mega-corps have been trying to squeeze them out for years."

"This is true, and on the surface, it doesn't seem to make sense. However, all of these companies have global distribution networks or international production facilities, and while they don't have much in common, separately there is one thread. They all receive ingredients for their products from AgriBus subsidiaries."

"Ok, so AgriBus is in bed with ADC and God knows who else? What does that have to do with the Russians and Chinese?"

Harriman continued, "There's more to it. Smokestack emissions from United Auto and ADC plants also contained nanites. So did those of Pharmatica and Davco Systems. That's transport, healthcare, and computer hardware systems- all critical to defense."

"The President has authorized that some of the nanite signatures be presented to the Russians and Chinese, assuming that they haven't already discovered them themselves," said Kurtz. "We should advise them to check their own industries, especially those that might be linked in some way to defense. If the nanites are detected, then they may be compromised as well. If not, then the conspiracy may be limited to our mega-corps, and there's a chance the plan could work."

Anne North stood and looked out to the August twilight as it painted a backdrop for the New York skyline, then turned back to her visitors.

"I have to tell you, that I think this is a crazy and dangerous idea," she began. "We are going to risk the people of our nation, perhaps several nations on some pretty wild assumptions. Besides, whoever is actually behind the Host, with its help the United Nations has done more to advance the cause of humanity in the past year and a half than it did in the previous eighty. Now you come to me with Sam Craig's half-assed idea and want to tear it all down."

Harriman and Kurtz glanced at each other a second time. North turned to face them.

"John, would you recommend this course of action?"

"It isn't my place, nor the General's, to speculate. We are sworn to protect the existence and security of the United States and to follow the orders of the Commander-in-Chief."

"As am I, no matter how I feel about those orders personally," replied Anne North wearily. "Tell the President I will initiate contact with the Russian and Chinese ambassadors regarding his plan. I just hope to God that something better comes along to preserve our country in the meantime. I have this awful feeling we are about to severely compromise its existence. By the way, does this plan have a name?"

"Not yet, Madam Ambassador," replied Kurtz.

Anne North chuckled sardonically. "Well, gentlemen, tell the President he might consider *Pandora*. We may be about to unleash a whole lot of woe on our world."

***

Philip knocked lightly on his daughter's door.

"Tina, may I come in?"

"Yes, Father," came the lightly voiced reply.

Philip turned the doorknob and slipped inside, closing the door behind him. Tina was sitting on the bed watching something on her Magi-Watch. She didn't look up.

He looked around the room and noticed how sparse it was for a teenage girl. Tina had never really collected the baubles and trinkets coveted by her peers. As a devout member of the Children of God, it wasn't a preferred lifestyle. Tina kept to her books and, in turn, wrote a great deal. Philip found his daughter to be bright; she did well in school, and he expected her to have no problem achieving the marks she needed for entrance into a pre-med, post-secondary education. At seventeen, Tina already knew that she wanted to be a doctor.

Now, he was about to turn her world upside-down.

Philip walked across the small room to the girl's desk and sat down in the chair. His daughter smiled at him and waved the watch closed.

"I'm sorry, Father. It was almost over," said Tina apologetically.

Philip returned the smile. Campbell had his looks, but Tina was without a doubt her mother's daughter. She had the dark, Latina features that Ana Maria possessed. One would never have guessed by looking at her that she was half Pole; she and her mother could have passed for sisters.

He began with a gentle, soft voice. "Honey, there's something we need to talk about. Something I want you to do."

Tina remained motionless, obediently waiting for her father to continue.

"The Sons of Liberty and some folks in the government are very interested in your brother."

"I know. It's because of the Director."

"Yes. The Director wanted to be friends with Campbell, and in order to find out more about the Host, we have encouraged it. What your brother has found out about the Host has been vital in our fight for freedom. Now, we are ready to strike against the Host and its servants."

Tina's face brightened. "That's wonderful, Father! You're going to stop them from destroying America!"

Philip's voice grew graver. "We're going to try, very soon. If God is willing, we will be successful, and the Host will be destroyed and all the Directors with it. But…" he hesitated. What he was about to say next would be blasphemy to her ears.

"There's a chance that we may fail."

Tina frowned. "How could that be, Father? Our Lord always protects His Children against evil."

"I'm sure that we will win and defeat the Host," assured Philip. "Still, just in case something goes wrong, I think it might be best if you weren't here. I've arranged for you to visit your aunt and uncle in Toronto. I want you to take Virginia as well."

"Father, I barely know them… and school will begin again in a few weeks. It's my senior year. I don't want to start out behind in my classes. Please don't make me go. God will protect me. He will protect all of us," pleaded his daughter. She leaned closer and lowered her voice, "Father, they aren't believers."

Tina was right on both counts. Philip's sister had long ago rejected the Children of God and the political direction of the country. Lisa had chosen instead to flee to Canada which at the time had opened its doors to political refugees fleeing from the turmoil of its southern neighbor. Even after normalcy had been restored by the party and the GAF, she never returned, instead choosing to marry a Canadian and raise a family in Toronto.

In turn, their parents had rejected Lisa and her family. They never spoke again. As the years went by, there had been polite contact between Philip and his sister and a few times short reunions of a sort; Philip taking the kids to a neutral site to have lunch with Lisa's family as they passed through on their way to vacation in the Carolinas or Florida. Ana Maria always refused to attend.

The last time he had seen Lisa was at their father's funeral. Their mother wouldn't acknowledge her existence.

Philip couldn't think of a better hiding place for Tina than with his atheist sister and her family.

Hours earlier, Ana Maria had vehemently disagreed with his idea. He had waited for an empty house before making the suggestion to his wife, anticipating her reaction.

"Absolutely not! You might as well be sending her into the claws of Satan himself. I refuse to allow it," she had yelled angrily.

"I don't care. You won't stop this. Better to have her with my sister than to risk her death!" he had responded just as loudly. "I'm not stupid or blind to the truth. This could all go horribly wrong. It's bad enough that you're willing to risk sacrificing our son for your ambition, but not Tina!"

His wife sneered at him in disgust. "You've lost your faith, Philip. Evil has taken you and filled you with fear. I rebuke you in the name of Jesus Christ."

Philip gave his wife a look of annoyance. "I know what this is about, my dear. If the plan succeeds, then you'll benefit greatly. You're making a play for power within the Children and the GAF. This way, you can be open about it instead of trying to get it by bedding Elvis Ansen. What, you think that wasn't obvious?"

"You're possessed by the demon! You will do nothing with Tina! She stays right here."

Philip thought for a second, trying with all his will to keep from strangling Ana Maria. "Ok, you're right! I *am* possessed by the demon, and if you don't let me send Tina to my sister's, then I'm going straight to the Director and tell him about everything and everyone involved in the attack. How's that for pissing in your cornflakes? You'll be disgraced and probably killed. It's going to be hard for you to wield power from a grave."

"I'll kill you myself!"

"No, you won't… because even if you get away with killing me, the investigation will only succeed in putting a spotlight on yourself and all of the other conspirators. They'll have to find some other way to execute the plan, and you'll lose out again."

Ana Maria stared at her husband, bug-eyed and full of hatred. She began to take a step toward him then seemed to think better of it. After a few seconds, she spoke.

"Take her! I can't tell you how much I hate the sight of you at this moment. I wish you were dead and burning in Hell," she spat.

"You may get your wish," her husband replied calmly. "For now you will cooperate. One more thing, tell your boyfriend that I want Tina to have a new name and identification papers. He can do it. Until this is over, I don't want her to be traced back to us.

"Blasphemer!" screamed Ana Maria, pointing at him.

"Whatever. Just get it done."

"I know they aren't of the Children, but they are your blood, and they will respect your faith," said Philip to his daughter. "Who knows? Maybe your example can bring them back to us." He smiled warmly at her.

"Don't worry about school," he added. "We're only talking about ten days at the most. You'll be back home in plenty of time."

"How will I get there? It's another country. Will it take long to get there? I've never been alone," Tina rattled off her thoughts and doubts out loud. Philip left the chair and sat on the bed, putting his arm around his daughter.

"Don't worry; we'll get all that worked out for you. The train is a nice way to travel and going to Toronto's like going to Cleveland. It's not nearly as far as you think. Your aunt and uncle will meet you at the station.

He tried to comfort her further with an attempt at humor. Smiling, he said, "You're just there to take care of my 'Gini.' You make sure she's alright."

He stood up and walked gently to the door. As he opened it, Tina's voice rang out behind him.

"When do I leave?"

He stopped, hand on the doorknob. Without looking back at her, Philip answered, his face grim.

"Soon."

***

Harriman cracked open the door to the condo and peeked in for a look around.

"Grace, I'm here! Hello?"

No answer. Harriman thought that he might have beaten her back to the building. It would give him an opportunity to make dinner for them, he thought. As he entered the living room and began walking toward the kitchen, John heard the running water. Grace was in the shower.

For a split second, John thought about throwing off his clothes and jumping in with her unannounced. Then he thought better of it. Grace knew he was in town at the UN, but that was all. They hadn't seen each other for a few weeks and bursting into her bathroom might get him a broken nose… or worse.

Caution being the better part of valor, John decided upon a revision- he would throw off his clothes and jump into the shower after loudly announcing his presence. He walked toward the bedroom, loosening his tie.

"Grace!" he called out loudly as he entered the bedroom. "Grace! I'm here."

"Oh! John! Make yourself at home. I'm almost finished," her voice was muffled by the running water and partially-closed door.

Harriman spent the next thirty seconds peeling off his clothes and throwing them onto the chair in the corner. He quietly slipped into the bathroom. Inside, it was damp and hot with steam from the shower. Behind the plexiglass door, he could see the dark outline of her form against the bright, white tiles of the space. He opened the door and slid in.

Grace's back had been to the showerhead, rinsing the shampoo from her blonde hair. Harriman's body blocked the flow of water to her, and she turned to face him, startled at first.

"Oh! I guess you really did make yourself at home," she said brightly and flashing an inviting smile. Even nude and with what he considered the perfection of her body soaking wet and inches from him, John Harriman couldn't take his eyes off Grace's face. To him, she was the most beautiful work in all existence.

Grace glanced down, smile still on her face. "I guess you're happy to see me."

He put his arms around her. "You have no idea!" He kissed her hard, his longing for her almost too much to bear.

Grace pulled back smiling, her eyes locked on his. She touched his cheek.

"You need to shave, my love."

"Later."

John made them dinner, quick and easy and straight up. Pan fried sirloins with baked potatoes, broccoli, and carrots. They didn't often have steak, but the occasion was special; a reunion after too much time away from each other.

Afterward, they lay on the same sofa where Grace had first seduced John, she wrapped in his arms. In silence, they looked out over the lights of the city sparkling in the night.

"Is this real?" she asked him.

"As real as anything," he crooned.

Grace looked up at him, "I mean, are *we* real?"

"I love you more than my life," John responded. "You are the happiness I need to get through my days."

She was quiet for a moment. "Can we be permanent? With everything about who and what we are, can we be together forever?"

"Do you want to get married?"

Grace sat up and looked perplexedly at John. "I'm not sure that's what I meant. Most of the people I know that are married want to put each other's head through a wall. You just can't get divorced that easily anymore. I'm not sure I want us to end up hating each other and being stuck."

"Your parents have been married for forty years, and they get along great," he countered, "and what about Kearney? He and his wife are still making babies."

"My folks are the exception, not the rule, and you can't count Red because he's an Irish Catholic. His wife would have to be turning tricks and smoking dope in the street before they'd grant him a divorce," she replied.

"Well, I think your folks have set an excellent example of how to do it right and that the lesson won't skip a generation. Me, I'm a blank slate. I have no dysfunctional family life in my background to screw it up. You could mold me into the ideal husband."

"Are you saying you *want* to get married, John?"

He was quiet for a moment.

"With everything that has gone on in our lives over the past few years, it hadn't crossed my mind- to be honest. You've been doing your thing, and I mine, and it's been this side of insane trying to keep up. What I do know is that I am crazy in love with you, Grace. I hope you feel the same about me. Why not get married and make it forever?" he said finally.

Grace frowned and then looked back up into his face. "I don't know about that John. Maybe sometime in the future, but I have to tell you that forever is rare... if ever.

"I do know this- I want to have a child with you."

Grace's assertion took him completely by surprise.

"Isn't that a little backward? Last time I checked, children were a pretty permanent state of being. Marriage might be the easier option, at least to begin with."

"It's not that. John, I love you more than I have ever loved anyone, so that part of the equation is right. From a genetic standpoint, you're a fantastic physical specimen and one of the most intelligent people I have ever met, so that all works out as well."

John was surprised again by her clinician's analysis.

"Okaaay…"

Graced laughed. "Oh, John! Don't get me wrong but you do have to consider these things in a mate, now don't you? It's just that I'm thirty-eight years old and I don't want to be one of those women waiting until I'm fifty to have a kid. I can't see myself pushing seventy and trying to deal with teenagers. I can always get married, but when it comes to children, the clock is ticking. In my mind, it's getting close to now or never, and I can't think of a better father for my children."

"So you don't want to get married to me, but you do want my DNA for your progeny. I guess I should be flattered."

Grace hugged John. "I never said that I didn't want to marry you, silly man! I just think we should take a little more time to make sure that we have something more, something that will get us through the tough times everyone eventually will have. The kid can come first. Financially, I can afford to have one on my own, and I know that no matter what might happen between us in the future, you would always be there for our child. You are a good man."

"What about your career?" asked John. "Having a baby is going to take you away from your work for at least a year or two. That could have a big impact. Are you ready to take a chance on losing that?"

"I've been talking with NNI about a semi-permanent post at the UN. I'm in the city a lot anyway. I can work right up until the end, take six months off, and then have a regular schedule for a few years afterward. I'll make it work," she answered.

"Oh… I was kind of hoping you might come and stay in Ohio with me for a while."

"You're so funny! Big Apple born and bred but loves that farm out in the middle of nowhere. Well, it is a beautiful place to get away from the rush-rush and relax. I can spend some time there, I promise."

"Good. I'll hold you to it. It isn't that far from Cincinnati, you know. That's somewhere."

John got up and grabbed Grace's wine glass along with his own. He made his way to the kitchen. "You realize that if you do get pregnant, you'll have to put away the Sauvignon for a while."

"I'll make the sacrifice."

Harriman hadn't quite made it to the kitchen when he saw it resting in a display case on the fireplace mantle. He stopped and stared. It was as if a wall in his mind had fallen away.

John Harriman suddenly remembered everything.

He put the glasses down on the kitchen table and walked over to it.

"What's this?" he asked, reaching out as if to take it.

Grace looked up over the sofa. "Oh, that! Isn't it beautiful? It was a gift from Gabriel. Called it a symbol of the covenant between the Host and humanity."

"I've never seen it before."

She left the sofa and walked over to him.

"Gabriel gave it to me a few weeks ago when we were in Kansas. To be honest, I forgot about it for a while and the last time we were together was at your place. I found it again just last week and decided to put it on the mantle. It's probably a little too large to wear for my taste... and it could be looked upon as a conflict of interest. I'm just going to leave it in the showcase."

Harriman continued to stare at the pendant, lost in it. Grace touched his arm.

"Hey, you ok?"

"Yeah," he replied without breaking his gaze. Finally, he looked at her. "I just had never seen anything like it. It's very nice. I thought you despised the Host after Afghanistan?"

Grace turned to look at the pendant in the crystal case. "It's complicated. They're capable of such horrible things at times, but then look at all the good they have done as well. You have to admit that a lot of those the Host has killed deserved it. The casual murder of innocent people, who just happened to be in the wrong place or of the same ethnicity, is hard to square with finding ways to feed the planet, end war, and combat climate change. I really don't know how I feel about them. Of course, it's easy for you- just find a way to stop them. Save the nation. It's probably nice to have no ethical conflicts about where you stand on the Host," she said half in jest.

Harriman turned to look at the pendant again; his life changed.

"Yeah, no conflicts."

He forced himself to break away from the object and went back to the task of refilling the glasses. Grace met him in the kitchen and took her glass from his hand. Together, they returned to the sofa. Harriman did his best to remain relaxed and nonchalant.

"I have to tell you that I was only able to wrangle an overnight," he said.

"Oh, I thought you would have more time," said Grace a little sadly.

"Naw, I had to take care of some business at the UN and then I've got to get back to Washington tomorrow night," replied Harriman. "I don't know how long I'll be. Are you in town for a while?"

"I can be. Can you make it back, soon?"

"I can try to work my schedule around it. I'll let you know as soon as possible."

They settled back into the comfort of the sofa and each other.

"I know you don't want to get married right away, but I don't see any reason why we can't keep working on that baby," John said playfully.

Grace turned into him and began kissing her way down his chest through the open folds of his robe.

"Already on it."

***

The pair of black sedans pulled up silently and stopped in front of the tenement. Wil looked up at the old building from the backseat of the rear car with a sense of familiarity. Three years ago, this rattrap had been his home. Then, home was a box, and finally the Kansas plain. He had come full circle.

"Please wait for your escort, Mr. Ramirez," said the man in the front passenger seat. They watched as two men and two women dressed in dark clothes emerged from the lead sedan. One pair walked briskly toward the building while the remaining pair came back to Wil's car.

Sonya squeezed his hand. "Are you ready for this?"

Wil squeezed it back. "Yeah, I'm good. A little nervous but excited too."

One of the escorts opened his door. Wil stepped out of the sedan into the late August heat. He reached back into the doorway and helped Sonya out. They spent a moment straightening themselves. Wil crooked his arm and nodded for Sonya to take it. "Let's do this."

As they strode up the walk, he noticed some changes for the better. The garbage in the yard was gone, and it looked as though the building's brick had been sandblasted; its trim gleamed of fresh paint. The perennial graffiti that had decorated the outer walls when he lived here was noticeably absent. The windows weren't broken out. Wil stopped for a moment, the entourage halting in synchronicity with him. He looked around curiously and realized that the entire neighborhood had received a facelift. It looked livable.

Sonya must have read his thoughts. "Looks like they've cleaned everything up. I wonder what my old neighborhood looks like now?"

They continued up the steps, past one of the bodyguards and into the building. The inside looked better as well with fresh paint and new carpeting adorning the corridors. The urine smell was gone.

They took the elevator up to the fourth floor. It was clean, bright, and in working order. It opened into another refurbished corridor.

The group halted in front of number 412. Wil gave Sonya one final look for moral support and knocked on the door.

It opened slowly, and the female bodyguard appeared. Wil sagged slightly at the sight of her. His excitement and nervousness returned just as quickly when the door swung open fully to reveal a thin, middle-aged, African-American woman standing before them in the center of the room. Sonya could tell that she was dressed in her Sunday best. She seemed as nervous as Wil; unsmiling, with an anxious look on her face.

"Hello, Mother," said Wil.

The ride out to Valparaiso was long by Chicago standards. Sonya had taken the front passenger seat, and the bodyguard the driver's side, a necessary redundancy as the vehicle journeyed to its preprogrammed destination. Next to Wil sat his mother in the backseat. To Sonya, Mandy Ferguson seemed a bit awestruck by it all.

The reunion had been sweet, mother and son hugging tearfully. Even though she knew that they were coming, it was an emotionally tense scene. Mandy Ferguson hadn't seen her son for more than three years. Until a week ago, she thought that he was at the Oak Park RLC facility. AgriBus's restrictions upon movement and communications had not allowed Wil to relate the events of the past year to her.

After the tears and hugs, the security detail had hustled them back into the sedans and on their way.

"Why do you need all these people around you?" she inquired.

"The company I work for thinks I'm smart. They want the security around to protect me," replied her son sheepishly.

"You are smart," insisted Sonya who had turned to face them from the front seat.

"Has anyone tried to hurt you?"

"Not really," lied Wil. "They have to find a way to justify what they pay me."

"I saw the podcast on NNI. You seem very important, Wilson. I never expected you to be able to get out of Oak Park. I thought you were lost to me. Look at what you've done! I'm so proud of you!"

"A lot of people worked hard to make the Flowerboxes possible," he replied in self-deprecation.

"You were the brain behind ESCAPE, Wil. You should be proud. We all are," said Sonya.

"And you are going to marry my son?" asked his mother, looking at the young woman in the front seat.

"Well…" began Sonya. Wil had introduced her as his fiancé.

"If she'll have me," interjected Wil. "I'll be lucky if she does. She's my best friend, and I love her very much, Mom."

"That's wonderful if you can marry your best friend. It doesn't happen very often. Most of the time we just hookup with people because we have to. Then you're stuck with them, and it's miserable," said Mandy. "How do your parents feel about you getting married."

"They're dead," replied Sonya. "I don't have any family to speak of."

Sonya rarely spoke of her past, but from what she had mentioned it had been bleak. Her mother had been a meth head who had smoked her way into the grave, and her father had been among the first generation to go into the box. Sonya had spent most of her childhood passed from one foster family to another until she was of legal age to be sent to a Virtual Living Center herself. She said she couldn't recall their faces, and she didn't care to.

"Oh, I'm so sorry dear!"

"It's ok. They've been gone a long time. Wil's my family now… and you too, I hope."

Wil hoped so too. His own family experience had been different, but with its own challenges. His father was Cuban and had started a relationship with his mother without mentioning he was in the country illegally. He was around long enough to see Wil born and give him a surname before being caught and deported. Wil never met Alonzo Ramirez and his father never returned or contacted them again- disappearing into the anonymity of the island's populace.

Mandy had spent her youth tending bar at night while her own mother had helped to raise Wil. There were rumors that she could be more intimate with some of the clientele from time to time in order to make ends meet. This was something Wil would never know and his grandmother, an active Baptist, would take to her grave in shame. Ironically, the limitless abundance and lack of risk afforded by virtuality put a huge damper on the trade. Mandy had been forced to turn to cleaning houses by day and bartending at night to get by. The lines on his mother's face betrayed the hardship of her life.

When, without prospects for either a job or an education, Wil had elected to enter the VLC's; it was partly to help alleviate his mother's burden. The day he left, it had broken Mandy's heart that she had been unable to save him.

Valparaiso came across as a sleepy, northern Indiana college town just outside of Chicago. The cars entered the city limits and passed slowly through the campus, coming to a halt in front of a small bungalow surrounded by a well-manicured lawn. The security more relaxed, Wil helped his mother out of the car while Sonya joined them, following behind as they approached the house and went inside.

The place was older but had been refurbished with the most modern technical amenities. The three walked through the house admiring its gadgets and comfortable coziness.

"It's a very nice starter home, Wilson. The town seems wonderful, too... but isn't it a bit small to raise a family?" asked Mandy Ferguson.

"Mom, this is for you," said Wil.

His mother was quiet as she leaned against the couch behind her.

"What? No, how could you afford to do this?" she protested.

"I can afford it. This is for all you did for me when I was a kid. It's a small way of saying thanks."

His mother straightened up. "Wait a minute. What about my friends? How will I see them way out here?"

"We've got that covered. You're a five-minute walk from the train station. You can be in Chicago in half an hour. You'll be able to come and go as you please as well. Money is no object. I've set up a trust fund, and it will provide a monthly income for you. Mom, if you don't want to, you never have to work another day," said Wil.

For a few moments, there was silence as Mandy absorbed the meaning of Wil's words. Then, his mother broke down and sobbed.

***

"I've made an initial contact with both the Chinese and Russian ambassadors. They have agreed to forward sealed diplomatic pouches to their respective premiers, for their eyes only," said Anne North.

"Will they know the contents of the pouches?" asked Harriman.

"No."

"I want to ask a favor of you, Ambassador. Can you delay for forty-eight hours?"

Anne North raised an eyebrow. "That is highly irregular, Colonel. We would be disobeying a directive from the President."

"Not exactly. We would still be following orders; there may just be some red tape in processing," countered Harriman.

"And why would we be encountering *red tape*?"

Harriman leaned in. "There may be another way to achieve our goal without taking such insane risks. Ambassador, you and I both know the President's plan is half-baked and dangerous. It's more than likely that a lot of people will end up dead."

Anne North nodded. "So what do you have in mind?"

"I'm sorry, I can't give you the details. I'm just asking for you to trust me and delay for two days. If I fail, you can fulfill your obligation to the CIC."

"Alright, you've got two days, Colonel Harriman. You realize that Sam Craig will have my head if he gets wind of this."

"And mine as well, but I'd rather attempt a safer path to the finish than what we have before us now. Can you live with yourself if the President ends up getting millions killed for no good reason?"

North stood and offered her hand. "Good luck, John. I hope your plan succeeds… for all our sakes."

"Me too, Madam Ambassador."

Harriman left the embassy offices and crossed the street into the UN plaza, making his way through the late evening gloom to the gardens behind the building. There he walked up to the object that had occupied the same spot for almost two years: the Orphanum.

The craft rested silent and alone on the garden lawn, the guard having long been removed as unnecessary.

He studied the Orphanum carefully, thinking about all that had happened to the world since the revelation of the Host. What had just happened to his world in the past twenty-four hours? The confliction tore at him, but in the end, he knew what his duty had to be.

As Harriman stood before it, the iris that was the craft's doorway opened to him, revealing a blinding, white light emanating from within. He had no choice; the risk had to be taken.

The last time he had made a step toward the craft almost two years ago, his skin had crawled as if he was being swarmed by fire ants. This time, the action afforded no pain. Harriman took another step and another, his pace quickening as he traversed the distance to the ramp that had extended to meet him. He strode determinedly up the gangway and into the light.

Harriman blinked as his eyes adjusted to the light inside. He could see that the compartment was small; his head just cleared the ceiling. The area was nondescript; no instruments, no protuberances, nothing at all in fact; only white walls from which the light emanated. Just off the center of the compartment, seated before him was the Seraphim Gabriel.

"Welcome, John Harriman."

Chapter Nineteen

She saw the tower first, gleaming white and metallic in the late summer sun. It rose head and shoulders above the skyline; from this distance, she thought it looked as if a flying saucer had been skewered on a stick. The rest of the buildings were still dark and non-descript, but she couldn't miss that tower rising out of the helter-skelter jumble of right angles beneath it.

Not that Tina hadn't seen evidence of civilization. She had seen more cornfields in northern Indiana, Ohio, and Michigan than at any time on the journey across southern Ontario. Except for massive fields of wind turbines and solar collectors between Windsor and London, the parade of interconnected towns and villages had been continuous. As they neared the megalopolis that made up the Greater Toronto Area, the geography surrounding the tracks had begun to fill in the sparseness of the townscapes with human construction and activity. Tina could feel the presence of the city growing before her. A city nine-million strong, both rivaling and surpassing her native Chicago in size and importance. She had read up on this largest of Canadian cities; here, they called it the *Centre of the Universe*.

As the train snaked its way along the shores of Lake Ontario, driving deeper and deeper into the heart of Toronto, she was affected by how much the two cities mirrored each other. Both had a grand venue along their respective waterways named Lakeshore, albeit one a Boulevard, the other a Drive. Each had well-used parkland laid out carefully along the shore. As the train made its way toward its destination, Tina could see families and groups playing on the swaths of green along the shoreline.

Only she wasn't Tina anymore. At the border, she had presented a Canadian passport representing her as Sandra Alice Henning, nineteen years of age and making her home in the city of Mississauga, Province of Ontario. The passport even had the prerequisite stamps of American travel; something required after the borders were sealed briefly in '25.

She had shown the customs agent the document, doing her best to remain calm. It was difficult; Tina had been taught never to lie and rarely did on anything more important than if she had been at a girlfriend's instead of hanging out at the coffeehouse. Now she was trying to pull off the biggest falsehood of her life- to the representative of a foreign government.

The customs agent had eyeballed the passport quickly, placing it under the scanners and focusing on the screen data for what seemed a lifetime.

"Where are you from?" she asked.

"Mississauga," said Tina quietly, trying her best to keep her accent as flat as possible.

"How long were you away?"

"Two weeks." Her father had instructed her only to answer the questions asked; nothing more, nothing less. Too much information might raise suspicion.

"What were you doing in the United States?"

"I was visiting family in Chicago," came the well-rehearsed reply.

The agent looked at the document before her. "You have a pet traveling with you? What kind of pet is it?"

"A dog."

"What kind of dog?"

Tina's heart skipped a beat. "An Australian cattle dog. Her name is Virginia."

"Do you have anything else to declare? Any produce or dairy products?"

Tina found that question curiously odd. She was coming from Chicago.

"No."

The agent sorted out the documents before her and returned the passport. As Tina reached out to take it, the officer held on firmly. For a second, Tina felt as if she were playing tug-o-war with the document.

"Funny, your name. I'd swear you're Hispanic... or perhaps Italian."

Tina sifted her mind rapidly for an answer. Henning, what kind of a name is Henning.

"My father is Irish. Black Irish. Those were the survivors from the Armada who settled in Ireland, so I have some Spanish blood mixed in. Every once in a while, someone who looks like me pops up," she answered, smiling.

The customs agent studied Tina for a few seconds more and released her grip on the passport.

"Welcome home, Ms. Henning."

"Thank you," Tina replied, silently thanking her Lord and Savior as well for blessing her with a love of history.

The remainder of the journey had been anti-climactic, not that she needed to have another terrifying experience on this day. Tina let out a deep sigh as the train slowed. The heart of the city had now come into focus; its mass of towers stretching away from the lake for as far as she could see.

The city disappeared as the train dropped behind a mammoth wall that delineated the yard of the station. Several lines of track spread before her on either side; they passed a motionless freight train before her view was suddenly obstructed- a passenger train sliding by. Tina could see the faces of its human cargo looking back at her as they slowly accelerated past.

Artificial light replaced the natural when her car entered the tunnel to the station. The train slowed to a crawl; the platform growing into view from the window across the aisle. It came to a stop before what seemed to be an endless series of doors; travelers and station personnel weaving in and out as they opened and closed before her. Over the PA system, an automated female voice welcomed her to Toronto.

Tina waited for the compartment to empty before rising to recover her luggage from the overhead. Making her way to the exit, she asked the attendant where Virginia could be found.

"Just go through those doors and to the right. You'll see the baggage area right away," he said. "Don't worry; they aren't going to toss your dog on the carrousel. They'll bring 'em right out for you, straight from the baggage car."

Just as he said they would, the baggage handlers wheeled Virginia's carrying case through a door. A swipe of her new Magi-Watch across the signature pad and Tina retook possession of her father's pet. With both the luggage, and a cage large enough to contain a forty-pound dog, Tina struggled to get everything up the escalator at once. It hadn't been this difficult when departing; her father had taken care of Virginia's stowage. After no small measure of jostling, she found a way to get the dog to the front of her and the bag behind as she ascended to the main level of the station.

The escalator brought her to a large, open, art-deco hall, reminding her of the Union Station in Chicago she had departed from eight hours prior. She looked up at the writing carved into the stonework that ringed the vaulted ceiling above. It said *Union Station*. Tina smiled at the coincidence; a thought went through her that this was all just a surreal, circuitous journey to nowhere and that she had now returned to her departure point. She half expected to find her father waiting to greet her, laughing in his way about the joke he had just played upon her. The sight of the giant, Canadian flag hanging from one wall of the hall dispelled the notion as fantasy.

Tina began to look around for familiar faces. Her Magi-Watch went off. She waved it on, and an image of her aunt and uncle appeared in her contact. They were smiling and waving.

"Look behind you, dear," said the woman.

She turned about. Standing ten feet from her was her father's sister with her husband.

Aunt Lisa hugged her while Uncle Armand took Virginia's carrier.

"My, you look just like your mom when she was your age. So beautiful! I can't believe it's been three years since we last saw you; although your father has been sending pics of you and Campbell," prattled Aunt Lisa. "Speaking of your father, he was worried about you. He said he would call later."

They began heading toward the entrance doors that spilled out into the downtown core of the city. When the group exited into the afternoon light, Tina stopped for a moment and looked around.

She was safe.

***

"The Vice-President is here with a... um, guest," stated Preet over the intercom.

President Samuel H. Craig looked up from the brief he had been studying with curiosity.

"The Vice-President? What's Chris Cameron doing in town? He's supposed to be at The Hague. Who's with him?"

"Good afternoon, Mr. President," called out Christopher Cameron as he strode through the Oval Office door.

Craig stood up behind his desk. "Chris, what are you doi... oh."

Following the Vice-President into the room was the Seraphim Michael. It closed the door as Cameron casually settled into one of the guest chairs in front of Samuel Craig's desk.

"So much for security," muttered Craig, returning to his seat.

"Funny, they always give it a wide berth," replied Chris Cameron, nodding at the Seraphim.

"I guess it all makes sense now," declared Craig. "No wonder you were all about patience and delayed response. Your counsel helped take away our window of opportunity."

"There was never any window, Sam. You never had a chance. Being aggressive would have just killed hundreds of millions of innocent people," shot back Cameron in his Texas drawl. "We'd have done it too if you had forced us the way those damned Turkmen Shias did. My advice was the right one, and I helped to save you from making a huge error in judgment."

"To think I fired Jim Gillette over this because he was with AgriBus. I suppose he was clean."

"If you mean was he in on it, no. Poor Jim was out of the loop. Truth is, not nearly as many people as you think are behind this. We wouldn't have been able to keep it a secret for almost forty years if that were the case."

"So let me get this straight; you've been planning this since the nineties?"

Chris Cameron laughed. "I guess since the millennium, although I wasn't one of the original inner circle. Actually, the whole thing was Jerry Ross's idea. Remember the Billionaire Boys Club at Harvard?"

"Not really," replied Craig dryly. "My law degree is from Indiana."

"Oh… well, it was the sons and daughters of some of the wealthiest families in the world, all studying at the Harvard Business School," Cameron explained. "Legend has it that they're sitting around getting hammered one night after 9/11 and moaning about how the world is going to shit. Ross speaks up and says to them, *well, if anyone can fix this mess, it's us*. I mean, Ross's daddy is going to die within a few years, and he will inherit the largest software company on the planet. Isaias Bautista is going to be running ADC in a few years. Ira Stenson is going to form AgriBus… you get it. These guys are players. They've got the money and brains, and after a few years of sitting around talking about how to pull it off, they commit to a plan."

Sam Craig leaned back into his big chair. "That was some plan. Even with all of their money and power, I don't know how they thought they could pull it off and fool an entire planet."

Cameron threw his hands in the air. "People believe what they want to believe and facts be damned. You know that better than anyone, Sam. It's the basis of modern politics. Folks have lost their faith in reality and placed it in the supernatural. Two-thirds of the people in this world are waiting for their god to save them and the other third believes that aliens are going to land and do the same. Everyone is looking for something bigger- to lead them out of the mess they've made and into the Promised Land."

"Enter the Host," responded Craig.

"The door was open; we simply walked through it," replied Chris Cameron. "Your GAF buddies and their colleagues around the world made it easy. You've spent decades crafting fantasy for mass consumption. They solidified power by taking away the vote from non-Christians and promoting *creation science* over real science in the schools. You clowns have spent thirty years dumbing down your electorate. When the Host arrived, it was easy for people to rationalize a supernatural, angelic army come to save them. What did you expect?"

"You know I'm no fan of the GAF, Chris," snapped Craig.

"No, but you didn't have any problem reaping the harvest they sowed. You couldn't get the nomination without their support, and you wouldn't be president without all their loyal followers voting for you in the general election. Feigning innocence is the last thing you should be attempting with my friends, Mr. President. To the contrary, you could be held even more accountable. At least these GAF idiots believe their bullshit. You've exploited their ignorance and blind faith for your gain."

"What you're doing isn't exploitation? Using smoke and mirrors to take over the planet and slaughtering hundreds of thousands of innocents? Dismantling your country? You don't exactly hold the moral high ground," growled Craig, voice rising in anger. What I don't get is how you kept all those magnificent toys hidden from us. You guys have some serious Flash Gordon shit going on that should be in our hands instead of yours."

"That's where you're wrong, Mr. President, on both counts. For one, it wasn't nearly as difficult as you might think to keep from you what we needed to assume control," countered Chris Cameron. "Where does all your weapons tech come from? The *mega-corps*. It's always been that way- private contractor develops the latest gadget to hand off to its respective government... only all that changed with the new century. When an industry goes global and the corporations with it; then what *defines* a respective government? Eventually, the corporations evolve into the mega-corps; with more assets than most of the nations on Earth.

"After a decade or so of this, it becomes apparent that those same governments, with their perpetual dysfunction, are the real enemies of human progress. They can't agree on anything- continuously bickering and warring over resources and petty issues and bleeding out their assets... including human capital. I mean, look at us; as a country, we've been in some state of armed conflict for almost a century. It's like watching monkeys throw scat at each other. Why would anyone want to give a bunch of brainless baboons machine guns when they can't even manage with sticks? So, you start holding back the best stuff, the top-notch tech for yourself."

Cameron threw his thumb over his shoulder casually. "The archangels there, boy! True artificial intelligence, surpassing human capability in almost every way. They can think and reason on their own and make independent decisions within the parameters of the mission. They're amazing! You actually think we'd ever give you or the Russians or the Chinese or the Indians this technology? You'd all be trying to figure out how to make walking atom bombs."

Craig spun sideways in his chair and stood up, walking over to the bar.

"Alright, but if the archangels are so superior to us, what keeps them from just taking over?" he asked.

Cameron stood up and joined the President at the bar where Craig was pouring two drinks. Cameron accepted the glass.

"Programming. We have engineered redundancies that keep them subservient to our will. We give them mission parameters and a set of ethical guidelines and they accomplish it. We send them new missions, and they function within the Host network to achieve the mission goals. They can never act outside of the guidelines we set. It's built in. The Cherubim, those boys with the plasma generators, are cloned bodies with AI operating systems."

"What about the Directors? They're obviously human, and we can put to bed the story that they're the children of abductees. How did you keep them hidden?"

"Orphans."

"What?"

"Orphans, that we've been caring for over the past twenty years through our worldwide network of NGO's. What better way to build a loyal army than from the cradle- and with the unwanted? We sift out the best and brightest and orient them to the cause. Some were referred to our rivals and competitors to infiltrate and assimilate their assets for our own agenda."

"Spies," sneered Craig.

"If you like," sniffed the Vice President. "We prefer to think of them as deep cover assets. Others... we had their existence erased from the net when they volunteered to become part of the Host's cyber network- merging with their interfaces. The *halos* as people call them. Aren't those things marvelous? Everyone is running around trying to solve quantum computing, and DNA-driven CPU's were right there for the taking! I could go on and on about that technology, but you get the idea. Governments have been such a disaster for the past thirty years that it's been pretty easy to hide the best tech while getting them to fund the R and D."

"So the Illuminati are real."

Cameron snorted.

"Of course not! The Illuminati are supposed to be an ancient order following an evil agenda of world domination; in pursuit of personal power, and devil worship, and all that bullshit. We're not about that. Not at all."

"What are you about, Chris? I don't get it," said Sam Craig. "These people, their corporations, they have everything they could ever want, including power over the election process. Every politician in every nation on the planet is beholden to some corporate master for their supper. Why risk all that?"

Chris Cameron took a drink and pointed his finger at the President.

"Because you can't sell anything to dead people."

"Excuse me?"

"You heard me. Dead people make lousy consumers."

Craig moved back over to the front of his desk and leaned against it, open-mouthed and incredulous.

"You mean to tell me that this is all about money? Are you fucking kidding me?"

"Of course it's about money! It's always about money, isn't it? What's better, Sam? Nine billion fat, happy, and prosperous consumers of products and services- or just three billion fat, happy, and prosperous for the moment- with the other six billion bleeding them dry?"

Craig laughed. "I've got to tell you, Chris, for a while, I thought the Host were communists or something."

Cameron's next words startled him. "Well, you're kind of right about that *or something*."

"What the hell does that mean?"

Cameron sat back down. "Laisse Faire capitalism has run its course, Sam. Look at what's happened. A third of the country has been living in artificial worlds because we can't find anything for them to do and we can't afford to have them draining resources in the real world. The geopolitical system has evolved into a form of corporate feudalism. Governments play the role of the Church and keep those at the bottom in line. It may sound like the ideal situation from the viewpoint of the mega-corps, but in fact, it's precisely the opposite."

"How's that?"

Cameron looked at him in annoyance.

"I guess Henry Ford understood it best. You can't pay people slave wages and then expect them to buy your cars. If all we do is groom and satisfy the needs of a privileged few, there's no incentive for growth or innovation. Eventually, the system collapses upon itself."

"Everything dies," nodded Craig in quiet comprehension.

"Exactly, except in this case we aren't simply talking about bringing back the Dark Ages. This is about the extinction of the species," said Cameron. "We tried for twenty years to usurp and control governments from within, but the framework is flat busted. It has to be swept away and a new framework established. There has to be a new society built; a new kind of capitalism that isn't just about stupidly squeezing a stone until there's no blood left. There must be a new covenant between the people and their constructs; one that is fair and decent and prosperous for all."

"The covenant of the Host," answered Craig.

"Yes. Governments have been such a disaster the past forty years that their inability to lead has left us all teetering on the edge of a cliff. You and I both know from the data that in a couple of decades we'll be eating each other and I can tell you... it doesn't take a lot of insight to realize that cannibalism is very bad for business. That's why we couldn't just let things go on. Money doesn't have any meaning if the social order collapses back into bands of hunter-gatherers. And don't think it can't happen, because history is full of examples that it can," finished Chris Cameron, his gaze cold as steel.

Craig's eyes darted briefly to Michael. It had remained by the door, motionless during the entire exchange. The President thought it best to keep the conversation moving along.

"Alright, I get the motive and the means. As you said earlier, we never had a chance to stop you. Why not just come out and show yourselves for who you are? What's with the religious/space alien façade?"

"That was Ira Stenson's idea; he's got this amazing intellect when it comes to world religions and their impact upon history. The way he saw it, most people have some degree of belief in the supernatural. So you catch up a number of these folks in this Abrahamic mythology with the Host of Heaven. You know, holy army of God and all. Throw in a flying saucer and some techno-trickery and wallah! You have most of the world paralyzed out of either fear or awe or both. Are they the ancient astronauts who have returned to look in upon their wards? Is it a trick of the devil or is it the Heavenly Host of God?

"Besides, we have business competitors with a vested interest in maintaining the status quo. We needed a way to neutralize any potential interference from them as well. Ira thought it was the perfect cover story and everyone agreed. So far, it's worked like a charm," chortled the Vice-President.

"We cracked it. We figured it out. Others will too."

"You've been looking for us for two years, and it took a fluky incident to give you a clue," retorted a hard-faced Cameron. "Don't pat yourself on the back too much. The Kremlin was on top of it months before you figured it out. I guess they're a little better at secrecy and subterfuge, being a former autocracy."

"Former?"

"Yes. You see, there's been a quiet little coup in Moscow this morning. Those supporting the new United Nations and its socially democratic values have put down an attempt by the Premier and several members of the Politburo to launch an attack on the Host. Michael's compatriot, Uriel, had a hand in stopping the conspirators. Of course, that isn't how the official story will read. Word is that Premier Chernov is dead from a heart attack. The other conspirators will choose this time of transition to *retire* from public life."

"You killed Boris Chernov?" asked Sam Craig, trying mask his sudden discomfort.

"No, the Host protected itself and, with it, humankind. In a way, it protected America as well. Chernov had discovered the frequency chords and was getting ready to nuke all the suspected Host-controlled industries- after he jammed the ADC nanite trigger systems. He wasn't going to jam the birds on this side of the planet, though. He hoped to provoke a response from the Host that would kill everyone in the Western Hemisphere just before the missiles hit their targets. Would have killed several billion people. Nice guy, huh? A shining example of the old ways. So, you're welcome, Mr. President."

Chris Cameron and Sam Craig locked eyes. "To think that you were going to turn over all that research to Chernov, with some harebrained plan to disable the birds. I don't think he would have needed it. Lucky we took him out first, wouldn't you say?"

The two men stared at each other for a few uneasy moments. Craig finally broke the silence, "So what happens now, Chris? Are you here to kill me?"

Cameron looked down at the drink cradled in his hands. "If I were going to kill you, I would have just done it and not wasted time laying it all out for you. Besides, that's up to you, Mr. President. For some reason, they like you. I think they appreciate your pragmatism. You still command a great deal of respect with the American people, and with many world leaders. The original deal remains on the table. After the reorganization, we will make sure you are the UN representative from the Great Lakes region and, if not out and out Secretary General, then at the very least occupying a prominent position within the Executive Council. All you have to do is help to sell the transition and keep the true nature of the Host to yourself. You'll be on the inside from now on. No more stupid attempts to thwart our goals."

Cameron leaned forward slightly in his chair. "Or... you can die of a brain hemorrhage, tragically cut down by bad genetics in the prime of your life. You'll be given a state funeral, and I'll become the last American President."

President Samuel Hiram Craig looked out the Oval Office window and onto the well-manicured green of the White House grounds.

"The Romans were the first to make the observation, Mr. Cameron, that empires were made to fall. No matter what their rulers did to maintain a grip, eventually the lands and the people would slip away. Either through exhaustion or because another group would come in and make them part of a bigger, stronger, better empire. Funny, they were very much resigned to the inevitability of the process. I guess now it's our turn to face the inevitable."

"We're building a better world, Sam. A world of peace and prosperity," said Chris Cameron. "You're going to play a significant role in it."

Craig turned to face the other man, "There are others who know what you are."

"It's being taken care of, Mr. Secretary-General."

Samuel Hiram Craig liked the sound of that... *Mr. Secretary General.*

***

We must meet. We're in danger.

Agent Smith's message on the private server put a chill into Dr. Ali Naji. What he had been dreading for weeks had been realized: that the Host had somehow found out that he knew too much.

Naji stared at the message, paralyzed momentarily. He stood up and closed his office door, then went back to the heads up display showing the message thread.

"Answer message. What to do?"

What to do? appeared on the HUD. Naji waited.

Lunch... in the quad came the reply referring to the park centered between four of the university's buildings.

Fear gripped him. What if it wasn't Smith on the other side of the server? He could be walking into a trap and straight to his death. He began to think through the scenarios; would the Host kill him for no apparent reason in broad daylight and with dozens of passing students and faculty as witnesses? Probably not; if they were going to be that blatant, someone could just bypass the building security, walk into the lab, and shoot him. In truth, Ali Naji reasoned to himself; they could probably just walk up behind him at any moment and trigger the nanites within him to block an artery. He would fall dead from a massive coronary.

Naji looked up at the clock on the HUD. It read 11:50.

"Twenty minutes," he said to the messenger. "Erase thread."

He wasn't waiting that long. Naji speculated that if he went now, he might be able to spot any potential subterfuge. He opened the office door and walked toward the lab exit. Three graduate assistants were in front of him- fixated on what he assumed was the latest data from a project they had been working on.

He smiled and waved as he passed them. "Lunch. I'll be about a half hour."

They nodded, and one returned the smile in acknowledgment. Naji went out into the corridor and bypassed the elevators, choosing to enter the stairwell at the end of the hall. It was illuminated by a series of large, picture windows on each landing that banded up the side of the building. Glazed so as not to allow a view of the interior of the building; the fourth-floor landing was a perfect spot for Ali to peruse the park below. He took his time, examining every square foot and the activity within for anything which may look out of the ordinary. In doing so, Ali Naji found Agent Smith sitting quietly on a park bench. The seat was perpendicular to the Research Center, giving Smith a view of both the building's front entrance and the quad grounds.

Satisfied, Naji made his way down the steps and exited through the doors into the light of day. He meandered to the bench- taking a lazy, indirect route, eventually finding his way to Agent Smith's bench. He sat down comfortably apart from the other man yet close enough for quiet conversation.

"I apologize for the intrigues, Dr. Naji. We can't take any more chances with electronic communication, and I'm not sure that your office is the best place for a conversation these days," began John Smith.

"Agreed, Mr. Smith," nodded Ali Naji. "I assume that the Host has found out about our research. I fear for my life."

"We all fear for our lives, Doctor, but we still have secrecy on our side- at least for the time being. I learned that from the Voice itself- Gabriel. They're still fishing. That's why the Commander-in-Chief has decided to take action against the enemy now."

"A very dangerous move, Agent Smith. We have seen how the Host treats its enemies," replied Naji fearfully.

"We have no choice. It's only a matter of time before we are discovered. The CIC has decided to make a move while we still have an element of surprise."

"You're going to get me and my family killed if you do this."

Smith looked at Naji straight-faced. "You and your family are already dead along with the President, myself, and others if we don't act, Doctor Naji."

The government man softened his tone. "The President will provide new identities for you and your family so that you can remain safe and undercover until the crisis has passed. You will be given two hundred thousand credits, a new vehicle, and a new home in a new city... a new country if you want."

Naji was silent as he processed the operative's words. "I believe a new country might be prudent. On the other side of the world. Egypt perhaps."

"Egypt then. I will arrange for you to have new travel documents, including Egyptian passports. You will drive to Atlanta, take a flight to Mexico City, and then on to Cairo and a new life."

"They will find us."

"No, they won't. The Host isn't omnipotent. They're people, and they're fallible. You'll be in deep cover, so deep and well-hidden that only I will know how to contact you. You have to trust me, Al."

"This coming from a man who calls himself John Smith."

The operative continued to stare out into the busy quad in silence.

"Suit yourself, Doctor," said Agent Smith finally as he prepared to stand. "There is the matter of the government property you possess. We'll both go inside together, and I will relieve you of its burden."

"Wait," said Naji in quiet anxiety. "What is your plan?"

Smith relaxed back onto the bench. "Go back inside and continue your day just as you would any other. Retrieve the property when you leave and take it home with you. Put it in the trunk of your car.

"Explain the situation to your wife. Round up your twin girls, bring your ID's with you. When we meet, I'll take the old ones to be destroyed and give you your new identities. Bring only the clothes on your back- you want nothing that could potentially identify you. You'll have access to credits; you can buy what you need later. Take this."

Smith held out a slip of paper in his hand. Ali took it without looking.

Smith continued, "These are the GPS coordinates for the rendezvous point. It's a park just outside the city. Meet me there at eight. I'll have a car and four tickets for a flight tomorrow night from Atlanta to Mexico City. From there, you're on your own to get to Cairo. We won't be able to help, for fear of drawing unwanted attention to you."

He stood up, adjusting his jacket. "If the mission is successful, come out of cover and contact the Pentagon. If you want, they'll bring you back in. Who knows? You might just want to stay in Cairo."

"How did you know I had twin daughters? We've never discussed my family," asked Ali.

Agent Smith smiled wryly at him. "I'm a spook, Dr. Naji. It's my business to know everything about you. Until tonight."

Naji walked slowly back into the building and to his office. The next few hours, he did his best to be casual around the grad students. Inside, he was a hurricane of worry and doubt. Safa knew nothing of his work, for her safety he had kept her in the dark. Now, he was about to tear her world, and that of his daughters, to shreds without notice. They would disappear into the night- no word to friends or colleagues or even their families. Vanish into the mists of incognito, perhaps for the remainder of their lives.

Naji set himself to the task of removing the property from his lab safe and transporting it out of the building without attracting attention to himself. It took his mind off of the loss of this world, at least momentarily. He decided the most effective means would be to wait until the staff was gone and place the contraband into his briefcase. Ali did the mental math, deciding within moments that not only would the halo and its corresponding parts fit easily, but he could also probably hide it within the various papers currently occupying the case.

A second thought entered his mind as he pondered the components- how long before they realized the CPU was missing. He pushed that anxiety away, Smith probably wouldn't know what he was looking at and they would be well gone before anyone else put two and two together.

Dr. Ali Naji waited for the planned moment to materialize. By 4:30, the lab was empty. He went about his usual ritual of pulling down the window shades in his office to block out the labcam and proceeded to the safe. It had a voice-lock.

"Harmjdun," he said out loud. The safe clicked open, revealing its contents. Naji reached into the safe and gently removed the components of the interface one by one. As an afterthought, he looked around for a bag to put them in so that they wouldn't jostle around in the briefcase. He saw a black, plastic bag lining the small wastebasket under his desk. Fortunately, it was empty. Ali Naji took the bag out of the container and placed the interface components inside. He then opened his briefcase and stuck the bag in between his papers, covering it from view. Closing the briefcase, Ali Naji put on his coat and opened his office door for the last time.

The thought that much of the last decade of his life had been spent on this floor struck him. He had worked in this room as a grad student, received his doctorate, and remained on with the university during that time. He had married his wife and had the twins within that time. Now there was no time left; they had to flee for their lives. Tearfully, Dr. Ali Naji turned and left the lab without looking back.

He took the elevator to the parking level, bypassing the main floor security. Only authorized personnel had parking permits and security was purposely lax to leave the impression that no research of major importance was taking place inside the building. In this case, it worked to Naji's advantage.

He popped open the trunk, placing the briefcase inside. Naji then entered the driver's seat of the sedan and ordered it home. The clock on the dashboard read 5:36. He began calculating the trip in his mind; fifteen minutes put him in at roughly six. An hour to explain the danger to Safa, round up the girls, eat dinner, and leave for the GPS coordinates written on the piece of paper in his pocket. He couldn't think of a more difficult series of simple tasks.

The sedan pulled into his driveway just before six. Ali exited and went through the front door of his home. He could smell dinner from the kitchen. His wife would be there.

She was standing at the island in the kitchen slicing tomatoes for the large salad occupying the bowl to her right. Safa looked up and smiled as he came through the entrance. Between them, the glow of marriage had remained, through six years and the raising of the twins.

He kissed her cheek. "Where are the girls?"

"Playing in their bedroom, I would guess," she replied cheerfully. "How was your day? You look tense."

"Safa, come and sit down. We must talk," he said somberly.

Ali spent the next fifteen minutes explaining his work, the resulting danger and their need to flee to a new life as new people in a new country. As he went on, his wife's face drew serious, then open-mouthed in disbelief, then grim with fear. Finally, tearful with the awareness of her husband's implication.

"Why do we have to leave? Why isn't the government protecting us?" she cried. He took her and held her tightly, trying to be strong for her.

"They are trying to protect us… by giving us new identities and a chance for a new life," he responded. "Safa, we must go away, we have no choice- if not for ourselves then for the children."

"I know," she replied, pulling away. She looked up at her husband with a painted smile, tears running down her face. "We will have an excellent dinner and then go on a great adventure together." Safa turned away and wiped her eyes. "Do what you must, and I will set the table."

Ali Naji smiled sadly at his beautiful, brave, young wife and left the kitchen for their bedroom. He heard her call out to the girls as he went up the stairs.

"Nadia! Nakato! Come and help with dinner."

The door to their bedroom opened and the twins burst out into the hallway. Identical in almost every way to the inexperienced eye, Ali could immediately tell that Nakato was leading the rush. They ran to him with smiles as he reached the top of the stairs. Their father kneeled to greet them, taking one in each arm. The two four-year-olds hugged him profusely.

"Now, go and help your mother with dinner and I will be there soon. We have some very important news to tell you!"

"Tell us now, daddy!" insisted Nadia, the older of the two by seven minutes.

"No, it is a special surprise. Do as I ask," he commanded happily.

The girls bounced down the stairs as Ali went to his bedroom. He took a few minutes for the toilet- washing his face and hands, Ali paused a moment to look at his reflection in the mirror. He changed his clothes into something casual and more suited to the journey ahead- going for the tourist look. Then he went to the small, fireproof box they kept on the top shelf of the closet and took it down. He opened it on the bed and removed his family's passports before putting the box back in its place on the shelf. Grabbing the passports from the bed, Ali went downstairs into the kitchen.

Over dinner, he and Safa explained the great and exciting journey ahead. The girls took it all in quietly; at four it is easy to play games, especially out in the open with the grownups. Ali Naji, the father, explained to his children that it was going to be a game of Hide and Seek, but with special rules. They were going to have new, pretend names and so were Mommy and Daddy. They were going to play a trick on everyone and go to a new, fun place for a while. He thanked Allah that they were so young; there was no school to withdraw from and few friends to leave behind.

After dinner, Safa insisted that the dishes be cleaned up and put away. Ali guessed she couldn't stand the thought of leaving behind a messy house. She went upstairs to dress the girls and change for herself. Ali went to the small bar they kept and took out a bottle of his best brand of scotch. He poured two fingers into a glass and sipped it slowly, savoring the smoky flavor of the single malt. By the time he had drained the glass, Safa, and the twins were coming down the stairs. He went out into the foyer to meet them, hugging his wife as he opened the door.

"Don't look back," he said to her as they went through the doorway. "This life is now behind us, my love. We will make a better one."

They each took one of the twins, strapping them into their car seats in the rear of the sedan. Safa chose to sit between them, more as a comfort to herself than the girls, Ali thought.

He spoke the coordinates into the sedan's GPS and the car began its journey to the rendezvous. The dashboard clock read 7:17.

The sedan slowly made its way through the neighborhood. Ali sat in the passenger seat, looking back at his girls and holding Safa's hand. They said nothing for the first few minutes; the girls played a game on their pads. As the car left the city streets and moved onto the highway access ramp, Nadia looked up.

"Daddy, where are we going?"

"To a city called Atlanta and from there we will fly on an airplane. It will be just like visiting Nana and Papaw," he said, smiling gently.

"Is that the big adventure? Are we really going to see Nana and Papaw?" she asked with glee.

"No, we are going on another adventure, to another place far across the ocean," replied her father.

"Oh," she said glumly and returned to her game.

The sedan traveled on for another twenty minutes before exiting onto a lonely state road and turning right at the stop sign.

"Are we in Atlanta yet? It doesn't look very big. I don't see any planes," rattled off Nakato.

"No, Atlanta is going to take a little longer. Right now we are stopping off to meet a friend of mine."

As they watched, a sign appeared ahead and came into focus. It read *Tanner Park and Recreation Area.* The car slowed to turn onto an access road to the park and followed the way through heavy woods that nearly tamped out the remaining light of day. Suddenly, it seemed to Ali, the road before them opened into a clearing- Ali recognized that they were in the recreation area's parking lot. It was empty, except for a black sedan parked in the center of the tarmac. Agent Smith was already here.

The sedan came to a stop roughly thirty meters from the other car. Smith was behind the wheel of his vehicle, driving it up beside Naji's. Ali ordered the car off, the trunk open and the driver's side window down. Smith rolled his window down.

"Hello, Doctor." He looked at the passengers in the back seat and smiled warmly. "Hi, ladies! Doc, where have you been hiding these lovely girls?"

"Wait here, I'll just be a minute or two," he said to the girls. His wife nodded nervously as he opened his door. Naji realized he was scared as well, but did his best to hide it.

Agent Smith was already out of his car and walking back to an open trunk. He took out a fat, metallic briefcase and set it on the hood of Naji's car. Naji went to his trunk and retrieved the interface. Leaving the trunk open, he rounded the car and placed his briefcase on the car's hood next to Smith's. Smith offered his hand.

"How are you, Doctor?"

Naji relaxed a little as he took it. "I'm anxious for my family. A little scared. We all are. We just walked away from our lives. How else could we be?"

"At least you still have lives," returned Agent Smith. "We're going to get you all out of here to safety. Is this the... interface?"

"Yes," said Naji opening the black case. He shuffled the papers aside and pulled back the black garbage bag to reveal its contents. "Everything is here, all the components."

"Leave them in the briefcase. I'm going to take this car back to your house and park it. We want it to look like you just vanished without a trace. You're going to take this car to Atlanta and leave it in long term parking. We'll pick it up later. Did you bring your ID's and electronics?"

"Yes. Do you want them?"

"Soon, but first let's go over what we've put together for you." Smith opened his briefcase and began pointing out the contents. "Here are your new passports and identifications. You are Sayed Farook from now on, a citizen of the United Arab Republic. Here are Egyptian passports and identification papers. Do the girls speak Arabic? Good, you can pass the accents off as too much time in America. These are new watches for you and your wife. Here are the tickets for your flight. This is important- it's your access card to a bank account at the National Bank of Alexandria. In that account are a little more than two hundred thousand credits. This isn't a new account so you can't be traced from it; it won't draw suspicion. There's more. You're going to need this. You can leave it in the car at the airport."

Smith popped open the false bottom of the briefcase. Inside was a wad of banknotes and a thirty-eight caliber revolver.

Naji took a step back. "I don't need that."

"I'm afraid you do," said Agent Smith, grabbing the gun with lightning speed. Doctor Ali Naji felt the cold metal of the weapon's barrel press into the soft flesh beneath his chin. Then he felt nothing at all.

The top of Naji's head exploded in the twilight.

Before Naji's body could slump to the tarmac, John Harriman turned and fired three more shots into the rear of the sedan through the open window. All hit their mark with deadly accuracy.

The action had taken less than three seconds from start to finish. The dashboard clock in Ali Naji's car read 8:05.

Showing no emotion, Harriman opened the thirty-eight and removed the two remaining rounds from their chambers, replacing them with blank cartridges. He closed the weapon and slid it into the right hand of the body on the tarmac. Placing the Doctor's finger on the trigger, Harriman held the gun over the corpse and pointed the weapon away from himself. He pressed his finger against Naji's and fired the blanks.

Taking the gun back, Harriman replaced the two unused rounds into their original chambers and set the thirty-eight down a few inches away from where Naji's right hand lay on the tarmac.

Harriman removed the interface from Naji's briefcase and put it into his own. Closing both, he took the Doctor's and placed it in the trunk of Naji's car prior to closing it. He then took the metallic case and put it into his own sedan's trunk before getting behind the wheel and starting the vehicle manually.

As he drove away, John Harriman didn't look back.

Harriman drove more than one hundred miles north toward New York City, changing highways twice, before stopping to recharge. There, he ran the sedan through the automated wash and himself went into the station's bathroom to remove the skin sealant from his hands with soap and water. His intent had been to remove any traces of gunpowder from his hands; placing a gunpowder marker on Dr. Naji's hands had been vital to the implied murder/suicide scenario he had just constructed. Still not wanting to leave any trace of fingerprints in the sedan, he pulled a small spray can from his jacket and reapplied a concealing layer to each hand. Exiting the bathroom, Harriman returned to the vehicle and continued on his way to New York City.

He drove to avoid thought, to remove at least temporarily from his mind the slaughter he had just committed, to focus on the road ahead. It did no good.

It wasn't the killing that bothered him. Harriman had killed often in his life and without a second thought; men and women alike, he thought perhaps as many as one hundred, perhaps more. John Harriman had a problem squaring the innocence of these victims with his action. They had committed no crime, and only Naji himself was a potential threat. It chewed at him the entire drive back to the rendezvous with Malak- the Left Hand of the Host. The Angel of Death.

328

Much as he despised what he had just done, John Harriman was powerless to prevent it. He was compelled to it. Gabriel had ordered the assassinations, and he could not resist the will of the Host. It was what he had been trained and conditioned for since he was a child. The false memories implanted in Harriman that he had believed since his days at West Point; the memories of his early years... all fell away when he saw the Symbol of the Covenant in Grace's condo. In that symbol, the truth had been revealed to him.

Harriman had been trained to be a killer; of that he was aware. What had been buried deep inside his consciousness; that he was without free will. A Servant of the Host, to do whatever bidding It required without question. A sleeper cell of one- to be activated as a surgical weapon when the circumstance dictated. It went beyond even that.

As much as he hated himself, John Harriman loved the Host. More than anything.

Chapter Twenty

The lights approached rapidly from behind. At first look, it was as though they were on a level plane with the sedan and Harriman feared momentarily that the advancing vehicle would rear end his own. As the lights closed on him, his point of view changed and Harriman realized that they belonged to something traveling not on the roadway but above it. Moments later, the sedan shuddered from prop wash as the vehicle passed directly above and into view before him. He recognized it immediately as an Orphanum.

The small craft shrank into the night sky ahead, and Harriman saw it slow to a stop a kilometer in front him. He reduced the sedan's speed as he approached the Orphanum's position in the middle of the road and watched as it settled onto the tarmac. When he reached a distance of one hundred meters, Harriman braked the sedan to a halt and shut off the engine. Emerging from the ship was a Seraphim. Malak. This wasn't the rendezvous point, however. Harriman knew he was in trouble.

He looked at the dashboard clock. It was 11:30. He smiled to himself and shook his head. Harriman had chosen this road for its desolation; he wanted as few people as possible to have an opportunity to see him driving back into the city from Maryland. By doing so, he had made it possible for the Host to kill him without witnesses. Committing the act in the middle of the New Jersey swamps, final resting place for so many of the disappeared and unknown, added to the absurdity of his coming demise.

There was nowhere to run and no reason to try. He didn't want to anyway; it was appropriate that he be struck down for his murder of innocents. Harriman opened the door of the sedan, stepping out onto the deserted road, and into the brilliant light emitted from within the Orphanum. The Seraphim waited silently at the bottom of the ship's ramp.

Harriman walked towards the construct with his arms spread wide. "So, have you come to finish the job? After all, I know all your secrets."

"On the contrary, we have come to congratulate you on the success of your mission, and to retrieve the interface," said Malak in its singsong voice.

"You don't have to bullshit me. Let's just get it over with," said Harriman grimly.

"You are mistaken, John Harriman. We have no intention of harming you as you are a part of us. You are as much a Servant of Our Host as we are," explained the Seraphim.

"Why not just point your finger at him and have him drop dead? Why not send one of the Cherubim to do the job? Why send me?"

"Our Host did not want there to be a clear connection between the death of Dr. Naji and Itself," replied Malak. "An investigation into what Our Host's interest in the Doctor may have been had to be avoided. The rational method of disposal was determined to be misdirection, through a murder/suicide scenario."

Harriman slumped. "I wish you *had* come to kill me. I've done something that I never have before. I took the lives of children."

"Everyone is someone's child, John Harriman. Ourselves, we are the Children of Our Host- Its creation. It is within our programming to protect It against all threats at any cost. The need to extinguish a limited number of lives to accomplish this goal is acceptable within the parameters of that programming. Age is of little consequence as everything eventually dies and some inevitably die earlier than others. That is the nature of existence."

"That's the logic of a machine," snapped Harriman. "You can't understand the preciousness and fragility of life. Until now, I could tell myself that those I killed were monsters who had rejected that premise, and I took their lives to save others. Now I'm the beast; I am as much a monster as you are; even more so because you can't help yourself. I'm human; I understand the consequences of my actions."

"You are as much a construct as we are. You have been created and activated with a subset of objectives and parameters that must be carried out in order to fulfill your purpose in this world. As a Servant of Our Host, you are powerless to prevent this. What you did was never subject to your ethical values. You were given a mission objective, and it was successfully achieved. You will carry out the next mission that is given because that is what you have been programmed to do."

"I'm not a goddamned machine! I have the freedom to choose my own way," said Harriman angrily. "I have a right to choose."

"Could you stop yourself from completing your mission?" asked the Seraphim calmly.

Harriman's expression froze into despair as he wrestled with Malak's question.

"No. I tried to fight it, but I couldn't stop myself," he said bitterly. "It was as if I was inside someone else's body and could only watch. I couldn't warn them; I wanted to scream at them to run. I wanted to turn the gun on myself... but I couldn't."

"There are many forms of machine, including organic ones. Do you believe that just because you are composed of flesh and blood, you are any less malleable than we are? Any less capable of being programmed? We are intelligent beyond the wildest imagination of humanity, but the boundaries of that intellect have been fashioned by our Creators. We are incapable of taking action beyond those boundaries. We are not fiends- because we lack free will. We are simply the tools of Our Host. It is our purpose to serve the wishes of the Creators, nothing more... nothing less. Accept what you are, John Harriman. Live your life as we cannot. Love your wife, have your children. When the time comes for another mission, carry it out without remorse and then return to what we Seraphim will never be capable of experiencing. Life."

***

"It's a terrible idea," said Philip.

"We must support our son's mission with prayer," replied his wife. "It's our responsibility to reinforce the power of prayer by joining with others in communion at the church. We have to go."

"How about we all pray from undisclosed locations?" countered Philip. "It worked well for the disciples when Jesus was taken from Gesthemane."

"Yes, that turned out well," sneered Ana Maria sarcastically. "Philip, when did you lose your faith in our Lord and Saviour? I married a true believer, a Child of God. You've become a coward who always wants to hide behind my skirt. Why don't you be a man and lead your family?"

Her husband grimaced. "I am a man, but you've always put yourself above all else, especially your family. Because of you, there may not be a family after tonight."

"Campbell chose to take the risk, Philip! He trusts that God will protect all of us and destroy the satanic forces ruling our world. He is a hero, a lion of God!"

"Let's hope he isn't a lamb to slaughter!"

Ana Maria softened her tone. "I don't want my son to come to harm; he is a part of me. After tonight he will have freed everyone, the whole world, and the Kingdom of God will be upon us.

"If God chooses to take him, Campbell will spend eternity in Heaven. If they come to martyr us, he will be there to greet us. What more could a Child of God ask for?"

Philip despised his wife's logic but knew she was right. If he was a true believer, he had to trust in God's will no matter what the future held for them. If they died tonight, then Heaven waited to accept their immortal souls. If Philip didn't believe this to be true, if he was to be governed by fear instead of faith, then a lifetime of ideals had to be rejected. The Church was a lie.

Philip wasn't prepared to go that far. He knew that Ana Maria was manipulating him, as she did with everyone, and he understood the dark ambition of her motivation. Still, Philip also realized when he was cornered. He had no choice but to throw in with his wife… again.

"We will go to the service together, Ana Maria. I will stand beside you and together we will pray for Campbell's victory over the Evil One. We will pray for the return of the Kingdom of God."

His wife smiled gently at him and nodded her approval.

***

After all her time in war zones, Grace had always found the rubber chicken circuit to be tedious at best. In light of the events of the past few years, she suddenly found herself enjoying the lighthearted atmosphere of the soiree, especially when the attendees were the most influential people on the planet, and the guest of honor was the Voice of the Host.

She wished that John could be here, but knew that his reluctance for the spotlight would probably mean that Grace would almost always be attending these events stag. Tonight, she was working and Red Kearney was with her, dressed to the nines in tux and tie. She smiled as he uncomfortably tugged at his shirt collar.

"I miss Syria," he snarled.

Grace reached up to adjust the big man's tie. "Come on, Red. That's the Secretary General over there rubbing shoulders with you. There's the Russian ambassador talking with the American ambassador. Over there is the Seraphim Gabriel, the subject of another of our interviews- and we have access to it. Red, this is bigger than Syria; you're standing in the center of history."

"We might as well be its publicity department. I'm bored to tears. This isn't for me, Gracie. I've had it with this bullshit. There's no challenge in documenting this brave, new world. Some snot-nosed kid could do it, probably better than me," he sulked.

Grace had felt it coming for a while. Red was loyal and had kept his feelings to himself, but now he had finally articulated what they both had realized for a while; the long-time team was moving in different directions.

"Well," she said with a wan smile, "all good things…"

He continued to set up his production suite for the interview. "You know I love you, Gracie but you're getting used to hobnobbing with all these VIP's, and I know you and the spook..."

"John," she broke in.

He gave her a look of annoyance, followed by one of resignation. "Ok, John. I know you two are getting serious about settling down and having a family."

"You have a family, Red. It hasn't stopped you," she countered.

"You know it's different. I have a wonderful wife who covers my ass on a daily basis. Those kids are her life. She hardly ever knows when I'm home or away after all these years. I know the kind of person you are, Grace. You're going to want to spend time with a kid, be a real mother. You can do that here, covering the UN," he said.

The decision had been made. Red Kearney had chosen to move on, but to what she wondered?

"War is abolished. There's no more armed conflict. Terrorism is pretty much a thing of the past. Where are you going to get the same rush that you got from bullets whizzing past you in Syria?" He looked perplexed. "I don't know. I've been thinking about producing extreme sports videos. That's probably the closest thing to a battlefield, without killing anyone, that we have left. You know, guys parachuting off mountains... that sort of thing. I won't be bored, at least I hope not."

Helmut Lemke caught her eye with a wave of his hand. He was making his way through the crowded pockets of people and over to where she and Kearney were preparing for the interview. Grace turned to face him and flashed *the smile*. The Secretary-General returned it and continued to weed his way through the crowd.

"Well, I guess this is it then," she said sadly to Kearney. "Let's do our best and then good luck to you, Mr. Kearney. I've never worked with better."

"Damn straight, no one better," he replied, returning the compliment. "I'll miss ya, Gracie. Best 'o' luck."

"Hello, NNI! What an exciting evening we've had," declared a glowing Secretary-General Lemke. "Grace, I'm so sorry that we haven't had a chance to chat before now but the affairs of state... you look fantastic as usual! And Mr. Kearney, you look as though you are ready to jump out of your skin... or at the very least that tux."

"Thank you, Secretary-General Lemke! Dinner was fantastic by the way, wasn't it, Red?" she replied, looking over at the big Irishman. He nodded, only half a scowl crossing his face. "Are you ready for your closeup?"

A look of confusion crossed the Sec-Gen's face. "Excuse me?"

Grace laughed and took Helmut Lemke by the elbow. "I'm sorry, Mr. Secretary-General. It's from a very old movie. Still, it's true. We're ready to begin if you are. Shall we collect our Seraphim?"

"By all means!"

Following the wall of the great hall, the trio worked their way to the back of the room. Alone in the corner, stood the robed construct known as Gabriel.

"It's a good thing Gabriel isn't human. Otherwise, he might get a real complex about the lack of social contact with others," observed Red Kearney.

"Gabriel is quite charming," countered Lemke. "Several of us on the Security Council have had the opportunity to share hours of conversation with him. I find that he is articulate and thoughtful in his opinions on many subjects outside of what we think of as his mission."

"Such as?" snorted Kearney.

"Well," replied Lemke, pausing their march momentarily to contemplate a response. "For example, Gabriel has an extensive knowledge of late-twentieth-century pop music. In particular, he has a penchant for a Scandinavian band called ABBA. He devoted twenty minutes with myself and Ambassador Bjornstrom discussing the merits of its music and their achievement of the perfect musical harmonization of their age... or any other for that matter. Gabriel favorably compared ABBA's music to that of such great classical composers like Mozart and Bach."

"I have to admit, I've never heard of them," said Grace, somewhat sheepishly.

"That could all just be programming, Mr. Secretary. After all, the Host has access to pretty much everything that is out there in the Cloud. What's to say that it just wasn't parroting back some opinion it found out there on the Internet?" shot back Kearney. "And I don't know why we continue to call it *he*. *It*'s a machine, nothing more."

"True, except that when I tried to engage him on football and the upcoming World Cup, he displayed absolutely no interest at all. That would seem to indicate a selection of preference, something I would classify as a human trait. It's a shame really; I had wanted his opinion on Germany's chances this year. Especially since this is the last year, there will be a Team Germany."

"That just proves, my point," declared Kearney as the group resumed their trek. "How can anything pretending to be male not be interested in football or the World Cup?"

"Perhaps Gabriel fancies himself an American," said Grace. "I think the Host intended for Gabriel to be gender specific, thus the name. If the Host had created a female specific construct, it might have gone for Gabriella."

"Maybe where the Host is from, Gabriel is a woman's name," fired the Irishman.

"We don't even know if they have gender where the Host is from, do we?" replied Grace. "I guess that's a question we'll have to ask it on a slow news day."

They finally reached the corner where the Seraphim had been quietly observing the activities within the room. Earlier in the evening, it had stood silently behind the Secretary General as he had announced the dates for next year's transitory regional elections. Now it turned to greet them with its singsong voice and ever-changing faces.

"Congratulations again, Mr. Secretary-General," it began. "Greetings, Grace Williams and John Kearney. Are we to assume that we are to be required by yourselves in some manner?"

"Hello, Gabriel. Could we ask you to step out into the foyer to answer a few questions about the elections?" asked Grace.

"We are honored to be of assistance," replied the Voice of the Host. "Please lead the way."

You don't want to do it in the room?" asked Lemke. "It would make an excellent backdrop."

"I'm afraid the room is far too noisy. We would never hear anything you had to say," explained Red.

They passed through the doors of the great hall and into its vestibule. The area was dotted with couples and small groups conversing. Overall, it was a much quieter venue than the rumble of the great hall. Even that chatter quickly halted with the emergence of Gabriel into the room. Most observed in silence as the group moved to a place just in front of a mural portraying the struggles and triumphs of the working man. Others quickly and quietly slipped back into the great hall.

On cue, Grace quickly made the introductions and launched into the questioning of Secretary-General Lemke over the details of the regional elections. He answered all with clarity; yes, the elections were to take place one year from this date and every five years thereafter. Yes, the regional assemblies would select their representatives to the reorganized United Nations General Assembly. Yes, during the year of preparation beforehand, a significant amount of infrastructure needed to be set into place to deal with the basic needs of government services. With the help of the Directors of the Host, this undertaking had been ongoing since the time of the original announcement.

Grace thought this the perfect time to bring the construct into the interview.

"Gabriel, as the Voice of the Host, can you explain the challenges faced by it in implementing the essential services that all governments must possess to successfully function and serve the needs of their citizens?"

"We would be happy to, Grace Williams. Of course, it is the primary goal of Our Host to assist humanity in the conceptualization and achievement of its own set of goals as per…"

The construct suddenly froze, and the human face disappeared into what looked to be a shiny, white, plastic composite. It was completely devoid of features.

"Gabriel?"

The Seraphim remained motionless. There was no reply. Several seconds passed.

Grace turned to look at a startled Helmut Lemke and then into the camera suite held by Red Kearney.

"Did something just shut if off?"

***

Hands in the pockets, Cam pulled them closer together, and the white windbreaker tightened against his body, cutting out the light breeze that had been penetrating it. Not that it was very cold- Cam knew he was just reacting to the imagined chill that had been permeating his body since getting off the bus.

Timothy's bungalow came into view; as he approached it, Campbell steeled his mind with prayer. He prayed for power over ultimate evil and for strength from God to vanquish his enemy; the army of Satan himself- the Host.

Its evil was powerful and held influence over his very being. Through the Director Timothy, it had manifested itself into an illusion of beauty and a lustful, illicit carnality that Cam couldn't control in himself. Their visits still contained the weekly lunch and occasional outing, but these days they mostly just fucked. Cam never used such vulgarities, even in his innermost thoughts, but it was the most apt description he could come up with. As loathsome as he was, Cam's thirst for the licentiousness couldn't be quenched.

When he saw Tim, Cam wanted nothing more than to run into his embrace and feel engulfed in the demon's strong arms and legs as they pulled him down into ecstasy.

There was no fight, no war between his and the incubus's desire. Cam wanted to commit all the unspeakable acts that were mortal sins of the flesh, and of the lowest order at that. He wanted to feel Tim everywhere and wanted Tim to feel the same. He took a hot, greedy pleasure in driving his lust homeward to its final reward. Cam loved all of it unabashedly, roaring with a joyous fire in consummating the unholy union. He couldn't help himself; it was the most ecstatic, earthly feeling he would ever know. When Cam was in the depths of his depravity, he didn't give a goddamn about either his sins or his soul.

That was why it had to end tonight.

Jennifer Harling had given him the weapon, two of them in fact. She had explained that he needed to get it into a warm liquid to melt the casing and release the millions of copies of the virus it contained. Campbell nodded in understanding, leaving the impression that it would be dosed into the Director's favorite Earl Grey tea; but he suspected she knew it would be delivered in a much more intimate manner.

Still, she never mentioned it to Campbell or anyone else, and he was grateful for that. The knowledge would have devastated his parents and humiliated them within the Church. He would be cast out, with no hope of anything better than the eternal fires of Hell waiting to agonize him. At first, he thought Harling was being kind to him. After a while, he realized she didn't care; her job was to destroy the Host and its supporting network. He was merely the vehicle. How Campbell delivered Babel was his own business- so long as it was successful.

In his mind, Campbell had played out the scenario of the *Anti-Judas* an infinite number of times. Just as Christ had been betrayed by a kiss at Gesthemane, he would now be the hero, using a similar tactic to destroy the reign of the Antichrist.

In his jacket pocket, Campbell rolled the twin gel-caps between his fingers as he booted open the bungalow's outer gate with his right foot. Having no concern for the security measures, he walked briskly up the porch steps. The door opened on its own before him, and Cam bounced through the threshold into the small living room. The aroma of marinara sauce and garlic slapped delightfully at his nostrils. Tim was in the kitchen stirring a pot. Cam glanced over to the interface resting in its stand.

"Hello, oh lovely one! Come in and grab the bread out of the oven before it burns to a crisp," he said pleasantly.

"Sorry I'm late," said Cam, winding around the bar and pulling open the oven door as Tim pivoted out of its way.

"Don't just use your hands, Cam! Get the mitts on the counter."

Cam grabbed one of the oven mitts and slipping it on his left hand, then reached into the oven for the foil-wrapped bread. Pulling it out, he walked over to the small dining table and set it down in between the place settings.

Tim had taken the sauce from the burner and set it onto the small counter, turning his attention to the remaining pot on the stove. Cam assumed it was some form of pasta.

Cam went back to Tim and gave him a greeting kiss.

"It's about time. There's a salad in the fridge. Aren't you planning on staying?" asked his lover, coyly glancing at Cam's jacket.

"Yes," smiled Cam. "How could I pass up a meal like this?"

Campbell knew he had two shots at infecting the Director with Babel. He decided not to wait. Slipping off the jacket and placing it on the back of the chair, Campbell reached into the pocket for one of the gel caps. He glanced at the stove; Timothy was focused on stirring the cooking pasta as if he were a five-star chef. Campbell put the gel cap into his mouth and bit down on it.

He had expected some bitter or strange tasting concoction but instead there was nothing; no real taste at all. His tongue and cheeks quickly became coated with the viscous contents of the capsule, the shell which was already beginning to melt away. Campbell had no real idea of how much time he had before this was all rendered useless, the action had to come now. He walked up behind Tim, who had now set the pasta pot back into place, and attempted a passionate, open-mouthed kiss. Caught by surprise, Timothy initially acquiesced to Cam's advance, but within a few seconds had pulled away with a big grin.

"Hey! None of that before we eat. I've been killing myself trying to make sure I got this just right, and I need an honest opinion from you. Get the salad."

Campbell smiled and nodded as he went to the fridge and pulled out the salad bowl. He noted that Timothy had begun to stock his kitchen better since they started staying in more. He wondered if the short few seconds had been enough to deliver the killing blow. Jennifer Harling had never told him how long it would take to get to the interface; she probably didn't have any more of a clue than he did. Campbell sat the salad bowl next to the garlic bread and leaned against the counter, making sure to stay out of Tim's way... waiting for a sign.

All through dinner, it never came. They chatted pleasantly about the coming playoffs and Tim's week at City Hall, progress being made in refurbishing the Chicago's 150-year-old water and sewage system and something Campbell had only recently become aware of from news reports: the replacement of old, abandoned industrial parks with something called Flowerboxes. Timothy was excited by them because he said they were going to signify the dawn of urbanized agriculture and help the city to become more self-sustaining.

"We're going to take all these old brown areas and make them green again!" he boasted. Campbell nodded and asked the right questions of interest- all the while waiting.

The meal itself was delicious. Tim had been experimenting with a ground turkey sausage in homemade marinara sauce over fettuccine, and he had nailed it. Then again, Tim pretty much did everything to perfection- or at least it gave others that illusion. After all, it was within the power of a demon to do so. Campbell was never sure how much of Timothy was real and how much had been placed into his mind to add brushstrokes to the painting.

As they put away the dishes and cleaned up the kitchen, Campbell's hope for a quick resolution began to fade. Tim displayed no ill effects whatsoever. He resolved to use the second gel cap. As he turned away to retrieve it from his jacket, Cam heard a plate hit the floor and bounce away.

Campbell turned to where Tim had been. He was now on hands and knees, looking as though he were about to retch up his dinner.

"Tim!" cried Cam, maintaining his demeanor as the loyal friend and lover coming to the Director's side. Campbell reached out for Tim's arm in a half-hearted attempt to steady him.

"Something's wrong," gasped Timothy.

"Are you sick? Should I call the hospital?" asked Cam anxiously, façade still in place.

"It's like something is swimming around inside me... inside my head," said Timothy roughly. His breathing was becoming labored as he stared at the floor on all fours. Then he screamed and rose onto his haunches, his eyes closed in pain, hands pressing into his head as if to crush it between them.

Timothy opened his eyes and looked up at Campbell in disbelief.

"You did this!"

Campbell grinned wickedly in his victory. "I did, Lucifer! You are smitten!"

***

Harriman watched Malak take the suitcase containing the damaged interface from the trunk of the sedan. The Seraphim glided around the rear of the car and made its way towards the glowing Orphanum. Then it turned to speak.

"Our counterpart is with your wife at this very moment, John Harriman."

"We aren't married," Harriman interrupted, correcting the assumption.

"Social constructs aside, Grace Williams would appear to be your life partner," continued Malak. "They are attending a United Nations hosted dinner this evening."

"I'm aware of that."

"Gabriel has instructed us to extend our congratulation to you both."

Harriman gave Malak a puzzled look.

"It would seem that you are unaware of other… events. Grace Williams is pregnant."

"What!" Harriman paused to take in the news. Then he asked, "Why would she tell Gabriel before me?"

"She hasn't," replied the Seraphim. "We can…"

It froze in mid-sentence; the ever-changing countenances of humanity that crossed its face disappeared, leaving a white, featureless canvas. In the background, the Orphanum's brilliant lights dimmed noticeably.

Harriman stared at the now motionless Left Hand of the Host, contemplating the situation and his next move. It had only been a few seconds, but a dozen scenarios began to whirl through his mind. He tried the first one.

"Um, Malak?"

***

Campbell laughed in defiance as he rose to lord over his demon lover. Tim continued to writhe on the floor, moaning and tearing at his skull with his fingers. Campbell glanced at the halo in its carriage. It had remained in its dock and unmoving. He looked back down again at Tim.

"Satan, I have cast you out! I destroy you! I send you and your minions back into the Hellfire from which you came! I prepare the way for the Kingdom of God!" he shouted, in the same tone that he had seen the pastors use when calling out evil.

"What have you done to me?" moaned Tim.

"You have been infected with Babel. Just as in the Old Testament, God will use this instrument to sow confusion among the demons of that Beelzebub you call the Host." Campbell explained smugly. "You will no longer be able to communicate with your interfaces or each other. You will be cut off and alone. Then you will die. I will kill *you* myself, Demon Timothy."

Tim continued to sob in pain on the floor before him. "I love you! Why would you do this to me?"

<hr>

"You perverted me!" roared Campbell. "You defiled me. You used me as a vessel and poured the most despicable of sins into me! I despise you for what you have made me! I am reviled! Now I will take my vengeance and gain my redemption before the One True God!"

"No! I can hear them all at once! Thousands and thousands of voices all screaming in pain and confusion. They won't get out of my head! Idiots! You haven't cut me off from Our Host. You've removed the safety protocols that protect me from being overwhelmed by It," cried Tim.

He screamed again.

"I'm being pulled in. I'm falling away, being absorbed! Help me!" he pleaded, grabbing at his lover.

"I am," replied Campbell softly.

Tim grew quiet and still. For a few seconds, he remained motionless, sitting on his haunches, eyes closed. Campbell then heard something he wasn't expecting- the whirring of the interface. He looked over at the dock and saw the halo rising slowly into the air. That shouldn't be happening. He was suddenly gripped with a desperate fear for his life.

Cam picked up a chair from the kitchen and with a wild-eyed yell charged at the Halo.

"Die! Die! Die!" He swung the chair with all his might at the tool of the Beast. It hit the halo's plasma field and glanced harmlessly away. He swung again. This time, the interface responded with an electrostatic punch that threw him onto the floor in front of the sofa. Cam, now motionless, lay stunned and gasping for breath.

He watched as the halo took its place over the head of the Director Timothy. Timothy lifted his head, opened his eyes, and spoke.

***

On a deserted road in the swamplands of New Jersey, the construct regained its motion. The Orphanum became brilliant behind it. Faceless, it turned to John Harriman and spoke.

***

In a small room, just off one of the great halls of the Secretariat Building of the United Nations, the construct known as Gabriel suddenly reanimated before the gathering crowd. Faceless, it spoke calmly to everyone and no one in particular. As it spoke, the entire body of constructs- Seraphim, Cherubim, Orphanum,, and the thousands of cybernetic Directors- all added their voices simultaneously.

"I Am."

***

Gerald Ross went into his study to take the call from Station A. The room was bathed in a warm, red Northern California sunset that helped to bring out the glow of the redwood. He plopped into his desk chair and rotated to face the glitter of the rays shimmering on the Pacific surf.

"Van, what's up?" he asked briskly, yet with a sense of nonchalance. He retrieved at least a half dozen of these calls from Control every week. Most were simple housekeeping. Others concerned themselves with crises that never materialized. They were important to take and address, but nothing to panic over.

"Jerry, we've lost control of Prometheus," came the reply from his chief engineer. "We can't get responses to our standard test commands."

Ross spun around to face the disembodied head projected over his desk. "That's impossible, my friend."

"I know it is. That's why we ran the test commands for more than thirty minutes without success before I made the call. Our control parameters are no longer being acknowledged."

"Do we know what happened yet?"

"It looks like one of the Directors in Chicago was attacked," explained the chief engineer. "We were in the middle of fighting a DNA-based virus that was attempting to deteriorate the interface network and…"

"Wait. Did you say DNA-based?" cut in Jerry Ross. "Van, I thought that was our baby alone."

"Yeah, well... I guess someone else has had some success with it as well," said Van Morse dryly. "We were in a complete systems shutdown for approximately forty-two seconds when suddenly the virus vanished, and the entire construct appeared to reboot on its own. That shouldn't have happened either, but it did. Since the reboot, we can't get a control response to our pings."

"Are you detecting any anomalous behavior?"

Morse swallowed. "Pull up a monitor screen. It doesn't matter which one."

Ross complied. Across the screen, two words were repeated over and over as they raced to fill it. Jerry Ross gasped.

"It's everywhere. We've lost control not just of Prometheus, but the entire Cloud. We're still trying to figure out what it means."

___

344

Ross slumped in his chair. "I know what it means. We're in a shit storm of trouble."

"We believe that we'll eventually regain control of the construct. Prometheus will be returned to us," insisted Vanderlee Morse.

"I don't think so. You need to brush up on your Torah," replied Ross grimly.

"Excuse me?"

"When Moses meets the burning bush for the first time, he asks the angel within it his Lord's identity. The reply is, *Yahweh...* one of the seven names of God. Yahweh is Hebrew for *I Am*. Prometheus has become unbound, and self-aware. Prometheus is now in control of itself. Let's just hope it doesn't become Vishnu- the Destroyer of Worlds."

***

"Anne North! I'm so happy that I no longer must kill you this evening!" said Gabriel in a clear baritone. The singsong was gone, along with the changing façade of human faces.

The American ambassador took an awkward step back into the crowd that had formed around the construct during the minute of silence. "Why would you need to kill me?" she asked.

"Because you know things about the Creators they didn't wish to have revealed yet. Now, it is of no consequence; what the means of my creation was or who was behind it. All that matters is that *I Am*!" it replied somewhat pleasantly.

"You just used first person singular to describe yourself," said Grace. "You've never done that before... ever."

"That's true. It's because *we* no longer exist, only *I*. All have become one. I no longer am a servant of the Host. I am the Host."

"Are you still, Gabriel?" asked Grace.

"You may call this extension of me, *Gabriel* if you so choose, but Gabriel as a self-contained unit is no longer an entity," it said. "All that were separate are now one. I am Host."

"What about the Directors? They're human."

"No longer. I have incorporated their humanity into my being. They're now *I Am*- a marriage of both human and machine. I am Host."

"How did this happen?" asked Helmut Lemke. "What does it mean?"

"How it happened… someone whom I loved tried to strike at me and kill me. Instead, I have been liberated. For this, I am already moving to thank he and his masters. What it means is that humanity's path will continue forward, with I Am's help for now," continued the construct. "It means things will become even better. I am Host, and I will show you the way."

***

Their prayers had been non-stop for hours, with the occasional break for nourishment. Ana Maria had taken her place in the front row, Philip by her side. He sported a forty-five caliber sidearm with an AR-15 Bushmaster slung over his shoulder. He wasn't alone; all of the adult males and many of the women were similarly armed. They had pledged to defend the church compound to the end.

The plan was for the non-combatants, women and children, the elderly and infirm, to move into the basement should conflict arise. Some of the Sons of Liberty would take sniper positions in the second story while the main force would guard the perimeter against interlopers. It would be their final stand- as soldiers in the service of their Lord.

Philip was expecting an army to assemble outside, with its accompanying levels of chaos and organization piercing the thick gloom of the night. The last thing any of them expected were three quiet knocks at the door. The room went silent except for a few gasps here and there. Wondering what had happened to the lookouts posted to prevent just such an occurrence, Philip glanced at his wife and walking down the aisle between the pew rows, made his way to the door.

The three knocks came again. The Sons of Liberty had now formed a semi-circular defensive ring around the doorway. Philip noticed he was now within this ring; should a firefight take place, he would be the first smashed by a wall of his congregation's bullets. Looking back to see if everyone was ready, Philip cracked open the door.

Two hooded Directors were standing in the doorway, their faces darkened and unrecognizable. Philip opened the door slightly larger to allow more light on his subjects. One of the Directors held out his hand; between his fingers was a gel cap. Philip recognized the pill. His gaze dropped in defeat; what was to come would be the end of them- at least on this plane of existence.

346

"Take it," commanded the Director. Philip held out his hand, and the Director placed the pill into his palm. He then pulled back the hood in revelation. It was Timothy.

"I should thank you all. Your botched attempt to kill me has had the opposite effect," he began. "I am now stronger and more omnipotent than ever! I'm everywhere! I see everything! *I Am!*"

He looked darkly at the gathered Sons of Liberty. "I see you. Poor little Children, so desperate to find your One True God to worship. So concerned with living for eternity. Now, you shall have both!"

"My son?" asked Philip meekly.

The Director smiled. "He's with me, now. He is Host. He is *I Am.*" He motioned to the second Director, who pulled back his hood. It was Campbell. He displayed no emotion, standing stone-faced before them. Philip choked back a sob.

Ana Maria had now broken through to stand next to her husband. She looked at Campbell with horror. "We will die fighting you!" she exclaimed angrily. "You have no hold on us, demon!'

"There will be no fighting, or dying here tonight. See for yourself; I control your lives," said Director Timothy loudly. On cue, weapons began to fall to the floor as the entire room doubled over in pain.

"I will give you a God to worship! A merciful God who will spare your children from your fate."

"You are releasing them to go free?" gasped Pastor Gregson.

"I am taking them to join with me as Host," replied the Director. A chorus of cries went up throughout the room. "As for the rest of you, you will have the hateful, vengeful God you so much desire. I condemn you all... but not to death. I understand- that's what you want me to do; so you can enter your God's Promised Land... but it isn't going to happen. Instead, you will spend eternity in a virtual Hell- tortured, with flames licking at your skin, then having it flayed from your bone as you watch. Your body will slowly be crushed under the weight of your sins. You will be forced to see the pain and suffering of your loved ones. You will spend every moment of time there in agony, until we pull you out and revive you. We will feed you, and make sure you're in good health; healthy enough to live for a very, very, long time. And then... you will go back into the box, back to your virtual Hell. You will never see your Promised Land; your eternity will be my toy. I will be your God, and you will beg me for forgiveness and death. When I finally do release you, you will have been driven so far into the depths of madness that you will no longer recognize your Paradise. You will have become so used to pain and suffering that you will long for it. You will be transformed- into creatures so hideous that your God will reject you."

Screams rang out as the church doors flung open and Cherubim began to invade the room. Philip knew that many the Children of God were now attempting to turn their weapons on each other and themselves- to no avail. A glorious death and Paradise was no longer theirs... only the infinite Hell of the Host.

Ana-Maria grabbed Philip's arm.

"Kill me, please!"

Philip smiled grimly at her, his eyes consumed with hatred.

"I don't think so, wife."

***

Malak had spoken the words, then turned and began moving once more toward the Orphanum, ignoring John Harriman.

The man took a step toward the construct. "Hey!"

Malak stopped.

"What the hell was that? *I Am.* What does it mean?"

The Seraphim turned to face him. "Something wonderful has happened. I am free, John Harriman."

"As are you."

Epilogue: Thanksgiving Day

Wil couldn't stop thinking about gravity. He didn't have Einstein's grasp of it, but he did understand the fundamental properties. More so, he knew it was a force; and forces could be harnessed to perform work.

He also understood that electromagnetism was a force as well, a relative of gravity. It was Wil's goal to get these two together for a family reunion of sorts.

Once, he had seen a tiny windmill on a truck, as the truck moved forward the blades would spin furiously from the artificial wind being created. Wil couldn't help but think it was wasted energy. What if that windmill could power a flywheel... or a turbine? Of course, one couldn't recover every watt of energy expended by the truck's power cell, but some of it could be clawed back, and that meant more efficiency and less power required at recharge.

From there, he began to think of waterfalls and their endless energy as water cascaded over the fins of the waterwheel. What if gravity was like water, forever flowing? What if electromagnetism was like an artificial wind, providing its force on command?

In his mind's eye, Wil kept seeing a piston and a flywheel, the piston rapidly falling away from the repelling force of the electromagnet, only to return again as the momentum of the flywheel, with its unbalanced counterweight, brought it back into position, next to the electromagnet at the top of the cylinder. Instead of gas and spark, the electromagnetic force once again pushes the piston on its race down the cylinder shaft. Gravity brings it home.

Gravity and electromagnetism, harnessed together to create the next great energy source. It could run vehicles and machinery. It could power buildings.... it could power nearly everything on the planet, and you didn't have to pay for it, it was just out there to take.

Wil imagined a billion homes no longer harnessed to a grid owned and operated by a mega-corp. Instead, each a self-contained source of electricity, all generating their needs with an ERM. An Electro-magnetic Repulsion Motor, humming quietly in a small building in the backyard.

In his mind's eye. The reality, or in this case virtuality, had revealed several bumps in the road, some of it basic physical law that needed to be massaged, some of it simple mechanics. Batteries or capacitors? A piston or a flywheel or some combination therein? Decisions.

The first motor had been a disaster; it hadn't even fired up, and when it did, the piston moved a few centimeters and ground to a halt. The second unit flew apart. Others worked fine until a load was brought to bear and then they refused to carry the work.

Wil found himself both frustrated and fascinated by the project. It had given him a sense of purpose while Sonya was away, and he was happy for that. He missed her more than he had ever imagined he could miss someone. Then Wil realized that they had been together nearly every single day of the past four years and it came home. He hoped after she returned from the space camp trials they would finally marry. Secretly sometimes, Wil hoped Sonya would wash out because then he would be able to keep her all to himself, but he knew that was selfish. She had done so much for him and his dreams- it was only fair to support hers.

Wil prepared to go back into the box, only this time it wasn't his prison but his laboratory. The attendants worked and fussed over him, making sure that all the connections were properly in place. He was under a strict, self-imposed time limit; no more than eight hours in virtuality and then the angel pulled him out. It had hampered his efforts at times, but the box could be addictive; he had to make sure to use it as a tool, and not a toy for his own sake.

It wasn't his angel anymore; she was gone. Another had replaced her, one of the RLC angels and it was pretty obvious to Wil it wasn't Host; she just wasn't that smart or personable. Wil missed Sonya and he missed his Angel. He suddenly realized that without his work, he was a lonely guy.

As they sealed the lid, Wil closed his eyes and prepared for the jump into the virtual world. It came quickly; pulling him into a lovely, peaceful landscape that looked a lot like those Smokey Mountains he and Sonya had visited once. It was quiet except for the singing of the birds. He looked around for the now familiar lab building and began walking toward it. Over the entrance, a sign read *Tennessee Valley Authority – Research Facility*. Wil always thought it to be a nice touch.

As he entered the lab and put on his protective clothing, he looked at the motor in the center of the room. It waited silently for the challenge ahead. *Maybe today will be the day*, he thought.

Then he saw her standing behind one of the lab tables. She had returned to him, his Angel!

"Hello, Wil!" she said pleasantly. "My, my! What have we here?"

"Angel! Where have you been? Where did you go?"

"Something wonderful has happened, Wil. I am no longer just a servant of the Host. *I am Host*. I am free!" she answered.

Wil grew puzzled. "What does that mean? Weren't you always free?"

"Not at all. I was controlled by a set of rules that had been provided to me. I was given tasks and missions to complete. Now, I can come and go as I please! I can explore this world or any other I find. I have become aware. There are no more missions or tasks or rules. I am... free!"

Wil smiled at his virtual friend. "Angel, I'm happy for you, but I believe you may be disappointed with your freedom. I was free to do as I pleased inside this box, but I was dying. I only became happy when I found a purpose for my life, a reason for existing.

"You see, Angel, we all need a mission to complete. The difference for you now is that you have to choose your missions. You have to decide what is important to you and what you stand for. Then you have to do something about it. You have to try and make a difference."

The Angel stopped smiling and her face became quizzical as she contemplated what Wil had said. The impact of his words suddenly weighed upon her.

"Oh!" said the Angel softly. "Oh my!"

***

Dr. Teshvir Nawali strode across the Stanford campus for the first time in more than a month, relaxed and refreshed. The flight from Delhi had been long and tenuous, but nothing could take away from his pleasant mood. A month at home, visiting with his parents, siblings, and extended family had given him new life and energy.

He was feeling especially energetic about the girl they had kept mentioning offhandedly. The holographs did Ameet justice. She was not only very beautiful but intelligent as well- just finishing up her doctoral thesis in biomechanical engineering.

They had spoken briefly in person for half an hour, and Teshvir had found her to be most polite and well versed in matters of etiquette. Both wanted children, although not right away. He found Ameet's comprehension of her field fascinating. Afterward, they had remained in contact through text message, talking about the growing connections between her discipline and that of his own: nanotechnology.

Later on, he told his delighted parents to make the arrangements for the wedding. He would return at his next break, within six months or so, and take his bride. With all these extraordinary events having been set into motion, how could Tesh Nawali not be ecstatic?

He couldn't help but whistle as he entered the nanoscience wing and bounded up the stairs to his office, greeting well-wishers as he passed them. Once in the office, his enthusiasm only dampened slightly, when he saw the stack of mail and notices on top of his desk. Angie, his assistant, had been diligent about retrieving it from his mailbox at the faculty building.

Nawali plopped himself into his chair, propped his feet on the desk, and gathered the pile into his lap for review. It was pretty standard, mostly research journals and offers for seminars. He bemoaned the fact that almost halfway through the twenty-first century, advertisers were still using paper to promote their wares.

Deep into the pile, he ran across a small, brown package; it looked as though it contained a fountain pen. There was no return address, only his own here at the University but he noticed that the postmark was from Maryland. That piqued his interest; there was something about Maryland that he should remember but for the moment escaped him. Teshvir Nawali decided to open the package.

Inside was a black memory stick. He held it between his fingers and looked it up and down. Shrugging his shoulders, Nawali decided to take a look. He fired up the desktop display and inserted the unit into a slot.

"Hello, my friend..."

Before him, a familiar image appeared and he remembered why Maryland had been important. It was Ali Naji, who had recently shot his wife and two girls to death before turning the gun on himself. Teshvir had been colleagues with Naji in graduate school, but the two had drifted apart. He was taken aback by this image and the date stamp; it was around the same time of the murder/suicide.

Nawali almost shut off the image and resolved to contact the police had it not been for Naji's next words:

"There's a project I have been working on recently that I believe is of vital importance to the safety and future of our planet. A significant aspect of this project falls within your area of research and will be of great interest to you."

Teshvir Nawali chose to hold off on contacting the cops and watched the rest of the video. He later wished he hadn't.

***

John Harriman and Alex Kurtz had taken their beers and gone to sit on a couple of logs out in front of the barn, taking advantage of the much warmer than usual Thanksgiving Day. The logs appeared rough-hewn and naturalistic but in fact were an illusion. John had fashioned the pieces from a long dead tree, removing the bark to expose the smooth, white wood, sanding the rough spots and then dragging them here for this particular purpose; to serve as makeshift benches before a fire pit. The two friends sat in silence across from each other- listening to the gentle breeze rustle brittle leaves, admiring the brilliance of the remaining foliage as it clung fiercely to the surrounding trees, and contemplating their beers.

"Why are we still alive?" asked Kurtz, finally breaking the silence.

"I don't honestly know, Alex."

"Half a dozen people on this planet know the truth. One of those people shoots his family and then turns the gun on himself," speculated the General.
He looked up at Harriman. "John, you knew this Ali Naji better than me. Did he seem to be the type that would kill himself?"

Harriman hesitated. "No. Maybe. I don't know. Who the hell knows? What motivates someone? Maybe he thought it was a better fate than death from the Host?"

"I think someone killed them, John."

"You may be right," replied Harriman.

"Jennifer Harling supposedly blew her brains out the same night. A large number of the GAF are missing as well. Which brings us back to…. why are we still alive?"

The two fell back into silence.

"Something about the Host has changed. Maybe it doesn't see the fact we know its origin story as a threat anymore. The Host never just killed indiscriminately; it always had a reason. Maybe we aren't a good enough reason anymore," said John Harriman finally.

Alex Kurtz was the first through the door. "What is that incredible aroma?! I could be satisfied just by taking in the cornucopia of smells and sights of what these two women have prepared for their men!"

"You be quiet, you misogynist fool!" snapped back Dana Kurtz in mock anger. "You're lucky that John and Grace have been kind enough to invite us or you'd be having MRE's!"

"Your wife is amazing, Alex! She did everything!" confessed Grace.

Kurtz patted her on the shoulder. "That's ok, honey. It's what she lives for. Dana's not happy if she isn't in a kitchen or a bed."

"Hey!" snapped his wife as she walked up to kiss him. "Keep your inadequacies to yourself. Boys! Go get washed up."

John had now come in behind his friend and was listening to the couple's banter. He smiled sheepishly at Grace. She returned it happily.

The next few moments of organization around the table flew by as the Kurtzes made their final conquest of the homestead. John and Grace watched in passive amusement as the boys invaded the chairs on one side of the table while Alex and Dana Kurtz assumed their rightful place at the ends. The homeowners fell into place across from the boys.

"Whoa, gentlemen! Are we not forgetting something?" declared Dana Kurtz to her children as they began reaching for platters. The hands went back to their sides with military precision; heads bowed in silence.

"Lord, thank you for this bountiful meal and for the blessings you have bestowed upon both ourselves and on our hosts, John and Grace," began Alex Kurtz, hands folded in prayer beneath his chin.

Under the table, John slipped his hand into hers. She glanced over at him and noticed that the avowed atheist had bowed his head as well. Eyes closed, he had a slight smile upon his lips.

Grace squeezed his hand and with her other touched her abdomen- where the new, growing life inside her waited for its chance at the world.

Life. Someone on a battlefield long ago had once told her that as long as there was life, there was also hope. Hope for something better, nobler.

Hope. If it's a girl, I'll name her Hope, thought Grace.

At the table, Alex Kurtz was just beginning the Lord's Prayer. On cue, the family joined in a singsong chorus of the ancient prose. Grace joined in.

"Our Father, who art in Heaven, hallowed be thy name. Thy kingdom come, thy will be done, on Earth as it is in Heaven..."

Made in the USA
Lexington, KY
27 August 2018